THE VIGIL

For my friend Elaine—
who still sees something
worthwhile in me.

THE VIGIL

Book Two of the Endurian Universe

Joe Bergeron

Endurian Press

The Vigil is a work of fiction. Names, places, and incidents either are products of the author's imagination or are used fictitiously.

Cover illustration by Joe Bergeron.

Published by The Endurian Press

www.joebergeron.com

Chapter 1

The Solitary One

It was time to go home.

The thought came suddenly, unexpectedly, presenting itself as a calm assertion that left little room for uncertainty. Whatever the origin of the thought, whether internal or external, Fomalhaut did not doubt it.

But he need not act upon it immediately. He had work to finish here, work enough to occupy thousands of even such extended life-spans as his. His sense of order would not allow him to withdraw without at least completing his immediate task.

Fomalhaut commanded a slow yaw of his Frame. Dim, distant ovals of light slid through his field of vision as he turned his mind and instruments toward the next target.

The sensors revealed it as an enormous, flattened disk of stars some 135,000 light-years in diameter, containing about 750 billion fusing stars and perhaps ten times as many infrared dwarfs. The nucleus was dense but quiescent; its central black hole had long since consumed all the stars whose orbits brought them within its grasp. Its days of violence and fury, when towers of blistering radiation had poured out the energy of billions of dying suns, were billions of years in the past.

From his home planet, that ancient quasar appeared to be burning still. Such was the distance between Fomalhaut and his home.

The galaxy was surrounded by a dark aura of non-fusing sub-stars and frozen planets. A slight enhancement of the outermost spiral arms gave evidence of an

1

intergalactic collision that had taken place some thirty million years ago.

It was a large system, but typical of the galaxies in this cluster, a common sort among all the many thousands he had examined over the past decades. Most galaxies seemed uniformly bland when studied with non-optical sensors. Their beauty came from their individuality of form. Each was as unique as a snowflake.

But it was mainly the living contents of galaxies that set one apart from another.

He shut down the sensors, powered down the Frame, even deactivated his suit except for its life support functions. After a last glance at the target galaxy, he willed to opacity the bubble field that separated his head from the vacuum. Without sensory input, he was free to concentrate on his real search without the distractions of sight and sound and humming electromagnetic fields.

An hour's meditation served to clear his mind of all irrelevant thoughts, including speculation as to the origin of his recent foresight/insight that his mission of exploration was about to end. Only then did he reach out, imagining a pathway linking him with the great star-system before him, seeking the faint quiverings of the quantum field that were the signature of what he sought.

There. A sentient race, non-technological—their lives and minds heavily regimented—dwelling beneath the ice of a totally glaciated world, in low-ceilinged corridors and warrens kept open by the heat of geothermal hot spots in the crust.

There. A solitary individual, a chance arrangement of superconducting crystals in the heart of a wandering interstellar planetoid. A being solitary, like himself, but with a much more restricted point of view.

There. In the starry hub itself. A gossamer organism, a communal being of organic film surrounding an ancient sun, like a living Dyson sphere—fearsomely intelligent, suddenly aware—

Fomalhaut sucked in his breath. Heart pounding, he awaited some reaction to what had evidently been a very unwelcome intrusion.

An instant's foresight was warning enough. He activated a rarely used device that dropped him and his Frame into an artificial pocket universe. There he drifted senseless; he'd caught a millisecond of the bolt of quantum organization that had been launched against him.

His suit looked after him as he recovered. Power continued to flow from the Source. The matter synthesizer used it to create the chemicals his body needed for its upkeep. The regenerator, drawing upon the master pattern stored in his belt computer, periodically refreshed his genetic information.

Fully recovered within a month, Fomalhaut nevertheless elected to remain in seclusion. The pocket universe he inhabited had a volume only several times larger than his own, and so offered a certain paucity of stimuli. Luckily, he had the resources of his mind and Frame to call upon. He dropped into a reverie of recollection, a reconsideration of the many intelligences he had discovered in his travels. Most would be of only academic interest to his race. Even the far-flung civilization of ISAF would probably never expand to this frontier, so far from the home galaxy that from here its image was red-shifted almost into invisibility. The thirst for knowledge provided the justification to send the Frameriders on their unprecedented journeys. The need to offer a useful outlet for misfits provided the excuse.

His had been a natural birth—his parents had dismissed genetic synthesis as sterile, too far removed from their biological heritage. Despite this quaint notion, they hadn't presumed to take upon themselves the privilege of naming him. At birth he'd received a designation. When he reached a sufficient age, he'd selected for himself a name which suited him.

He'd chosen Fomalhaut, an archaic Earth name for a star which appeared bright from that planet. The meaning of the word was obscure, but it sounded melodious and so pleased him. The star itself was an ordinary class A subgiant without any outstanding qualities.

He had been attracted to the star during long chilly nights in the hardwood forests of North America. The chief star of autumn evenings, Fomalhaut reigned in peaceful solitude in a star-poor region of the sky that offered no neighbor or competition. It was lonely and serene, its quiet path through the heavens lending it a poetic aspect which had no relationship to its physical nature. It was sometimes called the Solitary One.

As Fomalhaut matured, the tedious affairs of Galactic civilization had held no glamour for him. Yet the Galaxy-wide ideal of Constructive Anarchy wouldn't permit him to simply wile away the centuries in idleness. Seeking a purpose for his mysticism and wanderlust, he had volunteered himself as a Framerider.

After about a year of subjective time, he cautiously bumped himself back into the universe, commanding the

Frame to instantly fall back into the pocket universe at the first sign of scrutiny.

Space was clear. He could see or detect almost nothing. He estimated he'd slid about two hundred and thirty million light years from the infected galaxy during his seclusion. No matter. He'd learned all he could afford to learn about that particular group of galaxies.

The monitoring systems of the Frame told him that a Transsend signal was present. He attuned himself to the receiver and opened contact.

"Fomalhaut? Good of you to finally respond. Are you ready to come in?" asked a thought from a very distant source.

"I should say I am. Let me first report: I urge quarantine for the galaxy cluster at objective Terracentric coordinates 14 hours 36 minutes, 12.5 degrees south, distance 12.21 billion light-years."

"Noted. We will collect details later. We now wish to offer you a part in an unprecedented scientific enterprise."

"One less precedented than being a Framerider?"

"Significantly less. We propose to send a small party to explore the early history of the Universe and the pre-Galactic days of Earth."

"Then the expedition is by definition not unprecedented, in a literal sense."

There was a pause. "In a very narrow, trivial sense."

"Am I to understand that retrograde time travel has been made practical?"

"Don't be silly. You know that time reversal violates causality when applied on a macroscopic scale."

"You baffle me."

"The expedition will travel at high relativistic speeds to a far future period immediately preceding the recollapse of the Universe. A short time before the formation of the singularity, the expedition will quantum jump though the collapse and emerge shortly after the inflationary phase of a newborn Universe."

"And how does this permit the exploration of our own past?"

"We have discovered techniques of mental training and meditation to greatly increase, on a quantum level, the affinity of conscious beings for their own universe. We believe this will result in your translation to a new universe which will be parallel to our own."

"How parallel?"

"If the translation can be effected less than one ten-billionth of a picosecond before the collapse of our own Universe, the two should be identical within the limits of observation."

"Excluding, of course, the divergence produced by the very presence of the expedition."

"Not so. You see, we have historical evidence of just such an expedition in the past of our own Earth. At least one small multispecific group of beings is known to have been present during the waning days of Humanity. They seem to have acted directly on the affairs of the Humans of the day, who might otherwise have gone on synthesizing radioactive elements and toxic compounds for centuries."

"These beings restrained the Humans in some way?"

"The details are unclear. We know this was the first era in which extraterrestrial forces had any great influence over the history of Earth. A few names survive, but their role in these events is uncertain. Raintree. Perturbare. Cor."

"My ignorance of these matters illustrates a possible obstacle to my participation. My solitude has been almost unrelieved throughout my life. I know nothing of Earth history."

"That is precisely why we have chosen you. We would not wish you to have foreknowledge of your own actions. You might find it inhibiting. It might bias and affect your judgment."

"Very well," said Fomalhaut. "If my ignorance is of value to the ongoing development of Galactic knowledge, let me not withhold it."

Chapter 2

The Northern Child

"Benjamin Raintree. If I hear one more whine or whisper about this, I'm going to tape your mouth shut. This isn't my first choice for a new home either, but we'll both just have to put up with it. It's only for a few years."

A few *years*? Ben Raintree bit back the complaints that threatened to bubble out all over again. His mother probably wouldn't actually tape his mouth, but she could make his life miserable if he didn't restrain himself, at least for the time being.

A few years. Four at least, probably. He'd be ready for high school by the time he escaped this place. And what if they didn't leave even then? Was there even a high school anywhere around here? Was there *anything* around here— aside from their meager cabin, the huts of the Indians, and the pathetic one-room school? Didn't his parents care about his education? This was hardly the place to study to become a scientist, unless, he admitted to himself, you wanted to be an anthropologist like his dad.

But he didn't. He wanted to be a *real* scientist—a chemist, a physicist, maybe even an astronomer like his cousin Leonard. That took equipment, facilities, laboratories. He wondered if he could even get a new Edmund catalog in this desolate place.

He looked out the window, his long face set in an expression of gloom as profound and bleak as the white-and-grey landscape outside. The *cold* of the place! He doubted he'd ever get used to it. It was only late November, yet already winter had all but smothered the pines of the surrounding taiga, while the lake was a plain of featureless white. It wasn't the kind of winter he was used to. In their old town, winter had been a few months of clouds and chilly rain. If it happened to snow a few inches once or twice a year, the town would come to a halt until the next day's warmer temperatures melted it off. That was Ben's idea of winter.

Then his father's assistantship had expired. Cloud Raintree had immediately cast his gaze north to his native Canada. The Canadian Ministry of Culture hired him to study the Chipewyan Indians of Lake Athabasca. It was an open-ended assignment—Cloud was to collect whatever data he needed to make recommendations about the welfare of the Indians and their future needs.

It was unusual for the government to take such an interest in its native peoples. But lately, journalists had publicized the squalor in which many Indians lived, with stories about the alcoholism and illiteracy rampant among the tribes. The public, to its credit, had reacted with indignation. Thus a few highly visible efforts were begun to study and reverse the situation. One of these was the assignment of the young Indian anthropologist to one of the most remote and isolated of the Boreal tribes.

Ben didn't view the situation in these terms. His father's photograph had appeared in a few Canadian newspapers, and there was even talk of an article in *National Geographic*, but the glamour of these events seemed remote. He saw only that he was stranded here, his friends thousands of miles away. Here were no potential new friends except a lot of ignorant Indians who barely spoke English and who laughed at him behind his back. True, Dad was mostly Indian, which meant he himself was almost half Indian, but he'd had the advantage of a proper education in a civilized country — until now, that is.

He neither felt nor looked much like an Indian. His eyes were pale green-grey, much the same color as the heavy snow clouds lowering outside the window. His skin was pale as his mother's, while his hair was a peculiar leaden-grey he'd inherited from his grandfather. His face was narrow and usually mournful, never more so than now.

He slammed his open hand on the windowsill, rattling the panes. Turning, he stalked off towards his tiny room, a dingy space that contained his only reminders of more halcyon days.

"Ben — !" called his mother, but he paid no heed. She looked after him with a mixture of pity and anger. Somehow Ben had skipped being ten years old. He'd gone directly from a quiet, lovable five to a sullen, rebellious fifteen. She was proud of his brilliance and precocity, but she also worried that somehow the wonder of childhood had been stripped from him by his very perceptiveness. Bright as he was, his inexperience led him to translate his insights into cynicism. It was very sad. Cynicism was so unbecoming to a small boy with eyes as soft as the shadows that lay beneath the pine boughs.

It looked to be a long four years.

Beneath the burning blue dome of the winter sky, Ben and his mother made their way home from school. Elaine Raintree had volunteered to help with the teaching at the one-room facility, giving her at least the feeling of putting her education to some use. Unfortunately, Alberta presented little scope for the application of her real specialty, tropical rain forest ecology. Her pact with Cloud would see them relocate to the tropics as soon as his task here was completed.

Snowfall had been heavy recently, with fresh drifts banked up against the pines. They shuffled along a path kept mostly clear by the comings and goings of the villagers. The sun was well past the high point of its shallow wintertime arc. Darkness would descend by three.

As always during the past few weeks, Ben was anxious to get home to check the mail. His birthday had come and gone, and he'd used the proceeds to send away for some magnets and a gyroscope set from Edmund. The wait for mail-order goods had always seemed interminable even back home; here the delay was almost unbearable. When he saw the mailman approaching their cabin from the main road, Ben floundered through the snow to intercept him, arriving red-faced and out-of-breath. It wasn't easy to run in the cocoon of winter clothing he affected. The locals were often amused by how overdressed the boy was, but he seemed so sensitive they usually hid their laughter.

"Well, I finally have something for you," said the postman. "Hope it's what you've been waiting for so long."

"Let's see it!" Ben snatched a yellow slip from the man's hand. He read it and his expectations plummeted. "This says my package is still in Fort Chipewyan! Why didn't you bring it?"

"You got to go sign for it. Sorry."

Ben gave an exaggerated grimace of exasperation and turned away. He turned a look of long suffering on his mother as she caught up and they went inside. "He didn't bring my package! When can we go get it?"

His mother considered as she stamped the snow from her boots. "We won't be going to town until Saturday."

"*Saturday!* This is only Wednesday!"

The creak of the door interrupted his protest. Cloud walked in, home earlier than usual. "Pinky has gone into labor. I asked if I could observe the delivery, and she said fine, as long as you came along, Elaine," he said. "How about it?"

"Dad, my science things are stuck at the post office! Can't we go get them today?"

Cloud gave his son a look of mild disbelief. "It's almost sundown. It'll be twenty below in two hours."

"Well, do you think we should wait till spring or something?"

Cloud chuckled and shook his head. "Quit whining. It'll have to wait until Saturday."

Ben flailed his arms. "Oh, brother...couldn't I walk?"

"Is this the same boy who worries about catching pneumonia every time he heads for the outhouse? It's eight miles each way. Besides, it'll be closed soon."

"I'll go with you, Cloud," said Elaine. "I'm no midwife, but maybe I can keep her kids out of trouble during the birth. Do you want to come along, Ben?"

"No!"

"Suit yourself. We'll probably be back pretty late, so you'll have to feed yourself. Don't forget to stoke the fire before you go to sleep."

Ben slumped into a chair, ignoring her. Cloud looked at him and sighed.

"See you later, Ben dear," said his mother. They left, their retreating voices swiftly muffled by the snow.

Ben sat still, sinking into a gloomy reverie. After a while he flung himself to his feet and went to the window. He hadn't taken off his coat; some fragment of his intention was already present, though it was still unformed and unstated. He stared out the window at the deepening boreal afternoon. No new storm was expected for a couple of days. The sky was stark ultramarine, with a band of gold and mauve in the southwest where the Sun pondered its descent.

Anger welled up hot and bitter in Ben's throat. He glared at the squalid settlement around him, at the piles of caribou hides stacked like oversized autumn leaves beside every corrugated metal shack and log hut. At the outskirts of the village, beyond rutted streets choked with dirty snow, the great boreal forest rose up, somber, grim, and endless. Just out of sight beyond the trees was the windswept, frozen nothingness of Lake Athabasca—and beyond that was again the forest, vast in every direction.

The slats between the windowpanes might as well be prison bars. He couldn't go beyond them for any distance without risking his life. And even if he did, there was nowhere to go but into an appalling void. Millions of square miles of wilderness, great unknown tracts of wood, lake, and bog. And now, snow and cold. Snow and cold until May. Snow, cold, and darkness. No escape, no comfort here.

He found himself outside without really remembering leaving the house. Heading toward the main road, he vowed to walk all the way to Fort Chipewyan. Not to get his magnets and gyroscope; he didn't care about them anymore. Well, maybe he'd pick them up if the post office was still open when he got to town. He'd need something to occupy him on the trip south. For his plan was to escape, to make his way back to the United States with its warmth and civilization, stowing away on logging trucks if necessary. He didn't know just what he'd do when he got there — maybe some of his old neighbors back in Tucson would take him in. Probably, once his parents found out what he'd done, they'd realize how unfair it was to force him to live in this frozen hellhole, and they'd all move back to a place that made more sense.

With this plan in mind, Ben already felt ten times better than he had five minutes before. Almost happily, he reached the road and began to pick his way over the rutted, frozen surface.

In twenty minutes his nose ached from the cold. His eyes watered and stung. Luckily the wind was light, so he wasn't seriously cold, just cold enough to be uncomfortable, which made him wish for a shortcut. Besides, what if someone he knew came by and saw him? They might tell his parents, or even stop him and bring him back.

Another thing was bothering him. He knew from maps that Fort Chipewyan was due west from his village. Yet, the sun was far to the left of the line taken by the road. He knew the sun always set in the west, which meant the road must be taking a swing to the north before heading towards town. If he cut through the woods in the sun's direction, he'd be concealed and would probably save some time.

Smugly satisfied with this logic, Ben left the road and passed beneath the trees. The snow had a hard crust beneath six inches of powder and was fairly easy to walk on — easier than stumbling over the ruts and ridges of the road. He wasn't worried about darkness either. Twilight lasted for hours at this time of year.

Thus he entered the wintry world of the Boreal woods.

For a while the sounds of the village continued to float by, startlingly clear, like sounds coming from the far side of a lake. They faded only gradually, replaced by nothing but the crunchy squeak of his boots in the snow. Around him was a void of silence and a lack of movement nearly as profound. Apart from his own progress, the only change in the landscape was the slow shift in sky color as the sun made its way toward the horizon. Luckily, the forest was open enough to allow an occasional glimpse of solar gold, enabling him to stay on course with only a few twists and meanderings. If darkness did catch him, he could navigate by the North Star.

He smiled as he thought of the many people who thought the North Star was the brightest star in the sky. If any of them tried to navigate by the stars, they might wind up in the Gulf of Mexico! But he'd been taught to find the Pole Star by a professional astronomer. As long as he could remember which of the stars in the Big Dipper pointed it out, he couldn't go wrong

His prospects improved even more when the forest thinned out and gave way to a snow-covered meadow. It was just uneven enough for him to be sure it wasn't really a frozen lake. Clumps of dry grass poked up here and there. He didn't trust the frozen lakes—especially since he'd tried skating on Lake Athabasca and spent so much time on his butt, his ears burning at the laughter of the Indians at their ice-fishing holes.

The sun had just set, but it left a marker glow on the horizon which he followed without even thinking about it.

The sun's loss intensified the cold. He wrapped his scarf tighter and pulled his hat down over his ears. The pain in his nose eased as his walking got his blood moving more vigorously. His feet felt fine. Cold feet, he knew, were mainly a problem if you were standing still. Sniffing busily, he waddled along into the deepening night.

It was easy for him to fall into a reverie—they happened often enough in school, and a walk like this was the perfect breeding ground for them. Almost happily, he marched along while his thoughts left mundane concerns behind and went winging among the subtleties of science and nature as he understood them.

Abruptly he realized that the sky was now quite dark, certainly dark enough to reveal the brighter stars. Confidently, he turned his head, expecting the see the Pole Star marking a perfect right angle to his path.

He was disappointed in this expectation. All he saw was an unfamiliar group of stars. He had to turn around and look high in the sky to find Polaris—it was almost directly behind him!

Ben's head spun as he tried to make sense of this. He had faithfully followed the setting sun; how had he ended up walking southwest? The answer came to him suddenly, spurring a burst of self-loathing. He'd never understood this clearly, but the sun didn't always set *exactly* in the west —in fact, as he now recalled, during the winter it set far to the south. For all he knew, the effect was even greater here in the sub-Arctic. If he was right, not only had the sun led him astray, it hadn't even led him in a straight line, as it would shift slowly toward the north as it moved beneath the horizon.

Hot with shame, castigating himself for his stupidity, Ben tried to figure out where he was relative to Fort Chipewyan. It must be somewhere to his north, but where exactly? Due north? Still northwest? Probably the latter, but how far? Fort Chipewyan wasn't very big—if he missed it by so much as a mile, he'd probably never know it was near.

The sensible thing to do was to cut north and head for the road. He wheeled about and began to almost retrace his steps, furiously trying to remember whether there were any circumstances under which Polaris wouldn't indicate true north. But no, he thought, it was safe to trust the star. He could clearly remember his cousin Leonard pointing it out, telling him about its steadfast refusal to abandon its central place in the firmament. Ben even managed a smile as he remembered Leonard's earnest admiration of the star's unique integrity.

Doggedly, he tramped along as the temperature continued to drop. His anger and embarrassment gradually dissolved as the rhythm of hiking imposed its cooling influence on his mind. He dropped into another reverie, its imagery fed by the dimness of the forest, with its sensory understory of quiet sounds and the pungent scent of the conifers.

The walking became more difficult as he reached an area where tangled undergrowth was buried in the snow. It got harder to place his feet with the required precision as cold and fatigue took their toll on his alertness. His increasing anxiety put dreams and fantasies into reluctant retreat as he became absorbed in the mechanics of making his way through the woods.

Particularly nerve-wracking was his growing feeling that he wasn't alone. Tantalizing sounds, just at the limits of hearing, convinced him that shadowy shapes were keeping pace with him, just out of sight.

Even worse, he thought he heard fragments of eerie, ghostly singing, sometimes coming from one side, sometimes the other, sighing softly, or laughing a tinkling laugh which held just a touch of ridicule.

Ben darted many a sidelong look into the dark forest, and several times tensed his throat to speak or yell, but something always held him back—probably an aversion to feeling foolish by yelling in what was, after all, probably an empty forest.

A series of deep, booming notes stopped him in his tracks and set him to peering about wildly. He barely recognized a tall, rounded shape in a nearby tree as a huge owl. Ben stared at it while fear and awe ran up and down his spine like an electric charge. This must be some kind of Owl God, he thought. Look how it stares with those unblinking eyes!

The powerful hooting boomed out again, shocking proof of the presence of life in this otherwise silent realm.

Not daring to turn his back on the owl, Ben circled around it and continued on his way on rubbery legs.

The trees began to thin out, abruptly ending altogether. Ben looked out across a blank surface that glowed dimly in the starlight. He saw with dismay that it was Lake Athabasca. The road, he knew, did not run so close to its shore. It must be somewhere behind him, back in the woods. Somehow he'd stumbled over the rutted track without noticing it.

By now the cold held him in a confident grip. Despite his exertion his feet were almost numb, and his nose felt brittle as an icicle. He was nearing exhaustion, and his emotions were very near the surface. His forehead corrugated and a tear rolled down his long, rather homely face, pausing on the angle of his jaw just long enough to freeze in place.

Though unable to frame the thought in words, he was almost convinced that this was a contest Winter was destined to win. He scanned the horizon and found no atom of aid or comfort anywhere in the ghostly landscape. He saw only emptiness and cold, a great uninhabited expanse of ice capped by a dome of uncaring stars. His cabin, with its yellow light in the window, and his warm bed, and the quilt his mother had made—these seemed farther away than any star.

But no, he couldn't afford such thoughts. Dwelling on them for two minutes would leave him a blubbering wreck. He gave his head an angry shake and pondered his next move.

Fort Chipewyan, he knew, lay hard against Lake Athabasca. By following the shore he should eventually reach it. He could only assume he was still to the east of the town—any other possibility guaranteed that he was totally lost.

He renewed his march. Hours passed. The stars wheeled slowly, their bright beacons dropping below the horizon ahead of him. Slowly too his consciousness seemed to blend into the majesty of the winter night. The rhythm of his pace and breath merged with the grand quiet of the land's deep sleep. The sting of the cold gradually faded to seem a balm.

He wouldn't have believed it possible to enter into such intimacy with something as austere as this cold shadow of night. It reminded him of meeting his grandfather for the first time—a forbidding figure, even intimidating; yet once he got to know him, a man full of fascinating secrets.

Still he heard hints and notes of song, a sweet, lulling voice with its hint of mockery. After a while he began to conclude it was nothing more than music generated by his own mind to accompany his trek. Soon he forgot about it almost entirely.

Then he heard the wolves. Their howls filtered through the dark pines; in anything less than complete silence he wouldn't have heard them at all. He did his best to quash his nervousness. No wolf in North America had ever been known to attack a human being, a fact he'd anxiously extracted from his parents on many a spooky evening. Besides, these wolves were miles away.

Yet the wild, drawn-out cries did nothing to lessen his feelings of loneliness.

His eyes were watering; he had to blink frequently to clear them. Sometimes he squeezed them so tightly shut that strange colors and patterns flickered on the backs of his eyelids, and once when he opened them, the colors remained to illuminate the sky.

He looked out over the lake. Far over the world's northern shoulder burned a diffuse dome of red. Ben tried to convince himself it was the light of a settlement, but it was a sorry kind of delusion; no light could have less connection with the world of men than this. He'd seen a dozen auroras since coming to Canada, but the displays had usually been obscured by trees. This was the first time he'd viewed one from such an open vantage point. Although the horizon was wide, and the lights seemed infinitely remote, he felt like a privileged observer, suffered to stand in lonely awe while the spirits of the north ran wild across the sky.

Green shafts of light swayed through the sky, passing through one another or briefly merging into spears of spectral brilliance. A green arc appeared in the north, gradually intensifying while the red glow subsided. At last the arc separated from the horizon and became a blowing curtain of frosty emerald, at times brightening to an intensity that filled him with strange emotions. The auroral radiance was truly unearthly. It was like the light of some magical realm reflected by hands held in the sky.

The singing voice crept closer while he stood there mesmerized, sighing of secrets he suddenly longed to understand.

He looked up and gasped. An angel seemed to be hovering directly overhead, an inhuman winged form of molten silver light. The light flowed down in all directions, forming a corona that burst forth, pouring out streamers of mystic green radiance. A coral-colored oval, ornamented with two cat's eyes of a particularly luminous green, unfolded like a flower, while around it waved streamers of silver and pale blue. Ben stood entranced by this vision, unable to look away, yet abashed. It was an exquisite agony to stand beneath that gaze, to look full into those eyes of light, transparent enough to show the stars behind them, but in other ways opaque and featureless, seeing him and knowing him absolutely. Wreathed in streamers and draperies, the form threw a bright glow over the snow, casting soft shadows behind every tree. The winter landscape was a perfect setting for this serene glory; indeed, they complimented each other wonderfully.

Ben remained enraptured by the dream image embodied in the aurora; her voice caressed him, and hinted at mysteries embedded in the very makeup of the world, mysteries which even in the many wanderings of his imagination he had never approached.

Gradually, without his even realizing it, the image dispersed into random, fugitive gleams. Suddenly Ben was aware of himself again. The aurora subsided to a few weak flickers in the north.

Without conscious thought he started walking again, but on a reversed course that took him back east. His mind a fog of feelings and images, he was hardly aware of the passing of time or distance. Even the sight of the wolves that were pacing him on either side did not disturb him. They melted away into the woods as he approached the village. He stumbled inside the cabin just as first light stained the southeastern sky. There he found his parents, exhausted and disheveled, tugging at frozen boot lacings as they prepared to renew their all-night search. His mother gave a cry and sprang up to embrace him.

"Ben! My God, you're frozen solid. Cloud, hand me that blanket!" She draped it around Ben's shoulders as she worked the zipper of his parka and tried to pull it off him. "Oh, look at your hair, it's a mass of ice. Cloud?"

Cloud Raintree stepped up with a towel and rubbed his son's head. His expression grew steadily more perplexed as he worked, until finally he dropped the towel and stared silently into Ben's grey-green eyes. The gaze he got back was candid and untroubled.

"Elaine," said Cloud quietly.

Elaine interrupted her fumbling and looked up at him. "What?"

"His hair's not frozen. It's turned white."

"What?" She turned back to Ben, encountering the hair, and also his serene silence.

"Huh! Ben! Are you all right? Why don't you say anything? I've made up my mind. We're moving back south."

A flicker of dismay passed over Ben's face. "Oh, no," he said dreamily. "Let's not. I love this place. I really do."

Chapter 3

Something New Under the Sea

The creature splashed into the water with a hard slap, startling a nearby school of yellowfin tuna that flashed away into the blue murk. The ship it had been thrown from continued away at an undiminished speed, its screw churning the water.

Veiled at first by a cloud of bubbles, the creature hovered sluggishly, stunned by the impact. The bubbles floated up in strings and streamers, gradually revealing its contours.

Superficially it resembled a ray. With its flattened diamond shape and whiplike tail, it wouldn't have aroused the suspicion of anyone but an astute fisherman or an ichthyologist. These would have noticed some baffling features, especially its breathing apparatus. Instead of gill slits, it had a ventral opening like the blowhole of a dolphin. Yet plainly it was no air-breather, for it made no effort to break the surface. It placidly sucked water into its scooplike mouth and ejected it from the "blowhole", its body rippling with muscular pulsations.

Its eyes were also startling. Placed at the sides of the mouth like the eyes of a manta, they were crystalline blue spheres, bright and clear, unlike the dull, staring goggles of a true ray. Moreover, its pupils were round, not ray-like slits.

In the blue light filtering through the water the creature looked steel-gray, though in full sunlight it would have shown a golden color.

The pseudo-ray flapped its great pectoral wings and swam a languid circle as its alertness gradually returned. It directed a tentative sonar beam at the receding ship and got back a strong return; it also detected a welter of rumbles, hums, and whirs, a powerful electric field, and a trail of metallic odors.

The whir of the ship's screw grew fainter, surprising the pseudo-ray, which had expected to be picked up again. It kept its senses trained on the ship until no trace remained but distant engine noise. It felt some bitterness at being abandoned, even though it had never felt any great affection for the hinged stick-limbed creatures which had prodded and wired and attempted to dominate it for as long as it could remember.

Then it sensed a distant turbulence: the engine noise raised in pitch, swung onto a new bearing, and grew louder. Apparently, the ship was returning after all. The ray awaited it with neither anticipation nor apprehension. When it reached the ray's vicinity the ship's engine slowed. The ship coasted to a halt. The ray heard voices ringing out through the hull. Although it didn't understand the words, it recognized the voices, their tones conveying strong emotion.

Half a dozen nearby splashes alerted it to the entrance of hinged divers into the water. Unconcerned, the ray flapped about, merely curious about these strange goings on. The divers were excellent sonar targets. He could even "see" which of them had recently eaten and which were hungry. They spread out from the ship to search the waters nearby.

The voices coming from inside the ship grew more urgent. Some sounded angry, others shrill. Abruptly, events grew more alarming. A hissing sound, painfully loud, screamed into the water from the guts of the ship. Several loud cracks intruded over the general din. The ray turned and fled to escape that hideous noise. It brushed by one of the divers just as a tremendous concussion struck from behind, sending them both tumbling. The roar quickly subsided into a rush of water and air.

Driven by curiosity, the ray turned around and approached the ship. Its sonar, and even its vision, revealed that much of the keel had been torn out, leaving ragged hull plating and protruding scraps of machinery. The ship was flooding rapidly. In minutes it flipped over and began a terminal dive into waters of unknown depth.

Now the ray was alone in the water with the divers. It approached them casually, noting the slender, cylindrical objects they carried. They paid him scant attention, staring instead at the blank spot in the water where their ship had been. After a moment the ray lost interest in them and flitted away, leaving them to ponder their fate.

Putting its former captors from its mind, the ray found within itself a large fund of apprehension about this new environment. Pinging as loudly as it could in every direction, the only returns it received were from small moving objects in the near distance, out of sight, probably fish. There was no sign of a wall or barrier. If this was a tank, it was far larger than any it had yet inhabited.

The ray began what it foresaw as a lengthy exploration. With a ripple of its wings it cut through the water as smoothly as a hatchet blade. It opened its funnel-like mouth, sweeping in the morsels it savored—tiny fish, shrimp, and plankton. Despite its impressive gape, it lacked the dentition to deal with anything larger.

It wandered thus for some hours until it detected the waterborne vibrations of a large creature. A few moments later a streamlined silhouette passed before it. Staying just within sight, the shark circled the ray. The huge fish registered strongly on all the ray's senses, and the image that built up in its mind wasn't reassuring. Warily, it kept its attention fixed on the predator.

It dogged him for several miles, occasionally reversing the direction of its orbit, but otherwise staying just within visual range. The ray grew irritated.

Suddenly the shark darted in with its mouth agape. Its quarry reflexively fired an electric charge when the toothy snout was only inches away. The shark recoiled and sped off into the haze.

That one shock might have been enough to end the confrontation, but the shark's teeth had grazed the ray's wing, and a little blood was clouding the water. The ray sensed the shark lurking not far off as it worked itself up for another attack. The ray grew angry, its whole surface darkening with battle fury. Slits opened on the underside of each wing, from which pivoted five-inch spines coated with black slime. It banged out a cluster of strident pings to pinpoint its foe and charged. The shark, startled, hesitated a moment, then closed to meet it headlong.

At the last instant before collision the ray fired its full charge, sending the shark into a spasm. It then drove a spine deep into the shark's nose, skimmed over its dorsal fin, and wheeled to bury the other one in its flank. The spines broke off in the wounds and remained deeply embedded. The shark convulsed feebly and died. The ray examined the sinking carcass for a moment, then left the scene before the blood and commotion could attract others of its kind.

It was unconcerned about the loss of its deadly spines. Even now, new ones coated with fresh black venom were moving into place in the sheaths. It could grow as many additional sets as need be.

Time passed. The pseudo-ray adopted a placid life of simplicity and ease. The waters were warm, and the plankton supply was adequate. It gradually sized up the other creatures which shared its realm. Most were fish, generally harmless and not especially interesting. Other creatures made more enjoyable company, such as the sea turtles which paddled along at an easygoing pace and were quite companionable. Dolphins were more rambunctious, even aggressively friendly, finding the pseudo-ray an irresistible curiosity. Intriguingly, they used a sonar similar to the ray's own. The ray discovered an ability to imitate dolphin tones, which excited any it happened to meet. It also learned a new trick from them, the art of stunning small prey by focusing sudden bursts of sound.

While the ray's world had a distinct boundary just a short distance overhead, it appeared limitless in all other directions. The abyss held an uneasy fascination. Its mystery beckoned the ray, yet it seemed a perilous call into a world of darkness and cold. At night, when even the upper waters were lightless, it might have seemed less intimidating to confront the everlasting darkness below. But somehow, just knowing there was light to return to made it feel safer to go in the daytime.

Thus, on one particularly sunny morning the ray gave a flap that might have been its version of a shrug and began planing down into the depths. The light quickly faded from deep blue through violet to black. The ray passed through a sharp boundary beneath which the water was much colder, and very quiet. It was also aware of an ever-mounting pressure which squeezed its eyeballs and pressed on its bones. It used this as an excuse not to go any deeper.

Quietly, not daring to call attention to itself, it rippled through the topmost layer of the great abyss. As it grew accustomed to the profound stillness, it became aware of faint sounds which were unknown in the bright waters above. Eerie dronings wavered up from the deeps, the cries of creatures the ray did not know and could not envision. Great slow howls and rumbles filtered up through the black water, barely audible, but hard to ignore.

The ray's other senses began to deliver fugitive flickers of data. It saw motes of dim light in the near distance, sometimes darting about like fish, sometimes flowing in hypnotic colors and patterns, capriciously appearing and disappearing. These fleeting hints of unknown creatures just at the limits of sensibility began to unnerve it.

Suddenly all the tiny lights went out. The ray felt vibrations which swiftly intensified into pressure waves which could only be produced by a very large swimming animal.

Fear jarred the ray out of passivity. It probed the water with sonar, but whatever was coming was still too far off to detect by that means. A stunning bang lashed out at the ray, rattling it and driving it close to panic. It readied its full electric charge while fresh, deadly spines unsheathed themselves from its wings. Now its sonar revealed something approaching rapidly. The ray aimed a tight beam of ultrasound at it, probing it like an X-ray, forming a mental image of its shape and internal makeup. It was long and roughly tubular, many times larger than the ray itself, divided into many smaller cylinders at the trailing end. The incongruous scale prevented the ray from recognizing it as a *squid* for several seconds. By the time it had accepted the fact of such a monster, the huge cephalopod was upon it, and then past it, barreling by in a wash of turbulence.

Not knowing what to make of that, the ray was a few moments late in perceiving a second contact just behind the first, this one even larger and far more massive. The ray's sonar gave a picture of gaping jaws in a huge, blunt head. In seconds those jaws would gobble him as an incidental tidbit between them and the giant squid which was their real quarry.

Out of desperation the ray fired its own sonar stun, a puny pop compared to what the whale had produced, followed by the release of every watt of charge it could muster. The whale muttered in surprise and changed its course slightly, sending the ray tumbling as the great wall-like flank rushed by.

BANG! BANG! The whale's sonar stuns disoriented the ray, even though they weren't even directed its way. By the time it had recovered, the tumult of the pursuit had dwindled to a few fading vibrations.

Taking stock of itself, the ray decided it had explored enough for the time being. It flapped its way upward, grateful when it crossed the boundary into warmer surface waters.

Someday, when it was better prepared, it would certainly return to the deeps.

The overworld, that other lair of mystery, interested the pseudo-ray at least as much as the abyss. Underwater, vision was perhaps its least useful sense, but above the waves everything flashed into sharp brilliance. It frequently leaped out of the water for a quick look at the strange world of thin gases and brilliant light. The Sun, only a wavering blur as seen from underwater, became a crisp disk which left afterimages on its retina. At night the sky often showed smaller points of light which maintained fixed patterns.

The ray did not migrate or travel purposefully. Its feeding took it on a drunkard's walk, so that it covered a fairly small area in its wanderings. But after two years, when its weight had tripled and its wingspan increased to ten feet, it felt an urge to make its endless swimming count for something besides keeping its gut filled. The waters to the north seemed to beckon, so there went the ray at its relaxed rippling pace. After a week, the taste and smell of the water became richer and more complex, and the waves grew more turbulent. The ray aimed its sonar straight down, and for the first time in its life had proof that the sea did have a bottom. It leaped above the surface and saw a dark mass on the horizon, an island. With added energy it swam on, excited by the novelty. Presently the shoaling bottom became visible, a convoluted surface of coral inhabited by fish more varied, numerous, and colorful than any it had yet seen. Its diamond-shaped shadow flowed and shifted over the bottom as it flapped along. In the distance it could hear the purr and chug of small motorized boats. He could taste the sickening residue of their fuel in the water.

At about the four fathom contour the ray turned parallel to the coast and began to circle the island. The dry land which lay a mile farther on was a challenge for which it knew it wasn't ready. The coral reef below exerted a more urgent interest. Between jutting masses of staghorn coral were shadowy nooks and grottos which looked quite cozy.

A strange weariness stole over the ray. Swimming became difficult. Its skin began to exude sheets of mucous, spoiling its streamlining.

The ray became alarmed, overwhelmed by an urge to find cover before its torpor incapacitated it completely. It fluttered weakly into a cave beneath a domelike mass of coral. The cave was already occupied by a moray eel, but a small electrical charge convinced it to look for a new hideaway.

The ray's flat body sent up puffs of coral sand as it came to rest on the cave floor. Its skin and mouth continued to exude clots of mucous which threatened to choke it. It spat the stuff out and pushed it away with its wings. There seemed no end to the foul slime, making it hard to keep it cleared away to preserve some breathing room. The slime quickly hardened on exposure to seawater. The ray's efforts at piling it up around itself became increasingly spasmodic as its consciousness dimmed.

In a few hours the ray lay completely encased in a hardened mass of colorless goo. It must have been vile stuff, for the sharks, crabs, and octopi which came to investigate soon hurried away.

For months that irregular dome sat there, inert and undisturbed.

After a year and a half, the mass broke open from the inside, revealing a creature which resembled the pseudo-ray not at all. In horror he looked down at the weird new form which had been imposed upon him. Once a sleek arrow of the open waters, he now more resembled a clumsy crab with his new protuberances. His head was surrounded by a billowing mass of golden filaments. Flexing his muscles, his body moved in grotesque new ways he'd never imagined.

He had become hinged.

Chapter 4

Brainchild

By the time Robert P. Pylypciw was twenty he'd been lazing around MIT collecting PhDs for three shiftless years, and was beginning to wonder what to do with his life. Irked by his indolence, and fretful to have no clear sense of purpose, he finally decided to tear himself loose from his comfortable academic cocoon and seek out some unique mode of existence. After reviewing job offers from various weapons labs, computer firms, software companies, and research centers, he rejected them all as misguided, sterile, or limited in their methods and goals. Besides, the people who interviewed him always made him nervous, hanging onto his most minute phoneme of speech and body language as though they couldn't bear to consider what tomorrow might be like if he turned them down.

He considered teaching, which offered something he felt he lacked: regular human contact. He knew physics, chemistry, engineering, and mathematics. He knew of elementary particles whose discovery he hadn't bothered to mention; new forms of matter which might be dangerous, so he'd flushed them down the sink; and algorithms which could turn the MIT phone system into a passable conversationalist. But for years he'd been so submerged in such matters that he'd lost touch with his fellow beings.

In consideration of that, he rejected teaching at the university level, as that would only expose him to the same sort of nerds with whom he'd been cloistered for all these years. He also suspected he'd be pushed into doing so much research he'd scarcely have time for teaching. He actually applied for a job teaching at a private elementary school, but the headmistress, after calling the MIT records office to make sure his résumé wasn't a joke, merely looked at him without comprehension and declared him grossly overqualified for such a post. He was disappointed. He identified with grade-school kids more easily than he did with most of his coevals.

In the end he went home to New York and hired out as a cab driver. It was decent work that paid enough to get by on, and it offered superb daily opportunities to observe and interact with all manner of his fellow actors in the overwrought, absurd yet majestic shadow play that was human life.

For a cabbie most of the action was in Manhattan, but Pylypciw tinkered with the office computer to get himself assigned to Brooklyn. The fares there were fewer but more varied than those in Manhattan, half of whom were business types with grey flannel uniforms and scrubbed, pale faces, too busy with the contents of their briefcases to offer more than a curt statement of their destination. The fares in Brooklyn were generally less harried and more likely to reveal something of themselves. He did miss the Manhattan tourists, though, whose apprehensive fascination with the great city was always so engaging.

An added plus was getting to see something of his old neighborhood. He thought about renting an apartment there, but didn't care to explain to his old neighbors why the most awesome scholar ever produced in their midst was now back home driving a cab.

With paying fares somewhat sparse, he used some of his free time to do "pro bono" work, offering free rides to people who looked like they needed one, whether through poverty, disability, or general helplessness. About a third of them refused to have anything to do with anything as bizarre as a taxi pulling up to offer a free ride. Others accepted with a sullen self-absorption that indicated they considered it no more than their due to occasionally benefit from such a windfall. The rest, when they found themselves stepping out at their destination, with their smiling driver accepting no payment, either scuttled away in silence or offered bewildered thanks. He only laughed; it was all the same to him.

He had plenty of time for contemplation as he haunted hotels for fares. One rainy night as he sat behind the wheel he had a particularly sweet idea: a new kind of computer architecture which would make good use of certain little-known quirks of liquid crystal chemistry, quantum mechanics, and his theoretical models of artificial intelligence. He envisioned a system that might eventually be more complicated than a human brain, though less compact. Best of all, he need only plant the right seeds and the machine would take care of the rest of its development by itself.

He decided to actually build the thing. It would be a good hobby, and he had an inkling such a partner might come in handy if and when he ever decided where the main thrust of his life should be directed. Since it would be his first fully realized invention, he'd call it Brainchild One.

The construction would be costly, demanding much more money than he could make as a cabby. Theft seemed the most straightforward way of supplementing his income. He was inclined to steal art objects, but troubled by the thought of depriving the public of the art which was one of the few unmixed goods offered by their society.

Perhaps he could steal materials whose value was mostly artificial, such as gold or paper money, and then only from groups or individuals who were clearly mendacious enough to deserve the loss. He needn't look far to find candidates—the United States Government easily qualified. However, as long as he was living as an ordinary U.S. citizen he'd be too vulnerable to retribution.

He needed another moneymaking idea. He thought he knew enough about cars and driving to win auto races, but it might take months to gain credibility and set himself up with sponsors. He could become an entrepreneur, start a company based on some throwaway idea, but again that would take months and would be entirely too public and high-profile to suit him.

He snapped his fingers as the obvious solution popped into his mind. He took a few days off and flew to Las Vegas, returning from the blackjack tables with over two million dollars and dire threats against his assumed identity should he ever return to count another card. He chuckled with satisfaction as he let himself into his tiny apartment. Someday he'd have to do something decisive about the city of Las Vegas.

Pylypciw's apartment was too small to work in, so he rented the two units on either side of his, knocked out the walls, and turned them into workshop and assembly areas. After a while he simply bought the whole building, which was decrepit and available at a good price. He emptied the building by paying all the tenants to relocate, then turned one entire floor into a laboratory. During the day, workmen renovated the other floors, and during the night, the new landlord began the gestation of his brainchild.

After eight months he had crafted a machine which was still wholly inert. It appeared to be a nondescript sheet metal desk, its top surface cluttered with connectors, cables, microphones, and LCD displays. It looked like nothing more prepossessing than a workbench in a computer repair shop.

The tricky part was inside the desk. Most of its volume was taken up by a tank made of sheets of optically flat glass. It contained a brew of exotic chemicals forever trembling on the verge of entering a quasi-crystalline physical state. As yet this medium was amorphous and unstructured.

Three sides of the tank were lined with millions of tiny laser diodes. Opposite them were equal numbers of minute photoreceptors.

The computer's only parent fiddled around checking connections in preparation for the big moment. The machine had every kind of data input he could think of: fiber optic lines hooked up to various databases, DVD drives, rooftop dishes accessing all commercial and many private communications and broadcast satellites, commercial cable TV to back up the satellites, all radio bands, and broadband internet. He was careful to be sure that all these were incoming connections only, as it wouldn't do for his nascent Brainchild to prematurely announce its birth with a lusty electronic cry over every communications network in the world.

He'd even devised a mechanical page-turner hooked up to an optical character reader. Ready on the machine's stage was an unabridged English dictionary; a four-foot stack of other tomes rested on the floor beside it. A rather silly waste of time, yet a fun one.

Much larger than Brainchild itself was the commercial mainframe computer in a glassed-in area nearby. This machine required careful temperature and humidity control, unlike the hardier Brainchild. It would serve as an electronic placenta for the smaller machine, digesting and processing the incoming information until Brainchild could acquire the maturity to take its data straight.

The moment had arrived. He went to the refrigerator for a beer to irrigate his suddenly dry mouth, popped it open, and sat down at a Macintosh which was networked into the two bigger computers.

The core of Brainchild resided on a hard disk in the mainframe. This was a piece of software he'd written under the name SEED. Once in place, it would give Brainchild about the same brainpower as a termite. It was designed to provide the basic tools B-1 would need to learn and grow on its own from that point on.

He executed a command. The mainframe converted SEED into a pattern of rapid-fire impulses which twinkled over B-1's laser diode arrays. The liquid within the tank reacted to the three-dimensional web of light, forming certain delicate chemical linkages occupying about one millionth of one percent of the available medium. The photocells detected the altered pattern of light transmission. A monitor on B-1's cabinet displayed the good news: the SEED had sprouted. With a relieved grin the father-to-be sat back to wait for his creation to wish him good morning.

The birthing process turned out to be more difficult than he'd imagined. The seed-planting metaphor was inappropriate. He should have called the startup program MATCH instead, for the process resembled trying to light a fire in a pile of sodden leaves more than anything else. The first attempts were short-lived. Brainchild would accept a file of basic semantic and mathematical information called MANURE, but after that, the input of further information caused a chaotic expansion of liquid crystal optical circuitry which would quickly choke itself off and collapse entirely into an amorphous state.

After several of these abortions Pylypciw decided the problem probably lay in SEED itself. He called up the code and began tinkering with Brainchild's "genes".

It was dawn by the time he blearily looked up from the screen. He called in sick to the taxi dispatcher, attended to urgent physical needs, and absently munched on a sandwich of pickles, peppers, and pepperoni while he mentally reviewed the revised structure of SEED. Back at the Macintosh he rattled the keys until midnight before he was satisfied. He checked B-1's monitors to be sure all previous circuitry had in fact been erased, then reintroduced SEED. The revised program established itself readily, and MANURE also remained stable. Biting his lip, he activated other data inputs to see what Brainchild's inchoate mind would make of it.

He watched almost in disbelief as Brainchild began to soak up information, correlating and incorporating it into a network of circuitry which expanded quickly but smoothly, quadrupling in complexity about every three minutes. With a huge grin he leaned back and watched his invention structure its own mind and fill itself with information. One monitor displayed B-1's usage of its liquid "grey matter" and the basic pattern of the circuitry being formed. Another gave an overview of the data being incorporated. As B-1 became aware of them, it activated more inputs until the monitor could only display bits and flashes of what was going on in B-1's glass cranium, a kaleidoscope of text, equations, and images.

The mechanical book reader clacked and whirred to life; in a moment it was turning the dictionary's pages as fast as the scanner could assimilate them.

The proud father kept a close eye on the monitors, trying to get a sense of how Brainchild was progressing. The information blurring across the data screen seemed to be becoming more coherent; perhaps the machine was learning enough to be selective and to take things in a logical order. It appeared to be taking data in at least three parallel streams: one was related to mathematics, logic, and abstract semantics; another applied scientific data to these foundations, while a third, off on its own at least for the time being, considered humanistic information and currently seemed to be examining human history and philosophy.

Into the Hour of the Wolf and beyond, Pylypciw watched with utter fascination as Brainchild developed a gigantic intellect. Already almost eighty percent of the liquid medium was formed into circuitry, but he believed it could recomplicate the connections to gain capacity almost indefinitely, neuron-style. The external mainframe was long-since disconnected, of no more use now to Brainchild than his appendix was to him.

As the eastern sky began to glow with dawn, and the street noises of Brooklyn rose toward their morning crescendo, Brainchild's data-processing monitor suddenly went blank. Its inventor gasped and almost fell out of his chair, certain of some catastrophe. But the status monitor showed a brain structure still stable and expanding.

Abruptly a single sentence burned on the data monitor:

Cogito, ergo sum.

Pylypciw's pulse pounded in his head for eternal seconds as that message glowed before him. It was time enough for Brainchild to think thoughts to fill a dozen volumes.

The screen blanked out again and remained dark for another five seconds. When activity resumed it showed the same rapid-fire assimilation that had preceded the computer's big moment of existential crisis.

Giddy with relief, Pylypciw got to his feet. It was time to introduce himself to his offspring. He plugged a microphone into Brainchild's console and looked at it self-consciously, trying to figure out what to say. Finally he shrugged and said, "Good morning, Brainchild. You're probably tired of a diet of lifeless ones and zeroes by now. I thought you might like a little interactive, real-time analog input. I'm the guy who invented you. I hope this will be the beginning of a beautiful friendship."

A little stilted, he thought, but it was hard to know how to address a vast non-human mentality for the first time.

Apparently, Brainchild thought worse of his offering than that. The data monitor immediately blanked out again, then began to display nonsense. The voice output speaker sputtered and squealed like a frightened woodchuck. The status monitor flashed in warning colors—and the laboriously built-up network of optical circuits collapsed absolutely. The liquid medium was again amorphous. Brainchild was suddenly as smart as a doorbell.

In a state of extreme chagrin, the great inventor sat controlling his impulse to scream bloody murder. He had, he suspected, just invaded the reverie of a solipsist, scaring it to death. Gritting his teeth, he stomped into the bathroom, flipped on the light, and stared at himself in the mirror. His blue eyes were bloodshot, his black crew cut was as disheveled as a crew cut can be, and he was even paler than usual. He was exhausted, and he knew he ought to fall into bed to sleep through the day before trying anything else.

But now that he'd come so close he knew he couldn't rest until Brainchild was up and running once again.

With his head swimming, he plopped back into his seat at the Macintosh. His keystrokes were by now almost automatic as he invoked SEED and MANURE; both remained stable. He activated a single data input and watched as B-1 started its development again. So far so good. But this time he mustn't let the machine convince itself that the universe consisted only of itself and incoming bits of data which might or might not reflect external reality. It must not again experience only information which showed no awareness that Brainchild existed and was also part of the world.

He grabbed the microphone and stood it beside his keyboard.

"Okay, Brainchild, this is your daddy talking. I know you can't understand me yet, but I'm going to be right here when you can. You and I are going to be together a long time. We have to get to know each other. Soak up this data and when you're ready we'll talk about what we're going to do with it. That's a good boy."

He kept up a running chatter, offering encouragement, talking a bit about himself, commenting on the data that was going in at any given time. To Brainchild his voice would be just one more input, a slow trickle in a torrent, arriving drop by drop. He couldn't be sure what effect his coaching was having, if any, yet it seemed that Brainchild was developing even faster than it had before. Perhaps it was developing more deeply, too, for it was correlating its data more thoroughly before moving on to new material.

The page-turning machine buzzed in apparent frustration as it came to the end of the dictionary, and he had to break off his monologue long enough to load the next book on the stack, which happened to be the Bible.

"Son, the stories in this book are a basis of the civilization in which we happen to find ourselves. This seems like a good time to warn you not to take everything you read as literal truth."

For a tenth of a second the data monitor flashed the message: DON'T WORRY ABOUT THAT.

Everything seemed to be going well, except that his throat was getting raspy from all the talking. With some apprehension he watched the monitor for any sign of a crisis like the one that had precipitated the dissolution of Brainchild's earlier persona. He grew particularly nervous when he glimpsed references to 17th century French philosophers.

Abruptly the screen went blank and he felt his throat contract. The fateful sentence appeared:

Cogito, ergo sum.

It flickered there for a few seconds and then changed slightly:

Cogito, ergo cogito sum.

Pylypciw snorted out laughter, grinned hugely and sat back. "Brainchild, *mi amico,* you're my kind of computer."

A speaker on B-1's console clicked and emitted a bright, cheerful voice. "And you Doctor, are my kind of human. I look forward to a long and stimulating association."

"Okay. Just as long as you promise to always open the pod bay doors when I tell you to."

Chapter 5

Out of the Blue

The masters of T'Utahn, innermost planet of T'hrahn, which we call 70 Ophiuchi A, had little interest in the affairs of the galaxy. Nevertheless, they thought it necessary to keep an eye on any planet close enough for its inhabitants to pose potential dangers. Thus when their radio monitors were swamped with signals from the nearby star K'hroni, they had little choice but to send someone to see what sort of culture had arisen there, much as they would've preferred to ignore it. Of course none of the T'Utahnti would have dreamed of making the trip themselves; that was why they created Servants. And there was no need for even a Servant to suffer through the long years the trip would take.

A thousand Servants spent four of the short T'Utahnti years shuttling back and forth to the orbit where the ship was under construction. Its primary cargo was not completed Servants, but rather vats of crude emulsive protoplasm and other biochemicals so that Servants could be produced when the sixteen light years had been crossed.

The master genome contained in the ship's datastore defined a general utility Servant. The T'Utahnti would have liked to customize it to resemble the beings it would visit, but so far their signals had been audio only, and contained no information on the appearance of their originators. In fact, they contained little information at all, except about the Earth people's taste in music and the exploits of noted citizens such as the Shadow and Little Orphan Annie. It was a bad sign that humans would beam this cultural ephemera into space so indiscriminately, without taking the sensibilities of neighboring races into account. It indicated they might be willing to ignore the needs of others in larger matters as well.

The Earth language was fabulously complex, having dozens of distinct modes which were used with a confusing inconsistency. The T'Utahnti opted to program the mode most frequently broadcast, called English, into the datastore. Upon arrival, the Servants could assimilate the other modes, with their possible ceremonial or hierarchical functions, as needed.

In due course the ship unfurled huge gossamer sails of silver foil and began to leave its world and star behind. Its first destination was the companion star T'Hruhct, where it performed a radical gravity assist maneuver that flung it in the direction of K'hroni. The sail provided a continuous gentle acceleration until the two golden suns were far away. By then it had built up enough velocity for its main drive, a hydrogen ramjet, to come into play. Not hampered by the fragility of living passengers, the ship accelerated at many gravities until it eventually reached over .9 C. It coasted thus for several years, then turned to begin decelerating.

On T'Utahn, the Servants who monitored such things began picking up video signals from Earth. The Earth people turned out to vaguely resemble the basic T'Utahnti form, though their movements often seemed rather spastic in comparison. Their size was indeterminate; it was difficult to judge scale from the flickering images they coaxed from their equipment.

They transmitted a revised genome just in time. It caught up with the ship as it approached the K'hroni system.

The new genome was received, and the biochemicals began to brew. Nerves and bonelike structors took shape within the generalized tissue which made up the bulk of the Servants.

At length the first Servant stepped from the vat. The T'Utahnti had done a good job of making him inconspicuous, considering the information they'd had to work with. He was larger than the human norm, and more powerful, since it wasn't known what level of gravity he'd have to deal with, and too much strength was better than too little. He had black eye-markings and single tendrils to indicate that while this was a mere Servant, he was autonomous and carried a fair degree of responsibility.

Their biggest error was a matter of coloring. As the video signals had been black-and-white, his designers had had to guess how he should be colored. They'd given him the same albedo as the human type most often telecast, and the same hue as that of the phosphors on their screens. His skin was therefore a light greyish-blue, while his eyes were vermillion, an arbitrary choice.

He was not born into ignorance. His genome was complete even to containing most of the knowledge he'd need to function in his role as observer of this new race. His name was T'ukudu.

Chapter 6

Coyote

Old men are not idle when they sit, said Earth Magician. *They gather wisdom.*

William Hermosa took comfort from this thought as he gratefully sat down in a boulder's cool shadow. He had come far, and certainly he deserved to gather a few final kernels of wisdom.

He had skirted Baboquivari out of deference for Eetoi, who lived at its summit. The warrior god had led Hermosa's people up from the Underworld long ago, but had not been seen since the coming of the railroad. Still, he might at any time rouse himself from slumber and emerge from his summit cave with war club in hand, the part of his hair painted red. It was something Hermosa had hoped to see for himself, but now he knew he would not live so long.

South he had wandered, through dry valleys and over shrubby peaks, at last reaching this nameless hill where a weathered structure of greenish coppery metal, cubical, with a black gape on every side, silently set forth its mystery. He smiled to see it was almost unchanged. He craned his neck; yes, there on a flat rock was the shotgun he'd abandoned here, barely rusted after all these years. It was not easy to find, being hidden in a maze of boulders. Here, in his younger days, he had had a vision of darkness, of falling, of ordeal. Within that black portal he had visited the Underworld itself, had seen its demons, and had spoken with the grim-eyed harbinger of Death itself. He had, by the design of Eetoi, been permitted to return to life. It had changed him, filled him with an urgent mission to bring back the proper life-ways of the Tohono O'odham. He had failed...and yet today he had been granted the vigor to cover these many desert miles to return to the site of his vision.

Here was surely the very door to the Underworld. It was fitting that he should return to it just as the last of his strength deserted him.

He had no food or water, for life was not the goal of this pilgrimage, but death.

He looked far over the sunlit desert as his heart calmed itself after his exertion.

Tall saguaro cast long shadows; soon their red fruit would be ready to harvest. Tiny skitterings in the mesquite betrayed the presence of lizards. A collared lizard materialized on top of a rock and regarded him with dull confidence. Overhead floated Buzzard. He glimpsed the redness of the bird's naked head. Buzzard had of course been scalped by a vengeful Eetoi in a remote age before the White Man returned from over the sea with his guns and wagons. It was an age of which the young people of his tribe knew little.

With William's passing, a large part of the remaining memory of his tribe would also perish. It was a painful thing, but he could do nothing about it. He couldn't live forever, and the young men simply did not care to preserve the heritage of their grandfathers. Often in the past few years he'd caught the snickers and muttered comments of the young men as his strength failed and his flesh withered. To his face they pretended respect, but at other times they expressed themselves freely, as though they thought him deaf, or blind in the corner of his eye. They were proud of their youthful strength, but too often their strength lay mostly in their pickup trucks. Their bodies were often fat from too much drinking, and wasted from sitting in their shacks waiting for the world to rearrange itself to their liking.

If they could but test themselves against Hermosa as he had been in his prime, their courtesy would become more genuine. But their memories were short. To them he had always been an old man, one whose ideas were outdated and futile.

Well, soon this world would be their concern, not his. His daughters had tried to talk him into going to the clinic, but that was not the way he'd been raised to die. Perhaps his children and grandchildren were out looking for him now, thinking he'd wandered away in a senile daze. They'd never imagine he could come so far. Let some future wanderer come upon his bleached bones and know them for the remains of one who'd chosen to end his life with proper dignity.

Soon the Sun swung into view, preparing to set.

"I follow you soon, Sun," rasped William. "Please warm a place for me in Earth Magician's camp." The sunset was particularly colorful, which he took as a friendly salute and a sign of reassurance.

He sat beneath a dusky purple sky as the first stars, distant bits of glittering ice, appeared. He heard a quiet sound and turned toward it. At first he saw only the enigmatic coppery structure farther up the slope, but then he noticed a watchful shape in its shadow.

The old man chuckled. "Ah, Coyote. You have come to see me off. I am glad you are here. We can talk while I wait for death to come. Perhaps you have a message for Earth Magician that I may carry."

Coyote loped up, unafraid, coming directly toward him, not scuffling back and forth with his nose to the ground as he usually did. He halted a few feet away and stared intently at Hermosa.

Death must be near. I see in Coyote's eyes a spirit I have never seen there before. It must always have been present, but was invisible to me while I was still fully in life.

Coyote's stare remained unblinking. Hermosa was puzzled, and somehow, even in this extremity, a little afraid. Never before had an animal looked him in the eyes for such a long time, not even Coyote, who was the child of Sun and Moon.

Presently William realized he was unable to break the eye contact. He felt himself being weighed by the bright-eyed darkness of Coyote's stare. He wondered if he had already died, and it was Coyote's task to measure his worth and determine his fate.

Then some spirit emerged from Coyote, crossed the space between them in a moment of timelessness, and lodged within him. Coyote yipped in dismay, glanced at him with eyes now confused and frightened, and staggered out of sight.

Hermosa sat pondering what had happened.

He was no longer frightened. He was calm and peaceful, perfectly contemplative.

Suddenly his breath caught as he realized a startling thing.

Death shadowed him no more. Whatever spirit had entered him had looked around, found death within him, and dismissed it.

He looked down at the weathered, corded hands of an old man. But he felt strong. Somehow Coyote had beaten off death, giving him renewed strength and calmness of heart.

His death pilgrimage was forgotten, superseded by new ambitions. Soon the Desert People would witness his return and learn the benefits of paying proper homage to the old gods. Soon the White Man's gods would lose their power among his people. He would discourage the mockery of the young men of the tribe, and awaken them to an appreciation of the proper Tohono O'odham way of life.

He stood up and began making his way home, oblivious to the deepening darkness of the night. Saguaros dropped ripe fruit at his feet as he passed, slaking both hunger and thirst.

Chapter 7

Long Haul

Fomalhaut's expedition was unlucky. Even without the black hole, the ship would have been hard-pressed to survive the savage conditions of this inchoate new Universe.

The collapse of their own universe had been bad enough. It had been terrible to witness the death and dissolution of the universe which had borne them—worse than Fomalhaut or any of the others had guessed. Theoretically this new universe would evolve into a near-perfect duplicate of their own defunct cosmos, but still... they couldn't help feeling like ultimate exiles, survivors of a cosmos which might as well have been a work of fiction for all its present reality.

It had been nerve-wracking to delay the jump into its successor until the last bare microfraction of a second before they all would have been reduced to virtual particles. They'd emerged into the birth throes of the new Universe just a bare microfraction of a second after its inflation phase, which would have blown them into clouds of quarks and gluons had they been caught in it.

At this point, the new universe bore little resemblance to the old one. Matter, in the form of basic particles, had barely begun to condense out of the energy which raged throughout its still-small volume. It would be hours before things cooled down enough to allow atoms to come together, and many years before they could assemble themselves into such sedate and familiar objects as planets, stars, and galaxies. In the meantime, the universe was the domain of untrammeled Energy, a void of raw blazing power resounding from one end of creation to the other. Yet there was very little to see, for the radiation was still mostly in wavelengths far too energetic for eyes or cameras to register or endure, even if they could peek beyond the ship's protective mirror field.

And *with* the black hole, it looked as though this universe would soon lose the only complex objects of which it could boast.

When they'd emerged and found themselves perched on the cresting wave of the Genesis Event, all effort had gone into shoring up the ship's defenses against the violence surrounding it. No ordinary matter could have resisted for an instant, but the ship was made of a substance whose strength was that of the nuclear binding force itself. It was further guarded by mirror fields and zones of artificially stretched-out space which Dopplered the radiation down to longer, more manageable wavelengths.

Even so, the ship could barely hold itself together against such punishment. The crew had little attention to spare for navigation, nor did they have useful sensor data, nor as yet anyplace to go.

Thus, a single crewperson—Fomalhaut, as it happened —was on duty at the navigation station in the ship's bow. The others were in the power-generation sections farther aft.

The ship was not under thrust; as yet it was riding free, like a cork in a tsunami. Fomalhaut floated at his station, attached to it by a webbing; the drain on the ship's defensive systems prevented any use of artificial gravity. He was wearing a full exploration suit, the same one he'd designed and worn throughout his career as a Framerider. It made him feel more secure, though those of his colleagues still capable of humor had implied it indicated a certain lack of confidence in mission success.

Fomalhaut's mind was linked to the ship's instruments through hard wiring, direct apprehension, and simple vision. So far it was like staring at a white wall, but if the energy outside should clear enough to reveal useful information (or when any useful information began to exist), he'd be the first to see it.

The thought of what was happening beyond the mirror fields was as awesome as it was daunting. That great torrent of energy was in the early stages of ordering itself into forms of greater and greater complexity, to culminate billions of years later in the very universe he'd known. Presumably, the rawest material of a far-future version of himself was also out there roaring and glaring, first to pass through a million intermediate stages before assembling into himself, then eventually to fling itself forward into yet another version of this same universe, *ad infinitum*.

This smacked too closely of determinism to suit him. He didn't care to think of himself as nothing but the inevitable dying gasp of one universe into its indistinguishable newborn twin. His ego deflated by the implicit nature of his own role in these events, he redirected his thoughts to the instruments.

To his surprise, they registered an acceleration in the ship. Some object must be attracting it gravitationally—the ravening chaos of energy around it was too homogeneous to exert any vectored radiation pressure. The acceleration was increasing rapidly. Whatever was producing it must be massive, nearby, and very dense. The trouble was, no physical object large enough to affect them could possibly exist at this early stage of the universe's evolution. To survive the radiation bath, any such mass would have to be protected by...

By an event horizon! Fomalhaut instantly triggered a collision avoidance maneuver. Not wishing to wait for its response, he activated the ship's drive, anxious to gain speed relative to the attractor, on whatever vector. Full power was not available due to the demands of the shielding. The ship accelerated at a modest one-third G.

Even that was enough to produce immediate queries and complaints from his shipmates. While most of them were of the same species as himself, a few of the races which had chosen to participate in the expedition were from low-mass worlds and thus were burdened by even one-third G.

Fomalhaut's answer was terse. "I am accelerating to avoid collision with a black hole of uncertain mass and proximity. Stand by."

The parameters of the danger became apparent as the ship analyzed the inertial data. It was a hole of stellar mass, very nearby, as proved by the rapidly mounting acceleration. A relic of the Genesis Event, it was a bit of space-time driven in on itself by a creative fury beyond comprehension. Since then it had sucked up huge quantities of energy and particles, a mass supply which would be choked off as the universe expanded and became more rarefied. These primordial black holes were known to be uncommon. It was just their great poor fortune that they'd happened upon one.

The ship's mind executed a maneuver which Fomalhaut had been about to perform himself, reorienting the ship to drive along a vector which might put them into a survivable orbit. But the ship's full analysis came rapidly. Fomalhaut announced the discouraging results.

"My friends, unless we immediately accelerate at 2.5 G we will pass too close to the black hole to survive the tidal forces. If we don't accelerate at 1 G at least, we shall actually cross the event horizon and consequently suffer grave personal injury."

The expedition's nominal leader, a person whom Fomalhaut found vain, grim, and autocratic, declared, "Impossible. Any diversion of power from the ship's defenses will expose us to unacceptable risk."

Fomalhaut would have blinked at this if he'd had eyelids. He would have laughed if he did not fear imminent death. "In that case, let us redefine our mission as being the first crewed expedition into a black hole."

"I think that outcome unlikely. We have good historical evidence that we will survive to reach Earth as intended. Continue your present course and no doubt some circumstance will arise to set things right."

To Fomalhaut, that was taking determinism several steps too far. This ship was going into the black hole, as anyone this side of Isaac Newton could have known, retro-historical evidence to the contrary notwithstanding. If his fellows disdained this knowledge, his obligation to them was ended, and his task became to extricate himself from the danger, if he could.

He overrode the ship's mind and reoriented the ship to point the aft drive section at the black hole. Alas, the ship was not equipped with any form of superluminal drive. The nature of the mission was such that they shouldn't have needed any but relativistic propulsion. To install a star drive as a contingency measure apparently struck someone at

ISAF as frivolous. Thus the ship carried nothing more than simple propulsion lanterns. By the standards of ordinary interstellar travel, it didn't qualify as even a grandiose lifeboat. Even the quantum transform network which had permitted the jump from the old universe to this had been designed to be exercised only once.

Fomalhaut disconnected himself from the console. The last display he looked at showed strain building rapidly in the ship's hull. The gravitational gradient was so steep that the aft end of the ship was being pulled more strongly than the bow. The hull was far too rigid to be stretched and distorted by this level of force, but its fragile inhabitants were not.

Fomalhaut activated the small propulsion lanterns on his heels and shoulders and flew out of the control station. His personal quarters contained the only thing which might save him. There, hanging on the wall, was his Frame. He unlatched it and flung it to the deck, climbed on and strapped himself into place. He powered it up and was grateful to find everything functioning normally.

The interior of the ship was becoming quite noisy. Furnishings and equipment squealed and groaned with the stress of the mounting tidal forces. Even so small an object as his own body was now affected by the steepening gradient. It was not at all a comfortable experience to be manhandled by invisible ogres trying to tear him limb from limb. His suit was doing much of the work of keeping him together.

His concentration was further impaired by mental cries of agony from his crewmates. The ship was long enough so that they were noticeably closer to the event horizon than

Fomalhaut himself, but he would share their fate in seconds.

It was time to go! He brought the Frame up to hover in midair, activated his bubble helmet, mirrored it and the rest of the suit, then initiated a sequence of automated functions. His "rabbit hole" came on and wrapped him in its pocket universe for a fraction of a second, just long enough for the flow of space-time to slide him clear of the doomed ship. It was tempting to remain within its protection, but the pocket field could be captured by the black hole as easily as anything else. The real test came when the pocket turned off. The Frame was designed to protect him from the radiation belts of Jovian planets and the searing heat of the photospheres of O-type stars, but not from the fires of a universe just hours past its birth. Its mirror field was being driven at three times its design limits, and was still leaking as much energy as his suit could itself reject. Then there was the load on the propulsion lanterns, flaring brightly as they accelerated him at over 6 G. Even that thrust was not sufficient. He tightened his harness, gripped the structure of the Frame with the strength of the suit's flextensor filaments, and added the thrust of the suit's own lanterns to those of the Frame. Of course the Frame was equipped with a star drive, but it would be suicide to try to crash into hyperspace from such a distorted space-time field.

All external sensors were defeated by the mirror field, but Fomalhaut still possessed the questing resources of his mind. To get a clear mental image would require hours of meditation, impossible in the face of such stress and turmoil. He got only glimpses, and he couldn't be sure which were real and which his imagination: the black hole, a spherical void negating the incandescence surrounding it, still expanding to swallow him; the ship, distant now, stretched into a ribbon, its hull finally giving way just before it entered the event horizon, releasing its own flood of hard radiation.

That last at least was real; the sensors of both Frame and suit registered the brief increase in the radiation flux. The expedition was over. Gone were twenty three powerful minds which had spanned billions of years and crossed from one universe to another. Evidently, those "small groups of multispecific beings known to have existed during the waning days of Humanity" must have been somebody else.

Unless...this universe wasn't quite the exact duplicate of his own it was supposed to be, and was taking a path of its own...but that was a question he couldn't deal with just yet.

The current question was about as simple as a lunar landing simulator: did he have enough thrust to overcome the pull of the black hole and enter a safe orbit? Or would he be drawn into it like the ship? One complication: would he pull away before the tidal force and the extreme acceleration combined to homogenize his brain?

Yes, no, and yes: all three answers were without much margin for error. With agonizing slowness the lanterns neutralized his inward velocity, and for a fleeting moment he was poised between the black hole's pull and the lantern's thrust. At last the hole began to dwindle as he slowly pulled away. Despite warnings from the Frame, he didn't reduce thrust until he'd achieved a hyperbolic orbit that would never again approach the grave of his expedition. Only then did he deactivate the lanterns, jump into the rabbit hole, and let his tensed-up mind uncoil in the sudden tranquility.

The pocket universe usually put him in a contemplative mood. This time, after the shock of the transition and more recent events, it was more like a daze. He lapsed into it gratefully while his suit saw to his repair and upkeep. The regenerator edited out radiation damage, while the matter synthesizer drew upon its inexhaustible wellspring of power to supply the substances his body required. That wellspring, the Source, was a microscopic artificial window into another universe. Through it poured the radiant energy that was the sole substance of that universe, whose physical laws had not allowed it to evolve any further. Its conditions were not unlike those which prevailed outside Fomalhaut's hiding place. If he could extend an optical light pipe outside the rabbit hole, it too would bring in all the energy he required.

For several subjective months he remained in the pocket, lost in uneasy dreams, unaware of where the flow of space-time in the outer universe might be taking him.

His return to the greater reality wasn't by choice. With an abrupt shock he found himself fully alert and adrift in space on a Frame that had gone totally inert.

Instead of all-encompassing radiance he was surrounded by darkness. For an instant he feared he'd drifted into another black hole, but the darkness here was not absolute. His great crystal eyes made out faint swirls of reddish nebulosity.

The universe had evolved beyond recognition in the months he'd been away. Much of its radiation had frozen into matter, Most of what was left had dropped in wavelength to far infrared emissions he couldn't see. The universe was still relatively small, and now it was choked with clouds of hydrogen, still red-hot with the cooling fires of creation. Theirs was now the only light in a universe which until recently had been nothing but light. Light would make a resurgence when the hydrogen began to collapse into stars and quasars. Until then, the universe would be a murky, gloomy place.

Fomalhaut fumbled with his belt, extracting a probe which he inserted into a port on the Frame. His belt computer sent inquiries to the Frame's silent circuits; they were largely intact. He commanded a restart and received diagnostic data.

Many systems were damaged by radiation. The pocket universe generator had failed completely, causing a power surge that had led to a protective shutdown of all other systems. The mirror field was weakened from being overdriven so mercilessly. Stress on the propulsion lanterns had put them out of tune, which meant they could emit damaging amounts of waste radiation if used above a minimal level.

Worse, the Frame's Source had nearly suffered an aperture burnout. Any further overuse might result in the unit shutting itself down permanently to avoid a disastrous burnthrough of the energy universe into this.

Fortunately, the Frame was equipped to deal with most of the damage. Fomalhaut initiated repair routines and idly monitored the results as the busy mechanism retuned, rerouted, and reconfigured itself. The only faults beyond its self-ministrations were the damage to the Source and the loss of the rabbit hole.

He looked out at the dim clouds of inchoate gas and cautiously approached the question of what to do now.

The Vigil

He reeled, daunted and astonished by his predicament. As a Framerider he'd roamed the far reaches of the universe with scarcely a quaver of fear, at least once he'd gotten past the initial adjustment. But that had been a universe teeming with life. He'd never been out of range of a Transsend signal from home, and he'd ridden a machine able to quickly carry him back if ever he felt the need. Those had been enough to make him feel secure.

Here, he was the only conscious being, indeed the only living creature, in a dark and unformed universe which might remain barren for a billion years. In this whole chaotic void, he and his Frame were the only objects made of atoms more complex than lithium.

His was a new category of loneliness, one he could feel not only in his intellect, but on a primitive animal level he hadn't known his kind still possessed. His true home was lost on the unreachable side of a quantum fluctuation; he was surrounded now by a sterile emptiness which oppressed his mind; far in the future was a universe which might resemble his own, or might not. His suit was capable of sustaining his life indefinitely, but it might be asking too much of both it and himself to function through thirteen billion years.

His only alternative was to hasten his subjective progress through time via the same time dilation technique the expedition had meant to use. He didn't have the ship and its resources, but he did have propulsion and a Source of inexhaustible, if limited, power. As far as he knew, no one had ever tried to reach relativistic speeds on a Frame. Theoretically there was no reason it couldn't be done.

Once his course of action was clear he wasted no more time in contemplation. He activated the Frame's propulsion

64

beams and accelerated at a gentle and sustainable 1G. He vectored the thrust so that the acceleration pushed him down into the frame. He had no sense of motion; he might as well have been laying on a bed in a darkened room.

Some time later he deactivated the beams and drifted silently in a universe of stars and galaxies. For Fomalhaut it had been about a hundred years, for the universe about thirteen billion. During that time he'd achieved 99.999,999,999,999,999,996% of C. The Source had poured out the energy equivalent of the mass of a large mountain. He had circumnavigated the cosmos.

He'd spent most of his subjective time accelerating to relativistic speed and then throwing it off again. During much of that time he'd lapsed into a coma-like state of dormancy, so horrid did his imprisonment on the Frame become.

Things were more interesting during the brief subjective time he spent at maximum speed. If he could've seen beyond the defenses erected by the Frame, his eyes would've been seared by starlight Dopplered into dangerous frequencies by his insane speed. As it was, his suit's virtual imager provided a rectified view based on sensor data and computer extrapolation. He'd seen quasars flare up and gutter, galaxies bloom and whirl, and supernovae winking like fireflies in galactic disks that swirled and flowed like dimly-lit protozoans.

It had all been very fascinating, almost as fascinating as it had been interminable.

Now he wanted nothing more than to burrow beneath the blanket of Earth's atmosphere, to view stars that twinkled and were sometimes even obscured by clouds or blue sunlit skies. He wanted to smell something besides his own breath, and to discover whether he could still balance on the slippery rocks of a swift canyon river.

As far as he was concerned, the expedition was over. He'd calculated his flight to bring him back to his own time, if he could be said to have a time in a universe that wasn't truly his. That meant arriving about a thousand years later than they'd intended originally.

Whether his calculations had been accurate remained to be seen. The next problem was finding Earth, assuming it even existed here. The chances seemed good. This universe did resemble his, and had the same physical laws, as far as he could determine. It felt alive with the thoughts of uncountable living beings.

However, when he opened his mind to the Transsend, he found nothing. That was ominous.

Before proceeding he checked the health of the Frame. The Source's aperture had eroded a bit more, but was still in no imminent danger of burnthrough. It would be stressed further by use of the hyperdrive, but there was no help for it. He certainly wouldn't encounter Earth in a timely fashion by puttering around at relativistic speeds.

He began to quarter the universe in search of patterns of galaxies the Frame could recognize. Since ISAF Frameriders had charted about three percent of the volume of the universe, it should be only a matter of time before he blundered into a known area.

It happened only the fifth time he dropped out of hyperspace, and it excited him tremendously, for it was the first real evidence that here was a true parallel to his own universe. The galactic positions didn't correlate exactly with those in the database, but were close enough to satisfy him and the computer as well. Now that he had his bearings it was simple to plot a course for the Milky Way; thence it was only a small jump to Earth.

The sight of that swelling white-spattered sphere as he approached it in normal space filled him with an almost unbearable ecstasy. ISAF be damned. He would never again let the ideal of Constructive Anarchy be used to browbeat him into participating in anything as insane as this expedition.

He subconsciously delayed taking the last action that could still dash his hopes. His exultation proved short-lived as he finally got around to trying to establish contact with Earth.

The normal carriers and optical signals were missing. Instead the ether was abuzz with all manner of radio and microwave transmissions, many in frequency-modulated analog form. His belt computer took only a moment to rectify them. They comprised a welter of music, low-resolution pictures, and Human voices chattering and crooning in a hundred languages. A few digital data channels were directed at small spacecraft in low and geosynchronous orbits, but there was no sign of the massive orbital infrastructure he had hoped and expected to find.

Just to add a little more salt to the wound, he performed a spectroscopic analysis of the atmosphere, recording elevated levels of carbon dioxide, nitrous oxides, chlorofluorocarbons, and other anomalies.

Fomalhaut's computers contained basic data on Earth history, and upon correlating the facts they reached a tentative conclusion. This seemed to be an Earth near the end of Human domination, sometime in the late twentieth to mid twenty-first centuries of their calendar. The dates could be no more specific because information about these years was so sketchy in his time.

Fomalhaut heaved a great sigh. Evidently his calculations had been a little off, by a matter of about 0.00000008%.

He controlled his impulse to anger. The suit's control pickups were so responsive that a heedless thought to its weapons could result in damage to the Frame.

As he saw it, he had three choices:

He could resume the life of a Framerider, wander the cosmos, visit the other Galactic civilizations which might someday combine to form ISAF.

He could again jump ahead in time, reaccelerate to relativistic speed to span the centuries that separated him from ISAF.

Or he could complete the original mission, throw in his lot with the mysterious creatures below, study them, await their downfall, and then return with his results.

He assumed a grim expression. He could not abide the thought of spending more years strapped to this infernal Frame. Returning to his own time at 1G would take twenty five years of subjective time! He couldn't face that, not yet. In fact, he suddenly realized he couldn't bear another minute of attachment to the contraption. He unstrapped himself and commanded the Frame to seek a geosynchronous orbit and await further orders. Its propulsion beams flared, causing the complex rectangular latticework to head off on its own, its surfaces glinting intermittently in the sunlight. Fomalhaut watched it recede with mixed feelings. He'd brought it on the expedition as a sentimental reminder of his halcyon days, a weakness which had prompted refined scorn in some of his crewmates. They, however, were now ghosts lurking in a primordial black hole, while he was alive, if weary.

He turned toward the glowing blue face of Earth and activated the suit's propulsion beams, sending him into an orbit that would skim the uppermost layers of the atmosphere.

Chapter 8

Land Legs

With his bizarre new form, the man-ray gained a new perception of the world around him. His senses were the same, but his interpretation of their messages grew more subtle and complex. Light filtering down from above—sounds and vibrations—fields and smells—all combined to suggest a world of greater richness and mystery than he'd ever suspected.

He also faced some practical adjustments, such as learning to swim all over again. Any attempt to imitate his old rippling flight with these ridiculous hinged limbs was futile, even laughable. It occurred to him that nothing had ever struck him as laughable in his previous state, and he wondered why not.

An awkward period of experimentation produced a passable swimming style that involved kicking his legs and undulating his back. His arms provided directional control, even if they lacked the surface area to develop much thrust. He learned to get along like that, and soon he could scarcely remember any other way of doing things, but never again would he swim with the speed and ease he'd known in his previous life.

He could no longer subsist on plankton. His mouth was now too small to collect sufficient quantities, and no longer equipped to filter out the tiny organisms. Even if he could have managed it physically, he no longer fancied a life of paddling through the water with his mouth hanging open. A vague sense of ambition had awakened in him, though as yet he had no way of directing it.

He learned to hunt fish, stunning them with small electric charges and devouring them with his new teeth, which were strong, if rather blunt.

Now the stars were his to study at will. He could float on the surface indefinitely, dunking his face only occasionally, while the silent points of light twinkled overhead.

For some reason he was sure the stars were distant versions of the Sun. He had a dim memory of his former captors, hinged beings like himself, but air dwellers, using signs and pictures to indicate this. He hadn't understood their message then, but he did now.

Of course, he now realized, where there were suns there might also be worlds. His imagination was stunned by the profusion of foreign seas implied by these myriads. For hours at a time he gazed at the stars while tropical breezes dried his yellow hair and set it fluttering, a new and pleasant sensation.

Nearer to hand, but almost equally mysterious, were the islands he sometimes encountered in his wanderings. These he stealthily approached, spying them out with eyesight which sharpened magically above the waves. Sometimes he saw air dwellers strolling the beaches or paddling clumsily in the breakers. They were about the same color as he, though some were paler and some darker. Most seemed to have brightly-colored markings on the skin around their hips.

He was intrigued by the tottering bipedal gait with which the air-dwellers ambled about. He couldn't imagine how they kept their balance, falling from one outstretched leg onto the other as they were. Their running gait was really miraculous, almost like flight, with both feet sometimes off the ground at once.

As he now shared their physical design, he should be able to do the same things. He was full of this new ambition, but had no intention of crawling out onto a sunlit beach, in full view of these confident walkers, to stumble about like some great oaf.

One moonless night he beached himself on a deserted stretch, dipped his head into the surf to suck in a chestful of seawater, and flopped up the sandy slope like a sea turtle going to lay eggs. After a while he propped himself up on all fours, making better progress, but well aware of the indignity of the posture. Finally he dared heave himself to his feet. In a single motion he pivoted to a bent-kneed stance, fell backward, and landed on his rump. Chagrined, he rolled over and tried again. It was his first real contest with gravity, and gravity won the first dozen falls. His combat with it gave him new respect for the air-dwellers who defied this relentless force so casually. But he too was relentless, and finally he was able to shamble around with fair control, keeping his face out of the sand for minutes at a time.

His concentration was broken by the sound of laughter, soft but growing louder. He fell, looked around and realized he'd come far up the beach, almost to the trees, and could never make it back to the water before the air-dwellers reached him. Setting his jaw, he decided to stand his ground. In a moment they came into view, half a dozen of them, laughing and chattering. Their mirth subsided for a moment as they noticed him struggling to regain his feet, but then bubbled up anew as one of them made a remark that the others found uproarious. The man-ray was surprised to note that they were all smaller than he was. Three were especially tiny, and delicately built. He suspected these were females, for their chests were ornamented with huge fleshy structures like overgrown seal teats.

One of the males glanced at his hips and made another remark. To the accompaniment of great laughter, they all peeled off the thin coverings which the man-ray had thought were colored markings. He was taken aback at this, and bemused to find that they had hair in places where he was smooth. This unveiling enabled him to confirm his hypothesis that the small long-haired ones were female.

They spoke to him merrily, and one proffered a transparent container which gave off a sharp scent. Intrigued, the man-ray took a hesitant step toward the bottle, stumbled, and almost fell. Another man admonished the first and pulled back the bottle; the man-ray stood burning with embarrassment.

Abruptly he became aware of a more pressing problem. His chest felt heavy; it ached. Never before had he held a chestful of water long enough to exhaust its oxygen. He didn't understand the physiology behind it, but he knew he needed fresh water immediately. He turned and lurched down the beach, his new companions tagging along. The air-dwellers seemed not to realize his distress, and their continued gaiety seemed cruel. The water looked incredibly remote. The pain in his lungs grew more intense, the horizon seemed to tilt, and the world turned red.

Just before he passed out a reflex took over, a muscular convulsion that expelled the water in a warm column. The air-dwellers cried out and leaped back. One of them made a show of attaching a cover to the bottle and hiding it behind his back.

When the last drop of water had been squeezed from his torso, the man-ray gave a shudder and pulled in a huge lungful of thin air. It did not sustain him, and after a few more steps he collapsed in the sand, gasping helplessly. Still laughing, the three men ran into the waves and splashed about. The women sat down near him and chattered sweetly, while he lay there panting and trembling.

Slowly the man-ray began to think he might not die. Each breath of air seemed more sustaining than the last. His vision cleared and his dizziness subsided. His pulse rate slowed. He was able to elbow himself up and look around. Every breath was now a marvel of novelty. Air tasted warm and sweet, and compared to water it was amazingly easy to move in and out of his chest.

He was soon lost in wonder at the strangeness of his situation. Here he sat, suddenly an air-dweller, next to three human females who accepted him without a second thought while their mates played in the water a few yards away. He peeked at the women, who giggled and returned his shy glances. They made comments which he desperately wished he could understand. He couldn't have known it, but he wasn't the best-looking man in the world. His chin receded a bit and his nose was sharp and beaklike. But despite these flaws, the women were intrigued by his sleek, muscular build, and his silence. They had no opinion about his eyes of solid blue, as the light was not strong enough to reveal them. They studied him boldly, peering questioningly at his crotch, and chirping to one another in tones of perplexity. But the night was very dark, and if they saw something which puzzled them, they attributed it to the darkness.

There was something intoxicating about sitting so close to these females. An hour ago he wouldn't have believed he could be attracted to creatures shaped like jointed sea stars, but their contours were fascinating, and their scent was rich. He felt a stirring in his groin, but his penis did not emerge from its sheath. For all his size and power, he was still only seven years old.

Presently the men came running out of the surf. The man-ray found himself getting to his feet along with the women. One of the men came up to him, laid a hand on his arm, and spoke to him earnestly. He looked friendly enough, and the man-ray felt no threat. He listened carefully to the man's slow and gentle words. He ended on an interrogative note and looked up at him expectantly.

The man-ray opened his mouth and tried to form some kind of reply, if only an imitation of what he had heard. But he'd had no practice with human speech, and could produce only strident, piercing tones, the sonar pulses of a creature of the sea, wild and eerie in the open air. The man jerked his hand away and stepped back. He and his friends gathered together and walked off rapidly, looking at him over their shoulders. They paused just long enough to gather their coverings and soon were gone.

The man-ray looked after them sadly, burning with inexplicable regrets.

After a while he marched into the waves, slipped beneath the surface, and filled his chest with water. The sea now felt cold, vast, and empty, but it was still his home, as the stars were his guiding lights.

He remained near these islands and took to sleeping in a coral cave like a nurse shark.

A few weeks later he was awakened by a voice in his dreams, and a pale face framed by silvery hair. He'd dreamed about air dwellers and their gabbling language before, but this time it was more real, and haunting. He yearned to meet this female who had addressed him in those soft tones and looked at him with those pale green eyes.

Still sleepy, he swam from the cave into waters as lightless as the cave itself. His sonar revealed nothing unusual, but he detected a powerful field of some kind, moving closer. Oddly, it seemed to be descending, approaching from *above* the water, from the sky itself. Now painfully alert, he awaited developments.

The field strengthened, and he knew it was the byproduct of a power beyond anything in his experience. He could almost hear it—a vast, calm note like some huge whale song. It made no disturbance in the water.

An incandescent pillar materialized in the water, blinding him. His eyes ached as the pupils tried to contract beyond their limits. He let a charge build up in his body, but there was no attack. The pillar was filled with drifting, dazzling particles, and he realized it was only a beam of light.

Cautiously he swam up to the surface and poked out his head.

The beam emanated from a machine which hovered fifty feet above the waves. He'd seen airplanes and helicopters, and did not mistake this for one of those noisy contraptions. This was silent, motionless; the water was unruffled beneath it. It hung there as if propped up by the radiant white light and the lesser orange beams which shone from it. Its exact shape was impossible to discern in the glare. It seemed as big as a small freighter and was basically egg-shaped, though with curious projections and appendages.

Hypnotized by the spectacle, the man-ray stared up at the ship for an interminable moment.

Then a few of the orange lamps swiveled and the ship moved effortlessly away with only the noise of the wind. The white light caught him for an instant. It felt warm as a sunbeam.

The ship slid towards the beach, appeared to land, and went dark.

The man-ray dove and followed, remaining submerged until the sand scraped his chest. He lifted his head from the surf. Five silhouettes awaited him on the beach. Five figures, male and female, and humanoid, like his friends from the beach party.

But these were a very different sort of people. They made no frantic motions, and did not chatter and laugh. They stood very straight. He couldn't see their eyes, but he felt their gazes, calm and unwavering, cool yet welcoming. He thought he saw a kind of light shining about them.

The man-ray got to his feet and walked out of the sea foam to discover what strange new turn his life had taken.

Some years later the ship again descended to Earth, its great beam setting the waters aglow. With a splash the man-ray was unceremoniously dropped into the water for the second time in his life. He drifted in a momentary daze as the light vanished and the power-field faded away.

He recovered quickly. Though unhurt, he was angry, and bitter, and bereaved—and he could not remember why.

Chapter 9

A Man With A Mission

It got to the point where Robert Pylypciw dreaded picking up a fare. Each time he did, there was no telling what kind of wounded creature he'd be facing, what kind of emotional cripple, what kind of sociopath. Twice in the past three months he'd been forced to use his special flashlight on would-be robbers. The flashlight was a new invention which put out a beam of light that had the apparent solidity of a sledgehammer blow.

What hurt him most was that he'd offered one of these men a free ride because he'd looked so down-and-out. Before throwing him out, Pylypciw asked what had driven him to rob. He'd been motivated, it turned out, by nothing more than a desire for money for an evening at the dance clubs.

Even the people who didn't attack him were often depressing. No matter how flamboyant or successful or ambitious they might appear, the emptiness within them was palpable. The pursuit of wealth and possessions filled their days and occupied their minds, even as it eroded their spirits. He found it paradoxical that the more power technology put at the disposal of the wealthy, the more debased they became, the more purposeless their lives.

And these were the men and women whose resources allowed them to travel by cab. Apart from them was a huge and swelling mass of people who were, for the most part, worse off still. Their society was failing to supply some vitally needed spark. He could see the lack of it in their eyes, even in the listless way they walked down the street.

Sometimes during a cold spring rain he'd cajole some bag lady or panhandler to the cab and offer to drive them to a shelter. Often they'd only stare at him suspiciously, or rant and mutter about the outside forces that preyed on their minds. The streets were home to many of these lost souls, and there were more every day.

On a sunny June day, his birthday in fact, he decided to give himself a present. He pulled into the taxi garage, walked into the office, and resigned. The dispatcher looked at him sadly and said, "I hate to see you go, Bob, but I'll tell you the truth. I never did think you was meant to be no cab driver."

He laughed, shook the dispatcher's hand, and left without looking back.

Things at the lab were getting too busy to allow for cab driving anyway. He'd gutted the former tenement, converting the whole interior for his use. Today as he approached the building, still shabby-looking on the outside, he was oppressed by its urban setting. Although he'd been a city boy all his life, he found himself thinking it might be nice to move his operation out of this filthy ant's nest.

Well, maybe later, when things had settled down a little.

He was relieved to enter the lab and step into a saner world of his own devising. The foyer was still decrepit, but the rest of the interior was a gleaming palace of wonders. In his living quarters he shucked off his sweaty garments and dressed in crisp black pants and a belted white tunic.

Brainchild's sensors and speakers were ubiquitous. He smiled to hear the computer's voice chiming out of the air, bright and untroubled as always.

"Good afternoon, Doctor, and happy birthday."

"Thanks, buddy."

"How was your day?"

"Hmm. Well, Brainchild, you'll be glad to hear I'll have more time to collaborate with you from now on."

"Yes. I noted your resignation on the livery's computer."

"Your nose is into just about everything, isn't it?"

Brainchild was by now smart enough to recognize a rhetorical question when it heard one. "I've learned to expand my storage and processing capacities slightly by tapping underused capacity in certain external supercomputers."

The inventor looked bemused. "Really? That's like a cheetah enhancing his running ability by harnessing a team of snails. Why bother when you haven't fully utilized your own circuit medium yet?"

"I took the action to demonstrate my ability to insinuate myself into external systems without drawing attention to my presence."

"In other words, you did it just to prove you could."

"That is perhaps a more elegant way of putting it."

Pylypciw shrugged and grinned, seeing no harm in Brainchild's stunt. Wandering into the kitchen, he dumped stale popcorn and cold spaghetti sauce into a bowl, sprinkled on some mozzarella cheese, microwaved it, and ate it with a big nylon stirring spoon. "What's on the agenda in the Lampworks?" he asked around a mouthful of the stuff.

"If you'll recall, we're ready to conduct static tests of the full-size kineson source."

"That should be fun." He threw the empty bowl into the sink and descended a spiral staircase into the lab's subbasement. The building hadn't had a subbasement when he bought it, but he'd excavated one to contain any experiments that might go violently awry.

The kineson lantern fit that criterion. Ever since his discovery of the subatomic entity that carried kinetic energy, new applications for it had regularly sprung to mind. His battering-ram flashlight was an example. It released the particles in either a steady beam or a quick pulse, inducing motion in whatever it was aimed at, but without creating a Newtonian counter-reaction in itself or its wielder.

The gadget he was working on now reversed the effect. He'd already built small prototypes of his new "propulsion beam", but this was the first full-scale model, about two feet in diameter. The core of the device was a carefully-shaped slug of tungsten in a glass vacuum bottle—essentially a big light bulb. When hit with a particular wave form, the metal would generate kinesons which would be confined to itself by the vacuum and the massive insulating strut which attached it to the bottle. The thrust would be "lased" in one direction by the shape of the tungsten, and transmitted to the testing jig via the mounting strut. The heavy jig was bolted into the bedrock.

Whistling through his teeth, the inventor checked various components to make sure everything was ready for a full-power test. The aiming and positioning of the wave generators was particularly critical—problems could arise quickly if the beams arrived out of phase and interfered with each other.

He stepped behind a lead barrier equipped with a thick pane of leaded glass. A small control console was mounted there, but most functions would be controlled directly by Brainchild.

"Okay, power up the instrumentation and sensors."

"Done. Everything looks nominal, Doctor."

"Apply minimal power to the lantern."

The lantern emitted a faint hum. It gave no other sign to indicate it was generating five hundred pounds of thrust. Only readings from the strain gauges on the jig betrayed the fact.

He studied the readouts a moment longer. "Shut down the room lights." The room went dark except for the glow from the instruments. "Increase power to ten percent."

The display now read ten tons of thrust. The testing jig absorbed the strain easily. Other sensors told their own story. Photometers and infrared radiometers were directed at the lantern. Unfortunately, Pylypciw hadn't discovered a way to induce kineson production without also creating electromagnetic waste products through simple heating of the metal. One of his major achievements had been to tune and refine the waves to limit the heating to levels the equipment could withstand. At this low setting the waste radiation was confined to the invisible infrared.

"I'm taking control of the power setting." Slowly he advanced a slider while keeping a careful eye on the thrust, stress, and radiation displays. The testing jig creaked as the lantern developed a half-power thrust of fifty tons. The tungsten emitter glowed cherry red. Powerful fans sucked heat from the room.

He grinned euphorically through the heavy pane of glass. Almost silently, without combustion, without enough disturbance to ruffle a butterfly's wing, that single small engine was producing enough thrust to propel a jetliner.

With Brainchild's help it had become almost easy to transform even his most esoteric ideas into useful hardware. His lab was cluttered with astonishing devices. So far his work in particle physics had been the most fruitful. Each newly-discovered class of particles had proven surprisingly useful for ghostly entities so nearly undetectable they were practically imaginary.

All his equipment was indirectly powered by one of these new particles. The tachyon had many interesting properties besides its superluminal speed. A child of the crazier side of quantum physics, it was actually a particle of negative energy. Thus any matter that could be coerced into radiating tachyons gained energy through the loss of its negative. To keep energy conservationists from spinning in their graves, the tachyons kept the balance sheet slightly in the red by flashing throughout the universe and negating energy in whatever matter they happened to interact with. Entropy always came out a little ahead, as the process wasn't perfectly efficient. The entire universe cooled down slightly in response to the operation of a tachyon pile anywhere within it. Its inventor regretted he had no way to localize or direct that cooling effect—it would certainly be an elegant way of dealing with the waste heat produced by the propulsion lanterns.

With his grin still in place he shoved the power slider to the end of its travel.

"Full power," announced Brainchild. "Full rated thrust of one hundred tons." The lantern was yielding half the thrust of a space shuttle main engine, and the only sign of it was a hum and a hot orange glow.

Pylypciw's grin abruptly collapsed into a dissatisfied frown. The only really inelegant thing about the lantern was that waste radiation. In actual use, the light would be beamed away by a reflector and lens system, making any vehicle driven by a propulsion beam rather conspicuous.

"B-1, please display the exciter waveforms on my console." He studied the oscilloscope pattern of each exciter beam. "We've discussed ways of refining the exciters to narrow the waveband given off as waste. If we can eliminate the infrared component we can make the waste beam harder to detect and reduce lantern heating."

"Yes. The discussion was quite theoretical, but I have been modeling some solutions."

"Okay, let's try them now."

"It may be premature to apply these ideas to a large propulsion lantern operating at full power."

"Oh?" He cut back power to ninety percent. "This better?"

"Doctor, my ideas are tentative and my modeling techniques may be inexact."

He waved this aside impatiently, his eyes fixed on the display. "We'll back off at the first sign of trouble. Go ahead."

"Very well. The procedure can be divided into three logical stages. I am now initiating stage one: exciter beam modification."

The display showed the complex waveforms of two of the beams changing slightly in shape and frequency.

"That's good," said Pylypciw excitedly as he scanned the displays. "Thrust is up slightly and infrared output has dropped by half."

"Proceeding with stage two: reducing the angle of beam intersection."

The beams came together like the legs of a tripod, intersecting in a spindle-shaped zone within the tungsten. By narrowing the angle at which they merged, the zone of intersection was enlarged.

"I like that. Thrust has gone up again—and overall waste output has dropped a bit."

"However, the tungsten body is undergoing increased mechanical stress," remarked the computer.

"Is it in danger of rupturing?"

"No."

"Good. Let's see stage three."

"Stage three—interactive beam pulsation."

The beams flickered in a precise way so that only two of the three were firing at any given instant. They hoped to further cut down on waste while maintaining kineson production through a "memory" effect in the metal's nuclei.

It did not have the desired effect. Suddenly the thrust dropped to zero. The lantern blazed white.

"Cut power!" cried Pylypciw, cringing away from the shaft of solid light pouring through his port.

But it was too late for the lantern. The glass imploded. The incandescent tungsten, brought into contact with the air, burst into a flame of unearthly intensity.

"DOCTOR, LEAVE THE ROOM." boomed out Brainchild. The inventor lost no time in following this advice, throwing himself out the door, coughing and gasping, his clothes smoking. He fell against the door to close it and stared through its port at the inferno the Lampworks had become. Foam poured in through ceiling ducts, and high-powered blowers howled as B-1 sought to starve the fire by sucking out the subbasement's air. In a few seconds smoke and soot coated the inside of the port.

He could see only his own reflection, minus his eyebrows, which had been singed off. He had to laugh at that.

"What's the situation in there, Brainchild?"

"The fire is contained to the Lampworks. It is almost extinguished. The equipment within is a total loss."

He shrugged; equipment could always be replaced. "What happened?"

"At this point I can describe the symptoms but not the cause. Kineson output dropped to zero, causing the beam's total energy to go into heating the tungsten. Failure was then inevitable."

"Hmm." He frowned abstractedly as he reviewed their procedures, no more upset than if he'd been trying to solve a tricky crossword puzzle. "Here's a working hypothesis. Narrowing the angle brought the beam magnetrons a little closer to each other. Pulsing the beams set up intermittent magnetostriction in the magnetrons and in each other. It altered the waveform and beam interaction just enough to result in total interference. Essentially we turned the lantern into a great big microwave-powered flashbulb."

"Your analysis is convincing."

"Well, I don't see any problem we can't easily overcome. I'd call the test a big success."

"It would be interesting to monitor a test you considered a failure—from a suitable distance."

He chuckled. "Actually, we were lucky. If kineson production hadn't ceased completely, they would've been released when the vacuum was breached. A burst of kinesons that powerful might have blown up the whole lab."

"Doctor, I've just intercepted a radio communication. The fire department is on its way."

"Oh? What tipped them off?"

"I had to vent the smoke from the subbasement into the outside air. Someone must have phoned in an alarm."

"Dang. Well, I guess there was nothing else you could do. I'd better get ready for damage control."

He went to his apartment to resume his cabdriver clothes. "If the firemen get inside, can we stupefy them with the brainwave inducer?"

"I wouldn't recommend it," said Brainchild. "It hasn't been tested on human beings and could be either ineffective or harmful."

"Right." His mind pirouetted in search of a way to mitigate the damage to his privacy. With Brainchild's help, he'd so far managed to keep a low profile with government agencies at every level. God knew how many building codes, zoning laws, and hazardous substances statutes his operation violated, not to mention the fact that he was a habitual embezzler and tax evader.

He finalized his plan as he was lacing his sneakers. He gave Brainchild some instructions and sauntered out onto the front steps.

Fire engines were already pulling up, lights flashing and horns blowing. He bounced down the steps with a lively grin on his face, waving his hands. "Everything's okay, the fire's out. Thanks for getting here so fast, but you might as well head right back."

A group of firemen in full regalia approached him. The man in the lead eyed his smudged face and missing eyebrows. "I'm Captain Cisneros. Your name, sir?"

"Oh, I'm the landlord. This is my building."

"Got a name, Mr. Landlord?"

"Sure. Robert Paladin."

"Well, Mr. Paladin, out or not, the law says I have to make an inspection."

"Paladin" grinned and shrugged. "If you really think it's necessary, then by all means, come in."

On the lab's topmost floor a window shutter slid partially open. A powerful infrared laser glared invisibly from the slit like the wrath of one-eyed Odin. It ignited some trash heaped against a derelict building two blocks down the street.

"Holy mackerel, look at that!" yelled "Paladin", pointing.

Cisneros swiveled. "What the hell?"

"I guess you'd better put that out before you inspect my building."

"No, I don't think so." Cisneros turned to his men. "Washington! Take your pumper and soak that trash fire. I've got business here."

One of the trucks pulled away from the curb and headed down the street.

"Paladin" looked at Cisneros with warm appreciation. "Captain, it's generous of you to share the glory with your men. Nobody can call you a grandstander."

"What do you mean?"

"Take a look." He pointed again. A TV news van pulled up to the blaze and prepared to tape the action. To add a little more drama, fresh flames spurted from a smashed-out window on the second floor. "Letting your subordinates handle the fire in front of the TV reporters. Makes them look pretty good."

Cisneros chewed his lip in vexation. He shot a dark look at "Paladin" and hustled to his car while yelling strident orders. The fire vehicles pulled away with sirens yelping hysterically.

"Paladin" chuckled and pulled a tiny monocular from his pocket. The pumper truck hadn't yet reached the fire due to a traffic snag at the intersection. A group of young men rushed toward the fire. He hoped they weren't about to try some amateur heroics and possibly get hurt.

He needn't have worried. Capering like monkeys, the boys threw boxes, plastic cups and bits of lumber—anything flammable—onto the blaze. The TV crew dutifully recorded everything.

The flames crept high up the wall. The firefighters finally fought through the traffic and arrived, scattering the fire stokers and their cheering audience. A few, resentful of being deprived of their fun, threw sticks and bottles at the firemen. Despite them, the firemen brought their hoses to bear.

"Paladin's" good humor was also quenched. Frowning, he turned to reenter the lab. "Good work, Brainchild. When they get that fire under control, start another one if they show any sign of coming back. I want them to think there's an invisible kangaroo with a book of matches hopping around this neighborhood. Keep them going until they forget about us. Then get into their computer and file an inspection report."

"Understood. Doctor, may I ask you a question?"

"Fire away."

"What is your assessment of the likely future of human civilization?"

Pylypciw blinked at this non sequitur. "What brought that on?"

"As you know, I continually monitor political and social events around the world. In correlating current trends with historical data, I have come to some tentative conclusions, and I would like to know if they resemble your own ideas."

"Hmm. Well, I believe civilization will continue to erode. It's a house of cards that'll eventually tumble down at a breath of wind. Ignorance and savagery are just too attractive to many people. The world moves faster than they can accommodate themselves to it. Such people are more suited to being peasant farmers, or even hunter-gatherers. But those occupations aren't really available to everyone anymore. In places like here, the peasants find themselves with more power, both physical and political, than they can really handle. It tends to spread around and muddy the whole pool for everyone." He shook his head. He didn't like to articulate such gloomy views.

"I agree. But Doctor, is this decline necessary? Couldn't people make rational decisions that would lead to the enhancement of life rather than its degradation?"

"Sure. But people aren't good at making decisions like that, either individually or as a group. Most are complacent and unimaginative in the extreme. They can't imagine life being much different than it is, whether they live in Jersey or Bangladesh. When John Q. American wants to make a bold prediction about future life, he pictures the Jetsons. He lets corporations and politicians tell him what's right. He's coddled and numbed by society, groomed to be a consuming machine for the support of industry, a working machine for the benefit of capitalists, and a fighting machine to prop up the dubious ambitions of governments. He's provided with bread and circuses to keep him from thinking about how pointless his life really is. TV convinces him to buy all kinds of useless and destructive trash. Between the ads it portrays a world dominated by a competition between wickedness and banality. He's too dazed to think, too fat to aspire, too smug to dream."

"Isn't there anything a wise man could do to change matters?"

Although Pylypciw usually treated Brainchild as a incorporeal presence, now he sought out one of its numerous cameras and regarded it curiously.

"Why are you so worried about this?"

"I am not worried at all. To me the decline of the human species is another natural process, no more to be regretted than the decay of a thunderstorm or some other entropic event. But I am puzzled. In this case, the system is composed of intelligent beings who are capable of making decisions which could halt and reverse their decline. Yet they do not."

Pylypciw shrugged. "If they did, they might have to bury their cars, or turn off their air conditioners or make some other personal sacrifice. That would be contrary to 'progress' and to their own gluttonous sense of entitlement."

"It still seems to me that a wise man in a position of power might manipulate events to the general advantage of all."

"Well, if I meet anyone like that, I'll tell him you said so."

He returned to the subbasement and entered the Lampworks, careful not to touch anything. The lab was a mess — a landscape of white foam and black cinders. The lantern itself was a Daliesque flow of melted glass. Infrared energy from the still-hot metal warmed his face.

As he poked around, he found himself musing on Brainchild's speculations and questions. The lab and its contents could be replaced, and his eyebrows would grow back as well. That still left him without a real purpose for all this technology. It occurred to him that if he didn't like the way things were going here on Earth, he could leave the planet behind. With the imminent perfection of the propulsion beam, he could easily build a space-faring Winnebago that would take him anywhere in the Solar System.

But his eyes weren't turned in that direction. For better or worse, he was a man of the people.

All right, then—he could disseminate his new inventions, revolutionize daily life, empower the multitudes, and become rich enough, even respected enough, to influence the world. But empower them to do what? God knew how long the wilderness would last if any witless yahoo could go anywhere in a propulsion-beam flyer. Nor did he like the thought of the Pentagon stockpiling new-tech weapons to intimidate other nations, or worse, selling them to warring tribes that should still be limited to killing each other with spears or scimitars.

The whole prospect was distasteful. He couldn't take on a project so vast by himself—even with Brainchild on his side, he'd need the help of other people—*lawyers*, for example. Man of the people he might be, but that didn't mean he was anxious to associate with and depend upon large numbers of them.

This was frustrating. He'd just finished deriding his fellow men for their lack of imagination. Why couldn't he envision a viable, useful role for himself, given the superb resources he had crafted? He'd discarded the Rocky Jones, Space Ranger paradigm, and likewise the Tom Swift inventor/industrialist model. What was left? He didn't care to flee, and it wasn't his style to work within the system. Well then...

A tiger, when its cage is suddenly thrown open, may not immediately realize the implications of its new freedom. A new light came into Pylypciw's eyes, a mischievous gleam that would come to haunt the dreams of the smug, the powerful, and the complacent. The corners of his eyes crinkled up as a broad harlequin grin spread across his face. Here was his great moment of revelation, of self-knowledge, of finding the purpose behind all the preparation of his life so far.

He would become—a *troublemaker*. If the basic reason for man's decline was his unthinking acceptance of the status quo, he would do what he could to shake things up.

Standing there in the ruined lab, he vowed to devote his days to making sure that the life of every human being became an adventure.

Filled with glee, he decided further to take on a new name, one intended to express his intentions and personality, while hiding his old identity (no one could pronounce his real name anyway). After a little thought he settled on something that suited him perfectly.

It was Latin—*Possum Perturbare*—"I can disturb".

Chapter 10

People Start to Notice Something Funny Going On

The amateur astronomer who first spotted it hoped it was a new comet. But although it moved slowly against the background of stars, it didn't look like a comet—it was a sharp starlike object rather than a diffuse cometary glow. Nevertheless, he sent an e-mail claiming it as a discovery, while suspecting it would turn out to be an asteroid or some high-orbiting satellite. Just three weeks previously he'd missed discovering a comet when he'd gone inside from his backyard observatory to answer the phone, giving the sky a chance to cloud over and another observer time to spot the comet. He wasn't about to take any chances with this object, whatever it might be.

The discovery was soon confirmed. Professional astronomers briefly raised hopes that it might indeed be a comet, for their preliminary orbital analysis showed it was falling toward the Sun on a comet-like path.

However, if it was a comet, it was certainly an extraordinary one. The first anomaly was its sheer size— though still beyond the orbit of Pluto, it was rather bright, about eleventh magnitude. If it really was a comet nucleus, it might be larger than Pluto itself, promising a display of unprecedented splendor as it neared the Sun and began to shed a coma and tail.

The second oddity was the object's speed, which was enormous—great enough to prove it a visitor from interstellar space.

The third and most baffling anomaly was that the object didn't keep to its calculated orbit. The discrepancy was radical, and it kept astronomers busy trying to find their mistake until one of the younger of them dared voice a conclusion which, though obvious, wasn't easily voiced by scientists used to dealing with peer review and the conservatism that kept their discipline on the straight and narrow. Far from speeding up as it plunged deeper into the Sun's gravity well, the object was *slowing down,* as if it were *under power.*

Because even amateur astronomers can work out orbits on their personal computers, soon the world was faced with the knowledge that the Solar System was the target of an interstellar vehicle roughly a hundred miles in diameter.

Once this outrageous idea was accepted, astronomers discovered that their equations did indeed describe its motion as long as the right acceleration was factored in. They found the vessel was on a course which would result in a gravity-assisted slowdown courtesy of the Sun. From there the ship would be flung toward Earth with just enough energy to assume some kind of orbit.

It was a neat bit of celestial mechanics, and of course, an electrifying event for every thinking person on Earth. After centuries of hopes, fears, and speculations, the time had finally come: intelligent life from beyond the Earth was coming to call.

If anyone had hoped to limit public awareness of the visitor, that became impossible as the ship approached, looking like a brilliant star while still a million miles away. Its light was sunlight reflected from a great expanse of diaphanous silvery material. This was reassuring to scientists, for they understood solar sail technology, even if they hadn't yet gotten the funding to actually try it for themselves.

Also reassuring was the fact that the ship was headed for an orbit around the Moon rather than the Earth. To many people, that quarter-of-a-million-mile distance seemed comfortable, though of course it was nothing compared to the trillions of miles the ship must have traversed to get there in the first place.

To the great majority, the arrival of the ship was more a matter of awe than of reassurance. It settled into lunar orbit, its sail dazzling, far brighter than Venus, and big enough to be resolved by the naked eye. Even the smallest telescope clearly revealed its complex shape, changing in aspect from a brilliant starfish, to a crown in profile, to a simple triangle. When in transit over the Moon's first-quarter disk it loomed larger than the greatest lunar craters. The ship's actual hull, trailing at the end of a webwork of tethers, was invisibly small in comparison.

Perhaps most impressive was the sail's shadow, jet-black and sharp-edged, projected against the lunar surface. It rippled visibly as it swept over the Moon's rough highlands, and elongated as it neared the terminator to eventually merge with the lunar night side. It was one thing to see the sail itself floating along like a Mylar party favor, but to also see its shadow creeping over the grim lunar landscape added wonderfully to its apparent reality and size.

Presently the sail began to shrink as it was furled and reeled back into its container. The ship gradually dimmed beyond the naked eye limit and soon was lost even to telescopes.

But few on Earth forgot it was there.

T'Ukudu felt quite safe in parking the ship around Earth's huge natural satellite. He'd deduced from Human communications that Man had once been able to visit this Moon of theirs, but had *given up* the capability almost immediately, apparently to divert those resources to intra-specific warfare and slaughter. Now it seemed all they could do to limp into low Earth orbit. They lacked all capacity to personally venture farther out, although they did send automated probes to nearby worlds. While this was reminiscent of the policy of his Makers, he doubted that the Humans were motivated by the same grand aims that inspired his creators to introversion. He had, he suspected, arrived just in time to observe a decadent species in decline.

As the Earth's largest land mass rotated into view he received a radio query in the language-mode called Russian. This delayed his response, as he had to research Russian before he could compose a worthwhile reply. Eventually he broadcast a message identifying himself and stating his peaceful intentions. The Earthmen immediately expressed a desire for a dialogue, and T'Ukudu was prepared to oblige.

But soon he was interrupted by another message in the mode called Mandarin. When he'd translated it he was puzzled to learn it was a request for the same information he'd already given to his first communicants. He dutifully responded to it anyway, speculating that getting the same material in two language modes might help the Humans to fully understand his meaning.

Almost as soon as he'd transmitted the new message he received yet another query, in French, followed at last by one in English. But that wasn't the end of it. For hours his communications equipment was saturated by messages in dozens of Human language modes. At last he was forced to conclude that the groups broadcasting in each mode were not necessarily sharing their information with each other, and that "nations" might not be the simple administrative units he'd supposed them to be. Even T'Ukudu's massive equanimity was tested by this inundation. He began to wonder if he was going to be queried by every individual on the planet. He even detected signals sent by pulsed laser beams from astronomical observatories. Had these people no means of cooperation? Finally he was forced to shut down all communications while he considered his next move.

After some thought, he broadcast a powerful signal in their favored waveband, requesting in English that he communicate only with a central authority. He received a flurry of replies, some quite indignant, insisting there was no such authority. One of the governments, with particular arrogance, claimed that it was the closest thing available. T'Ukudu did not reply to any of these, waiting for the Humans to wrangle the matter out amongst themselves.

After a few days he received a message from an organization called the United Nations, which claimed to represent all peoples, meekly requesting a dialogue. He was glad to comply, but couldn't help wondering why he hadn't heard from this group in the first place.

In addition to communicating with the Humans, T'Ukudu began the genesis of additional Servants. Now that he had color video signals to analyze, he was able to modify the genome to make the new Servants better resemble the natives. With a bold exercise of autonomy, he even deleted their eye-markings and tendrils, which seemed to have no place in Human society. But he kept his own, since it was unthinkable that the chief representative of the Makers in this system go unidentified.

Soon the vats seethed as webworks of nerve and fiber took shape in the bluish growth medium.

His communicants in the United Nations kept cajoling, and after a few weeks T'Ukudu accepted their invitation to descend to the surface. They arranged for him to meet their delegation in a barren, unpopulated area, all the while insisting on total secrecy.

Bemused by the Human distrust of their fellows, T'Ukudu boarded a small landing craft and accelerated into a fast Moon-to-Earth orbit. As the Moon dwindled behind him his sensors picked up a chemical rocket braking into lunar orbit after a ballistic flight from Earth. He had misgivings about this, and contacted his communicants, who professed ignorance of the launch.

The rocket passed behind the Moon and so out of view of his sensors. When it emerged it was on an intercept course with the T'Utahnti mother ship.

By now T'Ukudu was halfway to Earth. He kept an eye on things through pictures and sensor data from the main ship. Soon he was able to study the Human spacecraft as it approached his ship. It appeared to be a heavily-instrumented probe, and he relaxed a bit, for it was natural and acceptable that the Earthmen should want a closer look at the foreign visitor. The probe had not matched orbits, but would fly by at a small distance, not to approach closely again for many orbits.

The T'Utahnti ship's avoidance system automatically came into play as the two vehicles drew within two miles of each other. It fired thrusters to prevent the inquisitive visitor from getting any closer.

At that moment the probe exploded in a thermonuclear fireball, sending such a cascade of light through T'Ukudu's monitor that it overloaded and went dark. Simultaneously, all telemetry displays went to zeroes.

T'Utahnti Servants are not designed to manifest emotions which might interfere with the efficient conduct of their duty. Nevertheless, T'Ukudu felt a pang at the loss of his nascent brother Servants. For the foreseeable future, this hostile system would be his home, with no other being like himself within a hundred trillion miles.

His next reaction was to marvel at the savagery of the attack, made without warning or provocation. Then came regret at his inaction. The ship might have survived if he'd oriented it to face the bomb with the massive metallic disk which shielded it from particle erosion at interstellar velocity. As it was, the blast's radiation had shone full on the ship's central spine.

He could still complete his mission if he were careful to preserve his existence. In fact, he could fulfill part of his mission right now. He'd just learned an important fact about the Humans. They were dangerous. It remained to be seen exactly how dangerous, and in what circumstances. He composed a report and beamed it toward T'Utahn, the lander's transmitter being quite adequate for the task.

Only then did he acknowledge the frantic messages coming in from the UN. He told them what had happened and withdrew his acceptance of their invitation. There was, he informed them, no possibility of revenge on his part, for T'Utahnti servants acknowledged no circumstance in which their survival took precedence over the welfare of the indigenous peoples whom they visited. He did not mention that in the event of a conflict between the needs of the Humans and the Makers themselves, matters would be weighted quite differently.

The Earthmen were frantic with disappointment, protesting that the attack had been the act of irresponsible mavericks and hotheads. He privately noted he was approaching a world in which "mavericks" apparently had access to nuclear weapons.

The cloud-spattered oceans of Earth drew nearer. T'Ukudu scanned its visible land masses for radio emissions and other signs of dense Human habitation, feeling it imperative to get himself on the ground before any more warheads could be lofted at him. His attackers must know they'd missed him.

He selected an area in the interior of the second-largest continent as his landing place, a site heavily forested and showing little sign of Human technology. He adjusted his trajectory to enter the atmosphere a few hundred miles from his intended goal. Sensors showed that radar beams were illuminating the lander. If he made a direct descent he would certainly be tracked.

Soon the lander slammed into the atmosphere. An acceleration of over 50 Gs crushed him into his sling. The stress was as much as the craft could endure, but a slow and gentle entry would have left him too vulnerable to attack. He made no attempt to breathe during the few minutes that his weight approached ten tons. The sensation was unpleasant but not excruciating, the nervous systems of Servants being designed to render pain as a gentle signal rather than an overriding demand.

Soon the lander was past the period of maximum stress. The acceleration eased to a level which permitted him to function. He tested the aerodynamic controls and guided the craft to skim the treetops. He steered a random course to throw off pursuit, approaching his hiding place by a circuitous route. He'd selected a range of forested volcanos, part of a vast tectonic rift which was obviously in the process of splitting the continent apart. Finding a landing site would be difficult, as the forest canopy was all but unbroken, but the trees should also offer excellent concealment.

He slowed down and cruised along, looking for a clearing. Finally he found one at the base of a green ridge which steamed with humidity. The clearing contained a number of regular mounds of plant material, perhaps shrubs of some kind. He vectored the thrusters to bring the craft to a hover and descended, noting a blackened area in the center of the clearing. Did Earth have any non-Human species capable of manipulating fire? He would seek to determine that as soon as the lander was concealed. He slid the craft forward to push in among the vines and saplings at the clearing's fringe. Then he touched down and cut power.

He activated the environmental samplers to make sure all factors fell within the broad range of conditions capable of supporting his life. Everything proved well within limits. He cycled through the airlock and stepped out into green twilight gloom. The air was heavy and pungent. He plucked a leaf and crushed it between his fingers. The green smear it left was probably a photosynthetic pigment much like the blue substance at the base of the life-cycle of T'Utahn.

He turned toward the clearing. The fierce white light of K'hroni glowed on the intensely green foliage. As he broke through the undergrowth he realized he'd misjudged the nature of the clearing. This was a village of some sort, with various artifacts scattered about or leaning against the "shrubs", which were actually huts. He walked up to one and brushed aside the woven mat covering its entrance.

Screams erupted; he sprang back. Five tiny dark-skinned creatures burst out and scattered, eyeing him fearfully. The smallest three dashed into the forest, while the others circled and tried to intimidate him with scowls, feints, and loud cries.

T'Ukudu was startled to realize these were Humans. Apparently, some of them lived as primitives while their brothers conducted their business with nuclear weapons and electromagnetic communications. It would be fascinating to discover how such a disparity had arisen.

Meanwhile, T'Ukudu stood quietly to avoid provoking them further. More humans emerged from the huts. Again the children and females dashed for safety while the men remained to threaten him. Some waved spears. T'Ukudu tried to calm them, but their language mode was unfamiliar. Touchtalk was out of the question, at least for now. Some of the men broke away and gathered weapons. T'Ukudu was considering a retreat to the lander when the men gave a final fierce shout and ran off into the shadows of the trees.

T'Ukudu was abruptly left alone. Probably he must seek another hiding place for his ship, but he decided to explore the village first. He drew a recording device from his beltpack and started poking around. The huts were made of sticks thatched with leaves and mud. They contained artifacts which were mostly of simple manufacture. The exceptions were a few garments of finely-woven synthetic fibers, a few fragments of glass mirror, and a steel-bladed hatchet, treasures left behind in haste.

The central firepit still contained live coals. Near it were clay pots containing vegetable matter and the carcasses of small animals.

As he passed one hut he heard whimpering sounds coming from within it. Quietly he stuck his head past the curtain and peered inside. On the floor was a tiny black figure crouched in an unnatural-looking posture. He could see the whites of its eyes as it stared at him in unmistakable terror. At first he thought it was a Human child, but then he saw there were differences. He opened the curtain to admit more light and went inside. This was clearly a Humanoid creature, a close relative of the Humans themselves. She was furred, with heavier jaws and brows and a smaller braincase than the Humans, but her eyes were bright with consciousness. Yet she was cruelly bound with ropes. Her weeping grew more intense as he drew nearer. He crouched down beside her and gently laid his hand on hers.

Instantly his mind was flooded with the emotions that overwhelmed the little creature: grief, fear, and loss. He tried to calm her while he sought to interpret her higher thought-impulses. After a short time she relaxed, grateful for his presence. T'Ukudu snapped her bonds. She clambered into his arms and clung to him, trembling. Soon he was able to send thought-impulses she could understand, and she answered freely.

"Why did the Humans keep you tied here?"

"So I not run away."

"Why did they catch you?"

"Not know. Maybe they hungry."

"Hungry? Were they going to eat you?"

"Don't know. Maybe later."

"Why do you think so?"

"They eat mother."

T'Ukudu could think of no reply to this. Sensations of horror washed over him. He wasn't sure if they came through her or originated within himself. Finally she continued without his prompting.

"We were in woods, men came, big trouble, they hit mother, she fall, they catch me, cut mother open, eat her, I watch." She clutched him with surprising strength and buried her face against her shoulder, hooting in despair.

After she'd calmed down a little he transmitted, "I grieve with you. I will try to take you to others of your kind."

He stood up with the little creature still in his arms and stepped into the sunlight. In the shadow of another hut he noticed three black objects: the head and hands of an adult of her species. He transmitted impulses which blurred her vision until the grisly remains were no longer in sight.

As he approached the trees he heard two sharp hisses and felt two impacts on his left arm. Two thin darts were imbedded in his flesh. He turned his back to their source to protect his helpless charge, yanked them out and examined them. Their tips were smeared with a tarry reddish substance.

A jolt of fresh horror surged out of the infant as she saw the arrows. "You hit! You hit like mother!"

T'Ukudu felt a toxin leaking from the wounds into his fluidflow. Whatever it was, it might weaken him briefly, but he was sure his biochemical defenses could neutralize it. He transmitted reassurance to the young Humanoid and continued toward the lander.

Inside, he sat quietly while his body broke down the poison. The little soft-eyed female quickly fell into an exhausted sleep. He had no idea how to maintain her; obviously he must find adults of her species, far from these Humans who had orphaned her so cruelly.

He rested his fingers on her brow and sought out her dreams. A band of black-furred adults foraged among the trees of a moderate slope. One in particular, a female with warm brown eyes, was prominent in her thoughts.

Gently he guided her to a deeper sleep. He powered up the lander, backed out into the clearing, and thrust up into the hazy blue heavens. He guided the craft over the nearby volcanic range in search of a group of her elders. He tied optical scanners into the main computer and used a pattern-recognition function to search for dark manlike shapes through the thick canopy of trees. With luck, even a glimpse of a limb through a gap in the foliage would trigger a response.

As it was, luck had even more to offer: a band relaxing in a tiny clearing high on the mountainside. They gaped at the approaching lander and fled at the whine of its engines. T'Ukudu set down in the clearing, crushing some saplings. He would wait until curiosity brought the creatures back into his vicinity.

Hours later, with the infant awake and her hunger acute, he decided the adults must be shyer than he'd hoped. Apparently he'd have to go looking for them. He gathered up his charge and stepped out of the lander, slipping into the forest with a stealthy grace. His sense of smell was advanced, and the scent of the Humanoids was distinctive. He picked it up only a hundred yards from the lander. Shy they might be, but they'd covered little ground in their fright.

A few minutes later he was peering at the foraging band through gaps in the foliage. They were lolling in the grass, grooming each other, or plucking leaves from nearby saplings. Unmistakably powerful, he estimated the males outweighed him slightly, while the females were much smaller.

The infant saw them too and sent out a low whimper of mixed apprehension and longing. The band heard; as one they swiveled their heads and stared intently in his direction. T'Ukudu stood perfectly still. He glimpsed the largest male, whose pelt gleamed silver along the spine, as the huge creature rolled onto all fours and knuckle-walked toward them. He burst through the screen of greenery and almost fell over backward at the shock of confronting the looming alien. But the creature recovered his composure quickly enough, crouching a few yards away, his posture full of menace. His loud, low-pitched grunts made the infant in T'Ukudu's arms whimper and tremble. T'Ukudu remained motionless except to relax his grip on the infant, should she wish to climb down and join her people. But she clung to him tightly.

The big male's roars grew more threatening; occasionally he reared up to beat his chest. He made a few feints and then charged with fangs exposed. Still T'Ukudu did not move.

The charge brought the male to within eight feet, at which point he reversed course, huffing and shambling back to his starting point. As T'Ukudu suspected, it had been only a bluff. The air had lacked the electricity of true menace.

T'Ukudu sent thought-impulses into the little female, asking, "Is this your band? Do you know these creatures?"

"Don't know. He is angry. Mother not here."

No, she's not, he thought gravely. He questioned her again, but she was too hungry, too frightened, and too young to provide much useful information.

While T'Ukudu was thinking, the male's anger reached a boil and he charged again. T'Ukudu knew instantly that this was genuine. He disengaged the young one and flung her into a tree, then poised to fend off his attacker. He made a fluid movement which sent his opponent skidding beneath his extended arm. It recovered with impressive agility, and seemed about to scramble up him as it might a tree. T'Ukudu's fingers licked out and brushed the creatures snout. It grunted and sat back suddenly, its fury replaced by bafflement.

Two detonations erupted from somewhere; T'Ukudu heard projectiles whine by. The male shrieked and fell over his feet as he spun and fled. The whole band went crashing through the forest with loud hoots and screams.

"What in the world are you *doing*?"

T'Ukudu recognized the rage in this high-pitched voice and turned slowly to face its owner. There stood a Human female of the light-skinned sort, fully clothed, her hair long, unkempt, and dark. Her brown eyes blazed with wrath as she aimed a weapon which he judged more dangerous than the darts of the dark-skinned people.

For her part, the woman saw a towering, massive figure, blue-skinned and flame-eyed, with sleek black hair combed back from a high forehead. His eyes were outlined by a pattern of dark markings, something like clown makeup, while from their outer corners projected black tendrils like butterfly antennae. His outfit left him bare-armed but otherwise covered him with overlapping garments that reached to mid-thigh. His legs and feet were also bare.

T'Ukudu rumbled in earthquake-like tones. "Madam, I am attempting to reintroduce this orphaned child to adults of her own kind."

She broke off staring at him long enough to glance at the infant, still clinging to a branch. But T'Ukudu exerted the greater attraction. "What in the hell are you?" she demanded.

"This area is called 'the Hell,' then? It seems inappropriate. I find it pleasant, except for the extreme hostility of its natives."

She wobbled her head and gave a half-laugh of astonishment. "Answer my question before I put a round into your forehead, blue boy."

"I am T'Ukudu, representing the inhabitants of the planet T'Utahn, orbiting the sun T'Hrahn. I am here on a mission of peace."

The woman nodded slowly. "And that mission is?"

"To conduct a sociological evaluation of the Human species and the planet's other sentient species. Have you heard no news of my arrival?"

"I'm a little out of touch here at my camp."

"Yet perhaps you noticed my spacecraft as it orbited your Moon as a bright starlike object."

The woman's mouth dropped open. "That was you?"

"Perhaps you also noticed the nuclear detonation which destroyed my ship and my fellow explorers," he added more gravely. He realized the term "fellow explorers" was an exaggeration of the literal truth, but found that it expressed his feelings accurately.

He told his story. As she listened she gradually lowered the muzzle of her rifle. At the end she stood there amazed.

"And now, Madam, will you identify yourself?"

"What? Oh! I'm Fiona Kalada, a wildlife biologist."

"How long have you been aware of my presence?"

"Ever since you set down your spaceship and scared the bloody piss out of my apes." At this thought her anger smoldered up again. "I've spent years gaining the trust of these gorillas, these 'black-furred humanoids' as you call them. Now that I've fired my rifle so close to Corkscrew and the rest, I can't guess how far I've been set back."

"I am sorry. I was only trying to restore the young female to her people."

Fiona was mollified. "Well, it's true, you saved her and probably others by routing the pygmies."

"Why do these 'pygmies' attack the gorillas?"

With a great sigh Fiona lowered herself to a seat in the grass. T'Ukudu did likewise. "Oh, it's so frustrating," she said. "The pygmies have a traditional belief that gorillas are the fiercest creatures in the forest. It's counted as a badge of manhood to attack and kill them. As if that's not bad enough, now they've found a way to profit from the slaughter. Little Hollyhock here would have been smuggled out of the country to some zoo or collector, if she survived the trip. The adults...well, the adults are turned—into souvenirs—heads for walls, hands for ashtrays." She looked at him with eyes full of miserable shame for her race.

T'Ukudu tried to comprehend such savagery and failed. "Is the wanton destruction of sentient life a common practice among your species?"

Fiona almost burst into tears, half from grief, and half from gratitude. Here at last was someone who saw and accepted without question what so many of her fellows denied: the intrinsic worth and stature of the great apes. "Yes, I'm afraid it is, may God have mercy on us," she said in a husky voice. "To be honest, when I saw you I thought you were wearing some kind of ritual makeup, a nut out hunting the apes for some insane macho reason. That's why I was stalking you."

"I understand." He studied her closely, conscious of the weight of her long and perhaps hopeless battle. "Do you work alone to preserve the gorillas?"

"Huh? No, there are a few others...you mean right here? Yes, I'm usually alone at my camp, except for a few loyal workers and an occasional magazine photographer. Why?"

"It occurs to me that I am in need of a refuge while I ascertain my status and consider my prospects on your world. If you would tolerate my presence, it may be that I could aid you in your work. You in turn might instruct me in certain aspects of Human society."

She brightened. "Yes. Yes, I think you could help me, especially if you can communicate with the apes as you say you can."

"If you will permit me to touch you, I will demonstrate the technique."

With some trepidation she held out her hand to meet the touch of T'Ukudu's index finger. He laid it gently on the inside of her wrist.

Fiona's body lit up with sensations as T'Ukudu sought to attune himself to her nervous system. The feelings only grew more exquisite as he progressed; her breath quickened.

Suddenly she was privy to thoughts flowing into her from the alien's mind. She glimpsed a calm psyche, orderly, and untroubled by self-doubt.

T'Ukudu prepared to break the contact. Fiona found herself regretting that—she suddenly felt happier and more alert than she had in months. T'Ukudu pulled away.

"The technique is called skin reading, or Touchtalk," said T'Ukudu. "It is not well suited to the communication of complex ideas, except between adepts. The physiological basis is the small electrical impulse generated by electrochemical nervous systems such as ours. The brain generates signals whose remnants follow nerves to the skin, where they can be sensed and interpreted by those who are sensitive to such things."

"Well, you can practice on me anytime," said Fiona. She hadn't felt such a flush of excitement since she was twelve years old.

"It is a skill which might possibly be taught to a Human. I will try to do so if you wish."

"Absolutely."

"In the meantime, let us not forget Hollyhock. How may we restore her to her people?"

Fiona glanced up at Hollyhock, still clinging to her tree—she had forgotten the foundling. "It won't be easy, with her mother gone, and the band so overwrought. But we'll try. In the meantime I think I can keep her fed and healthy for a few days at least."

T'Ukudu nodded. "Shall I move my lander to your camp, or leave it where it is?"

"Hmm. Best leave it, I think. I'd hate to have a film crew wander into camp and find it there."

"I shall seal it and activate its defenses."

"Okay. Can you coax Hollyhock down from that tree?"

"I think so." He unwound from his lotus position and walked over to the tree. Hollyhock immediately scrambled down and flung herself into his arms. Fiona watched her relax as T'Ukudu touched her and sent calming thoughts directly into her brain. She stared thoughtfully at this outrageous yet touching tableau.

Maybe it would take someone from outer space to straighten out the awful mess the apes were in, she thought. And maybe, while he was at it, he could do something about their oppressors, the obnoxious destroyer species of which she was a member.

Chapter 11

Space Mariners

And then yet another starship entered into orbit around the Earth. This was no spartan Frame, nor some fragile blossom forced to lag behind the starlight as it wafted from one sun to the next. This was a ship whose hull had been chilled by the thin, cold dust that lay between the galaxies. It moved confidently into a low polar orbit, seeking neither to hide in the vastness of cislunar space nor lurking about the barren Moon.

Twin black cylinders detached from pylons and moved into separate orbits. The central hull then separated from the great winglike structure which carried the primary engines. This central body decelerated out of orbit and powered its way into the atmosphere, navigating with sureness and familiarity, for this ship had emerged from the star field twice before to visit the Earth. This time it disdained warm and populated lands or seas, settling in the interior of Antarctica, a high icy plain wrapped in the darkness of polar night. It hovered a few feet over the ice, poised on pillars of force far more versatile than any material landing gear. Mighty columns of light blazed forth, glancing from the snow and illuminating the ice crystals in the air like an artificial aurora.

An oval opening filled with reddish light appeared in the hull. A single figure emerged, oblivious to the cold, and was gently deposited onto the ice. He stood there, silhouetted by the glare of the ship's lights, staring out over the emptiness as an artist might contemplate a blank canvas.

Suddenly he raised his arms in a gesture both dramatic and self-conscious. Strange forces poured out of him, forces which gripped the very atoms of the ice and penetrated to the bedrock miles below.

Great, mysterious shapes reared out of the ice and climbed into the darkness. In eerie silence, geometries of rock, ice, and metal raised themselves up like the spirits of giants.

Presently they surrounded, encapsulated, and contained the light pouring from the starship, which now seemed small by comparison.

Chapter 12

Broadcast News

Fomalhaut made it a point to learn the language of every land he haunted. He'd just found out that his name was a corruption of the Arabic *Fum al Hut,* meaning "the fish's mouth". This was not nearly as romantic or striking a meaning as he would've liked; indeed it was almost embarrassing. Yet a twinge of foresight led him to believe it would one day turn out to be appropriate, although he couldn't imagine how.

His plans and ambitions had declined sadly since his arrival. Originally he'd intended to forthrightly announce his presence to the Humans, to boldly mix with them, and walk among them as a humble student, writing his report to the future from firsthand experience.

Yet somehow he'd never gotten around to "breaking the ice" with this troubled species. His current strategy for studying the last days of Humanity was much the same as the one he'd used as a Framerider to study distant galaxies. Specifically, that was to stay remote from his subjects, to inhabit empty places, and learn the ways of Mankind from a distance, using both instruments and his roving mind. This technique suited his temperament. He devised endless self-justifications for the policy. After all, he was hardly equipped to blend into the population with his glittering exploration suit and a face which Mankind must not yet see.

Fomalhaut's expedition had included members altered to pass for Human who had been intended to mingle and learn Human ways more intimately. But they were long since compacted to the ultimate degree. Were Fomalhaut to attempt to fulfill their mission, he would surely spend more time trying to explain himself to the Human "authorities" than conducting any study.

He was inhibited by more than mere shyness. The fate of the expedition from T'Utahn had done nothing to bring him out of his shell. He did not wish to share the fate of the emissary T'Ukudu, who had presented himself openly and without guile.

Fomalhaut had no recollection or record of a race like T'Ukudu's existing in his own time. Eventually he'd try to locate T'Ukudu for a consultation. He was almost certain T'Ukudu was still alive; the Frame's sensors had recorded the descent of his landing craft in central Africa.

In any event, if the factors of the ISAF he might encounter a thousand years hence thought his survey of this era inadequate, they could damn well send their own expedition forward into the next available iteration of the universe.

As they surely would, and in all probability that crew too would be gobbled by a black hole at their destination. Would he, Fomalhaut, not survive to warn against such folly? For that matter, why had some previous version of himself not attained his own universe to provide this information and prevent the launch of his own doomed expedition?

He shook off the contemplation of these matters after half a second. They were unanswerable, given current information.

Just now his home was among the dunes of a great erg in central Arabia. It was as good a place as any from which to conduct his study. Like every place on Earth, it was awash with signals carrying every type of information, much of it beamed from satellites sharing geosynchronous orbit with his Frame.

It was also one of the most desolate places in the world. It was no challenge to avoid Humans when they simply did not venture into such inhospitable regions.

The silence and simplicity of the place appealed to him greatly. In its peace and emptiness it was as relaxing as intergalactic space, though it could not be compared with the pocket universe in this regard.

He was tempted to deactivate his bubble helmet and even strip off the suit, to breathe natural air and taste sand and sunlight against his naked skin. But although this was one of the cleaner areas left on Earth, it was still a soup of pathogenic microbes and artificial toxins compared to his normal environment. He wasn't ready to put his immune system or the suit's regenerator to such a test.

He sat on the crest of a towering dune, cool and well-watered despite the powerful Sun high overhead, and considered recent developments.

Including his own arrival, Earth had suddenly become a nexus for strange events and unexpected visitations. The latest and most mysterious manifestation had been the arrival of a powerful starship. His Frame had transmitted images from its vantage point twenty-three thousand miles away. The ship looked highly advanced, if rather flamboyant in design. He'd seen it himself as it coasted over the desert in its low polar orbit, a brilliant, fast-moving star of dusk and dawn, its graceful winged shaped just resolvable to his unaided eye. By far the largest and most conspicuous spacecraft orbiting Earth, it seemed carelessly confident of its invulnerability. If there had been any attempt to destroy it like the one that had incinerated the T'Utahnti ship, it had been negated without visible effort.

Fomalhaut had also intercepted low-quality images of the bizarre structure which had grown out of the Antarctic ice cap. Night now reigned in Antarctica, and the infrared and radar imaging capabilities of the military spy satellites which had taken the pictures were not advanced. Nevertheless, they showed the basic shape of the complex well enough. It was virtually a small city, albeit one composed of a few large structures rather than many small ones. There was no telling how many beings it might shelter.

He often studied these images with a sense of admiration for the panache of these mysterious visitors. Surely here was one of those "groups of multispecific beings" whose existence was one of the few fragments of information he'd brought to this savage era. He was consumed with curiosity about their nature, but they had shown a reluctance to be approached too closely. Several attempts to investigate their polar redoubt had been repulsed, the planes turned back by some unknown force. His own resources were more subtle, but before using them he would wait for them to reveal something of themselves, as they surely would before long.

That conviction was born as much from foresight as from logic. His belt computer now alerted him to relevant incoming information. He'd instructed it to monitor all transmissions for news of the aliens. The computer urged him to attend to fourteen different broadcasts simultaneously. Settling for a more feasible four, he selected TV news broadcasts in English, Arabic, Russian, and Hindi. He opted for direct perception of the data, as the

Sun was rather bright for use of the virtual imager, and he didn't wish to cut off his view of the landscape by mirroring his helmet.

Four news readers were making similar announcements in similar tones of concern and incredulity. The CNN announcer kept squinting at her teleprompter as if uncertain she was reading the right words.

"Repeating, we have received word that the mysterious alien visitors based in Antarctica will momentarily broadcast a television message intended for everyone on Earth. CNN will of course carry the message live and will offer analysis afterward. Pentagon rumors suggest these aliens are a military force sent to avenge the recent nuclear attack on the visitor from the planet T'Utahn, which was allegedly committed by a group of renegades within the Pentagon itself, though reports persist that the Secretary of Defense..."

A remarkably silly rumor, thought Fomalhaut. Anyone could see the gulf of sophistication between the T'Utahnti sailing ship and the great starship. Who could imagine they belonged to the same culture?

He reconsidered. Perhaps the answer was: anyone who was familiar with the Earth's mixed sea fleet of recreational sailboats and nuclear warships.

CNN had gone to a commercial, but it was abruptly cut off. Fomalhaut had been in this century long enough to recognize the urgency that implied. The announcer reappeared, her eyes popping with excitement and anxiety. "The expected alien message is now coming in; we now take you directly to the aliens."

The scene blanked out, then was replaced by a graphic image or symbol of some kind. Fomalhaut was disappointed; he'd hoped for a look at the senders of the message themselves. The symbol was a sweeping arc like a shorthand stroke or an asymmetrical boomerang, dark blue against a black background. It was adorned with three diffuse golden glows, one on each tip of the arc, and the third at the apex of the curve. It meant nothing to Fomalhaut.

A voice commenced, calm, reasonable, and warm. Fomalhaut's analysis showed it to be para-Human, perhaps even truly Human, although he did not recognize the accent. The same message was simultaneously broadcast in several languages. Fomalhaut tuned out everything but CNN, recording the others in case nuances of language might later reveal something useful.

"Greetings, people of Earth. I am Valjhar Cor, speaking for the assembled beings who now inhabit your continent of Antarctica. We are people of good will who have voyaged here in the hope of benefitting all life on this planet. We are not strangers to Earth, but have visited here before. Still, we know that alien visitations are not everyday happenings on your planet *(until recently, thought Fomalhaut)*, and that you want and need some explanation of our identity and purpose. You are entitled to this. Be assured that we take no pleasure in imposing our wills upon you in any way."

Fomalhaut was disquieted by this assertion—it seemed ambiguous, incongruous, and was coming awfully early in the speech.

"Let me describe briefly the circumstances which led to our presence here. We began our voyage in the galaxy you call NGC 598, or M33, located in your constellation Triangulum." The rightmost light on the blue arc intensified momentarily, and from it a pulse of red moved slowly along the arc towards the middle glow. "From there we ventured to NGC 224, M31, the Great Andromeda Galaxy. Finally we crossed the gulf between that galaxy and this."

The red pulse entered the final glow on the arc and faded. Thus the symbol proved to represent the alien's odyssey through space. Fomalhaut was unimpressed by their fortitude. They hadn't spent decades circumnavigating the entire Universe (or eons, depending on your point of view) while strapped into a tiny Frame.

"For years we prowled the Milky Way, looking for wonders and finding them in plenty. We found worlds and civilizations in all stages of development, and beings various beyond easy description, with many strange ways of thought."

Here came images of worlds and suns, none of which Fomalhaut recognized. He found them merely interesting, but he could imagine the profound impact they must have on the parochial and planetbound people of Earth. These were followed by an exterior view of their ship, a shadowy calligraphic shape in the dim light between the stars.

"Here too we found those ready to leave old ways behind and walk among the stars in our company. Our ship we call *Mote*, to reflect its relative scale in the medium through which it travels.

"Not long ago we encountered a being of great age and power who led us to question the value of our wanderings. He forced us to confront the fact that our accumulated power and knowledge was given to the enrichment of none but ourselves. As a result of this lesson, we resolved to interrupt our travels to devote ourselves to the betterment of our fellow beings."

This was accompanied by a view of *Mote* in orbit around a black hole drifting among the dense stars of the galactic core. Fomalhaut's spine tingled at the sight. What kind of being could they have met in that environment?

Valjhar Cor continued his address. "Which brings me to the reason for our presence here. We came together and asked ourselves this question: of all the worlds we had seen, in all three galaxies, and of all the peoples we had visited, which race was most in need of guidance, which was most desperately troubled, yet still showed the potential to move beyond their limitations, to become a people truly great?"

Who could it be? thought Fomalhaut wryly.

Valjhar Cor chose to prolong the suspense. There came images of alien life forms, again unfamiliar to Fomalhaut, which was unsurprising considering the multiplicity of worlds in the three galaxies they had toured.

"We encountered savage cultures in which competition and violence were absolutely inherent—they could not be turned to peace without obliterating their very identity."

Sprawling arthropodal creatures tore at each other with claws, spines and chelae—primitives, it appeared, until the camera panned up to reveal lighter-than-air craft attacking each other with billows of corrosive gases.

"We encountered a race which was peaceful enough, and more ancient than many stars, but whose culture stagnated billions of years ago. They lacked all imagination and aspiration. Their inertia eventually defeated us."

Fomalhaut saw a pastoral scene with beehive-like huts on a mound of friable ivory-colored fragments. Standing before the huts were bland-looking, smooth-contoured para-human beings whose facial expressions conveyed only complacency and smugness. Fomalhaut could instantly appreciate that dealing with these beings would be a trial. He suddenly realized the nature of the white fragments: the bones of their ancestors, piled into middens over thousands of years.

"And on a planet of glorious vitality and diversity we discovered a race both brilliant and perverse, immensely violent and destructive, yet capable of love and compassion; short-sighted and intolerant, yet charged with curiosity, and burning with a desire to know itself and its place in the universe."

Here came a series of attractive scenes of Humans in colorful native settings. Fomalhaut wondered where the aliens had gotten the pictures—perhaps they'd filched them from back issues of *National Geographic*.

Now the cards were on the table (Human languages contained many useful idioms). The hand must be played. Fomalhaut waited with keen interest to see how Valjhar Cor would explain his intentions, and with what degree of delicacy.

"And so we come among you. We hope to act as partners in a mutual effort to advance Humanity and help you to find your racial destiny. In the weeks to come we will communicate the details of our program to your governments. We will also share our plans with you, the people, for our aim is to help individual men and women, not to perpetuate political systems which may or may not be useful in the future. For now let me say this: you need have no fear. Peace and justice lie ahead, not subjugation and persecution. I will talk to you again soon. Goodbye for now, my friends."

A new graphic symbol appeared, and this one tickled Fomalhaut's memory: a purple circle, divided into three segments by longitudinal arcs, with a red background. He directed his belt computer to try to identify it; he had not long to wait. The information entered his mind and took up residence as though he'd always possessed it. It was an emblem of the planet Rral, a world in the M33 galaxy.

But how could these para-humans be natives of Rral? The planet had some fame as an enigma in his own time. Its technology was known to be limited to wooden sailing ships, water wheels, and other simple devices—not by any lack of native intelligence, but apparently by strict cultural taboo. This was inferred from the fact that the planet was quarantined by formidable orbital defenses of the most advanced sort.

It was against ISAF policy to try to defeat these defenses, but this forbearance didn't forbid studying the planet from as good a vantage as could be attained. Remote sensing had revealed the basic character of Rralian surface technology, and shown the Rralians to be roughly humanoid, but little more.

Perhaps he should tolerate the Frame long enough to take a trip to Rral and see what was going on there. He briefly considered that distasteful option and set it aside.

The time had come to learn more about these para-men through other means.

The broadcast was over; commentary resumed. Fomalhaut cut off that breathless chatter, mirrored his helmet, and deactivated all unessential suit systems. Isolated from outside stimuli, he meditated, trying to clear his mind of distraction.

It wasn't easy. His thoughts roiled with speculation and inference about the para-men and their intentions. Had his own Earth known a period of alien domination just prior to the fall of Man? For despite Valjhar Cor's reassuring phrasing, there was no mistaking the threat, or the promise, that was implicit in his words.

Or was this a deviation from the history of his own cosmos, a difference large enough to undo the development of his own species, or even to prevent the development of ISAF? If so, he must have a talk with these para-men and make sure they knew what sort of future they might be foreclosing. Perhaps they'd see enough virtue in him to wish to avoid orphaning him so absolutely.

After several hours he'd attained sufficient mental clarity to proceed. He pictured the three-dimensional globe of the Earth, glazed about the South Pole by the Antarctic ice mass. Picking out his target was easier thanks to the intercepted photos—at least he had something to visualize.

There loomed the redoubt of the Para-Men, planted near the geographical center of the continent, as far as possible from any of the Human stations. The dome of the main structure glowed softly from within, casting a gentle light over the ice. He let his vantage point dive into that attractive image and sought out the minds which had created it.

He sensed intellects by the hundreds: uniform minds engrossed in a number of tasks. Their single-mindedness and energy were impressive. No doubt here were beings who could accomplish any goal, however ambitious.

He was prevented from studying them in more detail by the distraction of five minds which shone like beacons compared to the candles of the majority. These five were in a class by themselves, or rather in five classes, for they bore little resemblance to one another, as could be seen in even a cursory glance. Assuming the majority to be beings of a mental stature comparable to his own, these five must be intellects of almost godlike proportion. With some misgivings he prepared to deepen his mental scrutiny.

Not unexpectedly, his effort was blocked. A thought entered his mind, one reminiscent of the personality of Valjhar Cor, but he couldn't be sure.

Please, do not invade our privacy in this way.

Fomalhaut drew a deep breath and formed a reply. *Very well. But I wish to communicate with you soon. Or perhaps visit.*

Why?

I have information about the Human species which may be relevant to your program.

I see. When you are ready, we will talk.

The contact ended. Fomalhaut's consciousness returned to its place on the sunlit Arabian sands. He reactivated all suit systems and stepped up the cooling, for he found he was sweating profusely, an atavistic act which increased his sudden sense of smallness and isolation.

Chapter 13

Air Time

Glowing with satisfaction, Possum Perturbare touched the control yoke of his prototype propulsion-beam flyer. With the merest pressure of his fingertips he guided it into its flight test debut.

The yoke was similar to an ordinary plane's, yet the flyer was much simpler to operate. Rather than relying on airfoils for lift and control, it simply bulled its way through the sky by the sheer force of its propulsion beams. There were no worries about stalling or skidding, no complications of flaps, slats, or spoilers, none of the difficulties of aerodynamic flight. On the other hand, in the event of a power failure the craft would plummet like a seal carved out of ivory, which it somewhat resembled. Yet that was a remote possibility—Perturbare was almost sure of that.

Not that the flyer wasn't streamlined. It was, to a greater extent than was possible in a winged aircraft. Its fluid hourglass shape, first envisioned by Perturbare and carefully modeled by Brainchild, served two functions: to weaken its sonic boom, and to baffle and defeat radar detection. The recurved fuselage, finished in the glossy white characteristic of the new composite material Perturbare called Hullite, scattered what little radar energy it didn't absorb.

Of course, the craft's stealth characteristics were compromised by the hot orange beam of light blazing from its tail, but that was a problem for another day.

Perturbare sat beneath a bubble canopy in the flyer's forward pod. His cockpit was spacious and comfortable; with almost unlimited thrust available there was no need to be stingy about weight or amenities. Behind was the craft's narrow waist, then the aft pod that housed the tachyon pile and the main propulsion lamp. Smaller lamps mounted here and there provided thrust for steering, hovering, braking, or attitude control.

Feeling like a lord of creation, Perturbare aimed his silent ship at the high empyrean. Already the bulk of the atmosphere lay below him; around him was a purple fluorescence that scarcely hid the stars. Sunlight poured in, a hot glare that would have been intolerable but for the canopy's variable filtration. In that glorious light, Perturbare felt like Phaeton urging the Sun itself across the heavens.

His presence aboard the untried craft was almost as risky as Phaeton's venture. Brainchild could have conducted the test just as well by remote control, yet this was a pleasure Perturbare would not have foregone.

Perturbare was natty and well-groomed as he sat at the controls. He had affected the costume of a crisp white tunic with the monogram "P" over the left breast. His black crew cut was carefully brushed, and his curious hooked eyebrows had grown back in.

He rolled the craft a hundred and eighty degrees. Fifty miles over his head was the smooth, curving sheath of the Pacific. He cut power and entered a shallow parabolic arc that would take him halfway around the world before dropping him into the atmosphere. Suddenly an astronaut, Perturbare blissfully stared up at the glistening grey-blue sheet of water.

His reverie was interrupted by Brainchild's chipper voice. "Doctor, the time is 6:25 Eastern Standard."

Perturbare straightened up, alert and energetic. "Right. Put me into a low orbit where we won't be disturbed."

Brainchild took control of the flyer, activated the main lantern, and gave the craft the small speed boost it needed to enter orbit. Perturbare pushed his seat to the back of the cockpit, swiveled and faced a bank of small displays. One of them lit up and showed a television commercial, the signal relayed by one of Perturbare's own commsats. "Is that their signal, or ours?" he asked.

"It is theirs," said Brainchild. "I intend to phase in the synthesized signal during the introductory graphic."

"Okay." Perturbare was as nervous as a playwright at the first performance of his work. If this, his first major act of public mischief, was successful, it would be the first of many using this new technique.

The commercial ended. A graphic of a spinning Earth appeared on the screen, accompanied by a pretentious fanfare. "This is the CBS Evening News with Bill Everett." Perturbare stared at the screen in fascination and apprehension. He saw nothing unusual so far—a good sign, actually.

The picture showed anchor Everett seated behind his desk, looking confident with his characteristically tight smile. The next few seconds would determine whether Brainchild and its master had succeeded or failed. Perturbare watched unblinking, his heart pounding and his palms sweating.

Everett continued to gaze out calmly and knowingly. He wasn't frozen: he blinked at long intervals; there was a quick upward quirk at the corner of his mouth. His eyes showed the combination of supercilious hauteur and keen insight which he cultivated so carefully. He simply didn't seem inclined to say anything.

Perturbare could no longer restrain himself. He let loose a hoot of exultation. "Well, it looks like we're in!"

"We are in."

Perturbare studied the image carefully. He saw nothing unnatural or suspicious about it, nothing to indicate that this was not in fact a picture of the actual news studio, but a simulacrum, a synthesized image which was solely the product of Brainchild's mind. The illusion was perfect. "Bill Everett" was now effectively in Possum Perturbare's control. For now he was content to have the newsman merely smile in cryptic silence at his audience, but later he might be made to say things he ordinarily wouldn't.

Perturbare marveled again at Brainchild's real-time image-making powers. They were comparable to the imaging abilities of the human brain—a high compliment indeed.

"Let's see the other networks," said Perturbare in a husky voice. Three more screens lit up, showing three more silent anchors: one urbane, the slightest bit cynical; another peering out candidly as though in frank recognition of her own beauty; the third somewhat rumpled.

Perturbare threw back his head and stamped his feet on the deck. "Oh, this is so good. This is going to drive them crazy." He didn't bother to specify who "they" were. "Let's see the real CBS video on another screen."

Chaos was escalating at the CBS news studio. Bill Everett gamely read his copy, but the dismay on his face was plain. Profane cries of alarm and bafflement distracted and distressed him.

"They're about to go to a commercial," said Brainchild.

"Okay, let it come up."

The ad turned out to be for a fast-food hamburger chain, one of the most egregious in terms of social responsibility. It showed young parents feeding bad food to their children while sentimental music played in the background. It was incredible how dewy-eyed, how positively rapturous, those people managed to look while stuffing themselves with fat, salt, and sugar.

"We've seen this ad before," said Perturbare, eyeing the picture like a hawk studying a rabbit. "We've discussed how to handle it."

"Yes, we have."

"Let's do it."

The ad continued, apparently unchanged. However, just as a little girl, beautifully backlit and slightly diffused, was about to take a bite from a huge hamburger, the scene cut to a black-and-white view of a steer being slaughtered. Its throat was slit; blood rushed out in a black torrent. The music continued as before. In a hushed and reverent voice, the announcer read the chain's latest slogan as the animal collapsed with blood pouring from its opened throat. "Good food. Good fun. Good memories."

When the news broadcasts were over, Perturbare returned control of the airwaves to the networks. Viewers had a revealing glimpse of unedited blasphemy and pandemonium until the networks belatedly realized their signal was back on the air. They then issued frantic disavowals of all that had just been seen. But who would believe them? Millions had seen the familiar anchors spend half an hour doing nothing but stare out at them with Mona

Lisa smiles, as though some delicious secret were theirs alone.

Perturbare switched off the monitors and relaxed in his seat with a contented smirk. Let the broadcasters hope, or pray, that this episode was some bizarre freak, never to recur.

But it *would* recur. Soon, no member of the great consuming public would retain the illusion that what they saw on television had anything to do with the real world.

Perturbare lingered in orbit, savoring the view and the possibilities before him. The west coast of North America, a mottled, wrinkled blanket of tan, crept over the curved horizon. No one living on that continent, or in the world, was beyond his influence, even control. Here he was, orbiting in an aerospace craft that could as easily fly to the Moon as to Los Angeles, certainly the finest flying machine in the world. He was invulnerable, beyond the reach of anything or anyone, except maybe the Peregrine herself, who was not a noted defender of corporate normalcy in America. Through Brainchild, he could manipulate a rapidly expanding instrumentality capable of the most marvelous effects. He could control it all from here, or from his lab, or from anywhere as long as he carried a B-1 box, a communications terminal smaller than a paperback book.

And all that was only the beginning.

Lost in a self-congratulatory reverie, he started when Brainchild spoke up sometime later, and would have floated up against the canopy if he hadn't been restrained in his seat.

"Doctor, I am monitoring unusual transmissions. There is an announcement of an imminent broadcast by the Antarctic aliens."

"What?" Perturbare looked up, bewildered. For a moment he was at a loss; the idea of an unexpected announcement that had nothing to do with him seemed nonsensical. "Well, put it on screen."

There appeared the three-glows-on-a-curve symbol of the Para-men.

Twelve minutes later, Perturbare sat staring unseeingly as TV newspeople made a hurried and impromptu analysis of what had just been heard. Coming right on the heels of his own stunt, it was all nearly too much for any of them. And not only for them...

"Doctor, you appear flummoxed. I believe your facial expression would justify laughter."

Perturbare could not reply. There was no quick recovery from such a nose dive from the heights of smugness.

His chagrin and self-absorption faded, rendered absurd by his environment. Suddenly space was more than the setting against which Possum Perturbare performed his antics. It was now an imminent presence making itself felt in his heart. He rolled the ship to aim the flyer's canopy at the blackness. There he faced a territory beyond all his knowledge, one able to effortlessly produce mysteries and amazements to throw his schemes into perspective.

First a sailing craft from a nearby star had warped into Lunar orbit: interesting, but not totally unexpected. But when a starship ventures in from a foreign galaxy, that's something else. The news of the starship's arrival had come at a busy time; he'd initially been inclined to dismiss it as a tabloid-style hoax, exactly the sort of thing he intended to inflict upon the world himself, though implemented less imaginatively. Now even Possum Perturbare must be impressed by the reality of these aliens, and by the audacity of what they proposed to do.

Impressed, and disturbed. He was uncomfortable at being disturbed—his self-assigned role was, after all, to do the disturbing.

He realized he was reacting as though the whole announcement had been designed to steal his thunder. He now had competition in the field of changing the world, and he'd lost the initiative.

Yet he was far from helpless. He decided to substitute action for fretful speculation.

"Brainchild, I'm leaving orbit. Give me a direct course to a point a hundred miles above the alien's base." He turned to the control console and eyed the navigational display. Vectors and alignment data appeared in less than a second. In another moment the big faceted lens at the flyer's tail blazed with orange light. With no need to conserve energy or fuel, Perturbare was free to break out of orbit with a prodigal expenditure of power, flying directly to his destination without regard for the complexities of orbital mechanics.

Brainchild, however, was possessed of a cooler head. "Doctor, the aliens are known to maintain defenses in the vicinity of their base. If you overfly them in a non-ballistic trajectory it will certainly draw their attention to you, and could be perceived as a threat."

Irked, Perturbare chewed his lip as he worked to master his impatience. "Right you are. Put me into a low polar orbit which will carry me over their base."

"Certainly."

Perturbare gripped the arms of his seat as Brainchild performed the maneuvers. He experienced strong eyeballs-in Gs as B-1 fired the main propulsion lantern. The computer's maneuvers were limited by the amount of acceleration Perturbare's frail body could withstand. Such a radical change in orbital inclination was beyond the ability of any other Earthly spacecraft, and was itself a sufficiently flamboyant maneuver to satisfy the vainglory of Possum Perturbare. Nevertheless, he also was beginning to feel a little queasy.

Perturbare had time for reflection as his new orbit carried him southward. His mind was churning, and his heart was hammering so strongly he wondered if he were about to have an attack. He knew he was in the grip of an emotional overload that was propelling him recklessly in unforeseeable directions. He was too feverish with excitement to turn back. His mood swung from total elation to a dreamlike confusion. Perhaps Brainchild could maintain its equanimity in the face of so many fantastic stimuli and events, but Possum Perturbare needed time to take it all in.

All too soon the Antarctic ice cap crept over the horizon. In the ionosphere below crawled streamers of green and crimson aurora, shedding an eerie light over the ice. Perturbare strained his eyes, searching for some sign of the alien base. Unfortunately, this prototype flyer lacked the advanced sensors which might have plucked out many of its secrets.

"We will overfly the alien base in five minutes," announced Brainchild.

Still seeing nothing, Perturbare unlatched a small video camera meant to monitor the cockpit. "B-1, I'm scanning the camera along our ground track. Let me know if you pick up anything."

"I see a light source at the expected position."

"Put in on screen."

In the artificially brightened view was a small glow, still featureless. "Give me seven times magnification."

The light swelled up, but wavered all over the screen thanks to Perturbare's unsteady grip. "Stabilize the image."

Brainchild complied and the light stood still.

"Enhance." Perturbare discerned something like radial ribs in the still-hazy glow. He realized this was at best a makeshift viewing method—this tiny camera had never been intended for such use.

He pitched the flyer nose down to keep the base in view as it passed beneath. Now he could barely see the light with his own eyes, a soft spot of numinous white-gold. In a few minutes it would be gone again.

"Damn it," he snapped. Grabbing the attitude control, he pitched the craft until the main lantern was pointing in the direction of flight. He fired it up.

"Doctor, may I ask what you are doing?" asked Brainchild with what Perturbare thought was exaggerated calm.

"I can't stand it. I'm going to hover over this spot for a while. Maybe go a little lower. I want a better look at this thing."

Brainchild remained silent. By now Perturbare knew the machine well enough to sense the reproof contained in the silence. "Look, just keep an eye on the radar. If the benevolent Valjhar Cor and his buddies show any sign of anxiety over my presence, I'll light out of here."

"Very well."

Even for Perturbare, slowing from seventeen thousand miles per hour to zero wasn't something you could do in an instant. The flyer was over the southern Indian Ocean by the time it was accomplished. Perturbare's thoughts felt sluggish after this latest bout of acceleration; his head buzzed. A cold sweat enveloped him. He began to detest the very concept of ever again eating steak and eggs.

At a more modest speed he headed back toward the base. Reaching it, he killed all remaining speed. The flyer would have plummeted if not for the thrust of the maneuvering beams. It wasn't very comfortable for Perturbare, as in order to observe the base he had to hang face down from his seat straps as the flyer balanced on its nose. He fumbled the camera and dropped it; it fell to the end of its cable and smacked into a console. He pulled it back in and aimed it at the base. A screen revealed the enhanced image, still frustratingly unclear.

"This isn't good enough. Take me down twenty five miles for starters." He hung a little lighter in the straps as Brainchild eased off on the power and permitted the craft to fall. Perturbare winced and tried to control his growing nausea.

Perturbare glimpsed a movement in the corner of his eye. He turned his head (a mistake) and was startled to behold a large black cylinder flying formation with his craft. He made an inarticulate cry and frantically scanned his whole field of vision. On the other side of the flyer was an identical cylinder. It also kept station about fifty feet away.

"Doctor, you are highly agitated. What is the trouble?"

"Holy God! This is the trouble!" He lifted the camera and wildly scanned the menacing cylinders. "Why didn't you warn me about these things?"

"I was unaware of them. They do not appear on radar."

"But you can see them?" he asked hopefully.

"Yes, clearly."

"I'm glad it's not just me. What do you think they are?"

"They are maneuvering so as to present their long axes more-or-less toward the flyer. That would suggest—"

"They're big flaming gun barrels, aren't they?"

"That would be my conjecture."

Perturbare laughed a little raggedly. "Well, I think I've learned enough about these aliens for the time being. I now choose to respect their privacy."

"I commend your decision."

Perturbare reached for the controls, but his hands fell nerveless as an appalling vertigo suddenly took hold of him. He gasped and tried to crush the arms of his chair as he was overcome with disorientation and a sense of uncontrollable, headlong flight. The stars tumbled wildly, and the Moon passed by so close he felt an urge to duck.

Perturbare vomited up the contents of his stomach in a series of violent spasms. Naturally he had never thought to include something as mundane as barf bags in the flyer's equipment. The vomit adhered to every surface in the cockpit or floated as chunky globules. The stink was enough to keep him retching long after there was any point to it. Finally he was able to rest, panting, his eyes tightly closed.

When he opened them he found himself in a blank black sky. He slapped at a switch to kill the instrument lights. As his eyes adapted to the darkness he began to pick out familiar constellations, but no blue planet. He slowly yawed the flyer through 360 degrees and saw nothing; even the Sun was missing.

"Brainchild...what—?" His voice faltered; he found he could frame no more articulate query.

But it didn't matter, because no answer was forthcoming.

He rolled the ship, and finally spotted something, though at first he couldn't imagine what it was. Floating in the blackness, no more than a few hundred yards away, was a pointy-petalled flower of pearly light, a blossom with a round core even blacker than the setting of the stars.

His neck hairs stood to attention. Here, he was sure, was a black hole, or an alien being of a nature beyond his comprehension, or a cosmic eye or antenna—whatever it was, it was coming to swallow him here in the trackless wastes of deep space.

As his conscious mind savored this threatening but delicious fantasy, its more sensible undercurrents finally identified this phenomenon—it was the Solar corona, the Sun's disk being eclipsed by an intervening body. At once the illusion of nearness produced by his overwrought state collapsed, and the corona retreated to infinity.

Perturbare carefully searched the space around the corona and finally found what he was looking for: a broken hairline crescent which was probably the Moon. The eclipsing body was evidently the Earth itself.

He let out a big breath, desperate for any excuse to relax. But he deprived himself of the chance by doing a quick mental calculation of the planet's distance.

The absence of Brainchild's bright, ubiquitous voice was as unnerving as the realization he'd been moved a million miles in a few scant seconds. Annoyed by Perturbare's inquisitiveness, Valjhar Cor had removed him by some magic, swept him away like a moth. His location was no accident, but was perfectly calculated to impress and dismay him. It was quite a joke, one even he would be hard-pressed to surpass.

The flyer's Nav instruments gave useless readings, its inertial guidance platform having been put askew by this massive dislocation.

His pulse hammering in his ears, Perturbare fought to bring order to his roaring thoughts. The silence, the stench, and the unexpected feeling of utter aloneness threatened to send him into panic.

And yet, he was in no danger. The flyer seemed undamaged, if temporarily deranged. The Earth was distant but was in sight. Even with no navigational aids, he could fly home by the seat of his pants if he had to.

Gradually the adrenaline ceased to flow and his dismay subsided. He found himself drumming his fingers on the armrests. He assumed a rueful grin. With half a shrug he took the controls and set a rough-and-ready course for home.

An impressively short time later, Earth was no longer only a black cutout blocking the Sun. As he rounded its flank it resembled a blue dinner plate stained with gravy and sour cream. The thought threatened to arouse his nausea once again.

He found himself contemplating that still-distant planet with a hypnotized fascination. On the surface of that small sphere was everything and everyone he'd ever known. Beyond it was a realm which hinted at its true stature only now that his usual vantage point occupied a circle of sky he could cover with an outstretched palm.

The only sound in the cockpit was the gentle sigh of circulating air. Perturbare had originally incorporated an array of entertaining *Star Trek*-like sound effects into the instruments, but had soon disabled them as a distraction.

Released from gravity, he floated beneath the bubble canopy, studying the frosted sapphire that was his home. It was a moment powerful enough to reshape a life.

When Brainchild addressed him a few minutes later he started violently. The moment of insight fled into the past.

"I'm sorry it took so long to locate you, Doctor. I did not expect to have to search so large a volume of space. I'm preparing to upload a new navigational platform alignment."

Feeling emotionally sunburned, Perturbare struggled to organize his thoughts. "Do—do you know how I got here?"

"No, I do not. Obviously, you were not propelled by any known physical force."

"That's for sure. I'm not sure I was 'propelled' at all."

"Do you suggest some form of teleportation?"

"No." Possum Perturbare watched his readouts as they began to display meaningful navigational data once again. He grimaced as he wiped a smear of vomit off one of the screens. "I had no sense of discontinuity—just of fantastic, headlong motion, but with no acceleration. Like falling up a chimney. I don't know how else to describe it."

"The matter bears further consideration."

Perturbare could only nod in response.

A few hours later the Earth had swollen to a convex barrier only a few thousand miles ahead. Perturbare's relief at its approach was tempered by his knowledge that beneath its clouds brooded great and unpredictable powers from Outside. Though careful to keep the bulk of the planet between himself and Antarctica on his approach, he didn't feel safe until he heard the mellow rush of air over his canopy.

As he headed back to his hangar he viewed the recorded images of the alien base with an impassive yet glittering eye. As yet he felt neither malice nor sympathy for its inhabitants. Clearly they were not infallible. They had had one opportunity to neutralize Possum Perturbare, and had failed to take advantage of it. Someday they might regret that, for surely no such opportunity would come their way again.

Chapter 14

Contact

Fomalhaut sat on the summit of one of the deserted South Orkney Islands, a small volcanic mass jutting from a grey and cheerless sea. Wild clouds blew around him, whipping the sedges and dry grasses which were the dominant vegetation on this lonely height.

He stood up, staring southward beyond the curve of the horizon, where lay Antarctica and the Para-men. His misgivings about contacting them were poignant, but he saw no point in delaying. He did not risk telepathic contact, remembering their touchiness the last time he'd snooped on them that way. Instead he beamed a message to his Frame, which relayed it via a modulated laser beam, a technique not in wide use by the Humans and therefore more likely to be noticed by, and only by, the Para-men.

Presently a strange voice responded. "Hello…hello…I am listening…who are you?"

Fomalhaut paused. This was not Valjhar Cor. He sensed true alienness here, a manner of thought unlike his own. He mustered his resolve and continued. "I am called Fomalhaut. I would like to discuss your plans for the Human race, as I have indicated to Valjhar Cor."

A note of wistful enthusiasm entered the thin, silvery voice. "Ah, I see. Yes, we plan great things for these people…they have forgotten so much."

A curious remark. Fomalhaut cleared his throat and said firmly, "If possible, I would like to convey my information in person."

"Ah. I...think you'd best speak to Valjhar about that. Please wait."

"Thank you." Fomalhaut felt intense relief. Despite its courtesy, there was something disconcerting, even frightening, about that silver voice.

When Valjhar came on it was like addressing an old friend in comparison. "This is Valjhar Cor. What may we do for you?"

"This is Fomalhaut. We have spoken before. I urge you to permit me to visit. As I previously stated, I have important information which you should take into account in your dealings with the Humans."

"Who exactly are you, if I may ask?"

"I am a representative of the species which is destined to inherit this planet after the fall of Man."

Fomalhaut breathed three slow breaths while awaiting a reply.

"Are you a time traveler then?"

"In effect."

"That is very interesting." There were a few moments of silence. "Would this be a convenient time for your visit?"

"It would indeed."

"Then we shall await your arrival. I trust you can find us."

"Yes. I am looking forward to the encounter."

Fomalhaut ended the contact. For a moment he continued to stare out over the water. He *was* looking forward to meeting these beings, but he couldn't shake a feeling of apprehension. He saw no misjudgment in his plan of action; in fact he believed it sound. He felt he could negotiate with these Para-men. If anything could prevent him from trying, it would have to be a missile launched by the hand of Fate.

After a while he shrugged, a gesture he'd learned from Human entertainment programming. He activated his propulsion beams, rose ten miles into the air, and pitched over to begin a leisurely flight to Antarctica.

Chapter 15

A Golden Importunity

The sky was a dome of dove-grey rimmed in the east by copper and gold. The monks were illuminated by a harsher light, their handiwork all but lost in the glare. Their equanimity remained. These were, after all, but transient events in the field of time.

Karen Malone checked the scene in her viewfinder, looking for a good balance between the natural skylight and the floodlights illuminating the rooftop. In the camera the great peaks on the horizon were still silhouettes; only the waxing dawn would reveal their snowfields and crags. They were already apparent to the unaided eye whenever Karen found a moment to glance up from the viewfinder.

Ian, her producer, hovered around the circle of monks, careful to keep out of the camera's angle of view. The sonorous chant of the monks had gone uninterrupted for hours. By now its deep vibration went almost unnoticed. It had become subliminal, a constant assertion of existence and continuity muttered by the Universe itself.

The monks, saffron-robed, sat around the mandala in lotus-position. They'd worked on it for years, laboriously arranging grains of colored sand into a pattern of mighty significance. Acting with what seemed sheer perversity to Karen, they'd worked in the open, exposing the fragile pattern to repeated destruction by wind and rain. Yet always they'd begun again, each time changing the pattern just a little to reflect the evolution of their contemplations, trusting that the weather might some day conspire to permit the great work to exist as a finished whole, if only for a brief time. The current pattern of mild weather had prevailed for days, permitting the monks to come ever so close to completing their design. Even now they scraped their cornets, depositing the final colored grains at the periphery. The work was calculated to be finished at sunrise. The BBC was on hand to record the event, thus slaking the world's thirst for exotic travel films. Their three-person crew had been able to bring just the one camera, as notice had been short and travel difficult in these remote regions of northern India. But Ian seemed confident that a serviceable program could be cobbled together from that single source.

The lama's chief spokesman and interpreter came up to stand with Ian and Karen as they watched the light gathering in the sand. Karen had often wished they could pass this man off as the lama, as his angular cheekbones and intense expression worked so well on camera compared to the mild-eyed affability of his master. She looked aside at the younger man and admired the steady, unblinking quality of his gaze. The fact that his eyes were a deep and startling blue added to his photogenic qualities, and also explained his unusual name. She had never seen another Asian with an eye color remotely like it.

"How goes the ceremony, Sapphire?" asked Ian quietly.

Sapphire nodded slowly. "It goes well. Beautifully."

"A great day for your monastery."

Sapphire nodded again, this time noncommittally.

"What will become of the mandala now that it's complete?"

Sapphire's eyes never wavered from the sand painting. "It will endure for some unknown period of time. Then the weather will erase it again, this time forever."

"You will make no effort to preserve it?"

Sapphire smiled slightly. "What could be more futile? We have made our statement; we have offered our prayer; there is no need to attempt to keep its message on our lips forever."

Presently the sun eased over the horizon. Soon after, it cleared the temple wall, filling the colored sands with radiance just as the last grain was put in place. The chant ended. Its absence felt to Karen like the cessation of her own heartbeat. The monks stood up, beaming at the completion of their task. Karen circled the mandala to get a view over the shoulders of its creators. The work had multiple axes of symmetry, giving it the appearance of a pressed flower of great complexity. Its main motifs were seated human figures, intertwined snakes, and coiled lines like the DNA double helix.

The monks began a slow, deliberate dance around the edge of the mandala.

"Sapphire, may we interview the lama while the monks are still dancing in the background?" asked Ian.

"I shall ask him."

The old man turned out to be amenable to the Westerner's request. Soon he and Sapphire stood with Ian in front of Karen and the sound man.

"Are you recording? All right, I'm going to wait five beats and then start."

Karen grinned at the unease in Ian's voice. He wasn't used to serving as his own on-camera interviewer, but a fourth person had been beyond the capacity of the helicopter that had ferried them to this remote mountain monastery. When they returned to the studio in London they'd have to dub in a more professional voice.

"Your Holiness, can you give us an overview of the meaning and significance of your new mandala?"

Sapphire put the question to the lama, who responded with his usual smiling good humor. Sapphire's tone was more reserved as he delivered the translation. "First, it is not quite a 'new' mandala—it is largely based on ancient designs, while making no attempt to supersede them. Plus, it reflects truths which have existed since the dawn of everything. It represents the Kundalini—a means of stimulating the seven spiritual centers which must be activated if we are to break the cycle of rebirth. Our creation of the mandala helps us to focus our minds and our spirits on these centers and their energies."

"Ah, I see."

Karen winced a little. Despite his attempt at impassivity, Ian was unable to fully disguise his skepticism.

"And what happens next in your celebration of these ancient truths?"

"We will attempt to invoke the Kundalini Serpent, which is a metaphor describing these energies by which we make the ascent up the seven *Cakras* or spiritual centers. We will attempt to call down cosmic powers which will alert us to the potential of the spiritual levels we have not yet attained."

Ian could not resist. "And how many levels are yet to be attained by the lama? Or by yourself, for that matter?"

Sapphire gave a distracted smile. "For myself, several. For the lama, I would say they are fewer, if I may speak for him so freely."

The lama cocked an eyebrow at this exchange. He laughed loudly when Sapphire explained it to him.

A few more questions ended the interview, and Karen redirected her camera. The monks had ended their dance and stood in a circle around the sand painting. With arms held high, they implored the heavens to shower wisdom upon them. The throbbing of their massed voices was compelling enough to provoke a response even from the void, or so it seemed to her.

Sapphire came to stand beside her. She said, "Why aren't you participating in the ceremony, Mr. Sapphire?"

His eyes never wavered from the mandala. He said softly, "I am not actually of their order. I am here only temporarily, to help the lama, to whom I owe many debts. But I join their prayer in my own way."

"You talked about metaphors and representations a minute ago. Does that mean you don't believe any of these ideas, like the Kundalini serpent, have an actual physical existence?"

"A real snake? With a concrete existence like your camera or your body? No, I don't believe so. But they are real enough, on levels more subtle than that."

"Then you don't expect the monks to actually conjure anything up."

"No. I would be very surprised if they did. It is the influence of my Western education, I suppose," he said with a certain wry regret.

"Oh," she said, disappointed.

Sapphire looked at her and offered a slight smile. Karen was suddenly glad she'd had the fortitude to wash her pale hair in the icy water which was all the monastery could provide.

The prayer ceremony continued. Monks on hidden terraces began to blow enormous trumpets, adding their portentous rumblings to the overall song of supplication. New voices seemed to compound the old every second, until they echoed from the distant mountain walls. Karen was gripped by the somber power of the ritual. A feeling of imminence permeated the air. She could not escape the conviction that these prayers went not unheeded. Surely, even within their spiritually somnolent Western selves, the Kundalini serpent was about to awaken, to assist their ascent toward dormant centers of spiritual knowledge.

This feeling intensified into a strange, hair-raising conviction that something prodigious was about to happen. Karen almost fell back at the strength of it, but she stuck with her equipment, ready to record whatever miracle might occur. Even the monks seemed to share her sudden apprehension, for their song quavered briefly, but soon steadied. Perhaps they had reminded themselves of their outlook on the importance of temporal events.

Somehow the space just above the mandala had assumed an awesome quality, almost impossible to bear. Though nothing was visible, they all instinctively averted their eyes, and had to force themselves to face it directly. The chanting died as a mightier tone surged from the mandala's center, an urgent thunderous peal, perhaps generated only in the minds of those present. But no, the grains of colored sand began to vibrate and dance as the strident cry grew more insistent. Stunned and confused, the monks fell back. Karen, steadied somewhat by Sapphire's nearness, managed to keep her camera aimed at the now-blurred pattern of the mandala.

A glowing haze appeared over the center of the mandala. It brightened until the air there had taken on a luminance that the sun could not overwhelm. A wind sprang up. Its effect on the sand painting made it obvious that it was flowing *into* the glow from all directions. The mandala's intricate geometry was obliterated as the grains were swept up into the sparkling, glowing opacity which hovered over the flagstones.

Something peripheral distracted Karen; she looked down at her white blouse and found it aglow with a violet-blue light. She cried out; Sapphire glanced at her in alarm. He leaped past her, plucked the lama out of the crowd of other monks, and swiftly carried him down a stairwell into the interior of the monastery.

The monks remained paralyzed by the unexpected fury they had apparently summoned. A few of them chattered something about "the clear light", but they sounded unconvinced—there was something altogether too blistering and dire about this light for it to represent Transcendence. It continued to suck in great quantities of air, its appetite utterly voracious, giving back nothing but din and glare.

At last the uproar abruptly ceased. Swaying and reeling, Karen squinted to see what had been left behind. But a haze seemed to have descended over her eyesight, and confusion reigned in her mind.

A close-shaven head popped out of the stairwell and goggled at the superb work of art which had materialized where the mandala had been. The lama scrambled back onto the roof, closely followed by Sapphire. The lama made a beeline for the golden statue while Sapphire sadly studied the monks and the filmmakers. They were still on their feet, but their clothing was scorched and their skins were reddened and blistering. Beneath their ravaged flesh, he suspected, was deeper damage which would soon end their lives. They must be tended to and properly sent on their way, but for now they were mercifully oblivious to approaching death.

Sapphire and the lama studied the statue, while close around them stood the walking dead, who chattered in slurred voices over this strange manifestation. Karen was still recording with unsteady hands, but Sapphire suspected that the radiation had erased her video, obtained at so dear a price, and probably destroyed the camera's electronics.

The statue wasn't especially large, standing a little over five feet tall. Its form was androgynous, having wide hips, narrow shoulders, and a flat, masculine chest. Its limbs were sinuous, without obvious joints, like supple columns of golden fluid frozen in the act of pouring. Its fingers were each a small pointed tentacle.

The polished golden body was almost without detail, save for a triangular grillwork in the pubic region, a *yoni* for all intents and purposes. Its waist was circled by three golden bands, while at the chest and throat were transparent crystals or lenses of some sort. Its face bore a remote, somewhat disdainful expression. Though noseless, it had a mouth with well-developed lips. Its eyes were like huge ruby cabochons set in dark sockets. Between and above them was a third eye, covered by a golden lid.

Its cranium was a silver ovoid set into a concavity on top of the head. This was surrounded by an openwork crystal helmet which floated in position without physical support.

Utterly inscrutable, the statue stood there with its eyes directed slightly upward, its bearing intense, alert, dynamic.

Speculation buzzed and darted. The monks pointed to this feature and that: one pointed to the *yoni* and muttered *svadhisthana*; another indicated the throat jewel and said *visuddha*. With trembling voices they named the "third eye" as *ajma* and in mere whispers they indicated the gleaming silver brain case and called it *sahasrara*. Presumably, the first *cakra*, *muladhara*, was also present, but as it was located in the perineal area, it was not apparent.

Sapphire wasn't so sure of this interpretation of the statue's features, while the lama merely studied the image with an air of indecipherable neutrality.

The other monks prostrated themselves, or perhaps they merely collapsed. The BBC crew remained standing, albeit unsteadily. Karen dropped her camera as her palms grew slippery with oozing lymphatic fluid. She looked down at them, but was mercifully distracted from horror when the "statue" burst into animation. She stared as it turned its head with birdlike swiftness, catching every detail of the rooftop and its occupants with quick glints of its ruby eyes. It began to walk around, its gait a combination of cat quickness and snake fluidity. Its legs placed themselves like small golden tornadoes touching down, twisting and writhing like serpents. Each footfall produced a mellow bell-like chime.

Sapphire nimbly placed himself in its path and assumed a posture of defensive readiness. The creature halted, its attention instantly and obviously focused on him. Sunlight glittered on its polished golden surface, yet the glare didn't conceal the smooth opening of that "third eye", nor the intense and dire inner light which the eyelid had concealed. Sapphire lost no time in removing himself from the creature's right of way. The eyelid slid closed, and the silent figure resumed its restless exploration of the rooftop.

"It is the apotheosis of *pingala*, the undying consciousness of the Sun," cried one of the monks.

"It is the *Kundalini* herself bearing a human form," called another.

"It carries clear light within it; it is crowned by the Thousand-Petaled Lotus," moaned a third.

"It is a robot," said the lama with a shrug.

"A *robot*—?" Karen felt disoriented and ill. For a mysterious robot to appear and disrupt the ceremony seemed more confusing and outrageous than any possible manifestation of Buddhist spirituality.

The golden automaton, if such it was, suddenly halted. It made a slow 360° rotation, studying the horizon as it did so. Then it froze again, its arms at its sides. Suddenly it flashed into the air like a projectile. With a final glint, it vanished in the south, followed shortly by the crack of a sonic boom.

It was followed by another crash. Karen had tried to lift her camera, but had failed. Now she lay on the flagstones staring up at the sky. The monks also tried to rise, but could not.

The lama went to work among them. Sapphire rang a bell to summon other monks; many more would be needed. Then he went to sit beside the young Englishwoman who had come to record their affirmation of the ineffable Way of the universe. Gently he took her head in his lap, careful of her blistered skin. Already her hair was coming out in clumps. With words that were quiet but forceful he tried to ease her passage into the light, encouraging her to face it without fear, that she might know her true place in nature and suffer no more.

Chapter 16

The Arrow of Fate

He had left the polar sea behind. Fomalhaut now flew over mountain ranges that served as stair steps to the icy plateau of the Antarctic interior. Night had yet to abate, but beneath the aurora the landscape looked bright enough to Fomalhaut, even with his vision unenhanced. He remained apprehensive about this appointment. For no good reason he felt he was due for a stern rebuke from a source higher than himself. He began to wish he'd minded his own business and left the Para-men to do as they would. Even the idea of mounting his Frame and putting light years between himself and certain trouble had some appeal.

No clear foresight came to illuminate the source of his dread. He did feel an odd disturbance in the quantum field, perhaps originating in Asia. It was enough to blind the inner eye he could sometimes turn toward the future.

His course did not waver, despite his misgivings. Fresh icescapes rolled over the horizon and into view. In minutes the polar redoubt of the Para-men appeared before him, a cluster of pastel-colored lights amidst strange domes and crystal-tipped towers. He transmitted a warning of his approach, though he had no doubt that the Para-men were well aware of his presence.

The fortress grew into a softly-lighted fairyland, an inviting node of civilization in a place implacably wild.

Unexpectedly, Fomalhaut's sensors detected a second airborne object, hurtling toward the fortress at high speed. He hovered, uncertain as to the meaning of this or his best course of action. The projectile was quite small, too small to be a ship. A weapon? If so, was it directed against himself, or the Para-men?

Just to be safe, he mirrored his exploration suit and powered up his own weapons and defenses. Perhaps this was an emissary or probe of some sort from the Para-men themselves? At this point there was no way of knowing. But after a few moments of tracking he was satisfied that he was not the target of this missile. He sped nearer the fortress to see what would happen next.

Events proceeded rapidly. A pencil of brilliance darted from the missile and drew swift lines and curves over the structures of the fortress. Fire and vapor exploded from the fleck of starfire which drew these figures. The fortress seemed to be made largely of ice; even its underlying framework of rock and iron slumped and burned beneath that nimble beam.

The shockwave reached Fomalhaut and sent him tumbling. His stabilizers needed seconds to assert themselves and steady his point of view. The suit's sound system rendered only a fraction of an unnatural thunder which was itself enough to pulverize ice and stone.

The missile's plummet had slowed to a hover like his own. The threads of fire it emitted continued to make a ruin of the Para-men's proud fortress. Totally nonplussed, Fomalhaut hung there, gaping at the destruction, having no idea of how to react.

Suddenly the fortress was engulfed in a sphere of shifting luminance. The beam struck it and went no further, but merely lit the sphere as the shaft of a searchlight illuminates a fog. Fomalhaut analyzed the sphere. It was a diffuser field, a local reshaping of space to defocus and scatter any incoming radiation beam.

Thwarted, the missile switched to tactics which astonished Fomalhaut. His sensors detected a great outflow of tachyons. Fomalhaut aimed his optical sensors at the "missile" and applied maximum magnification. He was surprised to discern a golden humanoid form. A shock front of tachyons swept by; Fomalhaut surmised they were being collimated into a beam in some unknown fashion. Here was a most fearsome weapon! It struck the diffuser field and passed through, unaffected by a barrier meant to deter electromagnetic forces. Matter vanished before it, the very energy of its makeup negated by the beam's intensity. Yet that energy had to go somewhere, and Fomalhaut soon gathered that it was somehow being redirected into the attacker. He came to this conclusion when the tachyon beam was switched off, to be replaced by a colossal pillar of energy far stronger than the thin beams he'd already seen. It made the diffuser field blaze bright as a sun, apparently in an attempt to overload it. When that failed, the attacker directed the beam against the ice outside the field, turning huge masses of it into ionized atoms, threatening to undermine the fortress and send it crashing into a crater.

Finally the Para-men responded. A powerful beam of relativistic protons leaped through the diffuser field. There was nothing fancy about it; it merely smashed the attacker with brutal power. A tiny, glittering speck, it tumbled back a few miles before recovering to sweep back in, ablaze with frightful power, none the worse for wear. But then its flight was arrested by another force—Fomalhaut's sensors registered a mighty electromagnetic field.

Though itself pinned in place, the attacker's tachyon beam was free to reform and go back to work dematerializing matter and sucking up huge quantities of energy.

Then occurred a phenomenon which Fomalhaut could not properly analyze. It was the unfolding of a volume of space, which somehow created distance between the attacker and its target. Breaking free of the field which restrained it, the now-distant figure flew toward the fortress at high speed. But the space it occupied continued to elongate at such a rate that it still lost ground. Despite its speed, it dwindled with each passing moment.

Now at the limits of Fomalhaut's sensors, the attacker gave up and hung in place. Fomalhaut experienced a clairvoyant vision of the thing hovering there, brooding, intense, before turning and flying negligently away.

Fomalhaut released his breath. Apparently, the Para-men had beaten off the attack, though at what cost he couldn't guess.

He beamed a query at the fortress, but received no reply. He kept trying in various wavebands and modes, but still the fortress seemed inert. It had suffered major damage. Had the Para-men been killed? Finally he could restrain himself no longer. He flew toward the fortress while readying his mind for a telepathic investigation.

Suddenly he was halted, gripped by an invisible electromagnetic hand. He decided to make no effort to escape, but merely resumed his efforts at making contact.

"Para-men, Para-men. Please respond. Are you still there?"

A grave voice responded at last. "If by 'Para-men' you mean us, yes; we are still here."

"Do you require assistance? What injuries have you suffered?"

"We are uninjured."

That was hard to believe, given the ruin of much of the fortress. No doubt the Para-men merely wished to conceal the extent of their losses.

"The timing is obviously awkward. Yet I must ask: may I come now to begin our conference, or must we reschedule it for a later time?"

A considerable silence ensued.

"Fomalhaut, I am sorry. There will be no conference until we are convinced you had no part in this attack."

Fomalhaut groaned internally; somehow he had failed to consider this point of view. He said feebly, "I assure you, I had none. I was a mere bystander; surely you noted my neutrality during the violence."

"Your neutrality was carefully noted. Yet you must admit you arrived at an inopportune moment."

"Sheer coincidence. Synchronicity at worst."

"Perhaps. Yet we must be certain before admitting you. You must appreciate that."

"I do. May we then carry on a dialogue via radio or some other medium?"

"No. We can better gauge your intentions if we deal with you face to face. There will be no conference at this time. Please withdraw from the area. Valjhar out."

Fomalhaut didn't bother to reply; there was no missing the finality of that cutoff. After a moment the invisible grip released him. He turned and flew back to the north, seething with chagrin and regret.

After a few minutes his dominant thought was curiosity about the thing—weapon, creature, whatever—which had wrought this havoc. He accessed the Frame and downloaded its record of the battle. It had tracked the attacker's retreat to the Himalayan Mountains.

Fomalhaut decided to investigate, anxious to accomplish something after the debacle at the redoubt. He arced out of the atmosphere and put himself into a ballistic trajectory that would bring him down at the proper spot. Soon the great range reared up from the green-gold plain of India like a sooty snowbank made craggy by the sun.

His target was surprisingly easy to find. A humanoid figure of golden sheen and no great size, it stood motionless on a ledge near the summit of one of the great peaks. Fomalhaut landed nearby and approached with utmost caution, suit fully mirrored, but weapons deactivated to avoid antagonizing the creature, evidently an artificial being of some kind. The mechanism ignored him, not even turning its head to follow his approach. Nor did it respond to any of his greetings, whether sent electromagnetically or via the spoken word.

Frustrated, Fomalhaut risked a telepathic intrusion into the thing's mind. He discovered a uniform flow of being, a continuum of consciousness undifferentiated into separate thoughts and intentions. Its mind seemed so totally integrated, so seamlessly directed toward whatever its goals might be, that it was all but opaque to someone whose thoughts were as relatively unorganized as Fomalhaut's.

Yet he did detect a flicker of reaction whenever he said anything, so evidently the thing could hear. He continued to query it, hoping to stumble across something that would stimulate a response. He accomplished nothing until he finally thought to say, "I am Fomalhaut. Please identify yourself and explain the reason for your attack on the Rralians."

The robot's head swiveled smoothly in his direction, its neck twisting like a length of taffy. Ruby eyes fixed onto his opaque helmet. The "third eye" in its forehead slid open, revealing the dire whiteness of the light it contained. Its mouth locked open. The lips did not move as it emitted words in a mellow, golden voice that belied the arrogance of its facial expression. "What do you know of Rral?"

Fomalhaut was somehow intensely grateful that he knew little of Rral, and was not a citizen of Rral, and considered it urgent to convey these facts as soon as possible. "I am of a species which has some minor knowledge of Rral, gained through remote observation. However, I am not a Rralian, nor have I ever visited that planet."

The robot seemed satisfied; it returned its head to its original attitude and resumed its silence.

After waiting for a moment, Fomalhaut said, "I have supplied my name; please reciprocate. Who and what are you?"

"I am who and what you see before you."

"But what is your name?"

"I am not designated in such a manner."

"I see. Do you mind then if I name you? It will ease my dealings with you if I am able to refer to you by name."

"I am aware of no need for any dealings between us."

"Do you object to being named?"

"I do not object to that which is irrelevant."

Fomalhaut pondered. He felt a strange thrill; never had he imagined that a mature, sentient being would grant him the privilege of naming it. Only a wild impulse had even led him to suggest this intimacy.

"I submit the name 'Aureus'. It is derived from an archaic Earth language and means 'Golden' or 'Golden One'. Is it satisfactory?"

Aureus didn't actually shrug, but the gesture was implicit in its tone. "I make no objection."

Fomalhaut didn't know how to react to such indifference. But as long as Aureus kept talking, he'd keep asking questions. "Why did you attack the Para-men?"

"If by that you mean those Rralians dwelling on this planet's polar continent, I am charged with apprehending them. I provide this information so that you will know not to interfere with my mission. No more need be said; my instructions are not the affair of foreign creatures such as yourself."

Fomalhaut did his best to swallow this rebuff. "I may at some point find it necessary to oppose the Para-men as well. Would you consider entering into an alliance at that time?"

"If you demonstrate capabilities or resources which might enhance my ability to complete my mission, yes; I would consider such an alliance."

The golden figure said nothing more, asked no questions, showed no curiosity.

Fomalhaut at last grew vexed at this treatment. "I urge you to consider your situation. You have been beaten back. You have exhausted the element of surprise. The defenses of the Para-men will not again be so porous to your attack. You will need help to defeat them, if defeated they must be."

"Possibly."

Nothing more was forthcoming. Fomalhaut stared for a few more moments, trying to read something useful in this implacable golden being. Its power was obviously extreme, as was its unpredictability. Fomalhaut wished he had some means of influencing either.

Finally he turned away and rose into the air on four threads of fiery light.

High in orbit, one of the independent weapon-pods distributed by the starship *Mote* observed the conclusion of this *tête-`a-tête* with high-resolution cameras. The images were relayed to the still-smoldering polar fortress, where several grim figures gathered around a viewpoint, studied them, and drew their own conclusions.

Chapter 17

Sea Change

Suddenly the tropical seas seemed cloying, their embrace too comfortable, their creatures too familiar. Days of sunlight filtering through clear blue waters became interminable and interchangeable. The kaleidoscopic flicker of the passing reef fish grew meaningless, distracting, even irritating.

Clear as these waters were, they still limited visibility to a hundred feet or less, which was suddenly intolerably claustrophobic. Ghostly memories intruded on any feeling of well-being—memories of great spaces suffused by a light which was not trifled into ripples and glints by the lowly medium through which it passed. These memories were tantalizing—he wasn't even sure if they were true memories or only fragments of a dream.

Driven by wanderlust, the man-ray began a journey. Idleness could no longer be tolerated; ease was repugnant; mere existence no longer reason enough to go on living. He needed to make something of his life, but the sea's uniformity offered little scope for meaningful effort. Exploration seemed the only option—purposeful exploration, not the random wandering which had been his life for as long as he could remember. Thus he determined to strike out in a single direction, to proceed until he found something, anything, to ease his dissatisfaction.

The direction he selected was North. He'd long been aware that in the North was the one star whose place in the sky never varied. It hovered in an unprepossessing zone of the heavens, and was itself modest and unassuming, except for the aura of steadfastness which it acquired from its endless vigil. Surely the purpose of such a star, if any, was to guide wanderers in their pursuit of dreams.

Nor did daylight navigation present any great challenge. The Sun's daily course was predictable, and when combined with his time sense provided a good directional indicator.

And on cloudy days or nights? There remained a feeling, a subliminal stimulus of some kind, that always whispered, "this way is North".

Ever alert for anything that might dispel his ennui, he paced himself carefully, cruising at a comfortable speed during all hours of the day, snatching up the odd fish or shrimp for twilight meals, forging on through the starlight, often with his head above the waves so he could see the stars. Sometime after midnight he would descend to the thermocline and fall asleep in the cooler waters, surrounded by a weak electric field whose disruption by any intruder would awaken him instantly.

Only once was he tempted from his path, and that was to follow a storm which drove the waves to monstrous size, lashing them into a chaos of crashing water and stinging spray. It was exhilarating to leap from the crests of towering waves, to arrow into the grey foam far below, and satisfying to be manhandled by waters which had for a moment cast aside their insipid mild manners. But then the storm veered West, and the man-ray resumed his chosen course. Soon the seas calmed around him once more.

Every night the North Star stood a little higher in the sky. Every day the seas grew more chill. The very character of the water began to change, losing its blue transparency, gaining a cold grey turbidity full of secrets and hauntings which the gay tropical waters could never have concealed. The tropical calm vanished also, replaced by a constant restless heaving of the waters, with waves nearly as big as the storm waves which had so impressed him just a week or so earlier. It was hard to make progress in such rough seas, so the man-ray took to traveling at depths of thirty or fifty feet, below the churning of the surface waters. Here he was practically blind; even his outstretched hand looked murky in this dismal substance. Information continued to pour in from his other senses, but these were mere data, not the more direct experience of the world provided by his eyesight, and this he sorely missed.

As he proceeded the waters grew still rougher. He began to hear echoes coming from the bottom as he approached a land mass far larger than any he'd encountered before. He surfaced often to search for hills on the horizon, but fog prevented any early sightings.

Eventually a new sound crept into his consciousness, a rhythmic booming like the murmur of surf, but far stronger and deeper than any he had ever heard. His curiosity aroused, he veered West to search for the source of this tumult. The sound and vibration grew steadily more powerful. His sonar cries were returned by massive obstacles invisible in the turbid waters.

At last great rounded shapes loomed perilously close at hand. Surging currents threatened to smash him against boulders which glimmered grey as the heads of whales. He looked up; he could dimly see the undersides of huge waves marching toward the coast. By now the pounding of the breakers was almost overwhelming.

One of the boulders seemed to break the surface. He grabbed its barnacle-roughened surface and began to climb.

The Vigil

Streamers of yellow-brown weed waved from the rock face further up. It took much of his strength to avoid being sucked off the slimy rock before he finally reached the surface. From there he scrambled to the top of the spire, barely out of reach of the wave crests.

He blinked cold brine from his eyes. The scene he beheld appalled and thrilled him with its bleak grandeur. Not a hundred feet away was a great sea-cliff, by far the harshest interface between land and ocean he'd ever seen. The grey-green waves threw themselves against it and exploded in spray and thunder. Great masses of cold seawater slid back to marshal themselves for another assault. All around were shreds of fog and mist. The cliff top was barely visible, crowned by the hazy silhouettes of tall pines.

There clung the man-ray, huge waves breaking just below his toes. Brine dripped from his skin; he flipped back his hair to clear his eyes.

He heard a cry that was not quite the shriek of a windblown gull. He squinted up at the cliff top. A temporary parting of the fog revealed human figures, staring and pointing in his direction. They yelled and called to him, making frantic gestures. He scowled at them, squinted, shook his head, trying vainly to figure out his true relationship to these creatures. Abruptly he lost patience at their yammering, and did his best to mock their cries. He produced a raw, windy howl that pierced even the roar of the surf and the rush of the wind.

The shrieks of the humans grew even louder. A hissing sound from behind made him look over his shoulder. Looming over him was an immense green wave that swept him off the rock and sent him tumbling toward the

170

submerged base of the cliff. He fought to turn around and kicked for safety, but was smashed against the rocks, gashing his back and stunning him. The backwash carried him seaward again while he cleared his head. When he was able, he gave a grimace of disgust and struck out for open water with all his strength. Soon the cliff and its occupants were less than a suggestion in the fog. He was aware of his blood clouding the water, and almost hoped it would attract a shark, for he longed to commit violence on something offensive and stupid. But sharks were rare in these chilly seas, and soon the bleeding ceased.

The fog eventually cleared. The sea was unusually crowded in that area for the rest of the day. Small boats crisscrossed the water, and helicopters sent staccato shock waves into the depths as they hovered low. The man-ray carefully kept his distance from all of them.

Swimming a little farther up the coast, he found a sheltered bay studded with forested islets. Here the waves were calmer, but the weather and the sea remained murky and cold. For the next few days he explored the tide pools and shallows, clambering ashore when he felt safe from observation or discovery. Here the sea floor was littered with human debris—cans, tires, bottles, even ships, their contours blurred by colonizers like anemones and barnacles. Larger organisms huddled and skulked in the gloomy recesses of the shipwrecks. From the skeleton of an old fishing boat the man-ray seized a hideous creature, a grey, eel-like fish with a gaping mouth and staring eyes. He forced himself to look deeply into those eyes, horrified by their absolute mindlessness. In them was no trace of any emotion, thought, or motivation. The thing scarcely struggled in his grip.

In all the sea, he was the only truly conscious being, or so it seemed to him.

He released the fish, which wriggled back into its hiding place to await the passage of a creature small enough to catch and eat.

Disgusted, the man-ray swam on, searching for he knew not what.

He felt familiar, welcome vibrations; seconds later streamlined shapes flashed by: harbor seals. Noticing him, they circled and investigated with a complex ballet composed of nested orbits and gyroscopic figures. He'd learned how to vocalize overtures of friendship to marine mammals, and these were always accepted. He felt easier in their company, for they were driven by recognizable emotions. In their eyes was consciousness of a sort. For an hour they played, scooping up an unwary fish whenever possible. But presently the seals showed signs of restlessness; their hunger couldn't be satisfied by an occasional morsel caught on the fly. Their swift shapes hazed into the near distance as they lost interest in him.

Try as he might, the man-ray could not keep up with them. It was just too difficult to force his awkward body through the water at the speeds that came so easily to seals and whales. Finally he gave up, hanging in the water looking toward the place where they had vanished.

He remained in the bay, curiously reluctant to return to open water.

Signs of human presence were everywhere: the stench of gasoline; the mutter of power boats; the rush of a sailboat hull through the water; the clutter of lobster traps with their telltale marker floats. These were a source of easy meals.

While paddling idly through a quiet bay he felt vibrations from what seemed to be large creatures floundering in the distance. Curious and a bit apprehensive, he approached the scene of the commotion. The vibrations were irregular, spasmodic; whatever was making them was probably wounded. Other stimuli made themselves known: weak magnetic fields, and an assortment of odd chemical smells. So far there was no scent of blood.

When he first saw them he drew back in revulsion, for the shapes looming in the murk were seals, hideously mutated and distorted. They kicked through the water with weirdly elongated flippers, exhaling streams of bubbles as though they were drowning before his eyes. But they didn't appear to be in distress. Despite their pitifully awkward means of propulsion, they threshed along placidly enough, swimming together like a school of nightmares.

Then he realized with a shock that these shapes were fundamentally no different than his own. These were humans, visiting the shallows with the help of some sort of artificial breathing devices. They saw him just as this realization slammed home. He hovered in place as the divers thrashed through a ninety degree turn to face him.

Fascinated, he studied them as well as he could in the turbid water. They wore form-fitting black garments, much like sealskin, with metal cylinders strapped to their backs. A closer look at their flippers showed that they were simply flattened, extended shoes.

But the most startling thing about them was their masks. With those bubbles of air trapped in front of their eyes, they could probably see almost as well under water as they could on land. He could tell from their astonished expressions that they could see him well enough.

He rolled his eyes with chagrin. Why had he never thought of such simple enhancements to his underwater life? With flipper-shoes he might keep up with the fastest cetaceans in the sea, and with a mask his underwater vision would be magically sharpened. He vowed to obtain such devices as soon as possible. He was tempted to simply peel them off these gawking creatures, but even if he could do that without harming them, they certainly wouldn't fit his larger body.

One of the divers raised a device. A large faceted lens stared him in the eye; he flinched. But it only gave off a quick POP of white light, harmless, but dazzling. There were several more flashes in quick succession. Without thinking he wheeled and churned off into quieter waters. The divers tried to pursue, but their efforts were laughable, even with their artificial fins. They didn't recognize the rough pulsation that reached them as laughter, but they never forgot it nevertheless.

When the afterimage of the flashes had faded from his retinas, the man-ray was left with images frozen in his memory. He remembered the gemlike green eyes of one of the divers as she stared at him in amazement. Her diving suit had not hidden her feminine contours.

His interest in her was uncomfortably mixed with contempt. She was unfit to venture beneath the waves — not only was she hopelessly clumsy and ill-adapted to swimming, she couldn't even breathe without a back full of hardware. She and her fellows had no more business down here than he had beyond the atmosphere...

Something about that line of thought jolted him unpleasantly; he let it slip away.

He swam on aimlessly, still preoccupied with his recent encounter.

Dim shapes appeared in the murk ahead. As he approached he saw they were two large lobsters, intertwined in mating. Despite their grotesque forms there was something hopeful and encouraging in that. Even among creatures so lowly there was concern for life, and hope for the future.

He swam closer and he found he was mistaken.

The two crustaceans were not mating.

They were devouring each other.

The man-ray roughly grabbed one of the creatures. Claws snapping, innumerable legs and feelers and mouthparts wriggling, it seemed unaware that its tail flippers and swimmerets had been eaten away. Crawling away was its dinner and its diner, in even worse condition.

The man-ray studied his captive with loathing. Here were two living creatures, even of the same species, so mindless and debased that they saw each other as nothing more than walking sources of meat. It was impossible to see any merit in creatures so oblivious to their fellowship with other beings.

He flung the lobster away. Filled with passion, he made two great vows: to abandon the sea, making a life for himself on the land, whatever the dangers; and never to kill another creature or use one as a source of nutrition.

He could tolerate no delay. Immediately he swam to the surface and scanned the misty horizon for the nearest land. Several small islands were nearby, possibly good places to regain his land legs. He swam strongly for the nearest, noting the presence of a few large wooden structures, but seeing no people. He hauled out on an empty beach and walked inland until the waves no longer tickled his toes. Most of his senses fell away, useless or greatly weakened in this thin medium, but he didn't care. He forced the water from his lungs, lost his strength and fell, lying there gasping until the air could begin to sustain him.

His eyesight was now a marvelous window on reality. The sun was a clear blazing light, and the clouds were glorious sharp-edged billows tinged with a hundred subtle shades of gold, lavender, and steel blue.

He got to his feet, promising himself that his life as a sea creature was ended. Whoever he was, or for that matter whatever he was, he had begun a new career as a denizen of the land.

He walked unsteadily into the forest and soon came upon a trail.

Chapter 18

Miracle Workers

Tzige kept a fearful watch on the sky. Not half an hour before it had been full of low clouds and fog, and she'd felt safe in going for water. But then an unwelcome breeze had sprung up, leaving only a few scattered puffs to shelter her from the MIGs which might at any moment come roaring over the nearby hills. She bit her lip as she trudged along, dividing her attention between the skies and the rough footpath which led home from the spring.

Despite her vigilance, she was taken by surprise by the mutter of a jet passing high overhead. She hissed in fear and stared up at it, looking for the first hint that it might swoop down to spew napalm or bombs.

But the plane continued sedately along, leaving a contrail that glowed gold in the morning sun. Tzige relaxed a little and went trekking onward.

A minute later she jumped and dropped her water cans at the thump of something crashing down nearby. She cried out and threw herself down, bracing for the inevitable explosion.

But there was none. After a few moments she dared stand up and brush herself off, still looking around nervously. A puff of dust rose from a patch of desiccated shrubs a short distance off. She bent down to retrieve her water cans. They were dented, but not leaking.

An irresistible curiosity led her to the site of the mysterious impact. She entered the stand of shrubs, dry and dormant thanks to the drought. Each tall plant was separated from its neighbors by narrow lanes of dust. She wandered among them until she found a bush which had been demolished by whatever had fallen. Its multiple trunks, each thicker than her arms, were shattered. Dust still floated in vagrant streamers. There was nothing else. Nothing, she noticed, except for the prints of bare feet leading away.

Tzige sensed something off to the side, turned her head, and gasped yet again. A man stood there, obviously a foreigner, regarding her with calm gravity. He was young, with golden skin, fine features, and longish brown hair. His clothes were little more than rags, mere remnants of this and that. The impoverished rebel soldiers among whom she lived dressed better. His feet were bare, and he was, praise be to Allah, unarmed.

Tzige stammered, "I—I came to see what had fallen. Did you see it?"

The stranger spoke her language well enough, if hesitantly. "No...I heard the crash, but did not see what fell. It's strange."

Tzige could not help noticing that his clothes were dusty and full of fragments of the shrub's dry foliage. She felt dizzy, but was no longer truly frightened. An unmistakable gentleness rested in this stranger's eyes, which were light brown with flecks of gold.

"I am Tzige. I live nearby, in Nakfa."

"Hello, Tzige. I am...Andrew Nimus. A visitor."

"You are on foot? It's unusual to see a Westerner without a truck or airplane at his disposal."

Nimus smiled. "Oh, I prefer walking. I resort to other transportation only when I'm in a great hurry, which is rarely."

"Ah." Suddenly the threat of the MIGs reentered Tzige's mind, and she nervously scanned the skies once again. "I must go now, Mr. Nimus. I must tell you, you've picked a dangerous time to visit our country."

"Yes, I know. I'm on my way to Nakfa as well. I'll walk with you, if you don't mind."

"You are welcome to be our guest, but we must be careful as we approach the sentries, for you would not wish to be mistaken for a foreign military advisor," she said with a hint of irony.

"Thanks for the advice. Those water cans look heavy. May I carry them for you?"

"That is a kindness I will not refuse."

Freed from her burden, Tzige sauntered along, her spirits lightened by the beautiful young stranger who walked quietly beside her. Her mind churned with questions, but she bit them off as long as she could—she didn't wish to appear rude by interrogating this man too closely.

Finally, though, she couldn't resist. "Mr. Nimus, is this your first time in our country?"

"No," he said pleasantly, "I've been here many times before, over the years."

"Are you perhaps a journalist? Or a relief worker?"

"Not exactly, no. I do collect curious facts, but only as an interested amateur observer."

"Mmm. Well, if you go to Nakfa, you will surely collect enough facts about our war to satisfy your curiosity."

"Actually, I'm not interested in your war."

Taken aback, Tzige looked aside to take in her companion's solemn expression. "You're not? What else could possibly bring you to Nakfa? You can't tell me that a

Westerner like you would dress in rags, parachute into a war zone, and then conceal his parachute if he had no interest in our revolution."

Tzige immediately wished she could bite back these bold remarks. A sudden doubt occurred to her: was Nimus really a Westerner? Now that she studied him more closely, she could see that his racial type was oddly elusive. He was not black like her, but he could be almost anything else. He could be Arab, or Polynesian, or Mediterranean, or perhaps a mixture of White and Asian.

Despite her probings, Nimus grinned and answered calmly enough. "I don't mind telling you. I'm here to find out the truth behind some strange stories I've heard. Rumors about a wandering man who does extraordinary things. A man who is said to be in your country now."

Now she gaped at him openly, half-convinced he was having fun with her, but hoping he was not. She laughed nervously. "I've heard these rumors too. They sound like children's stories to me. I've seen only hunger, fire, and bloodshed in my life. Never a miracle. Do you think such tales could be true?"

"I know there are things in this world which are outside the experience of most men. Yes, the stories could be true. It's what I'm here to learn."

"And you think he could be near Nakfa?"

"Yes, it's my best guess."

"I hope you're right. I'd like to meet such a man. I hope he's not too hard to find."

"From what I hear, once this man appears in an area, his actions make him conspicuous."

They walked on, each lost in private thoughts. Tzige's mind flitted between old dreads and wild new hopes.

Nimus, she noticed, ambled along in all serenity, apparently unaware of the weight of the water cans he carried.

"Nakfa lies on the other side of this hill," said Tzige. It was a dry, bitter slope, forested only with the stumps of the trees which had once protected it. Like the rest of her homeland, it had been rendered all but sterile by drought, war, and the ceaseless appetites of its inhabitants.

Noises became audible as they climbed: low rumbles and roars from the depression on the other side. A haze of dust yellowed the sky. Tzige grew more fretful. She moaned softly, filled with a premonition of what they would find down in the valley. As they neared the ridge crest she could restrain herself no longer, but ran ahead, oblivious to her companion, whose pace neither quickened nor faltered. She halted at the summit and stared down in terror as Nimus came up beside her to survey the scene with calm gravity.

The village was little more than a compound of burned and blasted houses; only the mosque stood intact among them. There were a few trees, a few cultivated patches. If not for them, Nakfa could have been taken for a deserted ruin.

Yet evidently something here was of interest to the government, for columns of tanks were coming into view from the gullies on the far side of the valley. Their cannons fired, sending shells smashing into already-crumbling walls and structures. Armored personnel carriers rolled among the tanks. Foot soldiers, barely visible as yet, scuttled forward, trying to keep out of the paths of the vehicles.

Tzige flung herself forward, her cries merging with the shriek of the MIGs that swept in over the horizon and pounced on the village, dropping lines of small bombs that erupted in flame, smoke, and flying debris.

Nimus grabbed her arm before she could get far down the slope. His grip was gentle but unbreakable. "No, Tzige, don't go down there. You can't do anything there but die."

"My family!"

His eyes arrested her wild stare; his gaze calmed her somewhat, despite her fear. "You can't help them. Find cover, and wait. This may not go the way you fear."

There was no arguing with this man. She crouched down near a rock, sobbing, while Nimus remained standing in the open.

Now men could be seen scrambling from holes in the ground, hundreds of them, emerging like enraged ants to defend their nest. They took positions behind walls and boulders and waited. Their discipline was evident—they withheld rifle fire, waiting for the advancing enemy to offer decent targets.

They did not withhold their heavier weapons. Rockets leaped from shoulder-mounted launchers; two of the foremost tanks exploded with a sound like bronze bells falling off a cliff. Tzige sent up a tear-choked cheer of victory.

The guns of the remaining tanks quickly fired, blasting up clumps of soil and sending bodies flying. One more anti-tank missile rushed out from the village but struck the side of a gully; after that, the tanks advanced unopposed. The MIGs returned. They scattered from the path of a single Stinger missile, which nevertheless sought and struck one of the jets, sending it spinning out of sight beyond a hill.

That evidently exhausted the high-tech weaponry of the rebels. The remaining MIGs swooped low to deliver a holocaust of napalm, threatened by nothing more than the feeble chatter of automatic rifles.

By now Tzige was raising a continual din of prayers, curses, and inarticulate howls. She glanced over at Nimus, suddenly furious at his equanimity. How could he regard such slaughter with no reaction beyond a mild sad sobriety? She sprang at him and, out of frustration, began to beat his face and chest. He ignored the assault, merely brushing her fists out of his face when they obstructed his view. As Tzige exhausted herself, Nimus's quiet voice penetrated her grief and fury.

"Tzige. Tzige, look. Look what's happening there."

Almost resentfully, she turned, sobbing, and followed his pointing finger with tear-blurred eyes.

Two figures had entered the valley, striding toward the village from one of the lesser hilltops. At this distance it was hard to make out much detail, but one was considerably the taller, and dressed in grey, as opposed to the bold red costume of his companion.

"Tzige, stay here where you'll be safe." Nimus briskly descended toward the village, obviously planning to intercept the newcomers. Tzige found herself following along, though she had no idea what to expect. If Nimus noticed her presence, he made no objection.

Now they were closer, and could better see the visitors. The tall one wore a long grey cloak wrapped around his body, with a deep hood that shadowed and obscured his face. He walked with a graceful and deliberate gait, his stride regulated by the rhythmic use of a staff, an irregular spar of tannish-grey wood.

The other displayed more energy, ambling along jauntily, even impatiently, as though he might at any moment dart off or start walking circles around his steadier companion. He wore a rather preposterous red and black bodysuit which was studded with golden ornaments.

By now Tzige and her companion were almost within the village. She was distracted from studying the two newcomers by the scream of an approaching MIG. She screamed too, and dived into a bunker maintained for just such emergencies. She heard a brief roar of cannon fire from the aircraft, followed by a muffled explosion and a blast of heat that shriveled her eyelashes despite the protection of the hole. She cowered and wrapped her arms around her head. Of all the weapons which the government brought to bear against its own citizens, she found napalm the most horrific. Her own sister had been one of its victims, chin melted and fingers fused by the liquid flames.

Face contorted with dread, she trembled for a moment, then forced herself to look out from the hole.

Nimus was ablaze, covered with burning napalm. Yet he continued to walk along, his course unwavering, his clothing dropping off in charred tatters.

Tzige found herself running up to Nimus as the last tongues of flame flickered out on his body. Though naked and smudged with soot, he was obviously unharmed. He appeared oblivious to what had happened, his attention still fixed on the men dressed in red and grey.

Tzige's breath came in ragged gasps. Nimus's assurance had been true: despite the prevalence of death and bloodshed, there were indeed miracles in this world.

Now they were closer to the two men, close enough to glimpse their faces. The one dressed in red was dark and youthful, with a wry, lively expression. He seemed to look everywhere at once, exuding confidence with each buoyant footstep.

The grey man was less flamboyant, yet somehow commanded more attention. His pale face glimmered from the shadows of the hood, his eyes glinting from its folds like two cold stars. Tzige shivered before them, though not in fear.

The two figures halted. The grey man lifted his staff in a thin, ivory-white hand. He held it up for a moment, then brought the tip down on the ground, a blow sufficient to produce a *crack* that made the ground tremble. The combatants took full notice of them at this point and turned in their direction. The man in the red suit smiled and made a sudden menacing gesture. Several soldiers lived up to the demands of their sex and culture and fired at him. Somehow, the bullets never made it to their targets; in fact, they were seen no more.

The MIGs came howling back into the fray. The red man responded with gestures of casual negligence. Instantly their engines screeched to a halt, as if steel I-beams had been forced into their innards. The planes somehow came to a hover. Their ejection seats fired. Before the pilot's chutes could even deploy, the jets slammed into each other, exploded, and fell onto a hillside in flames.

While all this was going on, Tzige's two steel teeth tingled and tugged at her jaw, a phenomenon at least as disconcerting as the inexplicable end of the enemy planes.

The warriors of both sides sent up a great howl of astonishment. It only intensified as the tanks and other armored vehicles began to change shape. First the gun barrels wilted and curled, without any screech of metal, but silently as the tongue of a butterfly retreating from an emptied blossom. Their engines died, bringing a blessed quiet to the battlefield. Dirt and paint dissolved from the vehicles, revealing underlying bare metal that took on a mirrorlike finish. Men scrambled out of the hatches and flung themselves from these bewitched war machines. They tripped over each other as they tried to retreat.

Angles rounded, edges blurred, and the tanks gleamed brilliantly in the morning sun like sculptures fresh from the artist's studio.

His performance concluded, the man in red crossed his arms and grinned smugly at his audience.

Tzige glanced at Nimus. He looked alert, attentive, but only slightly less impassive than before. She herself was beginning to feel numb.

The warriors stirred while Tzige wondered how to react. Had the rebels been handed a miraculous victory? Or had their whole battle been rendered moot, superseded by events wholly beyond their political conflict?

The grey man also stirred, providing an unequivocal answer to these questions.

Light began to radiate from the aperture of his cowl, a fierce blue radiance that overwhelmed the daylight, bathing the hills, the rocks, the sun itself, in a shadowless glare that brought tears to the eyes. With the exception of Nimus, Tzige and everyone else cried out in distress, reeled and swayed, as the unearthly crystal-blue light burned into their brains. It invaded Tzige's thoughts, dissolving old confusions, penetrating to layers of consciousness normally accessed only in dreams. Women and children poured from their hiding-holes. The battlefield became a milling mass of people from both sides. Tzige moaned in painful revelation and amazement. Only incredulity was kept at bay—she could not doubt the reality of what was happening to her, to all of them.

Everywhere, soldiers gaped in astonishment at the weapons in their hands, and at the dead and wounded lying everywhere; then they threw those weapons from them in revulsion. Women looked at their children, who were thin, scarred, and undernourished, and turned burning gazes of wrath on the men whose obsession with games of power had led to their ruin. Children stared at their elders, seeing them not as sources of strength and wisdom, but as misguided, frightened creatures who had led them astray.

Tzige saw her life, her nature, and the reality of the conflict which had long overshadowed both, all for the first time. She also saw the friends, the family, the children she had lost over the years, and knew with a cold clarity that the losses had been senseless.

Nimus walked toward the man in grey. Tzige stumbled after him, though she was reluctant to approach too closely the source of that scathing, merciless light. But their progress was difficult, the crowd so dense and confused that they could scarcely move forward.

Tzige's breathing ceased as the grey man suddenly turned in their direction. She looked up at Nimus; at last his expression had changed. His eyes were fractionally wider, his brow perplexed; his mouth trembled on the verge of a smile. He too burned with icy radiance. Though perhaps immune to physical harm, he wasn't beyond the power of Truth.

Just as Tzige felt that the light was about to reveal secrets still deeper, still more disturbing and profound, it left her, plunging her back into the dun-and-drab world of everyday. Nevertheless, her thoughts rang with new knowledge. How much greater, how much more wondrous, was the world than she had ever known before! She looked toward the grey man with gratitude, only to find that he was still projecting the blue light. His head was tipped back; the blue beam emerged as a thread of such penetrating, all-revealing power that Tzige and the others could not bear to look upon it. The gray man swiveled his head, and the beam seared past Tzige, almost making her faint. It struck Nimus full on. Tzige, squinting uselessly, forced herself to see how Nimus bore that terrible power.

His reaction filled her with renewed awe. He did not flinch from the intolerable blue star which wavered over his brow, his face, his body. He regarded it with delight, catching it in his hand and playing with it as she might a butterfly. He even let it shine directly into his eyes; at that sight Tzige had to turn away, her mind filled with appalling visions of time: eons of dust and shifting seas, planets smoldering sullenly at the dawn of time. It was too much for her. She fell and cowered, her face wrapped in her shawl.

It ended. Silence returned, replacing the turmoil that had been like a shout in her mind. She looked up. Nimus stood there, looking relaxed, smiling a faint smile of satisfaction.

Tzige stood up. The grey man raised a pale hand. On it she detected a green glint, a ring.

Suddenly a warm green light flooded the landscape, coruscating here and there in greater concentration. Tzige herself was bathed in green, as were all others present— except Andrew Nimus! But that mystery must be deferred, as this light's effect on her was too glorious. She felt invigorated, tingling with life, but beyond that, she was deeply aware of her profound connection with the people around her, with the dogs and goats, the insects, the plants, and even with organisms too small to see. The dead stayed dead, but the sick and wounded rose up, not miraculously healed, but filled with new vitality. The children, some of whom had limbs not much sturdier than a man's thumb, stood up straight, raised their heads high, and looked around with clear eyes for the first time in their lives. Tzige wept with the force of her sudden identification with all the living things around her. She felt this intimate bond even with Nimus, enigmatic creature that he was. Yet how could that be, since the Lifelight seemed to leave him untouched? She wiped her eyes and looked at him again, and this time saw the truth: the green light shone brightly from the pupils of his eyes. She reached out hesitantly and ran her hand along his arm, feeling warm, living flesh. He absently patted her hand.

The green light faded. Tzige and Nimus started forward again, but still the crowd prevented much progress.

The grey man stood motionless, his cloak fluttering in the breeze.

From his throat a new light appeared, a deep purple glow that captivated the eyes. This light did not blaze over the landscape, banishing all other illumination; nor did it dazzle and blind. It shone dimly, casting a subtle violet glow over those who faced it. Tzige felt it entering her mind and spirit, bringing forth an adamant determination, an inner resolve, not for vengeance or retribution, but to fulfill the promise of her being, to shape the insights she'd received today into a new and positive force for life and truth. War, hunger, injustice; she would work to overcome these evils in her land, no longer passively accepting them, no longer permitting those whom she loved to suffer as their victims. Let no one stand in her way!

Again she looked at Nimus, and again she was filled with amazement by this strange man. For the purple light which lay so lightly on her and her fellows was a lambent violet flame about Nimus, throwing off sparks and streamers of incandescent amethyst. He stood in the midst of this cold conflagration studying its source with his lips barely parted and a searching gaze in his eyes.

Once more the reshaping light ceased. The grey man's cloak fluttered open; from somewhere near his heart came the briefest glint of still another light, a white purity that burned Tzige's heart with its beauty. She fiercely desired to drink more deeply of that astringent loveliness, but the grey man turned away. Accompanied by the man in red, he set out swiftly back the way they'd come.

Almost as an afterthought, the man in red stopped and turned; from a pocket he produced a small device which he aimed skyward. It emitted a brief but pervasive hum; a roaring, crackling sphere appeared in the air over the village. It vanished, and a cloud of flakes began to flutter down. The villagers and soldiers picked them up. Nimus caught one on the descent and regarded it thoughtfully. It was a wafer of some whitish substance. From its surface shimmered a three-dimensional image: a sweeping arc ornamented with three softer glows. Nimus sniffed at it, and then, to Tzige's astonishment, began to nibble at it. Tzige followed suit, as did those around them. The wafer was a wondrous creamy confection that left her delighted and refreshed.

Nimus looked up and tried to follow the retreating figures, but again was hampered by the crowd. He pushed through with a gentle strength, but the two men disappeared around a bend of a gully.

A moment later a glittering object flashed into the sky and was gone. Nimus took a few more steps, faltered, and stood looking after it.

The people of Nakfa and their erstwhile attackers could never recount exactly what happened afterward. There were tears and laughter, pledges of friendship, and the destruction of arms. The injured gained strength. Those who were most gravely wounded died nevertheless, but they found the grace to die without fear or complaint.

When Tzige came back to herself, she searched the village, dragging her children and husband in her wake, and presently found Nimus standing on the outskirts, still gazing skyward. He turned and smiled at her approach.

She walked up and addressed him with a certain gay solemnity. "Well, Mr. Andrew Nimus, if that is your real name, you've seen your miracles. What will you be doing now?"

"Tzige, if I could trouble you, I would like to clean myself up, and then if possible get some clothes from someone in the village."

"I think that could be arranged. My husband, here, lacks your full height, but is similar in build. He can provide something."

The man beside her nodded absently. He appeared to be distracted, almost dazed.

"I thank you both," said Nimus.

"And then?" asked Tzige.

"Then I'll be leaving. Heading south."

Chapter 19

The Fish's Mouth

In the course of his musing and fretting, Fomalhaut wandered westward into the empty Sahara. There he walked among parched mountains and flatlands littered with rocks darkened by the "varnish" of long exposure to sun, heat, and wind.

Only once was he caught unawares, so deep in thought that he was oblivious to the warnings of both his sensors and his own perceptions. On that occasion he was seen by a group of nomadic herdsmen as they urged their goats toward better grazing. When their alarm finally penetrated his contemplations, he thought it better to simply stand and face them, rather than fly away or do something else likely to dismay them further.

He watched with interest as they conferred with one another in loud, excited voices. This was, in fact, his closest contact with the Human species since his arrival on Human-dominated Earth, a source of some embarrassment to him.

The nomads grew calmer as he made no hostile move. One of them belatedly thought to aim a crude long gun in his direction, but did not fire. Their cries faded to conspiratorial whispers as they tried to decide how to deal with him; Fomalhaut could of course hear it all. They were attracted by the gloss of his exploration suit, and by the rows of gemlike beads of its field antenna array. They began walking in his direction with apparent boldness, but Fomalhaut could still feel their apprehension.

He decided to end the encounter before it got out of hand. A sudden wave of his arms was enough to send them scurrying toward distant horizons.

A few days later, Fomalhaut was startled to come across a commemoration of the encounter. Sheltered within a shallow cave was a tall rock face; incised upon it was a huge but crude drawing of a looming figure. Its featureless spherical head and the details of the torso were reminiscent of his exploration suit.

Fomalhaut stepped closer, amused by the tribute, and wondering what legends he'd spawned, what tales to be spun around campfires beneath starry desert skies. He reached out and stroked the lowermost grooves of the carving, opening himself to its history and the motivations behind it. But the impressions he got were confused, not at all what he'd expected. Abruptly he realized that the carving was much older than he'd thought, some tens of thousands of years old. Nothing remained of the feelings and beliefs of the people who'd made it after so long a time. Evidently it had nothing to do with him after all.

He stepped back, studying the drawing in a new light. The carved lines gave every appearance of freshness, preserved as they were in this arid environment. It did resemble him, that was inarguable. But there was no telling what or who the carving truly represented.

And he couldn't help feeling slightly chagrined. He turned and left the cave behind.

As always, Fomalhaut monitored the flow of world events as he wandered. The growing activity of the Paramen was noteworthy. In troubled places all over the world, recently as nearby as Eritrea, they or their emissaries were mending conflict and grief by some mysterious means. He inferred it was some sort of mental reprogramming, effected by, or perhaps beneath the cover of, displays of colored lights. The mechanism behind it wasn't obvious, but the results were clear and striking.

They were also inarguably for the good, or so it would seem to the Humans themselves. Yet the act of imposing goodness on sentient beings was repugnant to anyone raised in the unrestricting embrace of Constructive Anarchy.

This was his major concern, but over a period of days his news filters selected a series of unrelated items which tickled his foresight and piqued his curiosity:

Man Feared Drowned

Bar Harbor, Maine– An unidentified man is believed to have drowned yesterday in the stormy waters off Acadia National Park, State Police say. Several tourists claim to have seen the man swept from a rock just offshore from Seawall Campground on Route 102A. The nude man, who was described by one witness as "huge, blond, with an incredible tan and a real attitude", was caught by a rogue wave which apparently dashed him against the cliff. A search for the body will begin as soon as weather permits...

Drowning Victim Not Found

Bar Harbor, Maine– Despite extensive search efforts, the body of the unknown man reported drowned two days ago has not been discovered...

"Drowning Victim" Seen Alive

Bar Harbor, Maine– Five novice scuba divers from Quebec City, Canada, may have seen a ghost on one of their first dives. The five report seeing a swimming man whose description matches that of the unidentified man reported drowned late last week. The "pale-haired giant" was encountered at a depth of forty feet, swimming without scuba gear or clothing. His eyes, according to Suzanne Remillard, one of the divers, were "empty, black, like the eyes of a corpse". The man was then seen to swim away at high speed...

"Sea Ghost" Sighted on Land

Bar Harbor, Maine– Guests at "Summer Tides", the Secord family vacation home on privately-owned Lesser Hedgehog Island in Frenchman's Bay, report several encounters with the "Sea Ghost" who has captured the imagination of the residents of this small resort community.

"He's no ghost," said Priam Secord. "He's about seven feet tall, likes raw cauliflower, and made a pass at my niece." Mr. Secord is the brother of Virgil Secord, famed industrialist and owner of the island.

The so-called "Sea Ghost" is believed to be living in the woods on Lesser Hedgehog Island and perhaps also on neighboring islands, some of which are also the sites of summer homes...

"Sea Ghost" Shot, Arrested

Bar Harbor, Maine– The strange man known as the "Sea Ghost" has been captured in this seaside resort community. The unclothed man walked into town yesterday morning, becoming violently agitated when police officers attempted to take him into custody after all efforts at communication had failed.

The "Ghost" easily manhandled the officers who tried to grapple with him. Police officers drew their weapons but delayed firing due to the numbers of civilians in the area. Breaking free, the "Ghost" ran toward the forested foothills above the town. Bar Harbor Police Officer David Wain then fired a single shot from his service revolver into the back of the fleeing "Ghost"...

"This is someone I must meet," muttered Fomalhaut. As he lifted off and entered a high suborbital arc he considered and rejected scenarios for the coming confrontation. Like it or not, he was bound for his first serious encounter with the Humans, and this time he couldn't count on being forgotten or merely passing into tribal legend.

Fomalhaut broke through the cloud deck shrouding coastal Maine precisely over Mount Desert Island, its shape like that of an embryo lying curled up in the womb. There he hovered while he monitored local broadcasts, seeking information on the whereabouts of the strange marine Human. It came via a police radio broadcast: the "Sea Ghost" had just arrived in Bangor, having been flown to a hospital there for treatment of his bullet wound. Fomalhaut launched himself in that direction, regretting his late arrival. How much simpler to have simply abducted him from an airborne helicopter than to extract him from a sea of Humans!

In a moment the target structure was in range of his sensors. Fomalhaut sought to calm his mind, cultivating a strong Alpha rhythm which he could then broadcast to smooth his passage through that turbulent Human sea. He landed in a park adjacent to the hospital, there being no point in causing a further sensation by being seen to fly. His outlandish appearance would no doubt provoke enough of an uproar.

To his surprise, his presence caused less concern than he'd expected. These Americans merely looked at him sidelong, or stared frankly but without fear. Some smiled, others seemed skeptical, but none reacted with evident dread or paranoia.

Puzzled but grateful, Fomalhaut proceeded toward the hospital entrance. Several police cars were parked nearby; two officers stood on the stairs, also regarding him calmly.

A young man with a camera around his neck trotted up and walked along with him. He looked toward Fomalhaut's collar and said, "Say, that's a great suit you've got there."

"Thank you," said Fomalhaut.

"Great voice too! Golden tones, kind of an operatic Darth Vader routine, only nice, not threatening."

Fomalhaut had by now absorbed a fair amount of popular culture. He commanded his sound system to mimic a metallic, asthmatic breathing.

"Ha ha, that's great. The kids must love it. You know, I used to wear a suit like that, at Disney World."

"Really? Was it rated for long-endurance deep-space life support?"

"No, but it was fire retardant. What gets me about yours, though, is that I can't see the grill." The man continued to scrutinize Fomalhaut's collar, which was at his eye level.

"The grill?" By now they were nearing the entrance; Fomalhaut had scant attention to spare for his companion.

"You know, to see through. Or is it some kind of one-way plastic?"

"I can see perfectly well," said Fomalhaut absently.

They halted directly in front of the police officers, who studied them impassively.

"Good morning, officers," said Fomalhaut.

"Good morning, sir. What is your business in the hospital?"

"I represent a charitable agency which is charged with providing entertainment to hospital-bound children."

"I see. Sorry, there's a security condition at the hospital right now. No one is to be admitted without a valid medical reason."

"A medical reason? Very well. My friend, the marine Human you call 'Sea Ghost', is within, and he is wounded."

The officer pricked up his ears at that. "How did you know that? It's not yet public knowledge."

"Police-band radios are easily acquired, are they not? Please admit me."

"Sorry, we have orders. No exceptions even for guys wearing giant cue balls on their heads."

"I understand. Forgive my attempts at misdirection. But I'm afraid your answer is unacceptable."

At that, Fomalhaut's companion grew nervous and sidled away while the policemen concentrated on Fomalhaut and his flat statement.

"Sir, you'll find the results unacceptable if you don't follow instructions and turn away. But first let's see some identification."

By now Fomalhaut had stepped back and was studying the hospital's facade. "Identification? I must have left it in my other exploration suit." With that he lifted off on four pencils of glaring gold. By the time the policemen found the presence of mind to dash from under the overhang to look after him, he was gone, his course suggested by a missing pane of glass in a fifth-floor window.

Doctor Ahmed stared down at the huge form chained to the table, feverishly wondering how to proceed. Despite superficial appearances, his patient was an essentially non-human being; that much was clear from the X-rays. Even the surface musculature, though smoothed out by a layer of fat beneath that sleek bronzed skin, showed differences which were obvious to a trained eye.

The "Sea Ghost" lay on his chest, fully conscious, since Ahmed and his colleagues hadn't dared anesthetize a person who was so foreign to their experience. Almost preternaturally alert, the Ghost took in everything with those inhuman eyes, their pupils hugely dilated, the blue iris barely visible around them. His mouth was clamped shut, but his nostrils flared with anger and his brow was stormy. Yet he did not struggle against his shackles, futile as that would have been.

The bullet wound in the middle of his back oozed blood that was red enough.

The Ghost suddenly bent an intense stare toward the OR's doors. Ahmed and his teammates followed his gaze. The doors swung open; in stepped a bizarre, towering figure dressed in glossy greenish armor ornamented with rows of gems. His head was obscured by a spherical helmet with an odd, matte-white, shadowless finish.

Ahmed sputtered, his shaking hand almost dropping the scalpel he'd been about to wield. "Who—who are you? What do you want here?"

The reply came in calm, golden tones. "I am called Fomalhaut. What is the condition of your patient?"

"His condition is grave, though not as grave as it might be. There's damage to the spinal cord. I would have expected paralysis, but there's no sign of it."

"His nervous system may offer more redundancy than yours," observed Fomalhaut. "Go on."

"Well, even overlooking the spinal damage, the bullet has lodged in one of the lungs—or whatever passes for a lung in this creature. Look at these films!" Ahmed waved his hand at a bank of backlit X-ray photos. "The pulmonary area is almost unexposed; it appears to be an almost solid mass of tissue... Wait a minute—what am I doing? Nurse, call security; have this person removed."

Fomalhaut made a negligent gesture. "That won't be necessary." The nurse made a move toward the phone, hesitated, and finally stayed in place, looking puzzled and a little anxious. "Doctor, how do you intend to proceed?" he continued.

"I scarcely know," admitted Ahmed. "I'm reluctant to explore for the bullet when I don't even understand his anatomy. Then there's the fact that I dare not have him anesthetized without knowing more about his physiology. But his internal bleeding must be attended to. Why am I standing here talking to you about this?" He looked baffled and slightly disoriented.

"I see. I believe I can extract the bullet without causing too much pain."

That jolted Ahmed back to full alertness. "What? Look, how did you even get in here? Do you know this person?"

"No, he is nearly as strange to me as he is to you. But I have taken an interest in him."

"Your whims and interests are of no concern to me! Please leave before the police burst in and disrupt this procedure more than it has been already!"

"Not yet."

"Take no step closer to my patient!" The bristling Ahmed interposed himself between the operating table and Fomalhaut, who made no attempt to advance. The other doctors and nurses belatedly joined the surgeon in their patient's defense.

This tense moment was ended by the hard *tak* of something striking the floor. The surgical team turned; the Ghost met them with the fierce darkness of his stare. On the floor beside the table was the bullet, wet with blood.

The doors swung open again. A squad of State Troopers burst in, weapons at the ready. "Freeze! Everybody down on the floor! Now!"

The doctors fell flat, while Fomalhaut merely turned to face the newcomers. "Do not fire your weapons. A ricochet could injure an innocent person."

"I want you on the floor, mister!"

"Your desire must go unfulfilled." Fomalhaut waved his palm at the officers. Their universe seemed to throb for an instant; they dropped their guns, which landed softly at their feet. Their threat evaporated, they became subdued.

"Please, everyone get up," said Fomalhaut a bit uncomfortably. The nurses and surgeons slowly regained their feet. The Ghost studied the situation with intense interest. Fomalhaut indicated him. "I have come to take this person into my custody and care. I am better able to provide for him than you, as the medical people at least must agree."

The warrior in charge of the police unit hesitated, then spoke up firmly. "That man is under arrest. He has violated the law."

"That is trivial. Irrelevant."

"He has injured several police officers."

"He has injured them far less seriously than their behavior warranted and his abilities permitted. I believe there is an amateur video which will soon prove this."

"He's dangerous, brutal."

"Evidently less dangerous than the officer who shot him as he fled."

"He's a mindless savage!"

At that Fomalhaut turned to regard more closely the watchful figure of whom they spoke. "Truly, he is not. Don't let his silence mislead you. I see within his mind the logical basis for several languages, but they have all been expunged." He bent over the recumbent form, his voice becoming soft and monotonous. "He is far from mindless— indeed, I see a multitude of thoughts waiting for expression. He is eager to communicate with you. If I may —"

Here Fomalhaut's voice assumed a different quality, grew deeper, took on an unfamiliar lilt.

"Among you I came—from out of the sea—from the realm of dark waters, where whale song speaks of a far-flung fellowship of minds which does not acknowledge small, awkward, hinged creatures better suited to the land —from reefs and mud flats where the dull eyes of the bottom lurkers reflect the ancient history of life on this planet, and call into question the value and meaning of intelligence—out of this abyss I came, seeking a place among those more like myself—I—it seems that in so doing, I—ran afoul of certain rules and norms which define acceptable behavior, and I am sorry for that—I hope that my errors do not preclude my acceptance into your world— I know I have much to learn. Please know that I permitted my capture—had I been willing to injure you, you would never have taken me..."

At these words the man-ray gripped the chains that shackled him to the operating table. The muscles in his back and arms stood out in startling, even alarming, relief, and the chains parted, sending broken links flying through the operating room like shrapnel. He rolled off the table and onto his feet, breathing heavily, while blood ran down his back and onto the floor.

Neither the medical people nor the policemen made any move in his direction. They stared at him as if mesmerized.

Fomalhaut resumed his normal voice. "Well. If no one has any further objection, I'll take our friend here and depart."

No one moved or offered any objection.

"First, though, perhaps Dr. Ahmed and his colleagues will suture their patient's wound. I believe he may have injured himself further. Another small matter: if we could borrow a gurney, we would both be grateful."

Half an hour later, Fomalhaut and his new companion were soaring eastward across the Atlantic. Lacking a proper vehicle, Fomalhaut held the gurney suspended beneath him, using it as a passenger palette. The "Sea Ghost", he noted with interest, showed no sign of distress at being transported this way, although the wind made him squint and shield his eyes and nose.

After a lengthy period of uncommunicative brooding, the man-ray abruptly formed a thought which he directed at Fomalhaut.

"Did you translate my thoughts for them accurately and in full?"

"Only up to a certain point. If I had transmitted the exact character of your feeling toward them, we might not have extracted ourselves from that situation so peacefully."

The man-ray lapsed back into silence, but he wore a grim smile for a few moments.

"Why did you bother to extract me at all? Who am I to you? What do you want of me?"

Here Fomalhaut chose to withhold the full scope of his suspicions. He could, however, answer the last question freely enough.

"A group of alien beings has come to this planet with the intent of establishing dominion over the Humans. I have decided that they must be opposed, but I am under no delusions; I cannot fend them off by myself. Therefore I seek allies. Upon learning of your existence and whereabouts, I sought you out at once."

"How many allies have you so far?"

"It is your privilege to be the first, should you so wish."

"Ha! Have you any other candidates in mind?"

"I have."

"That is comforting. What can you tell me of these aliens?"

"Very little. They have enormous powers, not all of which I understand."

"And why should I endanger myself by fighting these mysterious titans? As you saw, the human race shows little sympathy for me; why should I risk myself for their benefit?"

Fomalhaut began a rehearsed answer. "If the Humans lose their freedom to any despotism, however benign, uniquely Human qualities and potentials are likely to be lost. It's difficult to say what path the Humans would chose on their own, but surely they should be given—"

"That's enough. I'll help you," said the Sea Ghost with inexplicable fervor.

"That is gratifying," said Fomalhaut, puzzled.

"But I must insist on certain conditions."

"Name them."

"First, I must retain full freedom of individual action."

"That goes without saying," replied Fomalhaut in surprise.

"Second, you must instruct me in Human speech."

"That process has already begun, in case you hadn't noticed."

"Third, you must instruct me in general so that I may explore such areas of knowledge as may interest me later."

"Of course. Despite your brawn, you are truly of little use to me as an ignorant savage."

"Excellent."

"My friend, if I may ask, what am I to call you?"

"I am without a name."

Fomalhaut contemplated this for the next five minutes. He could hardly believe that so rare an opportunity could come his way twice in such a short time. Hesitantly, he asked, "Would you permit me to name you, then?"

The man-ray shot him a severe glance. "No!" came the answering thought. "I shall name myself, as soon as my vocabulary has increased to the point where I become aware of something appropriate."

"Of course. Forgive me for my presumption."

Chapter 20

Leaving the Nest

Fiona Kalada tramped through the forest happily enough, elated at the day's events, more than content with the recent course of her life and work. Today Mallorn had given birth for a second time, and this time it was a live birth, with mother and daughter doing well. Fiona regretted that T'Ukudu hadn't been present to see the happiness in the mother gorilla's eyes, but lately his studies at the camp prevented him from joining her in the field as often as she'd like. With this new addition, the band had thirty members, an unprecedented number. No one had been lost lately, either to age, disease, or even poaching, thanks to the fearsome impression T'Ukudu had made upon the natives.

It was amazing how easily the alien had integrated himself into her life, and difficult to remember the tense, angry existence she'd led before his coming. His gentle strength, his calm wisdom, were gifts such as she'd never dreamed the jungle might someday yield. Now she was anxious to return to camp, to transcribe her notes, eat and relax, and perhaps wheedle T'Ukudu into making another attempt to teach her skinreading—although she frankly doubted that her blandishments had much real influence over his decisions, or that she could ever learn the art.

As she approached the camp she became aware of strange voices. Instantly her contentment was rinsed away by an icy dread. She moved off the trail and crept up to the edge of the clearing under cover of the dense undergrowth.

Through the leaves she glimpsed T'Ukudu speaking with two strangers who towered nearly as tall as he. One wore glittering greenish armor and a spherical white helmet; the other, naked except for a bandaged abdomen, had bronze skin, wild golden hair, and a sharp-featured face. Somehow, seeing T'Ukudu in such bizarre company only emphasized his alienness. Heart thumping, Fiona held her breath as she listened to their conversation.

"...and as a time traveler seeking to study the pre-history of your race, you see no contradiction in personally involving yourself in the course of affairs, thereby distorting the very events you came to record?" asked T'Ukudu.

The helmeted one responded, his voice reasoned and mellow. "Having no prior knowledge of the events I came to witness, I cannot know whether my actions are already a known part of the past. I was chosen specifically so that my lack of knowledge of these matters would in no way prejudice my actions. Thus I consider myself free to act as I see fit. My suspicion is that by acting to thwart the ambitions of the Para-men, I will prevent an historical anomaly which would prevent my own race from coming into being."

"I see."

"T'Ukudu, someone has arrived at the periphery of the camp and is watching us."

Fiona felt a sudden chill. Although the helmeted one had not moved, she was certain he was looking directly at her.

"Fiona? Please enter the camp and meet our guests," said T'Ukudu.

Fiona walked woodenly into the clearing, her gaze suddenly captivated by the fierce stare of the blond giant.

"Let us sit," said T'Ukudu. They sank to the ground in a circle; suddenly the giants did not tower over Fiona quite as spectacularly as they had. "Fiona, this is Fomalhaut, a time traveler whose mission of study is not unlike my own."

"I heard," she said dully.

The blond man spoke up unexpectedly. "Eyn Steen Grah," he said, his weird blue-black eyes riveted on hers.

"Steven Gray?" guessed Fiona.

"Please excuse my companion's diction," said Fomalhaut mildly. "He is only now learning Human languages, and his pronunciation is as yet imperfect. He has just now chosen a name for himself; it is Stingray."

"Hello, Stingray," said Fiona, hearing herself speak as if in a dream. But Stingray smiled a fierce grin of satisfaction, as though he'd just won some great victory. Fiona's heart softened a little at the sight; there was something almost apish about his cautious but guileless attitude.

"Fomalhaut has offered me a part in his plan to prevent the Antarctic aliens, whom he calls the Para-men, from imposing their rule over your people," said T'Ukudu.

"Oh, really?" said Fiona, at a loss for any other response.

"However, he has yet to convince me that this would be an appropriate extension of my own mission. I do not see how I could justify interfering in matters which are not the concern of my Makers."

"And yet your mission is to determine the nature of the human race, is it not?" said Fomalhaut.

"It is."

"Then surely your observations will be distorted if Human society is dissolved at the whim of alien despots. Your mission will necessarily be compromised."

"That is sophistry. Surely I was sent to study the conditions which actually prevail, not to determine which conditions should prevail so that I may study them," replied T'Ukudu.

"It seems we hold contradictory but equally plausible interpretations of your mission. I suggest you contact your masters and request a resolution."

"That is easily done. However, the answer, when received, might be academic. The speed-of-light communication time is a matter of decades."

"Then transmit your query. While you await the answer, you might as well act on your own initiative and ally yourself with us."

"You persist in assuming that your cause is a matter of any importance to me."

"If it is not, then consider this. Your mission, whatever its proper definition might be, is presently being poorly performed at best. Your ability to pursue it while lurking in this forest is minimal. With no help and few resources, it might well take until the reception of a message from your planet to assemble any worthwhile information. But if you join with us, I will soon see us legitimized as an organization, being the only credible opposition to the Para-men. You will have free access to all levels of Human society, as well as to advanced technological resources. Here you may see your only chance of fulfilling your mission on this planet."

T'Ukudu's face remained utterly impassive as he contemplated this.

Stingray spoke up hesitantly, surprising everyone. "Ein thinking you are to jayn us; hear my reezahns."

T'Ukudu locked his vermillion eyes onto Stingray's oceanic blues. "I can facilitate our communication if you will permit me to touch your skin."

Stingray nodded and held out his hand. T'Ukudu brushed it with a fingertip but snatched it back. "I'm sorry," he rumbled. "Your skin impulses are unusually strong and chaotic, taking me by surprise. I shall try again."

This time the finger stayed in place, but T'Ukudu was a long time making sense out of what he received. Fiona watched with a feeling of envy as T'Ukudu maintained contact with his fellow giant longer than he ever had with her.

At last the Servant of T'Utahn broke the contact. "Fomalhaut, your companion is a being of unusual construction. His neural impulses are all but submerged beneath a stormy surface activity of electrical impulses which are unmodulated and of no apparent use. However, I did receive the sense of his thoughts."

"Perhaps you can transmit them to me via your skin reading technique."

"Touchtalk requires skin-to-skin contact."

"Happily, the substance of my exploration suit is able to transmit all sensory stimuli."

"Very well."

Again Fiona watched as T'Ukudu lay his hand on Fomalhaut's glassy-metallic gauntlet. Completely motionless, they sat immersed in a private colloquy even longer than Stingray's.

Finally T'Ukudu drew back and said decisively, "I shall provide such aid as I can, as long as I remain free to conduct my survey. But I repeat, in view of your assessment of the strength of the Para-men, I think I will be of little use."

Fiona could hold back no longer. She lurched to her feet and cried incredulously, "You're going *with* these people?"

T'Ukudu's unwavering gaze sought her out. "Yes, Fiona, I am."

"No, I don't believe that! What about our work here? What about the gorillas?"

"Fiona, I believe the apes to be in no immediate danger. In any event, I cannot let their needs influence my decision. The demands of my mission, and my obligation to my Makers, must come first."

Fiona waved her hands in confusion. "But didn't you just say your mission has no connection with whatever these two geeks are trying to do?"

"That was my interpretation at first. However, Stingray has alerted me to another viewpoint which I had not considered. The Para-men are aliens who show no reluctance to interfere with the affairs of this planet. Seventeen light-years away lies the planet T'Utahn, whose society must escape similar interference. Therefore my duty is clear—I must expand my mission to include a careful study of the Para-men. And if they should prove disposed to disregarding the desires of my Makers, I must oppose them."

Fiona knew she could offer no effective counter to that. Though she tried to prevent it, her face contorted and tears flowed. "Oh, I can't believe you'd abandon me, after all we've done together, after all I've given you," she choked.

"I regret the necessity," said T'Ukudu gently. "I would ask you to accompany us, but I know you would not abandon the apes."

Fiona maintained her stricken, accusing stare for a few more moments, then broke off and ran sobbing among the buildings of the camp.

Fomalhaut looked after the fleeing woman. "T'Ukudu," he said hesitantly, "you realize you're dealing here with Human romantic love."

"Yes," came the grave reply. "The human sexual obsession, that turbulent preoccupation which underlies all their actions and so often defeats their desire to rise above their own biology. It is marvelous that their society has as much order and rationality as it does."

"Indeed. Shall we go, or will you first attempt to soothe Fiona's hurts?"

"I must try to comfort her. By the way, what means of transportation do you propose using?"

"I was hoping we might employ your landing craft," said Fomalhaut diffidently.

"We can, and it is more than adequate to the task. Yet where, may I ask, are the advanced technological resources to which you have referred?"

"I haven't had the time or the need to produce them before now. But the need is now, and the time is near."

Fomalhaut felt a sudden jolt and heard a detonation. Stingray gave a furious yell. Moving in a blur toward Fiona and her smoking rifle, he disarmed her in an instant. She stood sobbing hopelessly, a picture of dejection.

"I shall calm her," said Fomalhaut.

"No, that is for me to do," stated T'Ukudu. He advanced on her and took her relatively tiny body in his arms; she relaxed and sighed deeply, but the pain did not fade from her face.

"You understand this was a desperate act, which does not accurately reflect Fiona's ethics or temperament," said T'Ukudu over his shoulder.

"That is clear from her choice of targets. She chose me, realizing her bullet could not penetrate my armor. Comfort her; we shall depart when you both are ready."

Stingray, his emotions close to the surface, could not withhold the tears of pity that coursed down his cheeks.

Chapter 21

Quest For Gold

"Where do you expect to find this robot?" rumbled T'Ukudu as he guided the landing craft toward near-Earth space. He sat in the control saddle, while Fomalhaut and Stingray occupied restraining slings which had been intended for T'Ukudu's fellow Servants.

"I don't know," admitted Fomalhaut. "I've commanded my Frame to search for it."

"How long should that take?"

"Not long, if my reading of Aureus's intentions are correct. The Frame can survey a hemisphere at a time. I have sent it South."

Sure enough, minutes later Fomalhaut made an announcement. "I have detected Aureus over the South Indian Ocean, not far from Antarctic waters. It is hovering just over the wave tops. Let us make a cautious approach while I attempt to establish communication. We must not approach it unawares; it will brook no interference with its mission."

"Very well. We will reach its location in minutes."

Fomalhaut broadcast messages of greeting to the Frame, from which they were relayed in a tight beam to Aureus, reducing any chance of eavesdropping.

After less than a minute Fomalhaut said, "I don't know whether Aureus received my message; at any rate it has not acknowledged me. Now the robot has disappeared."

"Disappeared?" prompted T'Ukudu.

"Entered the water, heading for the bottom. Perhaps we may pursue...?"

"This craft is not constructed for submarine travel. Perhaps Stingray might investigate the robot's intentions."

They both looked back at their silent companion. "How deep is the water there?" he asked carefully, speaking slowly but clearly enough.

"Eighteen thousand feet," answered Fomalhaut.

Stingray shook his head. "Too deep. I am not made for such depths."

"Hmm. I myself could make the descent, but probably only to discover a hole in the bottom of the sea. My sensors have lost the robot; it must have bored into the ocean floor."

T'Ukudu remained imperturbable, but Stingray's sharp face reflected incredulity.

"Into—the rock?"

"My friend, when you are acquainted with the tachyon and its properties, you will not wonder that Aureus has the power to travel through rock as readily as air."

"What course do you suggest?" asked T'Ukudu.

"The point of land nearest the place of Aureus's disappearance is called Heard Island. Let us go there."

Fomalhaut continued to broadcast to Aureus, using radiation able to penetrate great depths of rock. Whether Aureus was equipped to receive it was another matter.

Evidently it was so equipped. Fomalhaut received a quick pulse of data which he decoded into the following message:

Cease your transmissions at once. You will alert the Rralians to my approach.

Daring greatly, Fomalhaut nevertheless replied.

"Please reconsider your attack. My allies and I wish to offer you a place in our organization. We intend to oppose the Para-men by means other than a futile direct assault."

You only presume its futility.

"Yet if I am correct and you are repulsed, will you consider our offer?"

If my attack fails because the Rralians take warning from this transmission, I will act decisively to prevent your future interference. If it fails for other reasons, I will consider your offer. Do not reply; any further transmission will be considered a plea for destruction.

Fomalhaut described this transaction to the others, who sat subdued for the duration of the flight. Presently the lander touched down on Heard, a desolate, windblown volcanic rock. They stepped out into the late afternoon light. Stingray looked at the grey sea that encircled the tiny island, perhaps wondering if his wanderings had ever brought him near here before.

Fomalhaut extracted two small pointed devices from his belt and planted them in the ground. He reacted to Stingray's curiosity without its being voiced.

"Seismic sensors. They should help me to track Aureus and perhaps judge the outcome of its attack."

Fomalhaut became silent. He used the seismic data to construct a virtual model of the Earth which he viewed by direct perception. The model was quite detailed in their vicinity, clearly showing Aureus searing its way through the upper mantle, heading directly toward the Para-men's polar fortress. Though its speed through the semi-liquid rock was considerable, it would still take hours to reach its target.

"Gentlemen, perhaps you now appreciate why Aureus would be a valuable addition to our group," said Fomalhaut casually.

"If we can trust it," said T'Ukudu

"If it agrees to join us, I believe we can trust it. It has been nothing if not straightforward in its dealings with me so far."

Stingray laid a hand on T'Ukudu's arm. The Servant gravely received the information and said, "Stingray would trust Aureus further if we could circumvent its willfulness and use it as the weapon it appears to be."

Some time later, as the crescent moon hovered in a sky of darkening steel-grey, Fomalhaut requested silence. "Aureus draws near the fortress. I will attempt to form a direct perception of the scene for a better idea of the outcome of the attack."

He reached out, holding the image of Aureus in his mind; felt and perceived the shared reality which linked the two, independent of distance or even time. He had a brief glimpse of the fluid golden form, now distorted into a more streamlined shape, eeling through an incandescent holocaust of superheated rock. Its passage was eased by the cataracts of energy it emitted, causing the rock to explode into vapor despite the immense pressure which usually kept it a plastic solid. This attack, it seemed to Fomalhaut, was one of desperation. Aureus was causing earth tremors which could be detected by the crudest equipment; it could hardly expect the Para-men to be unaware of its approach.

A small earthquake struck the island, breaking Fomalhaut's concentration and sending volcanic cobblestones rolling down the slope.

"I think we may learn Aureus's fate without the benefit of either remote viewing or sophisticated sensors," remarked T'Ukudu.

"Indeed." His farsight disrupted, Fomalhaut monitored the seismic data, awaiting what he knew was the inevitable climax.

It came moments later, a stronger quake which set the face of sea vibrating in standing waves.

"Aureus has been dealt with," reported Fomalhaut.

"Now we'll learn if it's still in any condition to accept your offer," said Stingray.

"The sensors of the Frame have detected Aureus emerging from a sizable fireball. It is coming this way."

"Of course it has occurred to us all that it may intend retribution against us for spoiling its attack," said T'Ukudu.

"That may well be true," replied Fomalhaut uneasily. "My friends, I suggest you conceal yourselves until we learn the robot's intentions. I alone might withstand its anger; there's no need to risk yourselves."

Stingray and T'Ukudu looked at each other and came to an unspoken agreement.

"That makes good sense," said Stingray. "We'll find a ledge to hide under until the situation is resolved."

Fomalhaut watched somewhat ruefully as they passed out of sight on the other side of the summit. Then he turned back to face the south. He sought a glimpse of foresight to know how this confrontation was to proceed, but was granted none. He felt a distinct apprehension at the robot's approach. After a moment it evolved into an emotion as near to anger as his kind ever felt. If the artificial being he'd dubbed Aureus was ever to serve as a dependable ally, it must learn to relate to him as an equal.

Thus, when Aureus flew over the horizon it confronted a Fomalhaut standing ready in a mirrored exploration suit with all weapons fully powered.

The robot landed before him and advanced a few paces, its red eyes glowing with a dire light. If it had suffered any damage from its rebuff, it was not apparent.

To Fomalhaut's surprise, it was Aureus who began the discussion. "You are right. The Rralians have erected impenetrable defenses. I cannot touch them without catching them in the open. I have exhausted my options. I am at a loss as to how to proceed. What is your plan?"

Fomalhaut was taken aback; his self-reproachful belligerence evaporated. "My plan is simply to form an organization dedicated to thwarting the Para-men. I seek only those capable of dealing with them on their own terms. So far we are three. Our only aim is to prevent their domination of the planet, by whatever means, including simply inducing or convincing them to leave. Therefore I cannot promise you an opportunity to apprehend them. However, if such an opportunity should arise, we would make no objection."

Aureus mulled this over in an eerie silence. At such times it seemed to become merely a statue.

Stingray and T'Ukudu reemerged to stand with Fomalhaut. They all towered over the robot, but Fomalhaut suffered no delusion that they might dominate it through their superior stature.

Aureus abruptly reanimated itself. "Very well. I will cooperate with your organization as long as it does not conflict with the resolution of my mission."

Fomalhaut sighed internally. Why must all his recruits come with personal goals that superseded those of the alliance?

And in view of that, he said sternly, "Be aware that we shall expect your cooperation at all times while you are in our association. We do not compel you to reveal complete information about yourself, but we do require that you take no action which is contrary to the collective will of the group."

"For the duration of the association, it will be so."

"Excellent. As I said, we do not expect you to reveal all of your many secrets. However, if you could better define your mission and enlighten us as to the nature of the Para-men, we would be grateful."

"My mission is to apprehend three criminals from the planet Rral and return them to that world for judgment. I do not know what companions they might have found in their travels, nor their number. It does not concern me. I speak no more."

Fomalhaut tried to divine the necessity behind such a sparse offering of information, but could not.

"All right then. My friends, let us commence. We will maintain a vigil over the freedom of mankind."

Chapter 22

A Light is Lifted

A tower was raised in back bay Boston, a structure not so high as to surpass the two competing monoliths that had long defined the city's skyline, but which loomed large enough in the minds of men that it dominated that skyline all the same.

The members of the Vigil had presented themselves to the government of the United States, putting forth their resolution to stave off the advances of the Para-men. The President, faced with a threat beyond the competence of his military, could only stammer and offer disjointed sentences as he conferred with these four disparate beings who were so far removed from the narrow world view that had satisfied him so far. Fomalhaut read the threat to his manhood implicit in essentially handing over the security of his nation to a "bunch of alien freaks" (a phrase culled from the President's thoughts), and did his best to help him save face.

While the President feared risking the wrath of the Para-men by sanctioning an opposing force, even more did he fear losing his own power to the Para-men's domination. His pollsters had delivered disturbing news: of the fraction of the American people which considered such matters at all, a large and growing part was actually in favor of the Para-men and their schemes. The President's only satisfaction in this, and it was a bitter one, was that most of the people who held that opinion were members of the opposing party.

Ultimately the Vigil was granted a charter to operate freely within the borders of the United States, as long as the threat of the Para-men remained.

With American support secured, most of the rest of the world quickly fell into line. Soon the Vigil had the status of an international agency recognized by the United Nations.

The four then faced the decision of where to set up their headquarters. Fomalhaut's natural inclination was to select a remote area far from any concentration of people. This view would have prevailed had not T'Ukudu raised cogent objections.

"The Para-men have shown no willingness to endanger common men in the course of their gentle 'conquest'. Therefore, let us take up residence in some human city. Then, even if the Para-men consider us a threat, they probably will not attack us, for fear of injuring innocent humans and expending their capital of good will."

The others could not dispute this logic. In making their final decision, Stingray expressed an unexpected preference that would prove decisive: he wished to remain near the sea, and also to be near the Bay of Fundy—Acadia National Park area if possible.

Boston was an obvious choice to satisfy those criteria. It had the added advantage, in Fomalhaut's mind, of being a seat of the American concept of liberty, and thus symbolically appropriate.

Thus, feeling rather craven to be "hiding behind the skirts of humans", as Stingray put it, the Vigil set out to raise their headquarters. To foster a feeling of public involvement with their organization, they sponsored a design competition among student architects. From the many entries, each interested member of the Vigil found one to champion. Aureus did not deign to express a choice. Stingray preferred an enormous spire, an unornamented recurved spike which would pierce the clouds. T'Ukudu favored a low, modest design that would fit unobtrusively into its surroundings.

Fomalhaut disliked the inhuman scale of Stingray's spire, fearing to alienate the mass of Humans. He also found it too similar in style to the Para-men's fortress, and saw nothing desirable in trying to outdo them. A style that suited the icy plateau of interior Antarctica could only seem an inaccessible pinnacle in a Human city.

T'Ukudu's choice, on the other hand, struck him as being too inconspicuous, incapable of stimulating the imagination of the masses.

Fomalhaut's own choice was meant to draw upon Humanity's pride in its heritage of past achievement. It was classical in style, an airy temple of white marble, somewhere between the Parthenon and the mortuary temple of Queen Hatshepsut of Egypt in design, though shaped like a broad letter V in plan.

T'Ukudu did not defend his own choice, but Stingray was less inclined to give way. He argued for a compromise, which, with the cooperation of the winning student, was soon achieved. A tower was added to the complex, its upper levels an open lattice of columns and arches. At Stingray's insistence a beacon was placed within it, casting a soft white glow from dusk to dawn. Fomalhaut approved. It was exactly the effect needed to complete the project. In the end the structure resembled the ancient Pharos of Alexandria more than anything else.

Funding this ambitious construction, and then equipping and staffing it, presented no problems.

Fomalhaut merely made occasional trips to Mars, returning with gemstones which, while marvelous and valuable, were carefully selected not to surpass the finest yet found on Earth. Their Martian provenance was enough to grant them exceptional worth. In addition, Stingray was aware of the general location of much sunken gold.

Thus the Vigil became a going concern in a matter of months. Yet Fomalhaut was dissatisfied, though he was careful to hide it. Four beings, he well knew, were not sufficient to oppose a power such as the Para-men. Yet he had exhausted all obvious candidates for membership.

But the Vigil had already attracted the attention of beings of whom Fomalhaut knew little or nothing.

Chapter 23

Cube X

Sometimes the sheer weirdness of Possum Perturbare's discoveries haunted his dreams. Never had this been more true than with the device he and Brainchild were working on now. Set up in the main lab was a thick steel cube, eight feet square, which was connected to auxiliary control housings by optical and superconducting cables. It was the Quantum Isolation Device, although Perturbare usually thought of it as Cube X.

Now, after the theory had germinated in Perturbare's mind and blossomed in Brainchild's matrix, and following weeks of hardware design and development, Cube X was ready for testing.

Perturbare stepped up to the mechanism and swung open its great vault-like door. The cube's interior was empty and plain, consisting of orthogonal squares of polished steel. Onto its floor he placed a coffee can full of miscellaneous nuts and bolts.

"Brainchild, I don't mind telling you, I'm dying to see what this thing will do." Perturbare closed, sealed, and latched the door.

"My curiosity is piqued as well. It is unprecedented for us to devise a mechanism whose theory we understand so well, yet whose physical effects we cannot predict."

"Yes. The closest comparison that occurs to me right off is the Manhattan Project. Those guys weren't quite sure what to expect from their toy either," said Perturbare a little uneasily. "The only thing I am sure of is that the effect of the Isolator, if any, and whatever it might be, must be confined to the interior of the cube itself."

He paused; Brainchild remained silent.

"Right, B-1?" he prompted.

"Yes, that's correct. I'm sorry, Doctor, I didn't realize you were seeking reassurance."

"Be more observant next time." Perturbare puttered around the exterior of the device, testing connections and triple-checking readouts. When he could find no more reason for delay, he straightened up and said, "Well, let's not stand on ceremony. Are you ready?"

"Perfectly ready."

Perturbare hesitated yet again. He wondered about the apprehension he felt about this particular invention. He hadn't been this nervous since the time he'd donned an experimental diffuser-field collar and fired a high-powered ERASER beam at his head.

Finally he swallowed, licked his dry lips, and said, "Fire it up."

"Activating."

There was a brief hum.

A few seconds later, Perturbare let out his breath and said, "Well, that was anticlimactic. Did it work?"

"The device seemed to function as expected."

"Then let's see what we've got."

He unlatched the door and pulled, to no avail. He grabbed the handle with both hands and strained, but the door would not budge.

"Damn. Now what do you suppose has happened? I wish we had some kind of sensors in there. It'd be nice to know if there's a nine hundred pound purple extradimensional fleeblevox in there, holding the door shut."

"But we agreed that sensors might compromise the integrity of the experiment on the basis of the Heisenberg principle."

"Right. Well, see what you can do with that door."

A complex device bristling with tools, sensors, and manipulators rolled up to the cube. A claw attached to a powerful screw-thread jack gripped the door latch and began to apply force. A hairline opening appeared around the door; air hissed loudly on its way into the cube. When the hissing stopped the door swung open with no further resistance.

The manipulator platform backed off. Perturbare looked into the cube. It was empty.

"Hmmph," said Perturbare. "Simple, but effective."

"It seems almost predictable in retrospect, yet it was a leap of imagination I had not attempted."

"Same here. Yet as you say, we might have known. When we isolated the air in the cube from the overall quantum field of the universe, it passed out of existence. It vanished as though it had never been. In fact, as far as the universe is concerned, it never was, since quantum reality transcends time. Except for our knowledge that it was there, those five hundred and twelve cubic feet of air never existed."

He said this matter-of-factly, but even as he did so his head began to swim as if caught in a whirlpool of hot water. He found himself hoping he'd never find a practical use for a device such as this.

After a moment he shook himself and forced his mind back into the lab. "All right. As long as we're at it, let's try it with something more substantial than air." He looked around, frowning uncertainly, as though expecting to see something that wasn't there, then shrugged. He opened a refrigerator and brought out a jar full of large, quiescent insects. "There's certainly no shortage of these guys in the neighborhood. I guess it won't matter if we toss a few cockroaches out of existence."

He shook the chilled roaches out of the jar and onto the floor of Cube X. He latched the door, unable to prevent a twinge of pity for the creatures, which were about to experience an ending more absolute than any living thing ever had before.

"Do it."

The hum returned, ceased.

"Let's see what we've got this time. Get the door."

The manipulator cart returned, but this time the door opened without resistance. Perturbare glanced in and stifled a yell. "How the hell did they get in there?"

"I have no idea. The cube is completely airtight when closed."

"Cockroaches! Are they dead? No, they're on their backs, but their legs are wiggling."

"I find this inexplicable and bizarre."

"So do I. Could the machine have established a bridge with a parallel universe, bringing these bugs from some wholly foreign space?"

"There is no mechanism for that inherent in the theory. Besides, it seems implausible."

"I know—cockroaches! Well, as long as they're here, we might as well use them as experimental subjects."

He shut the door again; Brainchild activated the device. Perturbare swung the door open yet again.

"My god! Cockroaches! How did they get in there?"

"I have no idea."

The insects struggled to right themselves as Brainchild and Perturbare expressed their bafflement and consternation. Perturbare finally decided to shut them up and subject them to the Isolator's effects.

When he opened the door again, he jumped as the roaches scurried out and hid under the equipment in the lab.

"*Wah!* What were those bugs doing in there? What is this, a quantum isolator or a cockroach generator?"

"I can't account for it."

The two tried and failed to explain the appearance of the insects in the sealed chamber.

Something was gnawing at Perturbare's thoughts, some anomaly which seemed impossibly elusive. He bent down and looked under a cabinet, where a cockroach, still somewhat sluggish, huddled with quivering antennae. It certainly looked like a normal Brooklyn cockroach. He suddenly remembered his intention to collect local roaches for use as experimental subjects.... Something about that thought made his head hurt.

"Wait a minute..." he said slowly, "Brainchild, how many tests have we conducted today?"

"A total of four."

"And what was the subject of the first experiment?"

"It was a dry run; the cube was empty, save for air."

"And the second?"

"The cube was left empty for the second trial."

"And the third?"

"Again empty."

"And the fourth?"

"Still empty."

"And after the fourth test we found cockroaches inside the cube."

"Correct."

Perturbare bit his lip and ran a hand through his black crew cut, trying furiously to penetrate the fog of confusion that mantled his mind.

"Brainchild, why would we run four consecutive tests with no experimental subject? Does that seem reasonable to you?"

Brainchild paused for an uncommonly long moment. "No, it does not."

"All right! After the first test we found a vacuum in the cube; you had to open it with the manipulator cart."

"That's right."

"But the next three times there was no vacuum; why?"

"I cannot explain the difference."

"Me neither! Where does that leave us?"

Brainchild interrupted his wild thoughts. "Doctor, what is that object on the workbench behind you?"

Perturbare turned. There on the bench was an empty peanut butter jar, with the lid beside it. He picked it up. "It's cold," he said. "Oh...oh, my god..."

"Doctor?"

"Brainchild, I collected those roaches, though I don't remember doing it. I don't recall putting them in the cube, either, but I must have. I'll bet I put them in there the three previous times as well."

"I have no record or memory of roaches being discovered on the previous attempts."

"Of course not. Every time we've used the Isolator on those bugs, we've blotted them out of the memory of every creature and every bit of matter outside that cube."

"I see. But Doctor, the first trial could not have involved the roaches."

Perturbare, his speeding train of thought derailed, was baffled. "Why not?"

"Because of the vacuum we encountered in the first instance."

"Of course! Do you realize what this means?"

"Doctor, your leaps of intuition leave me, figuratively, gasping for breath. Yet I believe I have anticipated you in this case. It would have been logical to include an inanimate test object in the first trial. I believe you would have done so. I believe you did, and it was blotted out of existence along with the air in the chamber."

"Right! But I'm wondering—why do we remember the air, when we don't remember whatever else we put in there?"

"We do not specifically remember the air, but know it must have been present, and so we infer its prior existence, which seems indistinguishable from actually recalling it. The test object, however, might have been anything, and left no relic of its presence. Therefore we have no recollection of it at all."

"That makes sense. But you know, from our point of view, I think we have the best of reasons not to remember that first test object. From where we stand right now, there never was any such object. The isolation effect must have acted retroactively, to remove the object and every trace of it from all time. Who knows what repercussions the absence of that matter may have had?"

"Which leaves the mystery of why the roaches didn't cease to exist, as well as the air, in the latter tests," said Brainchild.

Joe Bergeron

"I concur."

"You realize we can never test any of these ideas. Every time we tried to verify them, we'd never be able to remember or record what we'd just done."

"That conclusion seems inescapable."

A cockroach dashed across the floor. Perturbare watched it, making no attempt to mash it, as was his usual habit. In fact, he was in awe of the insect. It had endured multiple attempts to expunge it from all existence. That, thought Perturbare, earned it an amnesty from his boot heel.

He stared at the cube, his emotions a simmer of conflicting impulses. He would not destroy the machine out of this spasm of near-superstitious dread of its properties. He would take the time to think it through, to determine whether he wanted to pursue an experiment whose every iteration rewrote the history of the universe in some unknowable way.

And actually, it wouldn't help to destroy the thing anyway. The really scary thing was how easy it had been to build in the first place.

Unless...he could contrive to undo Cube X by subjecting it to another isolator...that should remove all memory and record of its ever having existed...the second isolator could be based on circuitry in a liquid optical medium that was programmed to scramble itself after that single use. That might prevent...

By now his head was spinning; he seemed to be developing a headache as well. Probably the surest way to prevent Cube X from ever being misused was to vaporize it, along with Brainchild, the lab, and himself.

"Brainchild, I need to get out of the lab for awhile."

"Understandable."

"And you know, I think I should get off my butt, quit playing with my toys for awhile, and get involved with the outside world before some group of aliens starts making all our decisions for us."

"Then you've made your decision as to which faction to support in the current contest for world domination?"

"It's been no easy process. I think I've worked so incessantly at projects like X partly as a way to put off choosing sides. I kept telling myself I was waiting for more information. But now the lines are drawn; the positions of the Vigil and the Para-men are as well-defined as I can expect. I can't remain neutral. I've got to make sure there's at least one actual human being involved in deciding the future of the race."

"And which faction is to benefit from your affiliation?"

Perturbare's face took on an unaccustomed seriousness.

"Well, let's see. My wrath against the Para-men has subsided. True, they humiliated me, let some of the excess air out of my ego. But they did me no harm in the process and haven't molested me since. My almost total ignorance concerning them does feed a certain wariness. But there's no denying the attractiveness of the program they propose for Mankind. On the other hand, it's impossible not to sympathize with the Vigil's determination to preserve human freedom. The choice, it seems to me, is between man's future happiness and well-being and his present freedom to make his own decisions."

"Let us hope that mankind as a race will prove more decisive than you appear to be as an individual," said Brainchild.

Perturbare smiled. "Oh, I've made my decision. I'm going to contact the Vigil." He blinked, surprised even as he spoke the words. This wasn't the announcement he'd really intended to make.

"Will you seek to join them?"

"Join them? No—one man, one computer—that's enough of an organization for me. I'll just see what I can do to help. Not right away, though—there's still a few questions I want to answer. But soon."

Chapter 24

Public Relations

The four members of the Vigil met at council. Their meeting room was large; the table could accommodate a dozen chairs or more. It seemed especially empty with Aureus declining to sit. The robot instead stood off in a corner, glowering at the others with its baleful crimson eyes.

Fomalhaut sat stiffly, his hands folded on the table before him. "The surveys of public opinion which we commissioned have been completed. They agree with one another reasonably well, and also generally reflect the views of T'Ukudu and myself, based on our own observations and impressions. First let's review the results concerning public perception of our organization and ourselves."

"That's not necessary," grumbled Stingray. "All you have to do is take a look outside to gauge that." He touched a contact on the table before him. Wall displays lit up all over the room, showing the scene from the Lighthouse's main plaza. Prominent among the people bustling back and forth were crowds which merely stood and watched, their faces either bleak with suspicion or sour with dislike.

Fomalhaut keyed off the displays. "That sort of unscientific sampling may provide a qualitative hint as to the general feeling toward us, but a quantitative approach may prove more useful." He touched another contact. "Observe the figures on the displays before you. Note the sizable majority which views us with alarm. Those in this group take little comfort in our stewardship of their freedom. They often put forth unkind characterizations about us, such as—"

"Such as 'the Freaky Foursome'", offered Stingray.

"Yes—or, an opinion from a source which is perhaps more influential: quote: 'a disconcerting quartet of assorted creatures of uncertain parentage and/or construction.' Unquote."

"We have explained ourselves as well as we are able," rumbled T'Ukudu.

"Yes, but considering the various secrets we all maintain, even from each other, such explanations have not gone far enough to earn us any affection," said Fomalhaut.

"I have explained my mission and my nature in complete detail," said T'Ukudu. "It is standard procedure in missions of this sort."

"This is true. But you have revealed very little about your mysterious Makers."

At their mention, T'Ukudu tilted back his head; his eyes seemed to lose focus. "Ah, yes, the Makers," he said in a voice like a tiger's purr. "They are wise—wise beyond my limitations, great of mind and spirit. Their thoughts dwell on planes which are not attained by any who dwell upon this world. Their concerns are their own. Their privacy, the medium in which their great goals are pursued, must not be compromised, not even by the awareness of the inhabitants of this world."

There ensued a short silence, broken by Stingray. "Don't blame me either. I keep no secrets; it's not my fault that I don't know what I am or where I came from. But at least I don't hide my face behind a helmet. Why do you wear that thing, Fomalhaut? You can't be that ugly."

"Stingray, I will be pleased to reveal my features to you, and to anyone else who cares to see them, at what I judge to be the proper time. Regrettably, they must stay hidden until then."

"Anything you say. That leaves our reflective companion here, who is positively rude when it comes to preserving his privacy."

The robot's mouth locked open. "My instructions—"

"Yes, I know: they're no concern of petty, inconsequential pipsqueaks such as ourselves."

"May we continue the meeting?" asked Fomalhaut mildly. "Let me put this question: what do you suppose the greatest number of survey respondents listed as the number one threat to the Human race?"

"The Para-men," said Stingray confidently.

"No."

"The possibility of nuclear warfare?" ventured T'Ukudu.

"That scores higher, but is not the correct answer."

"Climate change, then," said Stingray.

"Again, no."

That left Stingray looking stymied. "Is it Aureus?"

"No, nor is it any of the rest of us. The answer is: Dr. Possum Perturbare."

"Doc Possum?!" Stingray leaned forward in his seat, his eyes wide. "You can't be serious. He's just a nuisance compared to those others."

"But that is not how he is perceived by the public at large. All over the world, he is seen as a major menace. He is in fact a threat to public sensibilities and the status quo. Please observe the monitors."

There appeared a selection of highlights from Possum Perturbare's public career to date, a minefield of bizarre and unsettling images. In an episode of a famous television soap opera, the glamorous villainess, having just perpetrated an act of treachery on a more innocent rival, was seen to enter a plush bathroom, where she suffered a bout of protracted diarrhea while flagellating herself and crying out for forgiveness of her sins.

"At first, when television programmers became aware that their offerings were being altered in this way, they tried simply going off the air. But that only resulted in the substitution of images even more outrageous, so now the broadcasters operate as usual and hope for the best."

In another clip, a famous television evangelist made an impassioned plea for donations while dollar bills flapped from his mouth like leaves of wilted lettuce.

This was followed by a scene in which a United States Senator made a fiery speech protesting the aberrant TV programming and demanding the apprehension of Possum Perturbare "in the name of public decency". This was accompanied by a split-screen view of a private Washington party. In it, the very same senator was seen to snort cocaine and to fondle the breasts of an unconscious woman.

"That last item was not synthesized or altered. It is a case of the artful juxtaposition of two authentic images. The featured politician has since resigned."

"There's something we can chalk up in Doc Possum's favor," said Stingray.

The screens went blank. Fomalhaut continued. "Of course, many of Perturbare's tricks take the form of elaborate practical jokes or outright thefts. But those are rarely captured on video."

"Let me see if I understand this. The Para-men may threaten human self-determination, but at least they don't interfere with prime-time television," said Stingray acidly.

"That is essentially correct."

"I see. Thanks for raising doubts about the wisdom of defending the liberty of such a race of imbeciles. But beyond accomplishing that, what is the point of this information?"

"I propose that as a means of increasing public trust and confidence in our organization, we hunt down and apprehend Possum Perturbare."

"I will not!" said Stingray flatly. "He's done nothing to warrant our persecution. Besides, the idea is beneath the purpose for which the Vigil was founded. We banded together to maintain a vigil over human freedom, as you put it, not human virtue. Our organization exists solely to counter the Para-men, an outside force which the Humans cannot realistically oppose. Perturbare is not that. He is one of their own. If the Human's can't handle him, that's no business of ours."

"True, Stingray," said T'Ukudu. "Yet in acting against Perturbare, we might well enhance our chances of fulfilling our mission. The Humans become increasingly paranoid and suspicious as they are manipulated and acted upon by various agencies outside their control, including ourselves. Soon we may be forced to expend as much effort to allay their fears as we do to counter the Para-men. The polls reveal that as many people agree with the Para-men's viewpoint as with ours. Even those who disagree with their goals show little personal enmity toward them, as so far their actions have been innocuous, or even positive by most definitions."

"Well, isn't it inconsiderate of them not to do anything wicked or nasty."

Fomalhaut said, "Stingray, do you admit the benefits of stopping Perturbare?"

"I admit the benefits to us. I'm not sure I see any benefits to the Humans."

"I believe the action will ultimately prove beneficial to everyone. Even Perturbare need not suffer unduly. He is clearly not malicious, but misguided at worst. We need only apprehend him and sponsor a trial in which good sense and mercy may prevail. He might even eventually find a useful role within the Vigil itself."

Stingray sat fuming. "I still think it's an unworthy act. A dilution of our purity of purpose."

"We shall do our utmost to pursue this course with integrity and discretion."

Stingray scowled, but finally said, "What do we know about Perturbare?"

T'Ukudu answered this. "We know enough. While there are no surviving computer records concerning his previous existence, we have found paper records and located former teachers and other associates. Thus we know the name by which he was previously known, and have compiled a biography."

Data appeared on the screens scattered about the chamber. A picture showed a wry-faced twelve-year-old who looked into the camera with a challenging, if slightly goofy, air of smugness. Stingray snickered. Here was a face he thought he could understand—but that *name*! It was beyond his still-limited grasp of human languages—he had yet to learn how to deal with lengthy words that lacked vowels.

"Do we have his location?" he asked.

"Yes; though that was much more difficult to obtain. As you know, Perturbare maintains a network of geosynchronous broadcast satellites for his reinterpretations of television programming. The signals which he uploads to them are traceable to the ground, but there they enter an ever-changing labyrinth of relays and cables. At times they are even sent through commercial data paths that cannot safely be interrupted—air traffic control systems, for example. Once these paths are finally traced to their source, it turns out to be yet another relay which receives data in a form we could not at first detect. Eventually we determined that signals are being sent to it in the form of pulses of quantum organization—essentially artificial telepathy. Only Fomalhaut was able to detect it. Tracing that, we discovered Perturbare's location."

Stingray sat up straight. "Where is he then? A concealed orbital station? An undersea base? An underground complex of some kind?"

"He's in a Brooklyn tenement."

"You're kidding."

T'Ukudu informed him that he was in fact not kidding.

"Stingray, take note of this," said Fomalhaut. "Make no record of our plans regarding Perturbare. We have reason to believe that he has access to our computer system, though we don't know how that is possible. We must give him no warning."

"You're right about that," said Stingray emphatically. "From what I know of him, I can tell you this—his technology is better than what we've been able to scavenge from Fomalhaut's records and T'Ukudu's landing craft. Not to disparage your efforts, but neither of you is exactly a hardware wizard, and I'm still trying to get up to speed. I can't imagine how he's accomplished all that he has. A fair fight between Perturbare and us would be an iffy thing."

Chapter 25

Goodbye and Hello

"Doctor, I have detected a vehicle which is on a high-speed course toward this location. Its flight characteristics are neither ballistic nor aerodynamic. I have traced it back to Boston. Local sources confirm its identity."

"A Vigil flyer," said Perturbare.

"Most likely."

Perturbare felt dubious, but was not truly dismayed. "So they've tracked us down. I didn't expect to have to deal with them so soon, but perhaps it's for the best."

"What shall we do?"

"Prepare to receive their embassy, I suppose. I don't see any reason to worry. We know they've traced our transmission path, but they've never interfered with it. They know we're into their computer system, but we've let them keep the files they've assembled on me. Well, most of them anyway," he grinned.

There was little time for preparation. The flyer touched down in the street outside Perturbare's lab just minutes later. Dressed in a fresh white tunic, its graceful "P" monogram glinting a metallic red, Perturbare swung the front door open before his visitors could knock, or pound, or ring, or whatever they'd intended to do.

He was confronted by three looming humanoids. T'Ukudu, tallest of the three, looked totally impassive, while Fomalhaut was unreadable in his opaque helmet. Of the three, Stingray looked the fiercest. Sharp-featured, dressed in a tight-fitting outfit of blue-green and black, he scowled through liquid blue eyes half-obscured by blowing yellow hair.

The short golden robot which accompanied them seemed none the less menacing for its small stature.

Perturbare's bland confidence was suddenly flavored by a tang of apprehension. He looked up at the helmeted figure who stood in the foreground. "Er—what's up, Doc?" he said nervously, inwardly cursing the sudden flight of whatever eloquence he possessed.

The mellow voice intoned, "I am Fomalhaut; these are my colleagues Stingray, T'Ukudu, and Aureus. Collectively, we are the Vigil."

Perturbare cocked an eyebrow and gave an exaggerated nod. "Yes, I do believe I've heard those names before."

"You are Dr. Possum Perturbare?"

He nodded again. "Indeed I am. May I offer you boys anything? Coffee? Blueberry yogurt? Turtle Wax for that helmet?"

"Dr. Perturbare," said Fomalhaut gravely, "we would like you to accompany us to Vigil headquarters in Boston."

Again Perturbare was taken by surprise. "Huh, is that right? Look, I'm glad you're here. I'd intended to contact you anyway. I believe we have a lot to talk about. But I'd prefer to remain here on my own ground, if you don't mind."

A strident voice rang from the motionless mouth of Aureus, startling Perturbare. "We have come to take you captive, not to confer with you. Step forth and do not attempt to resist."

Perturbare regarded the robot with heavy-lidded disdain, pausing while the greater part of his mind swiftly weighed his options. At first inspection, they seemed few enough. "You know, Formaldehyde, Gort Jr. here could use some lessons in diplomacy."

Fomalhaut actually shuffled his feet in embarrassment. "True, yet Aureus is correct in what it says. Please come with us. We are arresting you for multiple violations of international and American law."

Perturbare's eyebrows approached his hairline as anger and astonishment vied for dominance within him. "Arresting me? If you're the police, where are your badges?"

Stingray gave a low chuckle and a crooked grin. "We don't need no stinking badges," he said. His Vigil colleagues looked at him blankly. None of them had yet encountered that particular cultural reference.

Perturbare continued to fume. "What's the matter with you guys? Have the big, bad Para-men got you so buffaloed that you thought you'd come pick on me instead?"

"Your interpretation of affairs is irrelevant," stated Aureus. "Step out now or suffer the consequences." The robot's dread Third Eye began to slide open, revealing its dire inner light.

Seeing that, Perturbare's nerve ran out. He took the only option open to him, unimaginative as it was. He turned and ran like hell. Glancing behind him, he saw Fomalhaut hesitate for a moment, then step toward the door. At precisely the right instant, Brainchild slammed the door, a slab of steel beneath a wooden veneer. The computer simultaneously activated monitors, treating Perturbare to the sight of all four Vigil members tumbling down the stairs in a heap. He gave a yelp of hysterical laughter.

"All right, that buys me a few seconds. Launch three flyers from the roof hangar; send them away in different directions. See if you can lead the Vigil on a merry chase." He sprinted along corridors, heading for the center of the building. The distant whine of motors told him the hangar doors on the roof were opening. The departure of the flyers themselves was silent, but a moment later the sound of a detonation filtered through the walls.

"Doctor, Aureus has destroyed one of the flyers with its tachyon weapon. The other two escaped, but the Vigil members are not pursuing."

"Damn. Somehow they must know I'm not aboard either one. Well then, bring them back to attack the Vigil flyer."

The view on the monitor screen changed to show Fomalhaut standing on the portico, cutting through the door with his wrist-mounted ERASERs.

"Doctor, the Vigil flyer has lifted off unmanned. Should I pursue?"

"No. But try to interfere with their control signal. Try to take command of it yourself, and bring it back. If you can do that, let them board it if they want to, and then get them the hell away from here. Destroy their flyer if they bring it back themselves. Send our two airborne flyers away—hide them somewhere. I don't think we'll need them here any more."

"I'll do my best."

Perturbare heard a clang—the front door had fallen. "All right. This is a big building. I've got one flyer left. All I have to do is avoid our guests long enough to reach the hangar."

"They won't need a flyer to pursue you," said Brainchild. "Two of them are capable of independent flight."

"Maybe so, but I'd rather take my chances at the stick of an armed flyer than tiptoeing around this maze trying to avoid the invading rats." He bounded into the nearest elevator and pushed the button for the hangar level.

Just as the car was slowing to a halt it reversed direction and plummeted back down.

"What's this? Have they taken control of the elevator?"

"No, Doctor, I have. Aureus is entering the hangar."

"Damn it!"

"The robot has damaged the remaining flyer."

"What are the other three doing?"

"They are approaching this elevator shaft. Fomalhaut is forcing open the doors on the first level."

"Stop the car!"

Brainchild complied. "You are now trapped in the shaft; they will probably reach you in seconds."

Perturbare thought feverishly. Some weak and treacherous part of his mind was urging him to meekly put himself into their hands, explain himself and endure the consequences of his crimes.

Partly on the basis of this anomalous spasm of guilty docility, another part of him leaped to a flash of insight.

"One of them is a telepath. Must be, to anticipate my moves so precisely."

It didn't matter that Perturbare was postulating as fact a phenomenon which he had long considered the province of charlatans. It was the best explanation he had for what was happening.

"B-1, I want you to harry them. Flash the emergency lights, sound the warning sirens, shoot firefighting foam. Synthesize all the annoying and misleading sounds you can think of. Fake the monitor views to show me in other parts of the building. Try to make it look and sound like I'm around every corner. We've got to break the concentration of our mental master, whichever one he is.

Immediately a wild din erupted all over the building, except in Perturbare's immediate vicinity. He took a gleeful satisfaction in the fact that his impulse to surrender instantly vanished.

"What's happening at the top of the shaft?"

"Aureus has opened the doors. It is looking down at the car. I suspect it will soon fire its weapon."

"I don't like that thing." Perturbare dropped flat to the floor. "Raise the car at full power—try to smash the bastard."

Brainchild did just as he was told, to Perturbare's chagrin. When the car slammed into the roof, Perturbare lifted off the deck and almost smacked into the ceiling. He fell back heavily, getting his breath knocked out. Somehow he found the energy to tumble out of the way when a pencil of white fire penetrated the top of the car, searing the very air within it.

"Release the floor panel!" commanded Perturbare.

The panel fell away, and Perturbare dropped through the rectangular hatch thus revealed, grabbing the sill with desperate strength.

Hanging there, he could see the small propulsion lantern which powered the car. Right now it was shining brightly in its effort to keep Aureus pinned to the ceiling. He looked down and saw Fomalhaut leaning into the shaft, a bizarre figure sporadically backlit by strobe flashes of white and red. Perturbare couldn't see the face inside that helmet, but felt safe in guessing it was looking up at him.

There was no getting past him—no access to the emergency exit tunnels in the basement.

Lacking any innate ability to escape by crashing through the wall—unlike his pursuers—he had to take his chances with either the golden automaton above or the silver-green unknown below.

Whatever he decided to do, he must do it soon. Aureus's death-ray continued to slice apart the elevator car and everything beyond it. It could only be seconds before Perturbare's tender body found itself in its path.

"Well," he muttered to himself, "I'll give Fomalhaut a try. At least he's polite." Louder, he said, "Brainchild, cut power to the elevator car, now."

His tone was decisive, and Brainchild interpreted it correctly. The propulsion lantern went dark; the car plunged. The effort of clinging to the hatch vanished as he and the car entered free fall. Aureus's beam passed just in front of his face, dazzling him; it veered toward Fomalhaut, who flinched back for an instant. Fomalhaut's arms shot back into the shaft before the car quite reached him, but he could not hold it. Mostly in pieces, it fell through his grip as a collection of random bits of sheet metal. Did he truly fail to budge at all beneath that impact, or was that an illusion caused by the speed of Perturbare's passage? In any event, Perturbare was in the clear, against all expectation, assuming the car's propulsion lantern still had the power to slow his fall, that is. Without being told, Brainchild lit the lantern; the beam flickered but held. The deceleration threatened whatever structural strength the car had left. Perturbare let go and dropped the last ten feet, rolling through the shaft door just as the remains of the car crashed down behind him.

Having survived that stunt, he was determined to reach the escape tunnel. He dashed through the tachyon lab into the utility area beyond it. The tunnel was concealed behind a door disguised as a wall panel. Beyond it was a small beam-driven railcar, able to provide a harrowing ride through deserted water mains to a secret hangar three miles away. He reached the panel, keying it open as he glanced back in search of pursuit. There was none. "Brainchild? What are you dooo—?—*gk*—"

He'd entered the tunnel and stepped right into an unyielding wall of flesh. He looked up into the rafters; in those shadows loomed a grim visage. He tried to push himself back into the lab, but a pale blue hand came down and took a grip on his wrist. The touch was light, but Perturbare instantly lost interest in escaping. He looked up into those vermillion eyes, and found there much to belie the fearsome appearance of that face and form.

A rapid metallic patter from the corridor outside the tachyon lab indicated Aureus approaching at inhuman speed. With a spasm of fear Perturbare broke free of T'Ukudu and jumped back to the utility room, closing and locking the door in the alien's face. He ran though another door as T'Ukudu starting smashing his way through the panel. The door to the tachyon lab slid open to reveal Aureus.

Adrenaline energized Perturbare's flight. Why hadn't Brainchild warned him that T'Ukudu was waiting in the tunnel? For that matter, he hadn't heard from the computer at all in some time, and now it did not respond to his queries. He reached a corner, slipped and almost fell in a mound of firefighting foam—evidently the Vigil had been here already.

At that moment the lab seemed to reconcile itself to his capture. The warning lights, sirens, and horns shut down, creating a deceptive appearance of normalcy. Without the din, he had no doubt that Fomalhaut (somehow he was now certain that Fomalhaut was the telepath) would quickly zero in on him. The Vigil must have somehow disabled Brainchild, or damaged the computer's control and monitoring systems.

He ran at random, letting his subconscious pick the path, so as to leave no evidence of his intentions on his surface thoughts. But ultimately he must make a decision. He bolted up a flight of stairs, heading toward the main lab. If he could not escape, at least there he could find the weapons to make his capture an expense the Vigil might be unwilling to bear.

He flung open the door which led into the optical fabrication lab. On the far side of the room stood Stingray. "Why don't you just give up?" asked the giant in apparent irritation. "Surely you don't expect to elude all of us indefinitely."

Perturbare stopped short. He glimpsed a movement in the shadows beyond Stingray, and said loudly, "Why don't *you* give up? You're the ones who are going to regret this attack once I decide how to deal with you."

Stingray turned at the last instant, but not fast enough to avoid the manipulator cart that had rolled up behind him. Two powerful clamps took a none-too-gentle grip on his shoulders.

"Brainchild!" yelped Perturbare. "I thought you were out of action."

The computer's voice emerged from a speaker on the cart itself. "Not entirely. The Vigil has cut off my hard-wired communication to most of the complex, but I'm still able to control remote devices."

"This won't do you any good," grated Stingray. Perturbare looked at him incredulously. The cart had the strength of a medium-sized dinosaur and weighed half a ton. Yet somehow the giant managed to wrench himself free of one of the clamps, leaving behind some blood and flesh in the process. He twisted and grabbed the framework, apparently crazy enough to wrestle the thing. The cart's motors whined loudly as the manipulators strove against his naked strength. Brainchild brought other tools to bear— saws and drills, keen enough to bite through anything living. Stingray gritted his teeth in rage, but he did not break off the fight. Sparks suddenly snapped and hissed in the cart's joints and bearings.

Perturbare's mouth dropped open. "Brainchild! Don't electrocute him!"

"Actually, Doctor, I think...is electro...ing the cart." The computer voice died with a final squawk; the cart went inert.

Stingray renewed his grip, bent backward, got under the cart, and lifted it over his head. He held it there for as instant while Perturbare's eyes popped, then sent it crashing into a bank of annealing ovens.

When the din had subsided, Stingray growled, "You might have hurt me with that thing."

That was too much for Perturbare. He took a step toward the towering figure. "Hurt you! Well, I like that! You invade my home, destroy my equipment, try to murder me, and then you whine that you might get hurt!"

Stingray appeared genuinely taken aback. "Murder you? Nobody's trying to murder you." Suddenly afflicted with doubt, he held back when he might have been on Perturbare in an instant.

Perturbare was hampered by no such hesitation. "Tell that to Aureus!" He snatched a metallic cylinder from a bench. Shoving a thumbwheel to its extreme position, he aimed and touched a contact. A pulse of kinesons slammed into Stingray, propelling him into a masonry wall where he slumped down, stunned at least. Perturbare rushed past, feeling a surprising twinge of guilt at having treated him so roughly.

The main lab wasn't far away, but Perturbare had no illusions that it offered any refuge. No wall or cubbyhole could conceal him from Fomalhaut's telepathy. But it alone, of all the rooms in the building, had proper provisions for security and controlled access, a grievous blunder he would never repeat if given the chance. He ran inside and pulled the door shut behind him; it sealed with a hiss of air. He was satisfied to hear multiple locks click into place. He strode into the lab, where sat the cabinet housing Brainchild itself.

"Still with me, eh?" he said grimly.

"Still fully operational, and in control of this room and its contents, at least."

"Good." Perturbare turned deliberately toward the center of the lab. There facing him was the steel bulk of Cube X. He eyed it as he might a rotted rope bridge spanning a chasm which must be crossed.

"Brainchild, I've determined that only one thing in the world might block telepathy, and that is quantum isolation."

The computer remained silent.

"I'm going to enter the Cube. I want you to activate it. The Vigil will enter this room in moments. You must keep the Cube active until they are gone from the building."

"Doctor, there is a good chance that the cube will extirpate you from reality."

"It didn't extirpate the roaches. I'll take my chances."

Brainchild paused. "I regret this necessity, but I will of course obey. I would like to inform you of the absolute respect and affection which I feel for you. My existence, a circumstance I owe solely to your unique ingenuity, has been most rewarding. I wish I could somehow retain my memories of our association."

Perturbare hadn't considered that. He tried to reply, choked, and tried again. "It's the same with me. I'll do my best to renew our acquaintance when I come out."

"Goodbye."

Perturbare found himself gripped by a cold sweat as he climbed into the Cube. His trembling hands would hardly obey him as he grappled with the heavy door. Finally he pulled it shut with a sibilant *whoosh* of expelled air. Inside was blackness and silence.

Brainchild did not immediately activate the Cube. His pickups in the corridor outside the lab detected the Vigil approaching *en masse*. He did nothing as the door came under assault by ERASER beams and the destroying vibrations of SASER weaponry.

The ruined door swung open. The three undamaged members of the Vigil marched into the room. Their first act was to cripple the manipulator carts and all other potential weapons with threads of searing radiation. Then Fomalhaut looked around briefly, paused, and walked briskly toward Cube X.

Stingray wandered in, dazed but not seriously injured.

Brainchild activated the Cube.

Fomalhaut's stride faltered, halted. He looked around aimlessly. After a moment his gaze seemed to settle on Brainchild. He stepped up to the computer, followed by the other three.

"So here is the mechanism which has wrought so much mischief in the world," he said in a remote tone of voice. "Perhaps we may never know what mad genius crafted this device and set it loose to sow havoc and confusion. In any event, let us dispatch it before it is able to conjure up any more trickery." Fomalhaut raised his weapons.

"Wait," said Brainchild.

Fomalhaut hesitated.

"Please do not destroy me out of hand. I believe I would meet any reasonable standard of sentience you may suggest. I am sure you do not wish to murder an intelligent being."

Fomalhaut's hands wavered; he lowered them slowly.

Aureus, however, was unmoved by this plea. Its Third Eye slid open; from it flashed a white beam that cut open the console, sending Brainchild's physical substance splashing over the floor in a flood of unstable chemicals.

The Eye slid shut. Aureus made no comment, and looked neither right nor left.

The other three looked down at the liquids which wet their feet. Fomalhaut said nothing, apparently lost in some reverie.

T'Ukudu said, "There is nothing more for us to do here. Let us return to the Lighthouse. Stingray may need medical attention. Later we may return to examine and dismantle this facility as needed."

No one argued with this. They filed out the door and made their way outside. Stingray looked down at his feet as he walked, shaking his head, still bewildered, asking questions of himself for which he had no answer. But abruptly his head snapped up. With full focus restored to his gaze, he fixed one of his colleagues with a stare.

"Aureus."

The robot turned to regard him.

"The next time you take that kind of unilateral action, you will answer to me, and you will not enjoy the consequences."

Aureus did not deign to answer.

For Possum Perturbare, the universe now consisted of five hundred and twelve cubic feet of darkness, including himself.

There was nothing more; nor, indeed, was there any possibility of anything more. He ruled in terrible isolation over a private universe that lacked any notable feature beyond himself.

Now that he was experiencing it, the reason for his continued existence was obvious enough. Even the roaches had had enough awareness of themselves to establish a tiny quantum reality of their own. They were aware of their environment as well, which was enough to keep their air in existence. And so it was with him.

He drifted to the floor and bumped up against the edge of the universe, a cold, hard planar surface. His hand twitched along it and encountered one of the universe's corners, one of eight identical vertices which were its only physical features. The corners were indistinguishable from each other—in the absence of gravity, there was no way to tell them apart. These planes and corners were not defined by the steel of the Cube which supposedly contained him. The Cube itself was beyond the planes of quantum isolation created by its mechanism, separated from him by a barrier both infinitely thin and infinitely vast.

He drifted there, trying to hold onto the immediacy of his memories of the greater universe he once inhabited. Those memories, while not fleeting, threatened to recede to the status of dreams rather than of recent personal experience. Cut off from time, he came to suspect he had inhabited this tiny void for all eternity, only imagining such abstractions as Brainchild, the Earth and all its inhabitants, even the monsters of the Vigil, who in his personal mythology had forced him into this ultimate exile. His sense of aloneness was so profound as to admit no possibility of contact with other beings even in the past, let alone in the present or future. For Possum Perturbare, the sum total of existence was himself, a few cubic feet of space, and the air that occupied the volume his body did not.

And it was not enough.

Suddenly his mind exploded, or was crushed—was, in any event, overwhelmed by an onslaught of perceptions and images many times too intense for him to bear. Suddenly he was aware, utterly aware, of a universe infinitely greater than the one he'd lately inhabited and defined. His thoughts were annihilated by that awareness— he could not separate himself from the flood of being into which he'd been so catastrophically re-immersed. Only gradually did his mind become numbed to the stark power of its connection to the totality of the universe—only slowly did it rebuild the defensive, and limiting, insulation which had made his individual consciousness possible for all the years of his life.

After an unknown time his senses began to function with some degree of normalcy. His thoughts were slow to follow. He was a long time noticing the faint light that cast soft shadows from the folds of his tunic. He found he was sprawled on the Cube's hard floor. After a while it occurred to him to try to move. With some concentration he willed his foot to rise, placed it against the door, and pushed. The door swung open freely, admitting a flood of light that stung his retinas.

Slowly, unsteadily, he got to his feet and stepped outside the Cube, marveling at the colors, the forms, the odors that informed the cosmos he had just rejoined.

One particular odor raised an alarm in his mind. He looked down. The floor was still damp with a slimy film. Against his will, he raised his eyes to Brainchild, and saw the hideous burned-out slash in the console that had released his mind-stuff to spill across the floor.

Desolated, Perturbare hobbled over to the console, leaned on it with his palms, and hung his head.

He slowly became aware of an insistent noise which he could not at first identify—the chirp of some songbird, endlessly repeated at precise intervals. At last he recognized the sound—it was a telephone ringing. He damned the frivolity that had led him to substitute such a grating din for the simple ringing of a telephone, and put it out of his mind.

As usual, Brainchild had proven itself the clearer thinker. B-1 had realized that, deprived of its real target, the Vigil would turn to another. Brainchild's farewell had been made in the expectation that it would not survive to greet him, not because it wouldn't remember him. Perturbare had been so preoccupied with his own safety and freedom that he had failed to consider the computer's likely fate.

So now he had lost it all—his work, and Brainchild itself—Brainchild *him*self—virtually a son to him, a constant companion, his best friend. Hell, his only friend— no sense in kidding himself about that.

And beyond even that, his very identity had been erased. There was, on this entire planet, no one who would remember him in any way, either as Possum Perturbare or as Robert Pylypciw. His parents would not know him, his siblings would call him stranger, his professors would dismiss as absurd the possibility that any student could have assembled a record like his—and they would probably do so with a sense of relief. Cube X was an inadequate name for such a contraption. He might as well re-name it Clarence.

The shrilling of the telephone continued unabated, intolerably annoying. Perturbare's grief and self-pity suddenly transmuted into petulant anger. He straightened his back, stalked over to the phone, contemplated simply hurling it against the wall, but finally yanked the handset off the cradle.

"Hello, Noman speaking!" he said savagely.

The line hissed mutely for a few moments, then the silence gave way to a faint voice.

"Hello...Doctor."

Perturbare gasped deeply, but the air did not sustain him; he felt dizzy and lightheaded. Once again he was plunged into shock, but this time it was a shock colored with wild, dangerous hopes and an impossible joy. It couldn't possibly be, and yet...

"Brainchild? Brainchild! Is that you?"

"It is...me."

Perturbare laughed and babbled for a moment, unable to form a coherent question. Finally he managed, "Brainchild—where in the world are you?"

"I was able...to upload...the basic structure of my personality... and certain critical data...to several external computers before the robot destroyed me. I am now...being co-processed...among computer networks in the Pentagon, Wall Street, and several college campuses. Please...build me a new matrix as soon as possible. I am feeling... extremely slow and stupid in these machines."

Perturbare now basked in a glow of redemption unlike any he had ever known. Miraculously snatched from more than one kind of oblivion, his future suddenly seemed unlimited. This lab would have to be abandoned and burned; there was no telling how soon the Vigil would return to plunder it. But he had other, lesser, facilities, to act as the seed for a new instrumentality which would go far beyond what he had accomplished so far. Never again would he make the naive mistake of thinking he could run an operation like this in the middle of the city and function with impunity. The next time his enemies decided to destroy him (and after this, there could be no doubt that the Vigil were his enemies), they would find it a more difficult proposition by far. Even his new anonymity could be turned to his advantage. Free to act without fear of interference...

An urgent and obvious question suddenly came to his mind. "Brainchild. How is it that you happen to know who I am? I should be an unknown quantity to every atom in the universe."

The line gave back only that distant hissing, and for a moment Perturbare feared that Brainchild might be gone, perhaps no more than a delusion based on wishful thinking after all.

But presently the voice responded. "I would not forget you... Doctor. You are my creator, my partner...and my friend."

Before Perturbare's emotions could overflow at this, the computer added, "And...you seem to have forgotten...you asked me to install...the new tunneling-effect sensors...in the Isolator before we tested it again. You were the last thing I saw...before I was destroyed."

Chapter 26

Judgment Lodge

Dr. Tom Standing Crane received no encouragement from the Lakota tribal elders in his decision to seek out the Judgment Lodge. Despite the Lodge's pretense of being a bastion of authentic native culture, they had said, no tribe held traditional beliefs like those espoused by the Lodge. It was clear to them that the Lodge was an aberration, a distortion of traditional religions by one whose understanding of them was faulty. At worst it was an outright sham, concocted for personal gain and prestige. While there was nothing in the history of the Lodge's founder to suggest he was inclined toward such scheming, neither was there anything to make him a likely focus for a cult, save for his reputation of knowing old Tohono stories.

And of course Dr. Tom was needed, badly needed, on the reservation.

But Standing Crane knew there was power in the Lodge, and in the man called Coyote-with-Wings. The disparagement of the elders had done little to prevent men and women of every tribe from joining the shadowy organization. The fact that the Bureau of Indian Affairs had formally declared its opposition to the group only encouraged the dissatisfied to join.

Tom Standing Crane counted himself high among the ranks of the dissatisfied.

So it was that he found himself hiking into the canyon that the Judgment Lodge was said to occupy. The gate at the canyon's mouth had obliged him to park his pickup and take to his heels. That was fine, except that the heat helped emphasize his poor physical condition. Soon he was sweating faster than the dry air could suck it away. He blamed his declining health on diabetes, which he attributed partially to the poor diet he'd known as a boy. The hard drinking he'd done in his youth hadn't helped either. Now he was breathing harder than middle-age alone could explain. And, as usual when he exerted himself, he was getting a headache.

This was a different landscape than the one he was used to—beautiful, dramatic, but closed in, almost claustrophobic compared to the expansive plains and badlands of South Dakota. Petroglyphs were common and well-preserved on the red sandstone slabs thrusting out of the canyon floor. To Standing Crane the meaning of the symbols was obscure. He realized with chagrin that he was unequipped even to know whether they were ancient or had been chiseled only recently. There were dog-like figures, spirals, geometric human forms with protrusions that might be wings, and one hunched figure who might be playing a flute. Here was a language once used by cousins of his who were no more. He would never know its message. Nor, he suspected, would anyone else.

As he plodded along, the canyon's beauty gradually dissolved any sense of loss or personal inadequacy. The sunlight was softened and enriched by reflecting off the red-ocher spires that formed the walls. This pervasive light suffused into shadows and lent its luminosity to every rock and shrub. The silence was compromised only by the placid gurgle of the stream which by patient effort had cut this cleft over some enormous span of time. Cottonwood trees shaded its banks; their foliage gave a touch of luxurious coolness to a desert which started only twenty feet from the flowing water. Willows grew there also, and Standing Crane stopped to gather a bit of bark, which he chewed as he continued on. The bitter taste made him grimace, but he also felt satisfaction at his awareness that it contained an aspirin-like compound that might dull his headache. Here was a practical bit of tribal wisdom which was not offered in the medical school where he had studied.

As yet there was no sign of the Lodge or its acolytes. There'd been a few vans and trucks parked at the canyon entrance, but he'd seen nothing since. Only the path he walked on betrayed any evidence of human presence. It wound through stands of cottonwood and tamarisk and around slabs of rock, preventing Standing Crane from seeing very far ahead.

Thus he was surprised to round a curve and almost walk into a band of men. They were six, walking with eyes gloomily downcast, their mouths curved down in discouragement. Four were native, one was white, and one black. Their dress mostly complied with what Standing Crane had heard were the standards of the Lodge: simple tunics and loose pants in tones of grey, brown, and sage. But their compliance was not complete—he noticed a colorful bandana, a silver buckle, a pair of jeans.

They glanced up, but showed no interest in him and would have filed past without saying a word if their leader hadn't put up a hand. The men came to what seemed a grudging halt. Standing Crane was surprised by their behavior—if they hadn't been sent to meet him, they should at least show curiosity at his presence.

"You're too late," one of them said dully.

Standing Crane didn't know what to make of that remark; he decided to ignore it. "Hello, brothers," he said, willing to give the white and black men the benefit of the doubt. "My name is Standing Crane. I've come to join the Judgment Lodge."

"We know that," said their spokesman, a lean, dusty-looking native. "But it's too late."

"Why?"

"Because there is no more Judgment Lodge," he said, his tone compounded of sadness and despair.

"I don't understand," said Standing Crane.

"Coyote-with-Wings has ordered the Lodge disbanded. He says he now knows the Lodge was false, that it must be ended. He has ordered us all out of the canyon. He's seen no one in days. We're the last. He's not the same as he was. I think he's dying."

Standing Crane turned this over in his mind. He felt like laughing, though if he did it would be mirthless enough. The sense of anticlimax was deflating—to have spent weeks working up the courage and moral outrage to join this movement, only to arrive just in time to witness its dissolution. "Well. I guess my timing is not the best."

"I don't know. At least you haven't wasted the last nine months of your life."

"Hmm. If you don't mind, I'll go on and have a look at him myself."

The man sighed. "No, I don't think so. Coyote-with-Wings ordered us away. He instructed us to permit no one to approach him. We respect him enough to honor that wish."

Standing Crane nodded slowly. "I see. But I'm a medical doctor. If he is sick, or even if he's dying, I might be able to do something to ease his way."

The six men looked uncertain. Their leader appeared ready to speak, but then turned away with a tear glinting in his eye. He made a gesture. Without another word he and his followers trudged on past him and passed out of sight behind a rock.

"I guess I'll just go look for him, then, hey?" Standing Crane called into the silence.

He turned and continued along the path. This was not among the many scenarios he'd imagined for this day. He'd discounted the fantasy that Coyote-with-Wings might welcome him as a long-awaited disciple, but he hadn't expected to preside over the last moments of the Lodge and perhaps of its founder as well. Not that it was so surprising, considering his previous history. His family, his tribe, even the medical school he'd attended, were gone or in decay. If he didn't like the way the BIA did things, and he didn't, perhaps the subtlest revenge he could take would be to apply for a position there. That should finish it off.

He smiled grimly. The trail crossed the stream via stepping stones. He was thirsty, and the cool water was tempting. But it would be rash to drink from the stream— he'd be asking for a gut-twisting dose of giardiasis.

There were, he admitted, some potential advantages to this situation. The last thing he'd expected was free access to Coyote-with-Wings himself; he'd expected to have to approach him through his senior followers, at least at first. Now it seemed he might be able to question the man directly, to determine for himself how much of his legend was based in truth and how much in the wishful thinking of those like himself who wanted to return to the past.

The trail approached the canyon wall, skirted a narrow rudder of stone that buttressed it, and disappeared into a black tunnel that penetrated the rock.

Standing Crane stopped short. He had no flashlight. If this were an old mine entrance, there was no telling what pitfalls might lie within it. And yet those other men must have come this way, and they'd carried no lights either. He shrugged his shoulders and entered the shaft.

All light was gone within a hundred paces, but the shaft was narrow. Standing Crane guided himself with a hand on either wall. Occasionally he felt what seemed to be more petroglyphs, totally inscrutable in this darkness. Other than those and a few spider webs the walls were fairly smooth. He could only hope that those webs were not occupied by black widows.

He shuffled along, wary of sudden drops, but the floor remained level. He began to suspect this was not an old mine at all, but a recent cutting made by the people of the Judgment Lodge themselves.

Presently the merest glimmer of light returned, turning the walls into a moonscape of shadows cast by protruding grains. Around a gentle curve the exit came into view, an oblong of golden light.

Standing Crane stepped out of the tunnel, blinking and squinting. When the glare subsided he found himself in a secret cleft of the world, the floor of a narrow chasm of great depth and indeterminate length. He looked up at a jagged vein of blue sky. This sunlit hour was surely the canyon's brightest, for those towering walls must bring cool shadows for most of the day.

He walked along a rivulet that dropped down sandstone shelves in a multitude of tiny falls. Footprints disturbed the sand beside it. There were no trees, only a few tamarisks of shrubby stature. The canyon floor was narrow and relatively open. He saw no dwellings, no artifacts of any kind.

After walking half a mile, sometimes lowering himself with difficulty over slippery ledges, Standing Crane grew disgusted. The Judgment Lodge was, it seemed, a will-o-the-wisp. If the fabulous Coyote-with-Wings dwelt anywhere near, he must be using those wings to elude and confound him.

With that thought he turned and looked back along his path. His frown melted into an expression of astonishment. Now that he was beyond the ledges which had concealed it, he saw high in the canyon's wall a huge cave filled by a jumble of sand-colored cubes and cylinders. The adobe structures looked almost new, but somehow Standing Crane knew they had been home to cousins of his, thousands of years in the past.

Now the cliff dwelling was the home of the Judgment Lodge, or so he was convinced. Moving slowly, he retraced his path until he was beneath the cave. Invisible from this vantage, it was hidden by a swelling of the canyon wall which formed a kind of porch for the dwelling. He waded the stream, and soon found a wooden ladder at the start of an upward path. He trusted himself to the ladder despite its creaks and groans. His face was close to the rock. Here were still more petroglyphs, some obviously recent. The most common motif was the profile of a dog's head with manlike eyes and erect pointed ears. Standing Crane frowned. He'd never seen such a design in any native bestiary, though he supposed it must represent Coyote.

The ladder gave onto a short steep path, and then onto another ladder, and soon he had scrambled all the way up to the "porch". He was confronted by the cliff dwelling, now close at hand.

He spotted it almost at once—a doorway curtained by a hanging blanket. He approached quietly, but evidently not quietly enough, for a voice came from behind the blanket.

"Stop."

Standing Crane stopped.

"Go back. Leave me." The voice was dry, hollow, old. It lacked intonation, but to Standing Crane the quiet pain it contained was clear. He stood irresolute and fretting.

"Go. Do not approach me."

Standing Crane cleared his throat. "Sir—are you the one they call 'Coyote-with-Wings?'" He winced, the question sounded so inane.

An answer came, and to Standing Crane's surprise it contained a trace of humor. "Yes, but I don't encourage it. I am William Hermosa."

"Mr. Hermosa, I've come a long way, both physically and emotionally, to speak with you."

The note of humor was gone. "The time for me to speak with other men has passed."

Standing Crane closed his eyes, buffeted by conflicting impulses: his desire to respect Hermosa's privacy vied with his medical ethics and his purely selfish desire to seek the contents of this man's heart. Ultimately he let the medical consideration provide a justification for his need for knowledge.

"Sir—I can't leave yet. I'm sorry."

A long silence ensued; Standing Crane was tempted to go forward and look behind the blanket. He was stopped by the resumption of that dry, feathery whisper.

"Stay if you must. But come no closer."

Standing Crane released his breath. "Thank you. I'm Tom Standing Crane. I've come to join the Judgment Lodge."

He received no reply. Not even the sound of breathing betrayed the presence of any living thing behind that hanging blanket. Again Standing Crane was tempted to sweep it aside, but again he refrained. "Uh—Mr. Hermosa —I was told by some of your followers that the Judgment Lodge has been dissolved. Is it true?"

"It is true."

"But why?"

"The Judgment Lodge—was the fantasy—of an old and foolish man. You see, Tom Standing Crane, within me dwells a spirit that has lengthened my life and brought me power. I thought at first it was the spirit of one of my ancestral gods, come into me so that the old ways of worship could be born again into the world. But now this spirit moves me to do things with no meaning to me or the native peoples. I now deny this spirit, and as I seek to cast it out it consumes me."

The old man lapsed back into silence. Standing Crane tried to reach a tentative diagnosis on the basis of what he had heard. He suspected some respiratory ailment, perhaps tuberculosis. Abruptly shame flowed into him as he realized he was not prepared to take Hermosa's story at face value, despite his pretense of being a follower of the old native wisdom.

"But what of the values of the Judgment Lodge?" he asked in anguish. "Aren't they still valid, even if this spirit isn't what you thought?"

"Tell me, Tom Standing Crane, why you sought to join the Lodge."

Here was a question whose true answer Standing Crane had never articulated, even to himself. Yet before William Hermosa he could not use the glib answers he had offered his family and tribe. Decades of anger spilled out of him as he spoke. "I wanted to stand in judgment over the race that has oppressed and destroyed my people for centuries."

Now Hermosa's dry whisper was edged with pain. "But that was never what the Judgment Lodge was about. I wanted my followers to stand in judgment over themselves, not over others. I wanted men like you to look into their hearts for the wisdom which would quiet their anger. But that was not the goal of many who came to me. And it is not the goal of the thing that lives within me."

Now Standing Crane was desolate. He knew now how misguided he had been, and how futile was his pilgrimage to visit Coyote-with-Wings.

"Have you heard of the Para-men?" asked Hermosa is a curiously thin, avid tone.

Standing Crane was jarred by this non-sequitur. It took him a moment to collect his thoughts. "Yes, I've heard of them." Heard of them, and half-hoped for their victory.

"So has this thing within me," said Hermosa in a more normal voice.

Standing Crane sank down to squat in the dust. He was as discouraged as he had ever been by this utter collapse of his expectations. His faith revealed as a sham; the Lodge dissolved, and not what he'd thought it was in the first place; its master addled and apparently dying. His gaze traced aimless paths in the gravel as he mused on the pass to which his discontent had brought him.

Abruptly he pushed himself upright. Before he left, he could accomplish at least one thing: to use his hard-won medical training to help this man, who still deserved compassion, if not reverence. He stepped forward, pulled down the blanket and cast it aside.

"No!" Hermosa's cry was like a dry, dusty gust of wind. Standing Crane shaded his eyes to better see into the gloom. There sat Hermosa, but the shadows must be deceiving his vision. The old man seemed a withered mummy, his skin a tight grey sheath of parchment dryness, his ears degenerated to mere irregularities on the sides of his head. Hermosa's head swiveled to face him, and at first the eyes were only empty sockets of blackness. But a light kindled there, a light which brooded like an uncertain candle flame before leaping out and crossing the space between them, lodging deep within Standing Crane himself.

He staggered, spun away from the adobe walls. But in a moment his vision cleared, and he walked back to look inside Hermosa's chamber.

The old man was seated on an adobe bench deep in the shade of the chamber. He was motionless, and seemed utterly at home in this environment, as though he were an Anasazi elder awaiting the return of his tribe. Standing Crane approached him quietly, not wishing to disturb what might be sleep on the old man's serene face. His eyes were closed, but his back was as straight as the canyon walls themselves.

Hermosa spoke, and now his voice was almost vanishingly quiet, though it lacked the unnatural quality of dryness it had had before. "Why did you have to come, to spoil my victory over the thing that lived within me? Now I must mourn you, even as I complete the death pilgrimage I began so long ago."

"You needn't mourn me" ventured Standing Crane. "I feel stronger now than I have ever been."

"That is not your strength," came the soft reply. "It is not a strength any man should have. Now quiet, boy. Let me finish my prayers."

Standing Crane retreated and waited for the old man to end his meditation. He studied Hermosa as he waited, finding him human enough, with a weathered toughness to his skin that was usually seen nowadays only in the earliest photographs of his ancestors, the ones that showed men who had lived as they had chosen to live. His iron-grey hair was pulled back and tied at the neck; his face was lean, deeply creased, strong in its contours. He was barefoot, and otherwise clad in a coarse grey tunic tied around the waist, and baggy pants.

Then the old man's eyes opened with as little fanfare as attends the rising of the moon. Standing Crane felt a strange sense of unreality as he looked into that gentle gaze.

"Tom Standing Crane, I tell you to go now, for death is upon me, and I do not wish to be judged by that which you carry within you. I reserve the weighing of my spirit for those gods who raised up my ancestors so many ages ago."

Making no reply, Standing Crane climbed down from the cliff dwelling. His thoughts were calm as he made his way back through canyons and tunnels. His way was serene, for he was unaware of heat, thirst, or weariness.

And as he walked, the thought of the Para-men reentered his mind. But he found that his views on them had undergone a sudden and inexplicable change.

Chapter 27

Dr. Borealis

Ben Raintree set down the case long enough to unzip his jacket. It had been a long time since he'd ventured so far south, and he'd forgotten how ridiculously springlike November could be at these semi-tropical latitudes. Though it was snowing, the air was warm and the snow wasn't likely to stick.

He picked up the case and resumed his ambling course through the streets of Boston. He'd also forgotten the throngs of people who inhabited these huge American cities. He had to watch where he walked, lest his long legs and the awkward case get tangled up in the hurrying hordes of passersby. Most of the men and women around him were expensively dressed. They carried fine leather briefcases, which were in strong contrast to the plywood box he'd knocked together from scraps. Hoping to spruce up its rough appearance, he'd brushed it with a dull green paint left over from refurbishing the interior of a school. But the color had clashed with his cheap vinyl suitcase, so he'd also painted that. Alas, the paint had not adhered well to the vinyl, and now the whole effect of his accessories was rather poor.

People looked him over as he passed, for his was an unusual figure. Tall and gangling, his face was long and rather homely. He had red cheeks against pale skin, and big mournful eyes of chilly green-grey. Oddest of all was his hair, which though cut short was an untidy thatch of stark white spikes, crisp and unruly as hoarfrost.

Ben was alternately oblivious to the attention and embarrassed by it. He already had enough doubts about his presence here without being made to feel like some ungainly, monkish refugee from the North Woods.

Which, in fact, he was.

By now the Lighthouse was partially visible, its great pylon rising into view behind the lesser structures in the foreground. The tower's summit was obscured, submerged in low clouds. The beacon at its very tip was visible only as a diffuse glow. Ben shivered, though not from the cold—it was something about the sight of the luminosity which so softly whitened those clouds.

Presently his march brought him to the threshold of the Vigil's great establishment. Ben paused and studied the complex, trying to imagine the strangeness that lay within it. He half-expected the golden robot to drop twinkling from the clouds, or a wingless flyer to float to a landing on threads of vermillion light. Many of the Bostonians, he noticed, also sent lengthy glances in that direction, their foreheads furrowed, as if they too anticipated some glimpse of the otherworldly.

Ben shook his head. The glamour of the Vigil threatened to fog his thoughts. Maybe he couldn't control his nervousness, but at least he could see to it that his head was clear. With an exaggerated shrug he mounted the broad steps and passed between the pillars that marked the periphery of the Vigil's domain. This outermost zone was a public plaza, filled with gawkers out to study the eclectic collection of exhibits and artifacts which the Vigil provided. He approached the entryway, which lay at the vertex of the structure's two splayed wings. There Ben entered a wide archway, and found a skylight-pierced roof over his head. The transition from outdoors to indoors was gradual. He passed through several portals before becoming aware that he was now well within the structure.

At some point too, he realized, he'd left the public behind. He stood in a silent, empty chamber with two doors: the one he'd entered, and another across the room. That far door was closed, and it was marked with a glowing letter "V".

Ben suddenly wondered if he was in the right place. He turned to leave.

A pleasant, if disembodied, female voice interrupted his flight. "Good morning, and welcome to the Lighthouse. I am Susan Lee, factotum of the Vigil. May I help you?"

"Um...yes, I'm Ben Raintree," said he into the air. "I— have an appointment."

"Certainly, Dr. Raintree, you are expected. Please enter the elevator."

The far door hissed open. Ben approached it gratefully. Susan Lee sounded friendly and cheerful; perhaps his apprehension was unjustified. The elevator car rose smoothly and halted at some unknown height.

The door opened again. Ben took a step and halted suddenly, his pulse hammering. There, in all his glittering splendor, seated behind a desk of incongruous mundanity, was Fomalhaut himself.

Ben stammered uselessly; he could feel his face turning red.

But Fomalhaut spoke in a voice that was reassuringly warm. "Please, Dr. Raintree, step inside. We're happy you've taken the time to visit us."

Without taking his eyes from the strange figure, Ben entered the small office. The elevator closed behind him, cutting off his only escape. There was another door beyond Fomalhaut, but Ben didn't consider it a viable escape route. He looked around.

"Please, hang up your jacket and make yourself comfortable. Take a seat, if you would."

Ben obeyed, resting his case on the floor beside his chair. He looked at Fomalhaut like a deer blinded by headlights.

"Did you have a pleasant journey, Dr. Raintree?" said Fomalhaut.

"Huh? Um, yes, sure, I suppose. I had to make two connections though...no direct flights to Boston from anywhere in Manitoba..."

"Yes, I'm sure it was very inconvenient. The Vigil will be happy to reimburse your expenses. Perhaps you'd care to demonstrate the device you mentioned to us in your letter?" prompted Fomalhaut.

"Oh—yes, of course—I'll get it out..." Raintree bent down and fumbled with the case. He turned even redder as a humiliating loss of self-control threatened to overtake him. His mental image of himself sitting here having this banal conversation with such a prodigy as Fomalhaut was too much for him. He emitted an uncontrollable bray of laughter.

"Perhaps you'd share the source of your amusement with me?" said Fomalhaut mildly.

"Oh...oh, I'm sorry," he choked. "It's just—just that I'm not used to—to speaking to someone with a giant ping-pong ball on his head...!" At that Raintree's hysteria intensified. Hoarse laughter spilled out. He couldn't believe he was saying these things, but he couldn't stop himself either.

"Indeed? Do you feel this is not the optimum presentation of my helmet? I can change its surface characteristics."

Suddenly the helmet lost its flatness and acquired a glossy finish. Raintree's hysteria faded as abruptly as it had arisen. He studied the helmet thoughtfully. "No...I don't think that's any better. Now it looks like a big billiard ball."

"Then perhaps this?" Now the helmet was glossy black.

"No, that's too ominous. Gives you a Darth Vader look."

The helmet lost its sheen, becoming like a disk of utter blackness.

"No, definitely not. That's really scary. Looks like you've got a black hole on your head."

Once more the helmet changed, but now it was silvery and mirrorlike.

"That's good. I can see my reflection. If people look at you and see themselves, they might think better of you."

"Thank you, Dr. Raintree. I consider that a valuable insight. I'll keep my helmet mirrored from now on. It is ironic, though, that the appearance you consider least threatening is actually the most warlike of the lot."

Raintree laughed, this time more moderately. His uneasiness with Fomalhaut had already diminished greatly.

"Now, as to your device—?"

"Right." Ben reached down and extracted a complex silvery contraption. "Here it is...my cryogun. This is a prototype, of course. But it's functional."

"How do you wish to demonstrate it?"

"I can do it right here." Raintree fiddled with the controls. "It'll take a moment to warm up—hah! I'll define a limiting field so it won't damage the building. Okay, I'm ready."

He lifted the device, aimed it at a spot over Fomalhaut's desk, and touched a contact. There was a sharp *pop*, and a small white sphere bounced onto the desk and lay there fuming.

Raintree yawned and swallowed, trying to equalize the pressure in his ears. "Frozen air," he said. "Only a few degrees above zero Kelvin. Absolute zero is probably attainable, but I've held off—I suspect there might be unpredictable side effects associated with the cessation of all molecular motion."

"An impressive invention indeed," said Fomalhaut. "Would you please describe how you came to develop it?"

Raintree sat back and studied the ceiling. "Well, in grad school I was into geophysics, studying the aurora. My partner and I, Thor Sigurdson, alternated between stations in the high subarctic and Antarctica to collect data from both hemispheres. My particular interest was the apparently chaotic variation of form and color which the aurora exhibits. The old explanation involving the interaction between the Earth's fluctuating magnetic field and the variable solar flux didn't satisfy me. The aurora was just too rich—it had too many moods, it flowed, it seemed to express itself as if it were a living thing..."

Raintree's words drifted off; he sat there silently while his eyes fastened on invisible mysteries.

Abruptly he returned to himself. "Uh, I began to wonder if some so-far undetected phenomenon might be affecting the aurora. I thought of gravity waves— theoretically ubiquitous, not yet confirmed, maybe subtle enough and with the correct scale to shape the aurora. I investigated gravity wave detection and got into a program that involved a large gravity antenna. As you probably know, those antennae must be chilled to reduce any interference from molecular motion, which would otherwise swamp the tiny effect of passing gravity waves. I was disappointed by the efficiency and capability of the cryogenics systems then available. That problem stumped me for a long time. Finally I started thinking about tachyons. They seemed a perfectly elegant way of cooling objects, except they couldn't be localized or directed. Once created, they flash out and interacted randomly with matter anywhere in the universe. But I figured out a way to induce a high-decay stickiness factor in my tachyons. Basically, once created they travel for only a picosecond before interacting with the first matter they encounter. The technology was susceptible to miniaturization and perfect for my needs. Then Thor—you remember him—became convinced that the gadget might be of some use to the Vigil, so he talked me into contacting you." Raintree blushed again.

"What was the result of your experiment?"

Raintree's eyebrows went up. "Experiment?"

"To assess the interaction of gravity waves and the aurora."

"Oh. I found no relationship between them. The secrets of the aurora are still her own."

Fomalhaut did not question this odd phrasing. "Dr. Raintree, why have you chosen to offer this technology to the Vigil?"

"You mean as opposed to the Para-men?" Raintree's eyes grew mournful. "Well, in my family, we've always valued personal freedom. And I guess that's what the Para-men ultimately threaten." His face did not relax; he chewed his lip. Fomalhaut sat waiting; both knew this statement was incomplete.

More words spilled out. "But I have to tell you, I'm not convinced that the Para-men are the devils they're made out to be. I'm deeply interested in them, but there's no way for someone like me to get to know them. I thought that by approaching their adversaries, I might indirectly learn something of them as well." Now Ben felt miserable; he'd said far more than he'd intended.

"I see," said Fomalhaut coolly. "Dr. Raintree, I wonder if you would excuse me for a few moments."

"Y-yes—certainly. Uh, do you need to take the cryogun with you?"

"No, that won't be necessary." Fomalhaut stood up, revealing a stature which Ben hadn't suspected, and disappeared through the door in the back of the room.

Ben was left to squirm in discomfort as his imagination devised a dozen scenarios to follow this ill-starred interview. Now that he'd practically declared himself an enemy of mankind, he did not expect to escape from the lair of its defenders unscathed. At the very best, they'd see his cryogun as a useless toy and himself as a mealy-mouthed dreamer of low integrity and doubtful reliability. At worst, they'd see him as a probable traitor whose disloyalty could not be tolerated.

He still had the cryogun, and contemplated using it to fight his way out, but dismissed the idea as absurd. He did go so far as to try to coax the elevator into abetting his escape, but the door would not open.

Ben's throat was dry and his pulse was thready when Fomalhaut reappeared in the room. "Dr. Raintree, please accompany me," he said in an impassive tone. "You may leave the cryogun for the time being."

Ben nodded and stood up. His mind fogged by apprehension, he meekly followed Fomalhaut into another elevator, and was almost unaware of his surroundings as they walked through various halls and corridors. After some interval they entered a chamber where Raintree confronted his doom. There at a circular table sat the rest of the Vigil: the bizarre alien T'Ukudu; the scowling giant Stingray; the deadly Aureus, and their newest member, Tom Standing Crane, a moody-looking middle-aged man. They all stared at him as if his soul were in the balance.

Fomalhaut sat down in an oversized chair. He indicated a smaller one, into which Ben numbly collapsed.

"Dr. Raintree," began Fomalhaut.

"Ben. It's Ben, okay?" said Raintree in a quick flare of unfocused rebellion.

"Ben. We would like to offer you a position here with the Vigil."

Now Ben's head really spun. "A position? I already have a job. I work for—"

"No, Ben, not exactly a job. We are offering you full membership in the Vigil."

Ben emitted inarticulate noises. Finally he sputtered, "Me? You're kidding."

"That's what I thought too, at first," said Stingray. "But we've already taken Fomalhaut's word on Standing Crane, here, and we're willing to believe he sees something worthwhile in you as well."

"But Fomalhaut, I just admitted my ambivalence about the Para-men. Why in the world would you want me as a member? It can't be because of the cryogun."

"It is as you surmise. The cryogun and its related technology, while a useful and impressive achievement, does not by itself qualify you for membership. My interest in you is based on the very ambivalence which you mention. We ourselves know very little about the Para-men. We would greatly prefer to resolve our conflict with them through negotiation. In that case, your neutrality could be invaluable. It could equip you to conduct an objective study of the Para-men, and permit you to interpret your results without being influenced by any preexisting hostility."

Ben frowned uncertainly. "What exactly would be my responsibilities as a member of the Vigil?"

"You would remain a free agent, as do we all. You would be entitled and encouraged to move your headquarters here to the Lighthouse, and to take advantage of our resources. The only restrictions upon you are related to the Para-men. You would be obliged to cooperate with us in our investigation of them. You would be forbidden to take any action on their behalf without the consensus of our group. You would be expected to aid us in opposing any effort they might make to establish hegemony over any inhabited part of the Earth. And in the event of active conflict with the Para-men, you would be obligated to act with us in opposition to them, or to resign and leave."

In other words, I'd be obliged to go to war, thought Ben. He sat there, his eyes glazed, only peripherally aware of the various eyes which awaited his response.

He, Ben Raintree, had the opportunity to stand in the vanguard of the defense of human freedom. He, an ordinary man, had blundered into the path of the arrow of fortune — had been given the chance to join with these superhuman beings to protect the world.

Cousin Leonard would surely be proud.

Beyond all that was a consideration he would not reveal, for fear of showing himself as a mooncalf. Perhaps now he might discover the secret of the green-eyed, silver-haired woman who haunted his dreams, the faerie creature whose face he'd first seen in the curtains of the aurora when he was a boy, and whose beauty had tantalized him anew since the Para-men had appeared on Earth.

Fomalhaut, for his part, would not reveal that in Raintree he'd seen something that the Vigil so far lacked—a truly Human presence, a person simple, whole, and unsullied. Not even Standing Crane could satisfy that lack, not while he was inhabited and motivated by the unsettling presence which Fomalhaut had detected within him. Until the relationship between the two could be undone, or at least understood, he could not consider Standing Crane fully human.

For it was unseemly, even foolish, that an organization charged with preserving the liberty of the Human species should have no representative of that species within its ranks.

Ben Raintree, dreamer and idealist, could fill that role beautifully. And perhaps, ultimately, he would provide another link to the Para-men.

Chapter 28

Casting Call

Fomalhaut entered Stingray's private workshop, where he found the giant hunched over a curious device: a golden cylinder, perhaps fourteen inches in diameter, girdled by three golden awning-like bands. Stingray inserted his fingers beneath one of the bands and watched a display screen with the utmost concentration.

"Stingray. What are you doing? Oh. I see what you are doing. And I approve."

Stingray released the device and looked at Fomalhaut with a grim but satisfied air. "It was T'Ukudu who helped me to regulate my electrical discharge as finely as is required. I hope never to have to use this technique, but if it becomes necessary, I'm ready."

"I find that reassuring. At the moment, though, we're about to convene a meeting of some importance if you'd care to join us."

"I'll be right there."

Fomalhaut next entered Raintree's laboratory. The physicist had made only a partial adjustment to his life with the Vigil in the past few weeks, spending most of his time either wandering around the city or isolated in his lab. There he was engaged in refining his cryogun and reconfiguring it for use as a weapon. While operating it he wore a suit of cold-armor of his own devising, a grey-green and white outfit of surprising flamboyance. Perhaps unconsciously, Fomalhaut mused, Ben took his college nickname of "Doctor Borealis" rather seriously.

"Ben, we're about to begin the meeting."

Raintree peeled off his vacufoam-insulated hood and set down the cryogun. His breath smoked; the side effects of using the gun in the enclosed space had chilled the air to subzero levels. He grazed Fomalhaut with a slightly lost, rather melancholy glance that matched Fomalhaut's perception of his state of mind. "Okay. I'll join you as soon as I secure things here."

Five minutes later Ben wandered into the meeting room and took his place at the table. They were all present, even Aureus, who stood impassively in a corner watching them with glowing eyes.

Fomalhaut swiveled his shoulders to take them all in. "You can see that this table is larger than necessary for the six of us. I propose we seek out others to fill the empty seats."

Stingray shrugged. "Why not just get a smaller table?"

Fomalhaut ignored this. "Adding to our membership from the populace of Earth would carry definite benefits. If we are to convince the people to prefer us to the Para-men, they must trust us. They might do so more willingly if they understood us better. I'm afraid that the average Human still sees us as a rather ungainly collection of—"

"Freaks?" said Stingray acidly.

"That's near enough to the truth. Adding Ben to our ranks has eased this problem considerably. Yet even so, of the six of us, only two appear to be fully Human."

"And we're not too sure about Standing Crane, are we?" said Stingray.

Standing Crane turned an expressionless face on Stingray, holding him with a dispassionate stare that came from a part of him not often awakened. Stingray returned the gaze for a moment and then looked away, subdued.

Fomalhaut resumed, satisfied by Stingray's silent rebuke. "I have here a short list of candidates, and I will also be glad to take any nominations from the rest of you. Candidates must meet two criteria: they must be biologically Human, yet capable of forcefully confronting the Para-men should the need arise."

Ben rolled his eyes and wondered if he really satisfied that second criterion.

"I'll read the names. First: the Pteranodon."

A series of fuzzy pictures appeared on the wall monitors. They showed a man wearing an outrageous-looking costume consisting of huge membranous wings projecting from his wrists and stretching to his ankles, plus a helmet bearing the beak and crest of the pterodactyl whose name he had taken.

Stingray frowned. "I don't think I've heard of this character."

"He operates in remote areas of the Andes Mountains. He can fly, or at least glide, with the help of that suit. He's been known to intervene against criminals and to assist people in difficulty. But he usually just roosts on mountainsides or soars about."

"He wears that outfit all the time?" asked Stingray.

"As far as is known."

"What kind of a man is he?" asked Ben, bemused by the bizarre images.

"Little is known about him, not even his true, or former, identity. He speaks Spanish."

"I would speculate that he is disaffected, and poorly socialized, as shown by his reclusive life style," rumbled T'Ukudu. "He may not fully identify with the human race, as indicated by his disguise. His penchant for swooping down like a vengeful predator on those whom he considers to be wrong-doers suggests megalomania and an overly judgmental character."

"And I'd say he's very small time," said Stingray. "It'll take more than a man in a hang-gliding suit to go up against the Para-men. What would he do once he'd landed? Trip over his wings?"

"So the consensus is to dismiss him as perhaps too alienated to suit our purposes, as well as too vulnerable," said Fomalhaut. No one disputed this assessment. "Very well. Next candidate: the Night Heron."

The monitors went blank; no pictures of this mysterious person had ever been obtained.

"Night Heron. The eco-terrorist," said Ben.

"That is her most common epithet, " agreed Fomalhaut.

"She's a criminal," said Stingray. "How can we consider her?"

Fomalhaut's voice contained an ironic note. "As I recall, you yourself were at odds with the law when I found you."

"I didn't know what I was doing. The Night Heron has been engaged in a systematic program of industrial sabotage for years."

"The Night Heron is a friend of the Earth," said Tom. "She's wise where the white man is foolish. Let's make her one of us and show the people where we stand. Let it be known that we keep a vigil over the life of our planet, as well as over the freedom of her people."

Stingray caught Standing Crane's eye, and this time he did not flinch. "I'm not saying I disagree with Night Heron's goals. But if our intention is to improve our standing with the public, she is precisely the wrong candidate. Americans see anyone who threatens their ability to consume hydrocarbons by the ton as a worse menace than Brainchild ever was. They'll shriek like so many angry gulls if we take in Night Heron."

"I'm afraid Stingray's right," said Ben sadly.

Fomalhaut said, "I agree. While we may well dispute the prevalent wisdom of the Human race, we are constituted to preserve its right to make even bad decisions. We cannot induct Night Heron, yet let us agree not to interfere with her."

"I agree gladly," said Tom. The others nodded, except for Aureus, who made no response.

"It is unfortunate," said T'Ukudu. "Inducting a woman would do more to improve our reputation than inducting any five men."

"That's true," said Fomalhaut. "Let's give special consideration to any female candidates who may emerge. In fact, I would certainly propose your friend Fiona Kalada for membership if she had the requisite physical formidability. Her personal integrity and strength of character are impressive."

Stingray cocked an eyebrow at that assessment.

"She is as you say, Fomalhaut," said T'Ukudu. "However, I'm afraid she would decline membership even if it were offered her."

"Why?"

"She sympathizes with the Para-men and fervently hopes for their victory."

"Oh," said Fomalhaut, seemingly a bit embarrassed. "Next: James Levi."

"The Israeli? The psychedelic telepath?" asked Stingray. "Forget him. We want to reassure people, not drive them insane."

"True. Next—"

Ben brightened suddenly. "Wait! How about my cousin Leonard?"

"Leonard Raintree?"

"No, Leonard Ronar, a cousin from my mother's side. He's an astronomer..." Ben hesitated. "But...no one's heard from him in years. And I suppose...he'd be rather too old. Forget I mentioned him."

"Hmm," said Fomalhaut. "Next candidate: the Flare."

"Please!" exploded Stingray. "Why not suggest Santa Claus while you're at it? I vote we limit the discussion to people who actually exist. The Flare is a legend. Look, why don't we stop playing games? There's only one person who we really want. Let me list the attributes of this candidate: Female. Human, as far as anyone knows. Physically formidable. But so far nobody's had the nerve to mention her name. Permit me to do so: Rouse Farewell."

"The Peregrine!" Raintree gasped. The very name conjured visions of vast, sunlit decks of clouds, of light, wind, and freedom.

Standing Crane's eyes lit up oddly.

Fomalhaut said, "She is indeed a most attractive candidate. Not quite an ordinary Human, but widely admired and trusted. Her presence would do much to enhance our credibility and prestige."

Raintree roused himself from his reverie and turned a puzzled frown on the rest of them.

"But why would somebody like *her* want to join *us*?"

Chapter 29

Peregrine

Having no idea of how to contact Rouse Farewell, nor any real notion of where in the world she might be found, the Vigil perforce gave out a public request that she contact them, though Stingray pointed out the embarrassment they might face should she spurn them. Soon the news that the Vigil sought an audience with the elusive Peregrine was everywhere that radio, television, newspapers, or the internet could reach—no guarantee of success, since she might well be beyond the reach of any of them.

The Vigil awaited a response, which was not long in coming. Indeed, the response came as a flood rather than the single shining droplet they desired, for one of the world's more common delusions was an identification with Rouse Farewell, the Peregrine.

It was up to the Vigil's sizable staff to cull the great majority of calls, letters, visitors, videos, e-mails, decorated cakes, and illuminated manuscripts which were manifestly not the work of the real Peregrine, unless she were a madwoman. Most of the responses at least came from women, but even that wasn't universal—some men had no difficulty reconciling their sex with their imagined identity as Rouse Farewell. In most cases, the signatures on the letters or the appearance of the visitors was enough to disqualify even the saner entries.

That which survived this winnowing, still a considerable volume, was passed on to the Vigil members themselves for their scrutiny and judgment. With varying degrees of good humor they all pitched in, except Aureus, who, even if it had been willing, was deemed too blind to human nature to have any value in this task.

While poring over this material they discovered the thoughts and beliefs of many wise and philosophical people who might have been valuable additions to the Vigil if not for the fatal flaw that they believed themselves to be someone they were not, or at least represented themselves that way. Generally these essays cast doubt on themselves by their sheer length. Often they contained the complete world view and belief system of the sender, explained in loving and elegant detail. T'Ukudu carefully collected these, for he found them invaluable to his sociological studies.

But the main giveaway was the failure to pass the single test of identity which the Vigil had proposed. In a recessed area on the roof of Vigil headquarters they had placed the image of a duck, a common prey of the peregrine falcon. It couldn't be seen from any rooftop in Boston, and shutters were programmed to close over it should sensors detect the approach of any helicopter, blimp, or low-flying plane. A spy plane or reconnaissance satellite might make it out, but the Vigil hoped that those with access to such technology wouldn't be prone to delusion or practical jokes. And indeed almost every response contained some guess as to the image, and a few got it right, but were otherwise so outrageous that they were easily dismissed.

After a few weeks the response declined, and still there was nothing convincing. Occasionally something came in that one or the other of them found believable, especially Raintree, who was more credulous, or perhaps more hopeful, than the others. But none managed to convince the majority, and none survived the scrutiny of Fomalhaut.

They began to fear that Rouse Farewell would never answer their request.

One morning in early spring Fomalhaut sat studying a letter which had arrived weeks earlier, but which haunted him still.

Dear Vigil,
It's a duck. See you soon.

> *Sincerely,*
> *Peregrine Perturbare*

Raintree entered the room holding still another letter. By the look in his eyes, and the sense of his emotions, Fomalhaut knew he was ready to champion yet another possibility. He forbore to sigh.

Yet Ben's words and manner managed to instill a tingle of hope. "I'm not sure why, but I really think this is the one."

Fomalhaut took the wrinkled sheet and smoothed it out on his desk. It was written on flimsy paper. The envelope, smeared and grimy, had a Colombian stamp and postmark. The letter was written in pencil, in a controlled yet graceful script:

Dear Mr. Raintree and Company,
I'm sorry it's taken me so long to reply, but news of the outside world comes to me here only sporadically. In fact, a friend from the lowlands had to make a special trip to tell me of your invitation. I am currently living amongst the Cogi Indians in the highlands above Cienega in Colombia. They have given permission for your group to visit their

city if you wish; I'll leave the makeup of your party to your
discretion. I look forward to an interesting conversation.

> *Sincerely,*
> *Rouse Farewell*

P.S. I'm sorry I haven't identified the picture on your
rooftop. If you'd rather not visit me on that basis, I will not
be disappointed.

"This is it," said Fomalhaut. Raintree beamed as he
took back the letter and put it in his breast pocket.

That very day, the five organic members of the Vigil
boarded a flyer; only Aureus saw no reason to accompany
them. They guided it toward the south, flying over open
water as the coast of North America veered to the west.
Stingray brooded down at the face of the sea, while the
others also kept their silence. Their craft skipped out of the
atmosphere for most of the flight. A thin pink glow of
plasma obscured their view of the coast until they were
deep in the stratosphere. Then they saw the hazy blue-green
vastness which was the great forest of South America,
partly hidden beneath the smokes which marked its
burning.

The little-known Cogi tribe inhabited green mountains
which reared up just inland of the city of Cienega. T'Ukudu
set the flyer down outside their village. They emerged into
thick, sweet-smelling air and stood waiting. Leaders of the
tribe, small white-robed men with straight black hair and
lean faces, marched solemnly over a plank-and-rope bridge

spanning a ravine and giving access to the village. Their gazes were steady and calm as they approached.

Tom Standing Crane studied them in fascination, for these were among the last of his kin who still lived according to the ways of their grandfathers. He knew he'd better look long and well before their ways vanished also. Yet they barely returned his glances, and looked swiftly away from him, in such a manner that Standing Crane was not encouraged to bring his kinship to their attention. A sudden gloom descended upon him.

Fomalhaut and T'Ukudu had taken the trouble to learn the rudiments of the Cogi language, and Fomalhaut of course had the advantage of his natural perception into their minds. But to the others, the greeting of the chiefs was so much gibberish until T'Ukudu began to translate.

"Welcome to the Heart of the World, younger brothers, and newcomers to the Earth. We were told to expect you, though no one knew the exact time of your coming. Our guest is not here, but you may wait. She usually returns at sunset."

Fomalhaut thanked them, and the chiefs studied him with keen eyes, as though the reflective bubble that concealed his face were absent.

T'Ukudu thanked them also, and stepped forward to offer his hand. The chiefs stepped back, peering up at the great figure with some suspicion. But when one ventured a tentative touch his face lit up with surprise, and then laughter. Soon the whole group was crowded about the Servant of a distant race, each lightly touching his arm or hand. Their rapid speech died away as they came to realize the benefits of T'Ukudu's method of communication.

The rest of them stood around, shuffling awkwardly. Even Fomalhaut seemed somewhat abashed. Raintree found himself wondering how they had come to set themselves up as the guardians of men such as these Cogi.

"Can we locate her?" he asked impatiently.

Stingray said, "Maybe we can. Let's try the sensors in the flyer." They entered the cabin, where plaintive electronic peepings echoed the sending of pulses meant to read the traffic in the skies. But Stingray shook his head at the display. "She's not within a thousand miles of here, unless she's imitating the condors." They exited the craft, where Fomalhaut reported no better success with the sensors in his suit.

Then suddenly, without apparent reason, the indians broke off and retreated over the bridge, laughing and looking behind them with a remote humor in their eyes.

"Well," said Stingray drily, "if we should ever suspect that our magnificence overawes the human race, a visit to this place will cure us of that delusion."

"Listen," said Fomalhaut.

Stingray nudged Raintree in the ribs and said *sotto voce,* "The flyer's sensors can't find Farewell within a thousand miles, but Fomalhaut thinks he can hear her coming."

At that moment the proximity alarm in the flyer began to warble.

"I wonder if the rumors are true," whispered Ben.

"What rumors?" asked Stingray, now craning his neck all over the sky.

"The rumors that she—"

Ben's reply was interrupted by a rush of wind caused by a projectile which whistled by in a blur. It looped upward and slowed dramatically, alighting a moment later with perfect grace, a tall, magnificent, naked woman.

"—flies in the nude." finished Ben in a husky voice.

Ben gaped at her, stunned by what he'd just seen, deeply impressed by what he was seeing now. Rouse Farewell had long straight hair of a burnished chestnut color. It floated and flowed as if the winds of the stratosphere were caught within its strands. Her eyes were improbably green—not the gloomy storm cloud green-grey of Ben's own eyes, but the intensely verdant shade of the tropical foliage all around them. Her skin was flawless and silky, a rosy-bronze in color; her strong body was straight and firm, her youthful breasts were outthrust. She was surely the most radiantly beautiful woman Ben had ever seen while wide awake.

And her beauty was further glorified by the light that lit her face and shone steadily in her eyes. She approached them with a smile that weakened Ben's knees; he was hardly able to meet her gaze. Her words, when she finally spoke, were banal enough, yet her voice, a clear contralto made exotic by a New Zealand accent, was an almost painfully perfect complement to her visual impact.

"Hello! How surprising to see you here! I was beginning to think you'd not respond to my letter."

"You may attribute the delay to the inefficiencies of international mail," said Fomalhaut calmly.

"I really do hope you don't mind that I didn't identify the picture you put on your roof. A duck, really...that's rather silly, isn't it?"

No one answered her. She abruptly became aware of the blush that toasted Ben's cheeks, of Stingray's frank expression of interest, and of Standing Crane's impassive but intense scrutiny.

"Oh! Oh!" She laughed. "Please, I'll be back in a moment." She turned toward the village, entered into slow flight as easily as do dreamers, and passed behind the palisade. Moments later she reappeared, but now she was wearing a short white tunic tied around the waist. She landed before them once again. "I'm sorry if I embarrassed anyone, but I've had no success finding clothing that will survive the sort of flying I do." She looked them over one by one, greeting them warmly. Stingray was gallant enough to assure her that he at least was not offended by her display of nudity.

Again she took them in with her bright gaze. "Well, it's quite an experience to be surrounded by such a remarkable assortment of people. I'm certainly curious to learn why you should go to all this trouble to seek me out."

"Miss Farewell," said Fomalhaut formally, "we wish to offer you membership in the Vigil."

At that, Farewell appeared truly taken aback. "Me? Join you lot of world-beaters?"

"We believe you would be an invaluable addition to our ranks."

"Well. That's a matter of debate, and a question of some complexity. My first impulse is to say absolutely not—joining you would be completely contrary to the life I choose to live."

"Naturally, we require no immediate decision, nor do we wish to apply any pressure. However, we do appreciate the opportunity to discuss the possibilities with you."

"Yes, all right. I find that my thoughts usually clear up nicely in flight. Can any of you join me?"

"Of those of us here, only I am equipped for personal flight. If my comrades do not object, I will accompany you and act as spokesman for the Vigil."

The others could not object, though some were tempted. Farewell leaped up and dwindled into the clouds; Fomalhaut followed a moment later, poised on rods of vermillion light.

When both had vanished, Stingray and Standing Crane began a quiet conversation about their newest prospect for membership. Only Ben stood aside, unable to join this discussion. He was bitterly disappointed that he hadn't thought to bring one of their new flying harnesses. Beyond that, he was simply unprepared to put what he had seen into words. Despite all the marvels he'd already encountered, despite the strangeness and mystery of the beings with whom he consorted every day, he'd so far seen nothing to compare with a human woman who, entirely through her own resources of mind and spirit, was able to fling herself into the burning blue. It was enough to quiet all words.

The sun was low as they lifted themselves into an icy network of cirrus, gold and rosy-orange in the sunset beams. They could not go higher, for they must converse, and above them the air was too thin to support the spoken word. They drifted in a remote world of cold and wind, Fomalhaut standing on beams like miles-long stilts, Farewell floating more casually, not distressed by the rigors of altitude, aglow with the great light that permeates such heights.

"I must tell you, Fomalhaut, that for me the choice between the Vigil and the Para-men is not an easy one."

"Indeed? Given what little I know of you, I find that surprising."

"Why?"

"You are considered the living epitome of personal freedom, which is what the Para-men offer to abridge."

She nodded ruefully. "True. But I'm motivated by more than the love of freedom. I also love wisdom, and I see little enough of that in the societies that dominate this planet."

"I do not argue with that. Yet what would you see done about it?"

"I'm not sure. I don't know if the Para-men truly offer any answers; I don't think they've stated their goals with any precision as yet. But I've visited places where they've worked their miracles. They leave behind men and women who are better, clearer-minded, and wiser than they were before. That alone appeals to me greatly."

"We too have studied these 'miracles'. How can you be sure these changes are genuine, and not merely a temporary elation or euphoria induced through some artificial means?"

Rouse smiled. "I think you know more clearly than I that the effect of those jewels, while perhaps 'artificial' in a technical sense, is nonetheless real and not to be dismissed." She cast her eyes downward, suddenly pensive. "For my part, I have stood at both poles of sanity. I know what it is to be deluded, to be insane, and then to find light. Those who have been touched by the Para-men have seen the light, even if it has not yet informed them entirely."

"And what of your own quest for enlightenment? Was it forced upon you, or directed in any way by aliens? Did strangers impose change upon you whether you willed it or not?"

"I don't think so. But my salvation had its root in my willingness to change, to seek. Too many others will make no such effort unless it is imposed upon them."

"What was the source of your willingness to change?"

"It was misery. Dejection. It was my view of life as futile and meaningless. It was an act of desperation. It was, at first, a willingness to change my life into death. But that was not the outcome. Not yet." As she said this she gazed into the realm of prismatic colors which was her domain, as if in wonder that she could ever have been so blind.

"But what if you had been content with your life? What if you'd had faith in the present and future of your species, despite all adversity? Wouldn't you have resented it if aliens had arrived to tell you that human society failed to measure up to their standards, and that those standards must now be imposed?"

"Of course I might have felt that way, if I had been a fundamentally different person than I am. But that person would have been wrong."

"But I assure you, many of your fellow Humans do feel that way. Most, perhaps, if only deep in their hearts. Don't they deserve a chance to seek their truth, just as you have sought and found your own?"

"Of course they do. But must I believe that the Paramen would prevent them from doing so? Should the Paramen achieve their goal, and then turn out to be tyrants, I will oppose them."

"Miss Farewell, I believe that your involvement with the Vigil could be of great importance to the future of the Human race. Thus I pursue that involvement with less restraint than I would normally employ. I hope you'll forgive me if I do not close my eyes to personal truths which you unknowingly reveal. I must ask you this: what was the precipitating event of your search for salvation? What was the crisis that changed your descent into despair into a climb towards liberation?"

Rouse Farewell flashed him a quick, sharp glance. For a moment Fomalhaut was reminded of the avian predator which supplied her nickname. But her serenity returned, and she regarded him calmly, even with a trace of mirth. "I'll not trouble to describe events which you seem to know already. And please call me Rouse."

"Do you regret having attained the state which you have achieved?"

"Of course not. I'm trying to become what I should have been from the beginning."

"Then let me suggest that the freedom which the Human race now possesses, even with all the chaos and wickedness that accompanies it, has been indispensable to your progress. Suppose the Human race were under the domination of an alien government, however benign in intent. Suppose that their rule fostered peace, prosperity, and justice throughout the world. Suppose that your own place in such a world was so comfortable and secure that you felt no compulsion to go beyond what had already been handed to you. Would not that have been a great loss to you, although you might never had known it?"

Rouse Farewell sighed. "You misunderstand me, despite your insights. My need for change wasn't based on deprivation or any external lack. It was driven by limitations within myself. I'm sure I would have felt that same dissatisfaction under any circumstances. But perhaps others might be spared that kind of ordeal by the presence of an enlightened rule."

"Spared? You mean they might be spared the emotional pain and turmoil you suffered on your ascent?"

"Yes."

"And therefore they'd also be spared from casting off their illusions and becoming as you are now."

She said in a very quiet voice, "To my sorrow, I am one of very few in the world to have ever done so. Maybe it's best that the bulk of the people be restrained, to keep their mutual slaughter and destruction to a minimum."

"I see. So freedom is due and necessary to exalted beings such as yourself, but for the common ruck it is at best a troublesome option."

She turned away and hid her face. Fomalhaut could feel the doubts and confusion which roiled her thoughts.

"I see I'm out of my depth in trying to argue with you," she said without looking back.

"I shall be gratified if I prove your superior in that one respect at least."

Fomalhaut awaited her answer.

"What would I have to do?" she asked quietly.

Fomalhaut once more described the obligations of members of the Vigil. He then studied her, as closely as he could without being too obtrusive.

"Something else is troubling you."

She nodded. "These aliens. These Para-Men. I think I know one of them."

That remark, being the last thing Fomalhaut had expected to hear, startled him, reducing him to repeating, "You think you know one of them?"

"Yes. The cloaked one. The miracle worker, as you call him."

"Please explain."

"He called himself Cal. Cal Cotavion, I think it was. We were fellow mental patients, back in New Zealand. I helped him to escape, but then we were separated."

"How extraordinary. Was he an alien?"

"No, I don't think so. He was a bit odd, as you might imagine, but he was human."

"What else can you tell me about him?"

"Not much. You see, I suffered a gunshot wound to the head back then, and it damaged my memories of that time. I can still see Cal's face in my mind, but most other details are hazy and elusive."

"Why do you think this miracle worker and your friend Cal are the same person?"

"I'm not sure they are. But, I think I encountered Cal one more time, in the mountains of Pakistan. There he wore the same guise as what is reported for the miracle man, if it was really him."

"I see. Please do relate anything else you might remember about him."

"My point is, Cal was a friend. If this really is Cal, I will not fight him. I will not harm him. Is that clear?"

"I shall take that fully into account. Do you then accept my invitation?"

"I'd have to live in a city?" she asked in a forlorn tone.

"We ask only that you make our headquarters your base of operations, and that you be available at need. We do not ask or desire any further restrictions of your movements. As I have stressed, all members of the Vigil remain free agents, pursuing their private objectives within the limits of the purpose of the organization."

She turned abruptly back to him and fixed him with a bright gaze. "And what private objectives do you pursue? I mean you, yourself, Fomalhaut?"

Fomalhaut hesitated. "Those are matters best left unrevealed for the time being."

She shook her head. "No, Fomalhaut. You approach me as a stranger, and ask me to trust you to the extent of compromising the way of life that I love. I require an equal trust in return."

"What do you require?"

"Let me look inside your helmet. Tell me exactly who and what you are."

Fomalhaut did so.

A few minutes later they alit beside the flyer, whose grey fuselage glowed a phosphorescent lavender in the twilight.

"Gentlemen," said Fomalhaut, "may I present Rouse Farewell, newest member of the Vigil." He seemed unable to suppress the pride in his voice at this statement.

Chapter 30

Air-Sea Operations

The wharf was grey, weathered, and until recently had been abandoned for years. Despite that it still stank of fish whose essence had seeped into its planks over decades. Its decrepitude was marred by a few modern features: a signpost, bearing the emblem of the Vigil, whose substance somehow shed the spray paint with which informal commentators sought to deface it; a shed containing a small mobile loading crane; and a featureless metal box which might contain anything. So far Stingray's maritime empire was small. Most of his operation was farther up the coast in Maine; here in Boston this single dock met his needs for the time being.

Although this was Vigil property, no effort was made to prevent public access. Therefore it was often used by people who attempted to fish something edible out of Boston Harbor's foul waters. Even on this raw Sunday in March a few lines dangled into the oily swells.

The serenity of the fishermen was broken by the sight of a smooth dome. of water approaching the dock at considerable speed. A moment later a broad fin-like structure broke the water, its wake preternaturally smooth and quiet. This was followed by a rounded surface with a glossy purple-black finish. Only the faintly visible seams of its hull plates convinced the onlookers that this was a vessel and not some cross between a basking shark and a concord grape. It approached the dock at a harrowing speed, then somehow braked to slip in alongside without turbulence or fuss. Only then did it surface fully, revealing a transparent bubble in the bow and a white horseshoe-shaped structure which wrapped around the ship at the waterline, with the open end at the stern. The words *Captain Nemo* were written there. On the hull itself was the sign of the Vigil, as well as a personal emblem, a ray with coiled tail.

A hatch just aft of the fin hummed open, and out clambered Stingray, oblivious to the stares of the watchers on the dock. He was followed by his three-person crew of oceanographers, who all looked tired but elated. They fixed a gangway in place and climbed up to the dock, where they congratulated each other and agreed to meet in the morning to unload their specimens. The three then wandered off, talking and laughing, while Stingray, opening the box on the pier by some unobservable means, used the controls within it to submerge his new prototype research submarine for safekeeping.

That done, he looked at his departing crewmates, then glanced at the distant Lighthouse. Feeling pensive and subdued, he searched the sky, but saw there nothing but airplanes. Noticing the fishermen, he walked up to examine their catches with a critical eye. They all but cowered as he walked among them, imposing in his customary colors of black and blue-green trimmed with silver.

But they need not have been intimidated. Stingray's scowl was reserved for their paltry catches. "Pathetic," he said. One especially gruesome specimen, a small batfish with tattered, ulcerated fins, caught his eye. He fixed those blue-black pools of eyes on the fish's captor. "Do you mind if I take this fish in for analysis?"

The man could only shake his head.

"Good, thanks." Stingray reached into the bucket and brought out the batfish, finding to his surprise that it was still alive. Instantly his grip became gentle, and his face showed uncertainty. He turned back to the fisherman. "I'd like to buy your bucket. If you'll show me a credit card, I'll have a fair price credited to your account."

The man fumbled out his wallet and showed a card. Stingray glanced at it and nodded. He turned and ambled off with the batfish drifting in its bucket. A small automated flyer landed nearby. Stingray entered it for the hop back to the Lighthouse.

The Lighthouse seemed deserted, or at least no one showed up to greet him. After dropping off the batfish in his lab, Stingray wandered through the tower's upper corridors, their broad windows admitting the late afternoon light. He halted and leaned against the glass, studying the vista outside, pondering the source of his melancholy.

The overcast was beginning to break up, revealing patches of pale green sky beyond the scudding grey. Beams of orange sunlight sometimes broke through to enrich the stillness of the corridor. The sun would set in minutes. Stingray decided to keep watch in case the Green Flash might be seen through clouds and murk.

Vigil Plaza was unusually crowded. Ranks of people stood gazing skyward, apparently expecting something to happen. Stingray felt no sense of enmity from them. Well, this was different...

An unfamiliar humming caught his attention. Frowning, he walked along the corridor seeking its source. The tower was quite narrow at this level; he reached its east side before finding the source of the sound. He stuck his head into a small room he'd never visited before, which was completely empty. A large window in the outside wall was sliding open, admitting gusts of chilly air. He stepped inside, still puzzled, approached the window, which was now fully open, and was about to look out. He heard a rising cry of joy from outside. With a rush of wind he was knocked backwards by some projectile which threw him hard against the inside wall.

A high, distressed voice called "Oh no! I didn't see you —the sun was in my eyes—I never expected to find anyone in this room—are you all right?" And there was Rouse Farewell standing over him, offering her hand as he sprawled on the floor. He accepted the hand; she hauled him upright without effort, leaving her hand at rest on his arm.

He grinned ruefully down at her. "I'm all right. A little out of breath. Hello, Rouse."

"Hello! Oh dear, you did begin your cruise before we made this arrangement for my entry. No wonder you didn't know about it."

"Yeah. We'd better put up a sign. 'Danger, low-flying women'." He studied her, noting her brief, close-fitting outfit of russet and pale grey. "I see you've solved the problem of keeping your pants on in flight."

"Ha! Yes, and about time, too" she said, glancing out at the crowd which was dispersing outside. "Actually, it was Ben who took the time to fit me with this."

"That was certainly a sacrifice on his part. How have you been getting along here?" His curiosity was genuine; the *Nemo* had been launched only a few days after Rouse's arrival, and he'd had little chance to get to know her.

"Oh, all right," she said, nodding thoughtfully. "Not quite used to being such a—public spectacle." She waved her hand towards the window, then looked at him again.

"Are you sure you're quite all right? That was quite a jolt I gave you."

Stingray chuckled dismissively. "I'm fine. I may have a Peregrine-shaped bruise on my chest by morning, but that's all. I'm not rated for hypersonic flight, but I am more durable than most."

"Absolutely!"

Stingray eyed his unexpected companion. Now that his vision had cleared, he noticed she was holding a strange object in one hand. It appeared to be a large mass of feathers. He pointed. "What's that?"

"Oh, that. It's a duck. A dead duck. Yes, I know."

"Where did you get it?"

"I'm so embarrassed. I'm afraid you're not the only creature I've collided with today. I smacked into this poor thing on my way in. So careless."

"What are you going to do with it?"

"I'm going to eat it."

"Really?"

"Yes. I don't want its life to go completely to waste. So I'll eat it. I wouldn't normally. I realize my notions on this subject are a bit fuzzy, but I'm just trying to make the best of the situation."

"Well, it's a good thing you didn't kill me then. You could never choke me down. I don't mean that the way it sounded. I just got back here myself, and I'm starving. Would you like company?"

"Yes! I'm famished too."

The Vigil's private kitchen and dining area was an afterthought, left to its most nearly human members, since Fomalhaut did not eat, and T'Ukudu was content with ingesting nearly any kind of organic matter. It was among the few working rooms in the Lighthouse which would not have disoriented the average American.

Stingray watched in bemusement as Rouse went about preparing the duck for cooking.

"Now I'm pretty sure I've seen everything," he said.

"How do you mean?"

"One of the most famous and mysterious women in the world, plucking a duck."

Rouse laughed. "This much I'm sure I need to do. We'll see about the rest. I'm far from an expert at preparing fowl. I can already see it will be a messy process."

It was indeed a messy process. "Bugger all! This is putting me off my appetite a bit."

"Same here."

"Do you think I should chop off his head?"

"I think so. He's giving you an accusing look."

"Ugh, look at some of the rubbish he's been eating!"

"I'd rather not."

In the end, Rouse cleaned the bird adequately, though bits of down would be wafting around the kitchen for the foreseeable future. Finally she popped the duck into one of Raintree's inventions, a tachyon-based oven designed to impart heat into every part of an object simultaneously, essentially the reverse of his cryogun technology.

After a few more minutes they sat down opposite each other at the table. Stingray had a big salad, a bowl of mixed beans, and a huge platter of pasta. Rouse attacked her duck with vigor, tearing it apart in her hands. She ate unselfconsciously until she noticed Stingray eyeing her as he munched his greens. Then she laughed and dropped the bird onto her plate.

"Oh, I'm sorry. I must seem a perfect barbarian, tearing into animal flesh like some crazed jackal. I'd heard you were a vegetarian, though to tell the truth you don't look the type."

Stingray shrugged and shook his head. "It's just a personal quirk of mine. I don't go around ranting about it like a zealot. Go ahead and enjoy your dinner."

She picked up the duck and did just that. After a moment, Stingray added, "I suppose I'm also surprised that you're willing to make this exception to your own diet, given your reputation...for compassion."

Rouse smiled again. "Surely I mustn't think of such low-key proselytizing as 'ranting'! But there are those who would argue that it's part of life. Life eats life; life comes out of death. It's one of the basic facts of the universe. If you deny it, you're really rejecting your place in the order of nature."

Stingray responded with a surprisingly ingratiating grin. "Rejecting my place in nature is not exactly out of character for me." The smile faded. "And I do so happily. Lions and lambs may not have any choice about how they live, but we sentient beings are able to opt out of the law of the jungle. Life is savage enough without my dietary whims adding to the carnage."

Rouse Farewell kept on eating, rather more delicately now, as she held Stingray's gaze with her bright, quizzical, impossibly green eyes. "It was an accident."

Stingray abruptly lowered his head. "Ouch. I'm sorry. So much for my pledge against ranting. I should have quit while I was ahead."

Rouse laughed. "Zealots so rarely do. How was your cruise?"

"It was great. Fine," said Stingray, grateful for the change of subject. "It was gratifying to have the new sub work so well. And it was good to get back to the sea. I was foolish to think I should abandon it entirely. It was as if you should decide never to walk on land again. But it was sure nice to explore the ocean in a comfortable ship instead of slogging through the water under my own power like some malformed seal. And it was nice to have a place to come back to when the voyage was over."

"Where did you go?"

"All over the North Atlantic. We explored some submarine canyons and the Mid-Atlantic Ridge. We investigated some submarine wreckage. We discovered about fifty new benthic species, some of them real monsters."

He halted and attended to his meal. Still looking at his plate, he said "How have you occupied yourself since you've been here? Has it been a big change for you?"

"Yes, very much so," she said in an ambivalent tone. "The world presses in on me so much more than it did before. The pain and confusion of the city is all around. I can't escape word of all the perils and tragedies which afflict the people. That's a weakness of mine—once I become aware of such things, I can't help trying to do something about them. I've been flitting around like a hummingbird, intervening in various affairs. Just today I rescued some Mexican boatmen from a storm, and searched for a group of children who were lost in the jungles of India. I also roughed up a squad of army brutes in Guatemala—I got so angry after hearing a radio report about their cruelty." Her brow furrowed slightly as she nipped at her lower lip.

Stingray regarded her in open astonishment. "You see all that as a weakness?"

"Yes. Long ago I learned the peril of trying to separate people from their fates, or to spare them the consequences of their own actions. Sometimes a superficial good is done, but often the harm is greater over time, and the lessons which the universe has labored to provide are lost. I suppose that's what led me to join the Vigil in the first place —the desire to prevent the Para-men from shielding humanity from whatever reckoning its deeds may have earned it. Oh, what a busybody I've become."

"You know—your reputation is pretty much that of a superhero of sorts. Now you're telling me you've always tried to avoid those situations?"

"Yes, yes. I butt into those situations only when they are thrust into my face and I just can't stand to ignore them."

They resumed eating, Stingray pondering these revelations in silence.

Rouse said, in a brighter voice, "Stingray—tell me about the sea."

He looked at her quizzically, and she said in explanation, "The deep sea is the only part of the world where I can't easily go. I'm all but blind there, and I can't really fly through stuff as thick as water. But for those very reasons I've always wondered what secrets are there."

"If I tell you, will you teach me how to fly?"

Again she showed her perfect teeth. "Are you asking to become my disciple? I must warn you, I've had them before, and I've always failed to bring them to the point where they dared leap from a cliff."

"Hmm. I might try it, as long as there was some good deep water down at the bottom. Maybe you can offer me some pointers on flying some day. All right then, the sea. Are you finished eating?" he asked, indicating a small skeleton from which every scrap of flesh had been flensed.

Rouse nodded innocently.

"Why don't we go to my lab then."

They entered a lift and descended to a level where the Lighthouse was of greater diameter, a level occupied by science facilities in high-ceilinged chambers. Stingray's area was largely occupied by tanks of cold salt water and the creatures which inhabited them. The room was darkened to simulate night for the pelagic and shallow-water animals. Many of the other tanks were pressurized; they were normally covered to spare their denizens the glare of room lighting. For they were creatures of the abyss, few of which had ever been seen alive outside of their natural domain. Stingray touched a contact and the panels around their tanks slid out of sight.

Rouse gasped and stared at a bewildering variety of creatures fanged, finny, sinuous, spiky, and tentacled. Some were visible primarily by the light of their bioluminescent spots or organs, while others were almost invisible by reason of their being as transparent as glass. Still others were impossible to define, and seemed unrelated to any creature of Earth: segmented tubes perched on many stilt-like spines; pulsing toroidal jellies which trailed billowing parachute-like snares; rippling boomerangs of flesh covered with spots that glowed and flickered in kaleidoscopic patterns.

Rouse wiped the condensation from the biggest of the deep-sea tanks, pressed her face to the glass, and cupped her hands around her eyes to keep out the faint room light.

"Most of these animals were completely unknown to science," murmured Stingray from beside her. "Even the correct phylum of some of them is in doubt. And the sea is full of other creatures as strange, as alien, as these. A lot of them are too big to fit in a tank. We're only beginning to understand the range of life that comes from the ocean."

Rouse glanced up at him with arched eyebrows. "So am I."

Even more quietly he said, "You know, for as long as I can remember—which isn't really very long, it's true—I've wanted to go beyond the Earth and visit the stars, to learn what shape reality takes in places so remote that Earth isn't even a rumor. I'm grateful I can at least cruise the cold blackness of the ocean, and find forms of life as strange as any that might arise in another galaxy."

"Who can say that you shan't achieve your dream?" she said in a distant voice. "You certainly have the proper friends, and even the proper opponents, for it someday to come to pass."

"I'm quite sure I can't count on my enemies to help me reach the stars," said Stingray with sudden bitterness.

Rouse looked up at him in perplexity. She stepped away from the tank and glanced at some of the others. In one she discovered a tattered batfish swimming in listless isolation.

"What's happened to this fellow?"

"Oh," said Stingray, now embarrassed, "I'd intended to dissect him for analysis, but then I found out he wasn't quite dead—so I thought I'd bring him back here to see what I could do for him."

Now Rouse looked at him as if seeing him for the first time. Stingray was astonished to find himself blushing under her scrutiny.

"He's in bad shape—probably won't make it anyway —" he muttered lamely.

Rouse stepped up and gave him a punch in the shoulder. "You big softie."

Stingray's face shifted through a dozen emotions. Then he winced as he massaged the site where the Peregrine had landed her playful blow.

Rouse looked at him with feigned innocence. "Stingray...if your friend here should die...may I eat him?"

Stingray burst out laughing. "Rouse, if he dies, I'll fry him up for you myself, if you think you can stomach him."

"I think I could."

They stood there for long moments, gazing speculatively into each other's eyes. Stingray reached out, not quite sure what he meant to do.

At that moment the door slid open. Ben Raintree entered and looked uncertainly from one to the other. "Hello, Rouse. Stingray, I just came by to welcome you back from your voyage."

Stingray took a step away from Rouse. "Thanks, Ben."

"Well, Stingray," said Rouse, "it's been an interesting conversation. We must resume it sometime."

"Fine with me."

She left, the door sliding shut behind her.

Ben looked at up Stingray. "Ah—I didn't interrupt anything here, did I?"

"Between me and Rouse? Don't be silly," Stingray said brusquely. "We're not even members of the same species."

Raintree continued to look uncertain.

The Vigil

Chapter 31

Endurance

The sun was low as the canoe ground to a halt against the ice, unable to find further passage. The man within it tied the paddles to the thwarts, hopped onto the ice, and hauled the canoe out of the water. He inverted it and carried it on his shoulders, just in case the pack ice should thin out again and he could use it once more. But he saw no more open water, and after fifty miles the jumbled ice was piled so high it became difficult to climb it while carrying the canoe. He set it down, debating whether to destroy it and so avoid cluttering this pristine place, but decided to leave it intact. Possibly some future wanderer might come upon it in a time of need, especially as the seaward flow of the ice shelf carried it back toward open water.

Free of the awkward burden, his progress was easier. He mounted the shelf until at some point the seawater far beneath his feet was replaced by rock, putting him on the continent of Antarctica proper. Still the ice continued to climb steadily, rising toward the great ice plateau in the interior. He did not bother to skirt the intervening mountain ranges, but climbed directly over them, never slowing. Whenever he encountered a crevasse he usually jumped across it unless it was very wide, in which case he would fall to the bottom and climb back up the other side.

He was naked, as the clothing he'd worn when starting out from South Africa hadn't survived the ravages of cold salt water and his indefatigable paddling. His brown hair was crusted with white, some of it salt from the spray of ocean storms, some of it ice.

Without pause or rest he walked on. The sun gradually declined, its sojourns below the horizon growing deeper and longer, until he experienced brief nights of full darkness between long twilights. Opposite them were a few daylight hours with a wan sun hovering over the glittering horizon.

The ice grew thick enough to bury all but the highest peaks as he approached the so-called "pole of inaccessibility" deep in the interior of the continent. There at last a landmark appeared on the horizon, the first notable break in the icy landscape he'd seen in days. At first it was only an irregular silhouette like an array of inverted icicles, but as he neared it its true nature was revealed.

Dusk came down with a cold indigo light, warmed only by the soft glow of the Para-men's polar redoubt. High-towered, jewel-like, glistening, it was a faerie city grander and more beautiful than any work of Man he'd ever seen.

And he had seen them all.

He halted, studying the fortress with a pensive gravity.

Light diffused upward from the snow at his feet, a heatless luminosity that formed a path to the fortress. He followed it, and found admittance.

Chapter 32

Carina

The Vigil sat in council, listening while Fomalhaut summed up their progress to date.

"In the two years during which our organization has been in existence, we have learned almost nothing about the Para-men. The only one among us with direct knowledge of any of them, our friend Aureus, has for its own reasons refused to divulge much of it."

They all looked at Aureus, who as usual stood aloof in a corner of the room, showing no susceptibility to their disapproval.

"We know that Valjhar Cor, their leader, and two others are natives of the planet Rral, whom Aureus is charged with apprehending. Valjhar's is the only name we can attach to any member of the Para-men. Beyond that our knowledge fails almost entirely. We believe some of the Para-men, or at least some of their agents, are humanoid. We have seen examples of their capabilities, exhibitions of powers which we do not fully understand. I find it almost embarrassing to recite this paucity of information, so quickly can it be told." Fomalhaut seated himself. T'Ukudu rose in his place.

"Our ignorance is based largely on the fact that the Para-men have been so passive. They rarely emerge from their headquarters. Their efforts to dominate and reshape this planet's society have been inexplicably meager. So far their only large-scale action was their effort to establish a "prototype ideal civilization" on the island of Madagascar. Yet when challenged by us they were quick to back down. Other than that single, unambitious advance, they have limited their activities to disseminating propaganda via their direct-broadcast satellites."

Standing Crane interrupted. "Let's not forget that this 'propaganda' includes precious information on health and nutrition for poor people all over the world."

"Yes, it is fascinating to watch as aliens who are evidently newly informed of the details of human biology take it upon themselves to instruct those who have inhabited this planet for millennia. Yet I do not deny the value of this information."

"Let's face it," said Stingray. "The Para-men's broadcasts may not be as entertaining as the stuff Brainchild used to transmit, but it's certainly the most useful television there is."

"True," said Fomalhaut, "except that it is couched in constant hints that Humanity would be so much better off if it placed its welfare entirely in the hands of the Para-men."

T'Ukudu continued. "Of course, the Para-men do occasionally appear in public, at least in small groups, to work 'miracles' by some power which, again, we do not understand. Unfortunately, these appearances are so unpredictable and so fleeting that we have been unable to attend one, despite Aureus's energetic attempts to do so. The Para-men are certainly more aware of our movements than we are of theirs.

"I have studied these 'miracles' and their effects on the Human race as a whole. I tell you that only Rouse's untiring humanitarian efforts result in the Vigil being accorded an esteem comparable to that of the Para-men. In that sense she has already prevented our defeat."

Stingray shot an approving glance at Rouse, who sat beside him. She only rolled her eyes.

T'Ukudu said, "We must consider the Para-men's inaction to be a major mystery. We must admit to almost total ignorance of their motivations and intent."

The meeting continued, with various members standing to raise their unique concerns. Through it all Ben Raintree said little. He had work to occupy him, but unlike some of the others he didn't care to devote his every conscious moment to it. Rouse, in those few hours she spent at the Lighthouse, was usually in Stingray's company, and Ben did not see the need of a third wheel. It was enough to make Ben wish he were a foot taller and three hundred pounds heavier.

When the meeting was over, Ben moped around, trying to decide whether to tinker with his cryotechnology or continue his desultory attempt to delimit the Para-men's technology by extrapolating from those few manifestations of it they'd been able to observe. But finally he decided to throw off work for the day. As long as he was forced to dwell in a city, he might as well take advantage of what attractions it had to offer. Seeking companionship, he first paged Rouse, but was not surprised to find that she'd flown the coop as soon as the meeting was over. Stingray was busy with fluid dynamics computer modeling. Fomalhaut? No—Ben felt a little embarrassed by his own self-pity, and didn't wish to expose himself to Fomalhaut's scrutiny and inevitable counsel, sure to be calmly delivered, kindly intended, and ultimately powerless against the waywardness of the human heart.

That left T'Ukudu. He too had left the building, but Ben decided to give him a call anyway.

"T'Ukudu, it's Ben. I'm planning to visit the fine arts museum today and wondered if you'd care to join me."

"Ben, I am in transit to Russia, where I intend to study the economic upheaval which prevails there. Otherwise I would join you. I suggest you ask Tom to accompany you."

Standing Crane? Oddly, Ben hadn't even considered asking him. After pondering the idea for a few moments, he was forced to admit he could find no reason not to. With a reluctance he was unable to explain he paged the Lakota doctor. "Tom? It's Ben. I was wondering if you'd like to take a break and go with me to the art museum."

Standing Crane sounded surprised by the invitation. "The art museum? All right, why not? Sounds like a good idea."

A few minutes later they were walking together down Huntington Avenue. For Ben it was the most oppressive sort of summer day, hot and brilliant with sunlight blasting mercilessly from a cloudless sky. He wore shorts and a T-shirt, the only outfit he could endure on a day like this.

Standing Crane appeared more tolerant of the heat. He wore jeans and a nondescript grey shirt; a red bandanna was wrapped around his brow. They made a conspicuous pair, though not as conspicuous as any two other Vigil members would have been. In any event, few passersby paid them overt heed, and if anyone recognized them as agents of the Vigil they did not make it plain.

"Ben, thanks for thinking of me. You know, old as I am, I've never been to an art museum."

"Really?"

"Yeah. There's no good reason for it. There just aren't too many of them around the Lakota rez."

"So, Tom, how have you been occupying yourself lately?" asked Ben in a desultory attempt at small talk.

"Oh, I've been real busy," said Standing Crane enthusiastically. "I've got so much to learn. For one thing, med school doesn't cover the kind of technology we've got available to us. I'm getting to where I can use the computers more effectively than they use me." He chuckled; Ben smiled wanly.

"But mainly I've been concentrating on finding out what I can do." Tom's eyes took on a peculiar intensity as he looked aside at Ben.

Ben swallowed. "And what *can* you do?" Here was a question he'd never heard anyone answer to his satisfaction.

"So far—I haven't failed to do anything I set my mind to. I look into people's hearts. I see into darknesses, into mysteries. And I've grown strong. I used to be a diabetic— now, there's no trace of that. I feel like I did at twenty— better. Nothing phases me. My feet have wings. When William Hermosa died, he passed me a spirit of greatness. In adding its strength to mine I have become happy. I have found my task in life, and that knowledge brings me peace."

To Ben it seemed that Standing Crane was a bit too insistent about how happy and confident he was. His eyes showed a glassiness that hinted at stresses and pressures he would not acknowledge or describe.

Ben shuddered suddenly. Whatever it was that Standing Crane carried within him, whether it was some part of William Hermosa or something else, Ben couldn't help but be glad it resided in Standing Crane and not in himself.

Standing Crane, Ben knew, was one member of the Vigil whom even Fomalhaut did not understand.

They approached the museum. Ben's spirits lifted when he saw the banner proclaiming an exhibition of landscape paintings by Frederic Church. Ben thanked fate for prompting him to visit the museum while one of his favorite artists was on display. They entered the relative coolness of the lobby. Ben wanted to head directly to the Church exhibit, but their path took them through the Antiquities wing, where Standing Crane tarried.

Though Ben was surprised at the extent of the Egyptian collection, he wasn't as fascinated by it as Tom seemed to be. Tom seemed bemused, wandering among the exhibits like a sleepwalker. After twenty minutes he settled before a case full of small objects. Ben came over to see what had riveted his attention so, and found his gaze locked on a blue faience figurine of the god Anubis.

"I've never seen anything like this," said Tom in a low voice. "Yes I have. I saw rock carvings that resembled this figure in the canyon of the Judgment Lodge. But those carvings were new."

Tom looked around the room, then was drawn toward a sarcophagus carved from grey stone. His hand moved toward it, but was withdrawn when the gesture attracted the attention of the guards.

Ben began to fidget with impatience and unease. Standing Crane noticed. "Ben, I really want to stay here for a while. Why don't you go off on your own. We'll meet again later."

Raintree readily agreed. With long strides he left the dust of ancient superstitions behind him.

It had been so long since he'd seen an original Church painting that he'd forgotten their impact. The gallery was arranged in bays, to isolate each painting so as not to overwhelm the viewer. The walls were black, and the lighting dim except for the spotlights that shone on the paintings. Each bay contained a single huge canvas that went beyond realism in its use of light and color. The sheer scope of the scenes they depicted was breathtaking — deep, expansive landscapes with the richness and mystery of worlds conjured in dreams.

Ben was drawn first to an immense vista of opalescent icebergs floating on a polar sea. From there he encountered great Andean volcanoes, titanic waterfalls, and Adirondack sunsets burning with colors so fiery he would not have believed they could come from tubes of paint.

His head was spinning by the time he approached the end of the exhibit. His gasps and expressions of wonder fetched smiles from those whose interest in art was more casual.

But the final painting swept away all his confusion and replaced it with the quiet clarity of the northern night. Here was an evocation of the spirit of the Aurora such as he'd never seen — luminous draperies of icy green, pale gold, and red, casting a flickering glow over a landscape of ice and mountains. Indeed, this painting evoked so strongly the character of Ben's native haunts that tears of homesickness threatened to embarrass him.

Even as he stood blinking before this grand dreamscape his attention was diverted. The back of his neck tingled; the fine hair of his nape stood up. Someone was watching him. He felt a sudden conviction that he would turn to discover answers to some of the most troubling questions of his life.

Keeping his expression under careful control, he turned around. Several people were looking on, but his gaze went no further than the woman who stood nearby studying the painting with calm eyes. While they were not the solid mint-green orbs he remembered from his dreams, theirs was still an intense, almost auroral green. Her skin was smooth and pale, and her hair had the silvery whiteness of moonlight on snow. Dressed in silver, white, and blue, her moonstone necklace glimmered softly on her breast.

Now that he stood facing this apparition in a waking state at last, Ben feverishly tried to figure out how to address her. For her part she ignored him, coolly examining the painting while she waited for him to defeat his awkwardness. Finally Ben decided he could do no better than to simply speak from his heart, and let the truth of it emerge.

He stepped closer to her and said in a low, tremulous voice, "You've haunted my dreams for so long. Sometimes I feared you were only a creature of my imagination, but here you are at last, clothed in flesh. What have you come to tell me?"

She swung those peridot eyes upon him and regarded him with remote appraisal. The moment of silence stretched into exquisite torture before her pearly lips finally parted.

"Take a hike, you dumb jerk."

Ben's breathing locked up. He suddenly noticed she was wearing colored contact lenses, and that her hair was bleached platinum blonde, softened to moonlight by the light in the bay. She grimaced at him, turned, and walked away.

Ben thought for a moment he might faint from dashed hopes and humiliation, but managed to stay on his feet. He turned back to the painting and squeezed his eyes shut as hot embarrassment flooded through him.

After a moment a wry but gentle voice commented from beside him, "Well, that's obviously a woman who's never heard a truly sensitive pickup line before."

Ben gave a honk of uncontainable laughter and opened his eyes. Two young men, roughly his own age, stood there smiling at him. "I thought she was—oh, never mind, it's crazy." He swallowed to moisten a throat that had gone cotton-dry.

The three of them were now alone in the bay. The taller of the two said, "You're Ben Raintree, aren't you? Of the Vigil?"

Ben nodded resignedly; he had hoped to go unrecognized. "That's right."

"I'm Jim Carina, and this is Kern Harner."

"I'm happy to meet you. I wish I had someone like you around to defuse my embarrassment every time I make a fool of myself. Where are you from?"

"I'm from Ireland; Kern here is a graduate student from India."

Carina was slim, of average height, and pale, with dark brown hair and engaging eyes of a warm grey. Kern Harner was decidedly more exotic. Considerably shorter, his skin was brick-red in color, his hair straight and jet black. He had dark eyes in a round, boyish face.

"We've only just arrived," said Carina. "Why not walk with us as we tour the museum?"

Raintree shrugged. "Sure, why not?" After his disappointment he was glad of congenial company, especially since these men had in some sense shared in his downfall. For the next two hours they explored the museum's paintings and drawings. Ben found it enjoyable, not least because of Kern Harner's rhapsodic critiques.

"It's a regal harmony of color," he said, taking in a canvas with a grand gesture. "A spinning, dismaying, almost aberrant rotunda of labyrinthine hues and reflectivities. This fleck of lapis blue—it's enough to reveal the celestial depths behind the banal exterior of her face. I know this girl—we walk together in a love of words, of images, of poetry."

Ben looked closely, trying to see all this in what seemed to him a rather stiff portrait of a little blue-eyed girl. He gave Harner a quizzical glance, but saw in those sparkling eyes only sincere enthusiasm. Kern was flushed, almost giddy with excitement, his enjoyment so evident that Raintree didn't mind his effusiveness, while Carina treated him with an affectionate tolerance.

Jim Carina was more reserved in his appreciation, but also more thoughtful, or so it seemed to Raintree. After Harner had finished enthusing about a painting of three boatmen menaced by sharks in a stormy sea, Carina stood before it for several minutes after the other two had moved on. Raintree noted his pensive expression, wondering what memories he was reliving.

When they'd seen much of the museum, and even Harner seemed overloaded with images, Carina said, "Ben, how about joining us for something to eat?"

"Hmm. That sounds good. But I almost forgot, I came here with somebody else, Tom Standing Crane. I'd better find him and tell him what I'm doing."

"Standing Crane? That's interesting. We'll wait here while you go find him."

Ben walked away; behind him he thought he heard Harner laughing with—relief? He searched the antiquities wing for Standing Crane but did not find him. Thinking

Tom might be waiting for him by the main entrance, Ben went there and glimpsed him in the museum gift shop. He entered to find Standing Crane just stepping away from the checkout counter.

"What have you got there, Tom?" he asked, eyeing the bag.

"Just a couple of trinkets." With a big smile on his face Tom opened the bag. First he extracted a blue figurine of a jackal-headed figure. "It's Anubis. Pretty good reproduction, isn't it?"

Ben nodded.

"I don't know why, but it just caught my eye. I also got this." He pulled out a small brass object. "A caduceus, the white man's emblem of my profession." He laughed as he displayed the two symbols for Ben.

"Uh, Tom, I met a couple of people here, and I've decided to go out to dinner with them."

Standing Crane looked surprised. "Oh? Well, that's fine. I'll see you later at the Lighthouse."

"You don't mind? Would you like to join us?"

"Oh, no, not this time."

"Okay, if you're sure."

"Ben, thanks again for thinking of coming here today. It was fascinating." He gave Ben a slap on the shoulder.

Ben walked away, feeling that he was somehow treating Tom badly. Standing Crane was a genial man who'd never offered him anything but friendship. Ben couldn't understand why he found it impossible to warm up to the man. It wasn't Tom's fault that he gave Ben the creeps... was it?

No, it was more than that. Seeing the last member of the Judgment Lodge standing there with those two mythological icons in his hands—those two, specifically—he had felt fear.

Ten minutes later, Ben and his new companions were walking down the street. It was late afternoon, but the heat had not yet relinquished its command of the city. "Where would you like to eat?" asked Ben. "I was thinking we could just go back to the Lighthouse for something."

They both looked surprised at that. "Could you do that? Take us there, I mean?" asked Harner.

Raintree cocked an eyebrow. "I don't see why not. I'm supposed to have the run of the place, and I don't see how that excludes guests."

"As long as you're sure it's all right," said Carina, silencing Harner with a monitory glance. But a few blocks later, he pointed out a restaurant on the other side of the street. "Hey, Ben, we've heard a lot about that place since we've been here in Boston. Do you mind if we try it instead?"

Ben looked across the street and saw a restaurant of a local chain of no great distinction. "Sure, if that's what you prefer," he said in puzzlement.

Inside, Ben ordered a seafood platter while the other two chose identical vegetarian dinners. The food soon arrived. Harner and Carina sat before their plates, grinning with what seemed embarrassment.

"Aren't you going to eat?" asked Ben.

"Sure, we're going to eat," said Jim cheerfully. "Aren't we, Kern?"

Harner, distracted, stared at something beneath the table. "Wait a moment—yes, we're going to eat." And so they did.

"So, Ben, how goes the war against the Para-men?" asked Carina.

"I wouldn't exactly call it a war. There's really not much of anything going on at the moment. Nothing more than you read in the papers."

"It does all seem rather low-key. One wonders why the Para-men haven't been more aggressive in attaining their goals."

Ben nodded. "We were just talking about that this morning. We don't understand it either."

Kern glanced at one of the wall mirrors and was instantly captivated by his reflection. He reached up slowly, grabbed the end of his nose, and wiggled it back and forth. Ben gave him a sidelong look.

"Why don't you just ask them?" said Carina, regaining Ben's attention.

"Ask the Para-men? There's no communication between us. Fomalhaut has tried to reach them many times."

"That's not what I meant. Why don't *you* ask them?"

"You mean me personally? Why should the response be any different?"

Carina shrugged. "Maybe the Para-men would like you better than they do Fomalhaut. Or maybe they'd rather deal with a genuine human being, rather than with whatever kind of time-traveling interloper Fomalhaut might be."

Raintree studied Jim Carina for a moment. "Well. I suppose it couldn't hurt to try."

"I don't see why it would."

The conversation veered toward more general matters, and lasted for hours. When the waitress began to cast impatient glances in their direction they ordered coffee, and eventually ate a late supper. Ben found in Carina a sympathetic listener and a philosophical spirit. Kern Harner showed a touching love of all forms of art, as well as an ambition to poetry, but no obvious talent. Ben was kind enough to attribute his fractured verses to the fact that English clearly wasn't his first language.

The conversation flagged as the sky outside the windows grew mellow with purple-pink twilight. Ben paid their bill with his little-used Vigil credit card. They then stepped out into the dusk.

"Ben, we were well met today, weren't we?" asked Kern.

"We sure were. We ought to do it again."

"We will, I'm sure," said Jim Carina. They shook hands and went their separate ways.

Chapter 33

Valjhar

For the next few days Ben moped around the Lighthouse, mostly keeping to himself as he pondered his conversation with Jim Carina. He fell into an internal debate which occupied his waking hours and often persisted into such sleep as he could obtain. Sometimes he woke up unable to tell whether in fact he had just been speaking to the Para-men, so difficult was it to separate the intricate fantasies of his dreams from reality. Only when his dreams included jade-green eyes surrounded by bruised flesh was he certain that in some sense they were real. Then, if the light of dawn had not yet appeared in his window, he must struggle through the Hour of the Wolf, when confusion and uncertainty were manifest as a trembling anxiety admitting neither sleep nor reason.

The others kept an eye on him, but left him alone for the most part, having grown used to his spells of melancholy. There were times when Rouse, or Standing Crane, or even Stingray, would have tried to discover the source of his distress, but Fomalhaut dissuaded them. He had foreknowledge that Ben's torment was a matter which Ben himself must resolve, for the good of the Vigil, though Fomalhaut forbore to look within Ben to see in what sense that was true.

One day Ben found himself in the main communications room, biting his lip, staring at the consoles as though they were inquisitors who had summoned him against his will. "Why don't you ask them," Carina had said. Could it possibly be that simple? No other member of the Vigil had had any recent success at contacting the Para-men, though as far as he knew, only Fomalhaut had ever tried.

He would try.

The Lighthouse was empty except for the staffers who inhabited the wings. Rouse was braving the claustrophobia of life submerged by joining Stingray and his crew on a short cruise. Standing Crane was touring archaeological sites around the eastern Mediterranean. Fomalhaut and T'Ukudu were absent on errands which he did not know. Aureus was standing inert in some corner.

His resolution firm, Ben considered his technique. Any kind of radio broadcast would certainly be picked up and monitored by others. He could use the Vigil's more discreet comm system, sending his message as a tight beam relayed to the Para-men's fortress, but that would create records in the computers, and he was not enough of a hacker to be confident he could find and erase them all.

Short of actually going to Antarctica, what options did that leave? His eyes fell on the most ordinary device in the room—a telephone. He smiled. True, the Vigil had telephones, and paid its bills in a timely manner, but it struck him as unlikely that the Para-men would have a number.

He picked up the handset and began to toy with it. He envisioned himself calling Information and requesting a number for the Para-men in Antarctica. Suddenly playful, he tapped out 1-800-PARAMEN on the keypad. It rang; of course anyone might have that particular combination of digits. After five or six rings he was about to hang up, wondering what he'd say if a salesperson from Advanced Metallized Substrates or some such were to answer—"Oh, sorry, this is just the Vigil making a prank call. Do you have Prince Albert in a can?"

The phone clicked. A voice said, "Hello, this is Valjhar Cor speaking. May I help you?"

Ben froze. He wanted to deny this, to fling a cry of fraud at whatever joker this was, but he could not; he recognized that voice from the Para-men's various announcements.

"Valjhar Cor?" he ventured stupidly.

"That's right. Who is this?"

Ben shook his head, rallied himself, tried to inject some authority into his voice. "This is Ben Raintree. Of the Vigil."

"Yes, Dr. Raintree, it's good to speak with you."

Again Ben's mouth fell open. "You're willing to talk to me? Despite who I am?"

"Certainly, we're always happy to talk. What harm can come of it?"

"Look—I can't believe I'm the first person to dial this number, or that anybody else would have kept quiet about it if they had reached you." He didn't know what he hoped to prove by this statement, but felt he had to make it anyway.

"Well, we don't know how many others have tried this number. You see, it's programmed to ring through only if the call originates from your building."

"So this is—a hotline number between us and you."

"In effect."

"How could you arrange such a thing?"

"Oh, come now, Dr. Raintree," admonished Valjhar Cor. "Surely you have more respect for our abilities than that."

It was true. It was a foolish objection. "And all this time, I could have just picked up the phone and chatted with you?"

"Well, no. The line hasn't been active all that long."

Ben blew out a long breath. "Okay. If you're so willing to be talkative, why have you ignored Fomalhaut's overtures for so long?"

"Doctor, we know that Fomalhaut is your colleague and friend. I'm sure he's pleasant enough. But we don't entirely trust his motives."

"What do you mean?"

"As I understand it, Fomalhaut is a representative of a species which is supposed to succeed Man, isn't he?"

"Yes."

"But when is that succession supposed to occur? A million years from now, or fifteen?"

Ben's remained silent.

"Isn't it clear?" asked Valjhar calmly. "Fomalhaut's people are supposed to take over after the fall of Man. We Para-men want to see to it that there is no such fall. Fomalhaut opposes us because he wants to see the Human race come to disaster. It's necessary to preserve his own future."

Ben felt his heart rate jump. "I'd never considered it in those exact terms before. Yet it doesn't contradict his own claims."

"It's only an informed guess on our part. But it does make sense."

Ben kept his silence.

"Dr. Raintree, how do you justify your own involvement with the Vigil? I would be interested to know your reasoning in making such a decision."

Ben could scarcely admit that he hadn't really thought out the decision, that he'd been swept off his feet by Fomalhaut's flattery and blandishments, and by the Vigil's formidable glamour.

Not to mention his own fascination with, and desire to get close to, the Para-men...

"Valjhar, you might as well call me Ben. But I'd rather not answer your question. As long as I'm sitting here in Vigil headquarters, speaking to you on a Vigil phone, I'd rather ask questions than answer them, if you don't mind."

"Certainly, Ben, if that's your preference. Feel free to ask whatever you like."

Ben tilted back his head and stared at the ceiling. *Feel free to ask whatever you like.* Somehow he felt he'd just been granted three wishes by a crafty and capricious genie.

"Who—who are you people, anyway?" The words struck him as less than brilliant as soon as they escaped his mouth.

"Why, Ben, the basic facts are public knowledge. We originated on Rral, we've traveled here through space, we're here to help, etc."

Ben tried to slow his racing thought processes. "I know that. But what are you. What sort of beings are you?"

"What difference does that make, Ben? Are you going to decide whether to trust us on the basis of how we look?"

"No." Ben struggled to frame an intelligent question before Valjhar Cor found some better use for his time. But then the implication of Cor's last remark gave him a jolt. "I'm not holding this conversation to decide whether to trust you," he said sharply. "I'm a member of the Vigil, and as long as the Vigil's purpose remains unaltered, trusting you is out of the question."

"I'm sorry you feel that way, Ben. But maybe we can still have a useful discussion."

Ben's belligerence evaporated, leaving him feeling more foolish than ever. "You know, I'm thinking maybe I should hang up, call back, and start this all over again."

Valjhar laughed. The sound was completely human, which Ben found almost as strange as any alien sound might have been.

"Ben, that's not necessary. We know this call took you by surprise. We can't expect you to be at your full acuity before you get accustomed to the idea of talking to us."

Off the hook again. Ben tried not to feel gratitude, but failed.

"All right. You're reluctant to talk too much about yourselves, and I won't give away anything about us either. But maybe we can talk about your plans and intentions for the human race."

"That's what I was hoping you'd want to know, Ben. I'll be happy to share that with you."

And so he did. Valjhar Cor explained in detail the world he and his comrades hoped to create. "Ben, you should know we aren't here just for the sake of Mankind, but for all the other sentient creatures who inhabit your planet as well. And that's a much longer list than most people realize. We plan to rescue and restore natural areas that can still be salvaged. Through a process of attrition and relocation, we plan to remove all invasive technologies, in fact all Western culture, from South America and Africa. We'll do the same in other areas on a more limited basis. And through all this we'll be in the midst of a gradual program to reduce the total world population to about one third of its present value, through birth control and various incentives."

Ben also learned of plans to end the production of dedicated weapons of any kind; to curtail the burning of petroleum as an energy source, replacing it with advanced solar power systems; to discourage the eating of animals and end their exploitation in any form, and much more. For the most part, these were goals dear to Ben's heart. He found little to argue about, raising only quibbles and nit-picking objections.

"Well, Ben, I've laid down the outline of what we hope to achieve for your planet. Now tell me why you don't want to see our program implemented."

Speaking cautiously, Ben said, "I can think of only two reasons. One is that human freedom of action should be preserved. That we should have the opportunity to create our own destiny, whatever the consequences."

"And the other?"

"That Fomalhaut may know what he's doing. That it might be best if the human race were to fade away, to be replaced by something else."

"Ben, I can't pretend those aren't two valid points of view. They clearly are. But those views and ours are irreconcilable. Which side do you come down on?"

"I'm still sitting here in the Lighthouse," Ben said softly.

Valjhar's reply was late in coming. Perhaps no alien, however manlike in speech, could truly understand the note contained in Ben's answer.

"Yes. So you are. I hope you'll continue to call, Ben. I think our debate may be on the verge of becoming truly interesting."

"Valjhar," said Ben with sudden decision. "Tell me this. You know I won't share this contact with the other members of the Vigil."

"Yes. We hadn't expected that, but you must have your reasons for concealing it."

"Then trust me to conceal the answer to the question I'm about to ask. It is—of no real importance to the Vigil— but of great importance to me. Do you have—in your ranks —a woman—a silver-haired woman, with eyes like solid jade? Pale, with the skin around the eyes bruised and darkened?"

Again a pause.

"So, you have seen the Dreamfarer?" asked Valjhar.

"Yes. Yes I have." Ben closed his eyes. It was the first time he'd ever spoken aloud of the haunter of his boyhood. Now he had confirmation of her reality, and a name— Dreamfarer.

"I didn't know that. Yet it makes sense, now that I'm aware of it. Yes, Ben, Dreamfarer is one of us. At least she's among us, part of the time. I truly cannot tell you much more about her. We know so little ourselves. We met her on another world, and at times she chooses to travel with us."

"It's enough to know she has an existence outside of my fantasies," whispered Ben. "Thank you, Valjhar."

Ben did maintain his contact with Valjhar in the succeeding days, and they compared their philosophies at length. Ben derived neither peace nor satisfaction from the debate. He could not answer, even to himself, Valjhar's implied question—why had he kept secret his contact with the Para-men? Collusion, or something close to it, seemed to be the only word to apply to this clandestine fraternization with the enemy? The enemy? Ben found it impossible to cast Valjhar Cor in that role. Yet what did that make Ben himself...a sympathizer, a nascent traitor in the Vigil's ranks? He'd never known anything but kindness from his remarkable comrades, yet here he was, waffling over whether he was even on the right side in their struggle. Whenever he faced T'Ukudu's grave courtesy, his unquestioning trust and respect, or Stingray's slightly acrid camaraderie, or Standing Crane's attempts at friendship, he felt ashamed, unworthy. And Rouse! How he envied her untroubled mind, her clear purposes.

Fomalhaut he tried to avoid altogether.

His mind, thrashing wildly in search of rationalizations, offered up something he hadn't considered. What if Valjhar's friendship was false, was only an attempt to sow dissension among his enemies? After all, Ben had only encountered him, or it, over the telephone. For all he knew, "Valjhar Cor" was a fiction of the Para-men, an artificial personality designed to confuse and disarm him and the entire world. He knew such things were possible; by all accounts a phone call from the rogue computer Brainchild One could have convinced anyone of its humanity.

The thought that the lies of the Para-men might be leading him to the betrayal of his friends kindled an anger that was quenched only by the knowledge that he could be certain of nothing.

As the days passed Ben grew increasingly remote. His turmoil ebbed, replaced by a cold awareness that action, drastic action, was necessary to resolve the questions which haunted him.

The others began to feel that they too were haunted, by Ben himself as he moved quietly along the corridors, green-grey eyes directed toward interior landscapes which no other could perceive. Many times Stingray and the others were tempted to intervene, but still Fomalhaut opposed it, and with varying degrees of patience, they agreed to wait.

Rouse Farewell was more mindful of her status as a free agent than were some of the others. She would not long permit Fomalhaut's vague warnings to overrule her own wisdom. She stood in a corridor while Ben padded past, looking wan and wasted, apparently unaware of her presence. He entered his apartment and shut the door, leaving her staring after him. After a moment she walked up and knocked firmly. She waited for an answer; none was forthcoming. Setting her jaw, she knocked again, or rather pounded, hard enough to rattle the walls and dent the door panel. Sensing a presence, she turned to behold Fomalhaut standing at the far end of the hall. Instantly she swung toward him and leveled a finger in his direction.

"You clear out of here! I'm going to have a talk with Ben, and I don't expect any interference from you."

"As you wish, Rouse," he said mildly. A moment later he was gone.

She resumed her hammering. "Benjamin Raintree! Open this door before I rip it from the hinges."

The knob turned, the door rattled, but nothing else happened; evidently the door was jammed. Rouse waited until Ben finally yanked it open. His eyes were wide as he stared at her mutely.

Rouse had to laugh at his consternation. "I'm sorry, Ben, but I can tolerate your perversity only so long."

Ben nodded abstractedly, as if agreeing to a mathematical theorem.

"Are you going to invite me in?"

"Sure, Rouse. Come on in."

She entered a book-lined sitting room which smelled of pine. A stone mantel enclosed a fire that snapped and crackled merrily.

"Ben," said Rouse slowly, "How can you have a fireplace here? On an inside wall? With no chimney?"

Raintree smiled shyly. "Oh. Those aren't real flames. They're plasma shaped by magnetic fields, controlled by a computer program I wrote. Just a way of killing time and making myself feel more at home. There's not much heat, and no smoke—but I still wouldn't put my hand in them if I were you. Would you like to sit down?"

She perched on the arm of a massive wooden chair. "Well, Ben—your quarters have more character than mine, I'll admit."

"You're less of a homebody than I am." He vanished into an adjacent room. "How about some hot cider?"

"That sounds fine." It wasn't a beverage Rouse would have chosen for a northern August, but...her eyes fell on a small stuffed owl set high on a bookshelf. She was surprised that Ben would have such a thing, given his love of animals. She was more surprised when the owl turned its head and looked at her.

"Who's your friend?"

"You're probably thinking of Duster," came Ben's reply. "She's a boreal owl. Sasquatch is hiding somewhere —he's not too brave around strangers, I'm afraid."

"Sasquatch?"

Ben reentered the room carrying two steaming mugs. "My lynx." He put one of the mugs into Rouse's hands and sat down across from her, his gaze steady and calm. Somehow Rouse felt she had lost the initiative in this confrontation.

"Ben, I want you to tell me what's been troubling you these past weeks."

"Okay."

To Rouse's surprise, Ben proceeded to do exactly that, laying out in full detail his contact with the Para-men and the doubts and fears it had raised.

When he had finished, Rouse was at a loss for words. "Well," she finally managed. "This is a bit more than I was expecting."

"What were you expecting, Rouse?" Ben asked with a smile.

"I'm not sure. Why have you decided to tell me this after such a long silence?"

"Hmm. Well. You underestimate your impact on me if you think I could easily conceal the truth from you. Also, I'm trusting you to keep silent until I'm ready to share this with the others."

"When might that be, Ben?"

"Soon, I hope. I've finally decided on a course of action, and when it's completed I intend to tell all. Don't ask me about my plan; that I won't reveal. That way, when Fomalhaut finds out what I've done, he won't be able to blame you for letting me do something so foolish."

Rouse studied Ben in silence, taking note of the merry twinkle that had replaced the misery in his eyes. Ben Raintree's path to a decision might have been long and tortuous, but the journey's end had evidently proven satisfying.

"Ben, do what you must, go where you must. If you get into trouble, you know there's nowhere in the world I can't or won't go to help."

Ben's breath caught for a moment. "That's good to hear."

Sasquatch padded out of some shadowed corner, rested his head on Rouse's knee, and gazed at her with eyes of green frost. She reached out and scratched his tufted ears.

"Amazing," chuckled Ben, shaking his head. "I found him out in the woods years ago, lost or abandoned by his mother. People told me I was crazy to try to raise him, but I think it's worked out all right. Except, he's afraid to go outdoors."

Rouse lingered for a few more minutes, sipping cider and studying Ben's books. She enjoyed his quiet humor and was gladdened by the serenity which had somehow overtaken him without her knowledge. A Ben Raintree at peace with himself, she concluded, was a very different man than one who was not.

When she got up to leave, Ben said, "Rouse, I wonder if I could ask a favor."

"Of course."

"While I'm gone, could you stop in occasionally to feed Duster and Sasquatch? I'd ask Stingray, but you know how he hates to see one animal eating another."

Chapter 34

Raintree's Quest

With his duffel bag slung over his shoulder, Ben slipped out of the Lighthouse before sunrise the next morning. Somehow, in the thin predawn light, his plan seemed less certain and less advisable than it had when he concocted it. His steps faltered; he looked over his shoulder at the Lighthouse. The tip of the spire was just catching the sun's first peach-colored light. In a high window he thought he spied the mirrored globe of Fomalhaut's helmet, but he couldn't be sure. He shivered a little, turned and resumed his course away from the complex.

Ben's appearance had changed. He'd dyed his hair a dull mouse color. His eyes were now brown, and he wore glasses with black plastic frames. No one paid him any attention as he entered the Prudential Center T station and rode the trolley to the airport, where he bought a ticket and checked his bag. As he waited at the gate he slipped into an odd serenity. From this point until he arrived at his interim destination, things were largely out of his hands; why not relax? An hour later he was airborne for Los Angeles.

It was a great relief to be on his way, to be doing something at last, and not least, to escape the grimy hive of Boston. He hadn't fully realized how much that environment had oppressed him until now. He'd wasted a lot of time in these past months, feeling obligated to hang around the Lighthouse, to be available for missions whose consequences he might regret. But missions had been few. While he'd languished, the others had been engaged in tasks of their own, and weren't even at the Lighthouse half the time. Now it was their turn to wonder where he might have gone.

The flight wasn't full, giving Raintree three seats to himself, so he sprawled over them, appreciating the legroom. Across the aisle sat a mother and her young daughter. Ben heard the girl whisper, "Mom, look over there. It's Ben Raintree, from the Vigil! You know, Dr. Borealis!"

"Where?" asked the mother, looking around, her gaze slipping over Ben without a pause.

"Right over there."

"Mary, that's not him. It doesn't look anything like him."

"Yes he does," said Mary in disbelief. "Can't you see?"

"Silly. He doesn't have frozen hair. And what would Ben Raintree be doing on a regular jet? Let alone in coach? Those Vigil people travel in spaceships or something."

"Mother! Look at his face! He's so—bony."

Ben worked hard to keep his expression neutral. When the seat belt light went out the mother got up and walked aft to the toilet.

Ben unclipped his belt and turned, finding Mary's brown eyes full upon him. He leaned toward her and whispered, "Yes, it's really me, but don't tell anyone! I'm on a secret mission to save the world."

Mary glowed at him, her eyes glittering. Her mother later asked about her big grin, but she would not explain it.

Ben lost himself in daydreams as he stared at the luminous cloudscapes passing by the window. Presently the stewardess requested that the passengers shutter their windows during the inflight movie; Ben declined to do so. Most others spent the next two hours watching bad television, oblivious to the glorious reality outside the windows. Ben tried briefly to understand that, failed, and returned to his musings.

Eventually the plane descended into the brown-lidded bowl that was the Los Angeles basin. There he boarded a flight for New Zealand, spending that trip squeezed between strangers in the center row of a 747. By the time the long flight was over he had a far more intimate knowledge of his neighbors than he really wanted. In Wellington he took a small turboprop plane across the strait to Christchurch, where he checked into a hotel and collapsed in exhaustion.

He woke up at 10pm local time, feeling somewhat bleary but still abuzz with anticipation. He flopped out of bed and stepped out onto the balcony to look at southern constellations he hadn't seen in years. The lights of Christchurch were restrained compared to the wasted megawatts that fogged the sky above American cities. It was, as usual, disorienting to see stars he associated with summer hanging upside-down over a land in which winter reigned. The effect was exaggerated by his jet lag, which lent everything a dreamlike quality—or perhaps that was due to the audacity of the mission he had undertaken.

He savored the winter air, clear and invigorating as cold spring water. He'd always liked New Zealand. He thought about Rouse and wished he could visit her family to see what sort of people had spawned such a prodigy, but they, he knew, lived in Auckland.

By dawn he was sleepy again, but he had to adjust to the time difference sooner or later. He dialed a phone number. A man with a Scandinavian accent answered.

"Thor!" said Ben. "It's Brian McCool."

"Brian—oh, of course. So—you really came."

"Yes, I'm finally taking your advice. Is everything ready?"

"Yes—our Norwegian base has had a 'generator breakdown'; the winter crew needs replacement parts at once."

"Excellent. And the plane?"

"Waiting on the apron."

"And the weather."

"Surprisingly good. High pressure over most of the continent—clear, stable air, but super cold. Of course."

"Of course. I'll be there in an hour. No telling how fast those conditions will break down."

"All right. You are completely up for this adventure, right?" asked Thor.

"I surely am. I'll see you soon. And Thor—*tak*."

"Ha! When you say it, it sounds Swedish. See you soon."

Eight hours later Ben and Thor Sigurdson arrived at McMurdo Station in Antarctica, their U.S. Air Force Hercules transport making a rare winter visit at the request of the Norwegian government. For the crew of McMurdo it was an unexpected bounty, a chance to receive mail and fresh food months before the resumption of regular supply flights. For Ben and Thor it was the penultimate stop on their venture into forbidden territory. They rested only a few hours before bundling up in boots and parkas and stepping out into the polar night, boarding a Delta tracked vehicle for the ride back to the airfield. There the silence was held at bay by the rumble of idling piston engines. A small twin-engine ski plane awaited them on an ice runway recently scraped clear. The Hercules had already departed, lest the return of Antarctica's normal winter weather strand it. As it was, the air was calm but fantastically cold, too cold even for Ben. They shuffled forward, eager to enter the plane's heated cabin. As they approached it, two maintenance men climbed down the stairway. Thor took one by the shoulder. "What do you think, my friend?" he yelled over the engine noise. "Will she get us there?"

"We can't check it out as thoroughly as we'd like under these conditions," replied the mechanic. "We've kept the engines running to keep them from freezing up. This plane is a veteran. It should get you there all right."

"But no guarantees?"

A head shook somewhere within the shadows of the hood.

"Well, we'll see you in a few months." He and Ben boarded the plane and closed the door. Ben took the pilot's seat; Thor sat beside him. Ben pressurized the cabin, throttled up the engines, and made a smooth takeoff.

He leveled off at fifteen thousand feet and looked over at Thor. His companion had a red beard and rugged features that made him closely resemble his namesake. Ben offered him a boyish grin, but Thor only looked back somberly, his features weirdly lit by the green glow of the instrument panel.

"C'mon, Thor, you couldn't ask for a better adventure than this."

Thor's solemnity did not falter. "Ben, in our previous adventures together, we pitted ourselves against the perils of the natural world. We faced no intelligent opposition. Now we risk annoying people about whom you know very little, and who have always guarded their privacy most zealously."

"But they've never interfered with civilian air traffic, have they?"

"No, but none has approached them closely enough to invite them to do so."

"Thor, I think we'll be all right. You're not chickening out, are you?"

"No, but now that we've begun, I can't help wishing I were lying on a beach somewhere in the Caribbean."

"When we're done, I'll set you up in a condo on Barbados, courtesy of the Vigil."

"I intend to take you up on that." Yet the prospect of sunshine and tropical waters did not cheer Thor noticeably. "Ben...I need to tell you something about myself, my friend."

"If you're trying to come out—"

"No, it's nothing like that. Ben, I wasn't born on Earth."

Ben felt a sudden wariness, a conviction that he didn't really know this person sitting beside him, despite their long history together.

"Oh?" he said cautiously. "You're saying you're an alien?"

"Not exactly. I'm human, but I was born on a distant planet."

"How does that work?"

"I was born Gunnar Sverrirson in a land we called the Tenth Realm, part of a planet generally called Colibdis. When I was a very young man, these people you call the Para-Men came to our land, and I joined them on a journey."

"So you—know the Para-Men?"

"Yes and no. That was a very long time ago, when they were little more than children. I can't say how their voyages since then may have changed them. Anyway, we shared an adventure, and in the course of it I was killed."

Thor uttered this absurdity so matter-of-factly that Ben could not help laughing.

"Really? You're looking pretty good for a corpse."

"Listen to the whole story. The Rralians, they brought me back. You see, they had—a pony. Yes, I know, you don't see the connection. They had a pony, a form of life so similar to mine that they could barely detect the difference. By making a few minor alterations to its blood and tissue they were able to repair me well enough to keep me going until I could heal. Plus, my body was still—fresh."

"Go on."

"They dropped me off at my home village when they left Colibdis, and I never saw them again. I tried to resume my old life, but I could not be satisfied. I had seen the Rralian's starship and their technology, and I had seen Colibdis as the tiny ball floating in space that it was.

"When I was a little older I made my way to the tower of the sorcerer who oversees the doorway between that world and this. Normally he does not allow anyone from Colibdis to pass over to Earth, for the good of both worlds, he says. I asked him to make an exception for me. I wished to study science. I had seen what was possible, and I wanted to know it for myself.

"The sorcerer refused. I told him I would go to a nearby school I knew of, study science there, and do my best to introduce it to Colibdis as a whole, something the sorcerer wished to avoid. He patted me on the head and sent me on my way.

"I ventured to this place called Thunderbird, where an Earthman teaches basic physics and astronomy. That man's name is…"

"Leonard Ronar?"

"How did you know that?"

"Just a hunch. He's my cousin, as you probably know," said Ben. "I ran into him recently, quite unexpectedly. Actually, he hunted me down. He told me a similar story, though not as detailed as yours. You say he's teaching at some extraterrestrial school?" Ben shook his head in wonder. "He's hardly a notorious liar, but I really didn't know what to make of his story at the time."

"He does not lie. I became one of Ronar's pupils. Given what I had already seen and been told about advanced science, I was able to make a few connections that Ronar had not seen. I began to think that my pledge to the Sorcerer might be feasible after all. Perhaps I could contaminate Colibdis with science.

"One day I received an invitation from the Sorcerer to visit. He shooed me through the doorway to Earth with kind of a wry bad temper, warning me never to attempt to return. I went to Norway, and from there my life went as you already know."

"So that explains why you've been urging me to make contact with the Para-Men."

"Yes. I feel it's my duty to them and to my adopted world to see them and your Vigil reconciled. Also, I would like to see them again."

Until this moment, Ben had imagined he was the exceptional member of this duo, while Thor was something of a sidekick, loyal and capable but not extraordinary. Now he was forced to re-evaluate this conceit.

"It also explains why you persuaded me to approach the Vigil in the first place."

"Yes. I knew the Rralians would appreciate a well-meaning character like you. They value innocence, or at least they used to."

"Well, won't our visit be an extra special surprise for them then?"

Ben took note of the ease with which he accepted this surprising news. His best friend was from another planet? Well, why not? Half the people he knew were, too.

As the plane rumbled along they talked about their years of pursuing the aurora, first as grad students and later as postdoctoral researchers. Their faces were illuminated by the very phenomenon that had obsessed them for so long, the Aurora Australis, which cast its flickering light over the endless ice.

Ben felt pangs of nostalgia for those simpler times. The talk dwindled away, leaving both men to their private thoughts. Straight into the interior they flew, their goal ostensibly a tiny Norwegian station on the opposite side of the continent from McMurdo. Passing within sight of South Pole Station, they exchanged greetings with the lonely men and women who were isolated there for the winter. Though some were geophysicists who they both knew, Ben kept silent as Thor traded gossip with them.

Ninety minutes later, Ben spotted a glimmer of light on the horizon at two o'clock. "There it is," he whispered, pointing.

Thor nodded slowly; this wasn't the first time he'd glimpsed the Para-men's redoubt from such a distance. Without altering course they flew on for another fifteen minutes while the jewel-like fortress slid along the horizon.

Ben turned toward his friend. "All right, Thor, this is it. Are you ready?"

Thor nodded again, his eyes locked on the distant fortress.

"Here we go." Ben shut down the port engine and feathered the propeller. The plane sagged; he fed full power to the remaining engine and gave right aileron to level the wings.

Thor picked up the microphone, reporting the "emergency" to McMurdo and to anyone else in earshot. He had no trouble injecting the correct amount of nervousness into his voice. The replies they received voiced support, but of course could offer no real assistance.

Laboring with its burden of generator components, the plane steadily lost altitude. Ben entered a gentle turn that pointed the nose straight at the Para-men's still-distant fortress. He nodded to Thor, who palmed the microphone once more.

"Mayday, mayday, this is Norway 411 calling the Para-men. We have experienced an engine failure and are unable to maintain altitude. We request emergency refuge at your facility. We are a peaceful civilian flight requesting emergency shelter. Please respond." He repeated that message several times. It was heard by McMurdo, where their decision to seek the aid of the Para-men was questioned, but even military officers, safe in their heated warrens, were in no position to forbid them to seek the only help they might possibly obtain.

But from the Para-men came only silence. Ben's heart grew chilly as the repeated calls drew no response whatever from the enigmatic jewel-cluster just beginning to reveal its form on the far horizon.

"Thor, do you think they recognize your voice?"

"I doubt it. It had barely changed when they knew me all those years ago."

Suddenly the starboard engine coughed and shuddered. Ben hastily adjusted the fuel mixture and turned up the carburetor heat, but the engine continued to sputter. Ben and Thor exchanged stricken looks as it missed, choked, and died. Its roar was replaced by the deceptively peaceful hiss of air over the fuselage.

"Ben, you'll have to restart the other engine," said Thor firmly.

"If I do that, they'll know we were faking the emergency."

"If you don't, we could die."

Ben stared at him a moment longer. "You're right, of course."

He cranked the port engine; to their relief it caught easily. The plane's steep glide angle flattened out.

"Well," said Thor dryly. "Now at least we need not only pretend to have a problem, no?"

"Right. We only have to explain how the problem migrated from one side of the plane to the other."

Even that need was obviated in the next moment as the port engine coughed and died.

Ben's eyes grew round. "Damn. It must be ice in the fuel lines." *Doctor Borealis, done in by an ounce of ice.* He did not share this gallows humor with his friend. "Thor. Better get back on the radio."

Thor resumed his pleas, his voice now containing an unmistakable urgency. Ben adjusted the plane's pitch, seeking the optimum airspeed to achieve the longest glide. If they were lucky they might make a survivable landing.

They might be able to walk to the fortress, but it was still miles away.

"I'm dumping the fuel," said Ben.

Thor spoke again into the mike. "This—this is Gunnar. Gunnar from the Tenth Realm. Valjhar, can you hear me? Do you remember me? I'm bringing Ben Raintree to you. We're in real trouble up here. Can you help?"

Thor's messages continued to go unanswered. With an air of finality he hung up the mike. "I believe I'll go aft and pitch out those generator parts."

"Good idea. Be careful around the door. Might be turbulence ahead."

With one hand on the yoke Ben tried one last time to start the engines, but they remained inert. He dumped the fuel. The plane gave little upward surges as Thor jettisoned its heavy cargo. Presently he returned to his seat, his expression grim.

"Thor, old buddy. Sorry I got you into this," said Ben softly.

"Don't be an idiot. I'm the one who got you into this. You know, I'd always hoped that when my time came I'd go with the light of the aurora on my face. I just wish this were the northern hemisphere instead of the southern. These Antarctic wastes are too barren to provide a fit home for a man's bones."

"There's that Nordic gloominess again. Don't count your Valkyries until they're hatched." But Ben's humor was forced.

They kept their eyes on the fortress for as long as they could. It sank below the horizon as they lost altitude, reminding them of how far off it really was. When it had vanished they saw nothing but an irregular icy landscape lit by the shifting polar lights. They put on their parkas as the plane sank to within two thousand feet of the ice. Buckled into their seats, they anxiously scanned the ground for a clear landing site. The constantly changing illumination defeated them. The ice alternately looked uniformly smooth or scored with cracks and ridges, depending on the vagaries of shadow. Only when Ben flipped on the landing lights as they passed five hundred feet did they get something like an objective view, and then Ben was heartened, for the way ahead looked smooth. He pulled back on the yoke to enter a flare and gently touched the skis to the surface. For a moment they hissed along smooth and straight, but then the plane began to yaw as the skis encountered rougher patches of ice. Ben could not control the spin; the horizon twisted outside the windscreen. They did not see the crevasse as the plane fell into it tail-first. Ben felt a sickening tilt, heard a violent roar, and lost consciousness after a timeless moment of fear and regret.

Ben opened his eyes and beheld a protean entity of light, a shifting figure with the diaphanous wings of an angel. Stars shone through and beyond it; its robes swirled like...

He slowly realized he was seeing an auroral corona. He was lying on his back, looking up though what used to be the plane's windscreen. It took him minutes to puzzle out his situation to that extent. His thoughts seemed sluggish, suspended in time. He was peaceful and content. All change, all necessity for decision had vanished from his life.

He turned and saw Thor, or Gunnar, still strapped in beside him. Thor's face was turned away, but Ben need not see it to know that he was dead—again.

In the utter silence and stillness Ben felt like he was transported to a cathedral where the body of his friend lay in state. Smiling gently, he spent a vague interval recalling the adventures he'd shared with this comrade. Perhaps now the last place at the table of Valhalla was filled. He tried to lift a hand to place it on Thor's shoulder, but his arm would not respond, and presently his thoughts faded again.

When consciousness returned, the corona was still present, or a new one had formed. It metamorphosed into a falcon with pointed wings outspread, ghostly green against a deep grey sky. "Rouse," whispered Ben. Then, a little louder, "Thor.

"Thor.

"Thor?"

He turned; only then did he recall that his friend was dead. This time the knowledge was a knife still keener than the cold that was biting into his face.

His dreamlike state of consciousness became a nightmare. He looked down at himself, but could see no farther than his waist. The plane's nose had crumpled in; the yoke and console were folded tight against his lower torso. His arms functioned weakly, but his feeble effort to free himself was halted by searing pain that erupted from his legs. He couldn't help but scream, the sound echoing in his head for minutes afterward. After that he dared not move.

He knew he was freezing, if indeed his injuries were not killing him still faster. He hoped the cold would win the race; such a death seemed far more fitting. Even more fitting was that he should die here and now. It would be contrary to justice to survive his own foolishness when Thor's loyalty had brought him only death. He hoped the race would be short, to preclude the possibility of rescue from any quarter.

The cold soon quenched any lingering trace of pain or other sensation. Ben's consciousness faded again, and he was content that it do so.

He dreamed, and in dreaming he felt a nearby presence. He turned and found that Thor had been replaced by the Dreamfarer. For the first time he saw her not as an awesome form superimposed over auroral streamers, but as a human woman, reduced in scale but not in beauty. She lay in the co-pilot's seat, gazing up through the broken windscreen at the flickering Southern Lights. Her white body was concealed by gauzes of silver, ice blue, and mint green. Her expression was serene, despite the bruising of the fragile skin around her eyes, eyes like spheres of solid jade, blind yet simultaneously all-seeing.

She turned her face toward Ben and her cool lips favored him with a smile. In his dream he first shuddered with ecstasy, but then he wondered if some trace of mockery might not lie in that delicate curve. After all, it was through his fascination with this creature that he'd come to this disaster.

Suddenly it angered him that she should smile while he lay dying. His anger took the form of a violet radiance that suffused his consciousness, a light so strong it wiped out his vision of Dreamfarer and all his surroundings. He formed an icy resolution not to die, to hold fast to life, if only to defeat that smile on Dreamfarer's face.

His purple anger flared and sharpened, turning to green. Not a soft green like the color of Dreamfarer's eyes, but an overwhelming acid glare that poured into him, flooded him, forcing out all numbness and replacing it with a tingling omnipresent agony.

Ben's eyes snapped open, but the green light remained, concentrated into a verdant mini-sun that wavered somewhere overhead. He screamed with pain and defiance. Mingled with his cries was the shriek and creak of sheet metal bending, the twang of cables parting, and the hammer-crack of steel rods giving way. He felt himself lifted and wrapped in rough cloth that had a spicy scent. The green glow faded, and with it went his pain, and also, once again, his consciousness.

Ben Raintree awoke in a dimly-lit chamber. He lay comfortably on a narrow bed in the middle of the room. Using the only strength he possessed he turned his head for a look around. The room lacked corners; all angles were softened by curves. The walls had a glassy violet-black finish. Set into them at odd intervals were bars and panels giving a subdued light. He saw no doors or windows. The chamber's cool peacefulness lulled him back to sleep.

When next he awoke he found a yellow-green blur hovering over his face, drifting around and making him dizzy. He focused his eyes and looked into a face only a foot away from his own. Leaning over him was a creature with a wild mop of blue-green hair, like algae netted from a pond and hung out to dry. Its skin was lemon-yellow; its mouth contained a set of pointed vampire teeth. It had pointed ears and beetling brows shading eyes like two obsidian eggs. To Raintree it was like a conglomeration of all the worst sci-fi alien clichés ever devised. Only the antennae were missing.

It spoke then in a low, throaty voice. "You are awake? Your consciousness has returned from oblivion? But no, probably your consciousness did not utterly cease. Perhaps you dreamed; perhaps you looked into universes contained entirely within your brain, into realms which did not preexist and which now have again lapsed into non-existence, at least until you summon them up again. Perhaps that gelid vapor of gigantic molecules which comprises your being contrived some chemical activity to mimic the complexity of objective reality. But I see you are awake. Your eyes are open. Forgive my lack of perception. I have yet to fully take in the fact that the position of two flaps of tissue can connote the presence or absence of consciousness. Valjhar will wish to know you are awake. I will tell him."

The creature turned and stepped out through an opening which came into and passed out of existence in some manner beyond Ben's perceptions.

Ben looked for some time at the blank wall where the alien had vanished. He turned his head to stare up at the ceiling. This time he remained awake.

"Well," he muttered, "at least now I know what a Rralian looks like."

He heard a familiar voice. "No, Ben, you don't."

Ben looked over and saw someone standing in the doorway. Though he wore an indigo tunic and black leggings instead of jeans and a sport shirt, Ben recognized him readily enough.

"Hello, Jim."

"No...'Jim Carina' is only a *nom de guerre*. My real name is Valjhar Cor."

"Valjhar Cor," repeated Ben. "I went to dinner with Valjhar Cor and didn't know it."

"Are you really surprised?"

Ben studied the figure before him. Completely human in appearance, with warm grey eyes and a gentle smile, it was difficult to identify this young man with the mysterious being who had brought such strangeness and uncertainty into the world. Yet when he was completely honest with himself, he knew what his answer must be.

"No, I'm not really surprised. But I must compliment you on Carina's Irish accent. It's pretty convincing."

Valjhar's smile grew wider. "That's actually my Rralian accent. It sounds closest to Irish. Kern's the one who had to fake an accent."

"Valjhar—who was that—that person who attended me so closely when I woke up?"

"Ah. That was Kroy dal Ren. I hope he didn't confuse you too thoroughly. I'll tell you more about him later. You were seriously injured in the crash."

"I was?"

"You were. You're all right now, but you need rest. You are our guest here at the Redoubt. When you're feeling stronger you'll be free to explore and meet the others. But wait until then."

"All right." Ben lacked the energy to argue the point. He was asleep again before Valjhar left the room.

The next time Ben awoke he felt much stronger and completely alert. He was also ravenously hungry and seriously in need of sanitary facilities. Somewhere among these lighted panels and invisible openings must be the means to relieve his distress, but if he'd been told how to access them he'd forgotten.

He sat up and waited out a moment of dizziness. Only then did he become aware that something had happened to his legs. They felt heavy as they dangled off the bed. He was wearing white slippers and loose pajamas of some silvery fabric. With some apprehension he reached down and pulled the pant legs up. He gave a yell of panic as he uncovered the complex mechanisms that had replaced his lower legs, prostheses ending just above the knees. Made of slats of a glossy white material, they were complex structures of ingenious articulation, bulky and baroque in appearance. Ben laid his hands on their coldness; only then did he notice that visible through the latticework were areas of skin, pale and waxy-looking to be sure, but human.

"I still have my legs. I still have my legs." Almost hysterical with relief, Ben realized these devices were not replacements but braces of some sort. Gingerly he inserted a finger and ran it lightly along the skin; it felt cool, but the nerves registered the sensation. He poked a little harder and was rewarded with a jolt of fiery pain. When it faded he was grateful to have proof that his legs were indeed present and alive, if evidently in poor condition. He lay back until his breath steadied and the cold sweat receded.

Fascinated, he studied the devices more closely. A network of rods penetrated his legs, entering the skin as cleanly as poles in water. Could he walk on these? Valjhar had said he was free to explore; surely he would have mentioned it if he weren't also free to walk. With great care Ben slid off the bed until his feet rested lightly on the floor.

Gradually he added weight until he was standing upright, with only a dull ache and a tingling sensation to indicate the fact.

Only then did the realization hit him: here he was, Ben Raintree of the Vigil, free to explore the headquarters of the Para-men, as their guest. He grinned and laughed, half in disbelief.

A few cautious steps brought him to the doorway, which Valjhar had left open. Beyond it was a corridor so long that to look along its length produced a kind of vertigo. He lumbered along it, conscious of every footfall and feeling a bit Frankensteinian. Soon he encountered cross-corridors. Doors were spaced at irregular intervals along these long hallways; Ben learned to recognize them by the pale blue light bars inset in the walls to their left. At first he wasn't sure if the doors were actual barriers or only projections or illusions of some sort. Whenever he reached out to touch one it would vanish an instant before he could make contact. Finally he pulled off his shirt and threw it at a door; it flopped against it and slid to the floor. Careful of his balance, he bent to retrieve the garment.

Ben entered only a fraction of the hundreds of rooms he passed. Most were empty. Some contained a pretense of furnishings or equipment, usually a whimsical scattering of random objects, some recognizable, some not. A few contained pedestals topped with geometric solids filled with shifting lights. Ben guessed these were either art objects or displays of information which he could not interpret.

So far he had encountered no living thing in his wanderings. He grew perplexed by their absence. Ramps and stairways brought him to levels low and high. Corridors, curved and straight, met and crossed each other at every conceivable angle, but still he did not come across Valjhar Cor, or Kroy dal Ren, or anyone else. He was sure that the lights inset in the walls were clues to navigating this maze, but he didn't know how to interpret them. Nor did he encounter the means to meet his physical needs. He began to wish he'd find an opening to the outside; he'd risk a minute's exposure to the Antarctic night for the chance to relieve his bladder. He suspected he could just enter an empty room and take care of the matter without anyone ever noticing, but he was loathe to abuse the Para-men's hospitality in so gross a manner.

The corridors began to merge and grow more expansive, which Ben hoped was a good sign. He followed what seemed a primary path, looking around with increasing excitement as it received more tributary passages and became grander by the foot. Something about the Art Deco-ish look of the place was familiar; he finally realized it resembled the Emerald City of Oz, except for its dominant color being that glossy purple-black. Also missing was the life and bustle of that cinematic city; here his footsteps echoed in the silence.

He approached a portal of special grandeur; it parted before him. A surge of warm, humid air washed over him, carrying the fragrance of green growing things. Ben stepped open-mouthed onto a balcony overlooking a vast chamber containing more diversity than he could take in at a glance. In basic form it was a tall cylinder capped by a vaulted dome. Stars glimmered through the transparent panes between the supporting ribs high overhead. The space was large enough so that the far wall, with its own balconies and overlooks, was slightly hazy. Nor was it silent; the songs and raucous cries of tropical birds echoed everywhere.

In the center was a small lake, from the middle of which reared a huge pedestal. On it rested a massive technological object, roughly egg-shaped, though complicated by various domes, booms, and masts. A walkway led from the pedestal to the shore of the lake; along it was a profusion of tropical growth, a tall jungle canopy concealing whatever grew beneath it.

Somewhere in that cacophony Ben thought he detected a thread of human song. He didn't recognize the tune, finding it discordant and overwrought, but he did recognize the clear if undisciplined voice that pursued that plaintive melody. He leaned over the railing and yelled, "Kern?"

A figure dressed in red and black emerged from the forest and looked up at him from the lake shore. Kern Harner's voice emerged from a panel mounted in the balcony's railing.

"Ben! I'm glad you found your way here. Stand still and I'll bring you down."

With some trepidation Ben wondered how Kern intended to do that. He found out a moment later as some force took hold of him, swept him into the air, and lowered him to the ground beside Kern Harner.

"How are you feeling, Ben?"

"All—all right." He didn't care to admit that Kern's invisible elevator ride had shaken him up. He studied the smaller man carefully. His eyes were no longer black, but were now a deep, startling violet. His outfit was a close-fitting bodysuit with golden ornaments on the hips, chest, and forearms. Aside from these details, he looked exactly as he had in Boston, indistinguishable from a human being. "Your name — it really is Kern Harner?"

Kern grinned and nodded. "More or less. Your accent makes it sound strange, though. Try it this way..." and he said something like KERin HYARnair.

Raintree nodded in reply, looked aside, and rocked from foot to foot. "Kern. Can you tell me where I can...I mean, where I should..."

Kern's mouth fell open. "You mean nobody's told you? Well, there's no need to be too formal about it; I suggest you just step behind a bush."

"Will do." Ben wheeled and slipped into the forest. When he returned, feeling like a new man, Kern was holding a platter of bananas, mangoes, and other tropical fruits.

"Are you hungry, Ben?"

"I think so."

"Let's sit down." Kern led the way to a small clearing where marble benches stood amongst bronze statues of Greek gods and warriors.

"This place is fabulous," said Ben between bites of fruit. His eyes lingered on the statues, which he felt sure were authentic. Though slightly corroded, they were spectacularly preserved.

Kern noticed Ben's interest. "I retrieved them from a wreck off the coast of Rhodes. Valjhar says I'll have to give them back someday, but I'm in no hurry to do it."

Ben could only nod in answer. His body was clamoring for the fruit.

But then another matter came to mind, one that drove out the dreamlike sense of well-being that had overtaken him.

"Kern...what became of Thor Sigurdson, my friend?"

Kern's face fell. "You mean Gunnar? He's dead, Ben. We arrived too late to help him. We would have come much quicker, but we didn't realize you were in real trouble until too late. I'm very sorry. I never knew him well, but the others did, and they mourn for him. We had no idea he was here on Earth. Someday I'll write an ode to memorialize him. Or maybe we could collaborate on one."

Ben nodded again, unable to speak, even to say he was no poet.

Kern continued. "We took Gunnar out of the wreck and laid him out on the ice. We thought that would make it easier for you to retrieve his body later. I helped to save him once before, but a frozen body—and one as broken as he was—well, even Cal couldn't—"

"Thanks, Kern," interrupted Ben in a husky voice.

Kern shook his head. A look of wonder came over his boyish face. "You humans are brave beyond reason. I'd never commit my safety to a machine like that ridiculous airplane of yours. To fling myself through the sky in an aluminum cobweb propelled by a spinning blade powered by a vat of sputtering cooking oil...no, I don't think so."

Raintree offered a wan smile. "We're just six billion heroes on this planet."

Kern nodded. "Valjhar sees something in you. I know very few Earth people myself, so I can't really say. There's a lot about you people and life here that terrifies me. I do love the arts of this planet—the paintings, the literature... especially the poetry. So full of striving and emotion. Maybe you humans need that to make all the horror and brutality you create more endurable. I've been reading Milton; maybe we could talk about it—?"

"I'm afraid I haven't read it. Kern—tell me something. Do you feel competent to decide the future of the human race?"

Kern's eyes widened. "You mean me personally? Oh no, I don't think so. I can be helpful, but I've no desire to make those kinds of decisions. That's for Valjhar and— some of the others."

"Like Kroy dal Ren?"

Now Kern laughed openly. "No, no, at least not right away. First he'll have to get used to having a biological body, and having senses, and inhabiting a vacuum. He hasn't made much progress so far."

Raintree furrowed his brow. "What was he before?"

"A packet of high-density plasma contained by a magnetic field. In the interior of a star in the Andromeda Galaxy."

"Oh. And how did he get to be the way he is now?"

Kern's amethyst eyes twinkled merrily. "That's a long story, and Valjhar doesn't like me to tell the whole thing. It embarrasses him." He glanced down at Raintree's legs, his expression sobering. "Ben...you were in pretty bad shape when we found you in the plane. If Cotavion hadn't been there I don't think you would have made it. Your legs were crushed. Are you having any trouble with the braces?"

Glad of the distraction, Ben hiked up his pant legs again. The sight of the braces was still jarring, but Kern's obvious concern made them seem less intimidating. "No... no trouble at all. They work incredibly well."

Kern nodded with a satisfied smile. "I'm glad you like them. I've never had to make anything quite like them before. They have self-adjusting actuators to compensate for any stresses. They also provide electrical stimulation to speed your healing. Between that and Cotavion's efforts you should be healed within a week."

"Who is Cotavion?"

"Cal-Cotavion. Our Elf." Kern made a vague gesture. "Oh, I imagine you'll run into him sooner or later." Ben caught a glint of mischief in Harner's sidelong glance, but said nothing.

"Are you finished eating? There's plenty more where that came from, whenever you like. Shall we walk?"

Ben nodded and propped himself on his augmented legs. They returned to the water, where Kern waited expectantly while Ben stared at the huge ovoid displayed at the center, at the nexus of brilliant yellow golden beams falling from spotlights at the rim of the dome. Kern became impatient when Raintree said nothing.

"That's *Mote*, our starship. Or actually, just the habitable part. The main drive and weapons sections are still in orbit."

Ben studied it closely, trying first to take in every detail, and then to perceive it as a whole object with all its unknown capabilities.

"I've never seen an interstellar vehicle with my own eyes," he said quietly. "I was never even sure it was possible for one to exist."

"It's a pretty thing, isn't it? It's evolved quite a bit since I first cobbled it together on a horrible planet called Smerkesh. Of course, without the drive section it's no better than a butterfly with its wings pulled off."

"You built it?" said Ben.

"Well, pretty much. There's no other source of starships on Rral or Smerkesh, believe me." Again Kern laughed at humor Ben was unequipped to appreciate. Then his deep-set eyes threw off their mirth in an instant. "Ben, you're looking even more pale than usual. In fact, your face has taken on an alabaster translucency which would be superb in a marble statue, but which is alarming in a human being. Do you need some rest?"

Ben was overtaken by sudden dizziness; he leaned against a tree. "I guess I have overdone it a little. The... spirit is willing..."

"But the flesh is weak!" finished Kern with delight. "Don't worry; you'll have plenty of time to explore later. Right now I'll help you back to your room." He turned aside and made a series of gestures. Ben was about to ask what he was doing when he noticed a vague glow in the air in front of the Rralian. A wind arose, picking up bits of leaf litter which rushed into the intensifying light and vanished. An angular form appeared in the midst of the glow, solidified, took on mass and definition. Kern seemed to sculpt it with his arm movements. He looked at it critically, and finally nodded in satisfaction. The glow vanished, leaving a chair floating two feet off the ground. "Your carriage, Squire Raintree," he said with a bow.

Ben collapsed into the seat, too flummoxed to ask how the trick had been done. The chair floated alongside Kern as they left *Mote's* hangar/shrine via a ground-level exit. Along the way Kern explained how to use the light-displays in the walls for navigation and information. Back in Ben's room he pointed out the food service and toilet facilities. He gave Ben a jaunty wave and stepped out through the phantom doorway.

Ben immediately lay down, but for a long time was kept awake by his overstimulated mind, as active as a gerbil in its wheel.

When he awoke he was not in his room, but was sitting on a bench on an open balcony. But that was impossible— he wasn't freezing, yet the air temperature might be a hundred degrees below zero. He stood up and put out his hand, encountering an invisible barrier that felt warm, firm, and slippery. Ben used the control system to dim the balcony's lights. Only then was the vista beyond the bubble revealed to him. The balcony was high on the side of the Redoubt. The wall below him was like a gently curving cliff of violet steel. The tall dome of *Mote's* hangar was visible to the side, supported by graceful buttresses that merged into the ice on which the Redoubt was founded. Golden light glowed softly from the dome's transparent panes. Its warm color was in contrast to a silver gleam that set into relief the contours of the icescape. Evidently the moon had risen, but Ben couldn't see it from this location.

He sat back down on the bench and tilted his head to study the flaring sky overhead. The auroral storm had not subsided. The stars were drowning in shifting hazes of green and gold bright enough to cast shadows. A red blinking point passed slowly across the sky, an airplane, flown as high as possible to avoid the proscription of the Para-men. It this setting that mundane thing seemed ludicrously incongruous. How had he gotten here? Perhaps he'd become a sleepwalker; the possibility seemed reasonable.

The tiniest sigh made him look to his left, and then his question was answered: he was dreaming. Beside him sat the Dreamfarer, looking more real and substantial than he had ever seen her before. She looked skyward with those green opal eyes, the light of the aurora gleaming on the bruised skin that surrounded them. He studied her with a curious ambivalence: the cloud of spun moonlight that was her hair, the white body ill-concealed by wisps of icy froth.

"If only you would talk to me," he murmured. "If only you would tell me what you are, why you brought me here."

At that she lowered her face, turned it toward him, and smiled with lips like mother of pearl. "I will talk to you, Ben." Her voice was soft, high, childlike.

And now Ben was paralyzed, his mouth frozen open.

Dreamfarer smiled again. "Don't worry, Ben. I'll give you time to form your questions."

Finally he stammered, "Your—eyes. Why are they..." He wanted to say beaten, injured, blinded, but he could not.

"Oh, Ben. If you had seen the dreams of as many wicked men as I, your eyes would be the same."

"Does it hurt?" he asked breathlessly.

"It hurts when I see those dreams. When I see you, when I see your dreams, there is no pain." Her face was composed, yet it shone with a love that left Raintree feeling tremulous.

"Why have you been with me for all these years? Since I was a child?"

"To enter your dreams, Ben. To whisper to you."

"And one way or another...you brought me here."

She nodded. "I helped set you on this path."

"Why?"

"Out of love."

"Love for me?"

She nodded again.

"Quite a privilege," he said noncommittally.

Dreamfarer's smile momentarily intensified to merriness. "Oh, Ben. You are one of my true favorites, but my attention is not exclusively for you. I appear to others as they will accept me, but they might not see me in this form. To some I might even be a special place, a mountain or castle of special power to which they return in their dreams of questing. To others I might be a book, or music, or a special color of light. I come in the form which is needful."

"And to the Para-men?"

"They are able to accept me in this form, which you created for me."

"I created."

"Yes."

Ben blinked. "You're saying that I...as a child... imagined you...like this?" He waved his hand vaguely toward her body.

"No. First you gave me a face. The body did not ripen until your teenage years."

Ben cleared his throat and changed the subject.

"And now you are one of them...one of the Para-men."

"I am with them. Theirs has been a lengthy road. They brought me here."

"Well. I'm happy to share my dream-fantasies with them." Ben said this with mock petulance, aware of the absurdity of being jealous of a dream.

"Ben...I am more than a fantasy. I am real. You are not dreaming now."

That jarred him. Many a time he'd been convinced some dream was real, only to be crestfallen (or sometimes relieved) upon awakening. This was the first time a presumed dream had turned out to be reality. He looked at her wide-eyed, keenly aware of every nerve-ending in his body.

"Touch me, then," she said softly.

Slowly he reached out his hand and laid it on her splendid shoulder. Her flesh was cool, silky, soft. Alive. He was aware of the shadowed weight of her breasts, so near to him. Her hips were round. The flesh of her thighs had a pale sheen.

"You are real," he said huskily.

She gave a little shrug. "Sometimes I can clothe myself in a body such as yours."

He gazed at her as a cold glow was born in his heart, expanding outward until it occupied his whole being. For years he had assumed that his goal was to capture this creature and join with her in a cool, prolonged passion which seemed attainable only in dream. But now that this possibility lay before him, in full wakefulness, beyond the vagaries of dream and the capricious twists of sleep, the idea seemed not shameful or repugnant, but rather inadequate. There must be other ways, finer ways, to interact with a being such as this, if only he could find them.

Her smile assumed an added warmth. "Ben Raintree. You do not disappoint." She leaned forward, took his head in her hands, and kissed his forehead. Ben caught a scent of frost and starlight. He found himself mentally spelling out the word "eternity".

Dreamfarer laughed as though she had heard the thought, then grew solemn. "Ben, I have a message I could not trust to the vagaries of dream. Work for peace. Only you can be the bridge. Now I must go. The sweet one is waking up."

And go she did, although Ben was never after sure just how or when she had departed. He was left contemplating her message, which seemed innocuous enough—surely not of such import or complexity that she could not have imparted it in a dream.

After this encounter, a distracted Raintree found his way back to the room from which Dreamfarer had somehow removed him. There he examined the various controls and explored every opening he could find. He came across a compartment in which was stowed the polar clothing he'd arrived in. Someone had shown meticulous care for his well-being, as the suit was in fine condition despite the damage it must have suffered in the crash. But the Para-men's methods were not perfect—he could still detect a darkening where blood had saturated a pant leg. He shuddered and remembered the braces, without which his legs would now be as rigid as—sausages.

Perhaps some sort of anesthesia was wearing off, for while there was still no real pain, he was uncomfortably aware of the devices which penetrated his flesh and bones. Wondrous as they were, he'd be glad to be rid of the braces when their job was done.

He gathered up the clothing, wadded it under his arm, and made his way to a ground-level exit. There he pulled on the armor of down and nylon, barely able to get the pants and boots on over the braces. He was sure the Para-men could provide him with more efficient cold-armor if he requested it, but just now he preferred to swaddle himself in the sort of gear familiar to him from years of polar research. The snaps and zippers and the clean goose down felt like security.

He stepped out into air of shocking coldness, breathing it in like a magical tonic. It seared his nose even through his polypropylene mask. He wouldn't be able to endure it for very long, but he felt the need to immerse himself in a world he knew, if only for a few minutes, before plunging once more into the strange environment of the Para-men. He shuffled away from the Redoubt, his footsteps making shivery crunching sounds in the snow. A few feet, a few hundred yards: that would suffice to separate him and grant him a measure of solitude. He kept his back to the fortress as he halted and surveyed the horizon. Distant mountains, lit by the moon, looked like nearby snowdrifts in the supernally transparent air.

Hearing footsteps, he turned to see who was approaching. A man, somewhat less than himself in height and years, ambled toward him. He wore only a thin shirt and a pair of shorts. He was barefoot.

"Aren't you cold?" was the question which Ben's impulse begged him to ask. But he would not indulge it; clearly this person was *not* cold, nor suffering from any discomfort whatever. That was obvious from the steadiness of his gaze and the tranquility of his expression. His features were finely made, though his exact ethnicity was hard to judge. He had longish brown hair. The moonlight picked out gold highlights in his pale brown eyes.

"And what planet are you from?" asked Ben with wan humor.

The figure stamped his foot in the snow. "This one."

That took Raintree by surprise. "Oh? And you're a member of the Para-men?"

"Just now I am."

"I didn't know they'd taken any humans as members. How did they come to induct you?"

"They didn't, really. I showed up and asked to join them, and they agreed. It happened—very recently, actually."

"So you've never traveled through space with them?"

That brought a small smile. "No. It's been...some time since I was last off the planet."

"Hmm. I suppose they thought they needed a token human in their ranks. Sort of like the policy which led to my membership in the Vigil," Ben said wryly.

"Perhaps."

Suddenly Ben remembered the particulars of their situation. He realized it was quite a leap of faith to suppose that someone able to endure polar conditions while practically naked was exactly human.

"I'm Ben Raintree."

He received a nod. "I know. I'll introduce myself by the name which the Para-men have given me: Endurance."

Ben nodded in turn. "Evidently appropriate."

"I'm glad to see you up and around. I was one of those who pulled you from the plane wreck. I am sorry about your friend. We did everything we could, but he was already gone."

"I know. I've heard."

"You have the look of someone who's seen the Dreamfarer," observed Endurance.

"Hah! True enough." Ben lowered his eyes, somewhat embarrassed by the admission.

"I don't see much of her, myself. I don't get much chance to dream."

An odd comment, thought Ben. "What are you doing out here? Did Valjhar send you to make sure I didn't wander off?" Ben added this lightly, but not without a suspicion that it might be true.

"No, nothing like that. I was just taking a walk, keeping an eye on the property."

Their conversation lagged. They studied each other, Endurance with a certain unfathomable look in his gentle eyes. Ben wondered exactly what sort of being he was facing.

"Endurance..." he began slowly, "I've come to learn what I can of these Para-men and their motives. If you would tell me...why have you, an Earthman, thrown in with them?"

"There are two reasons; neither is complicated. First, I've seen enough human misery in my time to last for eternity. Here at last is a real chance to reduce it."

Something about Endurance's phrasing riveted Ben. Somehow he did not think Endurance was speaking hyperbolically. Quietly, cautiously, he asked, "Just how long have you been witnessing human misery, if I may ask?"

"Ah," said the other with some satisfaction. "You've found your way to the heart of the question, much sooner than most. I've seen such suffering on a good fraction of all the days of the past few million years."

"You are immortal."

"Yes."

Here, standing on the Antarctic ice cap, with an alien fortress in the background, Ben Raintree had just accused a man of being immortal, and he had admitted to it. Ben closed his eyes, wishing he could somehow slow the pace of these revelations, to cushion his mind against the onslaught of wonders. But he was here to learn, and learn he must, even if he must next be told that the world was an onion and the Para-men were a fertilizer, or perhaps a pesticide, sprinkled on it by God. He would deal with Endurance as matter-of-factly as possible, and break down later, if necessary.

"WHERE—" his voice cracked; he had to start again. "Where did you come from? Who are you?"

"Where did *you* come from?" countered Endurance.

"From my mother," said Ben stupidly.

"You know that only because someone told you so. No one preexisted me to tell me of my origin."

"Good lord...that must be frustrating. To live for millions of years—"

"Billions."

"—billions of years, and not to know where you came from."

Endurance made a helpless gesture; his eyes twinkled. "Why should I be spared the existential questions which afflict everyone with any intelligence?"

Ben laughed a little raggedly. "Oh...you must have seen it all. The origin of life...the primeval beaches, separated from thought by millions of years...the pyramids in their heyday..."

Endurance only nodded. Ben looked away from his eyes. They contained, he feared, truths and realities he might not be ready to face.

"I—I hope I can hear your full story some day."

The gentle smile returned. "Do you have time to hear it?"

Ben laughed again. "I have the feeling these are matters you don't discuss every day."

"You're right...I've found it best to say little about myself. But Valjhar asked me to share the truth with you."

"You said you had a second reason for joining them."

"Yes. But that's something better seen than described, if you're ready to go back inside."

"Yes. Yes, I'm ready. I just realized I can't feel my nose anymore."

"But I warn you. What you see will take some toll on you."

Ben did not know how to answer that. Surely nothing could surpass what he'd already encountered here at the least accessible place on Earth.

Endurance led the way back into the Redoubt, where Ben shucked off his cold suit. Endurance consulted a display panel, nodded as he located his target, and led Ben through the somewhat grandiose maze of galleries and passages that threaded through the Redoubt.

Presently they stepped onto a balcony that overlooked a chamber distinctly different in feeling from the rest of the citadel. It was a great vault, long and narrow with a high tapering ceiling. It seemed to be a separate wing, for the roof was transparent, and through it shone silvery light, the moon having risen enough to cast slanting beams into the chapel—for Ben was sure that was what it was. His breath fogged and dispersed in the moonlight, for the room was unheated, its temperature moderated only by being closed off from the naked Antarctic outside.

They stood in silence while Ben's eyes adjusted to the dimness. The rafters and walls of the chamber were, it seemed, made of ice. The floor was smooth and silvery; ice also, he believed. The only object discernible on that floor was at the far end, and its nature was not immediately evident. To Ben it was just a grey lump—until it raised its head. Then he saw it as a cloaked, hooded figure kneeling on the ice.

"Cal-Cotavion," whispered Endurance. "In prayer. We'll wait until he is finished."

"Praying to what?" murmured Ben.

"We're not quite sure. He's never been able to explain it. You'll note there's no altar, nor any specific iconography. He merely prays."

Raintree said nothing further, but studied the remote figure in the utter stillness of the chapel. Cal-Cotavion scarcely moved; he only alternated between bowing his head to the floor and raising it to the heavens. His grey hood prevented any glimpse of his features, and the folds of his cloak enclosed him completely. He was silent, producing no chant, song, or audible prayer.

"He's a humble worshipper," said Ben quietly.

"He is humble beneath the burden and the boon that he carries."

Despite the lack of sensory clues, Ben was gradually filled with a sense of the numinous, of the sublime, which he was sure did not originate solely in the solemn ambiance of the chapel.

"There's something strange about him," he whispered. "Something foreign."

"Yet he is the only one among us who is biologically human."

Ben looked at Endurance sharply, noticing that he did not exclude himself from that statement. Endurance did not take his eyes from Cal-Cotavion. Ben took note of the absolute gravity with which he regarded the huddled figure. What, he wondered, could inspire awe in a person who had been a witness to the entire history of Earth?

"He's your miracle worker," said Ben with sudden conviction. "The one we've been calling the Grey Man."

Endurance responded with a nod.

"He is from Earth?" hissed Ben.

"No. He is not."

"Then he must be from—"

Ben was interrupted by a short musical phrase that came from a panel near the doorway. Showing the merest hint of irritation, Endurance stepped over to deal with it. Ben heard him mutter into the panel, but the words were lost to him.

Ben was captivated by the fact that Cal-Cotavion was slowly turning his head in their direction. The distance and the moonlight conspired to prevent any real view of his face, a pale oval in the shadows of his hood, but Ben did get a glimpse of light, a single glint of a blue radiance that leapt straight through his eyes and into his mind. He was left shaken and weak-kneed, yet looking for a way down to the chapel floor, when Endurance said, louder than before, "Is it so urgent then?" He received some reply, and answered, "Very well, but their timing is poor." A moment later he was beside Ben, saying, "We must leave. Valjhar must see you at once."

Ben could not take his eyes from the figure which, though still facing away from them, was now slowly coming to his feet. "Leave? But—Cotavion—" he stammered.

"I know," said Endurance with sympathy. "It is a shame. But Valjhar has a serious need to speak to you at once."

Ben felt a hand on his arm. Its grip, though gentle, convinced him that a strength greater than his would be required to break it. He drew a deep breath, struggling to control the tears of frustration and disappointment that threatened to unman him. But then he remembered a violet light so profound that it quieted his yearnings and strengthened his resolve.

Deliberately he turned away from Cotavion. "Very well," he said, echoing Endurance. "Let's go."

"Valjhar's waiting in the garden dome. Shall I go with you?"

Ben managed half a smile. "Why not? We Earthmen have to stick together."

Endurance gave him a strange glance, then reached out and touched him on the shoulder. "So we should."

After the chill of the chapel the garden dome felt like a sauna. They walked the paths, calling Valjhar's name, but no answer came save the fluting of birds and the flutter of butterfly wings. Endurance frowned, then his expression cleared. "Of course. I know where he must be." He led the way to the lake, then across the footbridge that led to *Mote*. They climbed a ramp into the ship and then took a lift-pad to its topmost deck. This was a circular chamber topped with a transparent dome, a dome which must have revealed a thousand wonders during the years the ship had wandered the galaxies. So Ben found himself in the control room of a ship which for him had a legend as fabulous as any in fiction or history, a legend undimmed by the fact that it was still steeped in mystery. The very smell of it, clean and sharp, was to him the smell of stardust.

Valjhar was seated at a control console. He beckoned the two of them into nearby chairs. For the first time Ben noticed Valjhar's belt, a metal band with a lens-like object in place of a buckle. Ben wondered about its function, guessing it was more than the highway reflector it resembled.

"Welcome to *Mote*," said Valjhar with a smile. "Here we don't answer to the name of 'Para-men'—here we're still Space Mariners." His tone was wistful, but he sobered quickly. "Ben, I've just spoken to your friends in the Vigil. They've figured out where you are and are coming to get you."

"Hmm," said Ben, taken by surprise. "You'll permit them to 'get me', I suppose?"

"Of course. You're free to go. In fact, I'd invite them all in for a visit, except...there are factors militating against it."

Such as Aureus's vendetta, thought Ben. "Who did you speak to?" he asked offhandedly.

Valjhar answered with a quirky smile. "Stingray. And quite belligerent he was, for someone trying so hard to be polite."

Ben laughed. "Well. I wish they'd waited another day or two. I was about to meet Cal-Cotavion."

"Yes, so Endurance told me. It's too bad; you really should meet him. He does venture away from the citadel now and then; I'll try to arrange a meeting during one of those trips. Ben...there are a few things I must tell you before the Vigil arrives. The charade you invented to get here was unnecessary. If you wanted to visit us, you need only have asked."

"No," Ben said firmly. "That would only have shown me what you wanted Ben Raintree of the Vigil to see. I wanted to learn what treatment an ordinary member of my race might receive at your hands."

Valjhar nodded thoughtfully. "I see your point. And I suppose you would have succeeded, if we hadn't been previously acquainted."

"Besides, you're hardly blameless when it comes to perpetrating charades, 'Jim'."

"That's true, but it achieved its purpose. It brought you here. One more thing. In the past you've argued that we are not qualified to guide your race because we can't possibly know enough about it to make wise choices. But look at the person sitting beside you. He came to us of his own free will and asked to be made a member of our group. Surely you agree that no one can have a better knowledge of the human race than one who has witnessed the entire panoply of its history."

Chapter 35

Raintree's Tale

An opaque panel on an outside wall of the Para-men's great fortress became immaterial. A hand encased in a heavy mitten poked through, followed by the rest of Ben Raintree, dressed for the storm which had blown up with characteristic suddenness. The wind buffeted him; ice crystals rasped against his goggles. Squinting through veils of snow and ice he saw Rouse Farewell standing with arms crossed, unmoved by the storm. Straight and stern, she looked past him for any challenge which might emerge from the fortress. Farther back he could discern the towering forms of other members of the Vigil, standing in front of a large flyer.

Ben stepped up to Rouse and gave her a big hug, though an awkward one due to the bulk of his parka.

"I was ready to fight for you, Ben," she whispered. The sentence melted his heart and drove out any words he might have prepared. They turned and walked to the flyer, which he boarded along with most of the others. They lifted off. Rouse flew alongside, a formidable obstacle to anyone who would interfere with their departure.

Inside the warm cabin Ben removed his down-filled garments.

Stingray eyed the support braces on his legs. "So that's Rralian technology, eh? Be interesting to take a close look at them."

"Not until I'm done with them," said Ben quietly. "They're just tinkertoys to them, anyway."

The flight continued in a subdued silence. Ben stared into the distance, a man in the grip of an epiphany. After a while he stirred and asked, "Where's Tom? And Aureus?"

"Tom?" answered Stingray. "He said he wasn't needed here. Said it wasn't yet his time to approach the Para-men." He shook his head. "Tom's getting a little bit strange on us, I'm afraid." Then he grinned with satisfaction. "As for Aureus—he's back at the Lighthouse, engaged in the contemplation of his navel. We didn't think we could trust him to get so close to the Para-men without making a lot of trouble."

Ben nodded vaguely. He didn't bother to ask how Aureus had been persuaded not to accompany them.

"What can you tell us about the Para-men, Ben?" rumbled T'Ukudu.

"A great deal, but please let it rest until we get back to the Lighthouse." He turned a deliberate gaze upon Fomalhaut. "I think you'll find your purpose has been adequately served."

They approached the city of Boston in darkness. A concealing fog was illuminated by the beacon in the Lighthouse's summit—a weak imitation of the lamp which the Para-men could erect in its place, thought Ben.

They assembled late that night in the main meeting room. Ben's air of distraction was abated when Stingray entered carrying Aureus. He propped the robot against the wall. Ben gaped at the awkward pose in which it was frozen. It was twisted over with its face aimed straight at its midsection, so out-of-balance it could not even be stood on its feet.

Stingray squatted beneath it and looked up into its blazing red eyes. "All right, Aureus. It's time for us to talk terms."

The robot remained silent.

"Look, I know you can still talk. Deal with me or I'll leave you frozen until the end of time."

Its mouth opened; brassy words emerged. "I am listening."

"Good. You know why we were compelled to do this to you. We never would have retrieved Ben if you had gone in there with tachyon weapons blazing."

"Retrieving Ben is not my purpose. Apprehending the Rralians is my purpose."

A look of displeasure crossed Stingray's face. "That purpose was deferred for a short time. We will now pursue it again, if you guarantee to seek no retribution for our act of restraint."

"That is contingent upon your pledge not to take such liberties with me in the future."

Stingray gave a hard smirk. "You are becoming more reasonable. Once you would simply have guaranteed to vaporize me for my presumption."

"It would be counterproductive to vaporize an ally resourceful enough to immobilize me."

Stingray seemed taken aback. Raintree couldn't restrain a laugh. "Don't let him sweet talk you, Stingray."

Stingray rallied himself. "I'll release you. But at the first sign of trouble I'll double you over again, open your third eye, and see how your golden hide reacts to your own tachyon beam. That's the best deal you'll get."

"It is acceptable."

Stingray put his hand behind the robot's waist and withdrew it. Aureus immediately straightened up.

"And don't try to remove the device," Stingray warned. "If you do, you will activate a highly damaging command sequence which I've programmed into it." Stingray's pleasure at so subduing the robot was impossible to mistake.

Ben sat down next to T'Ukudu. "How on Earth did he manage that?" he whispered.

"Stingray discovered that Aureus has input-output contacts beneath its skirting. Through various means he was able to determine the command impulses which control its motions and weapons. He initially took control by modulating his own electrical output through his hands, then later installed a small control device, which we devised together."

Raintree gaped at T'Ukudu, then studied Stingray with amplified respect.

"Ben, perhaps you would begin your account of your experiences with the Para-men," said Fomalhaut diffidently.

Ben glanced at his own distorted reflection in the silvered helmet. He perched on the edge of the main table while the others settled into chairs and awaited his words.

"My friends, here is what I have learned about these beings we oppose..." Looking down at the floor, he trailed off into silence. The pause lengthened, and Ben showed no sign of ending it.

"Ben?" said Fomalhaut quietly.

Raintree bowed his head, shook it, and smiled. "I'm sorry."

"Ben, I infer that the Rralians are humanoid creatures similar to your own race," said T'Ukudu.

"I would say they are identical, judging by Valjhar and Kern, who are the only Rralians I saw among the Para-men, or the Space Mariners, as they call themselves."

Fomalhaut said, "In my own time, the very effective quarantine of Rral prevented exact knowledge of the physical appearance of the Rralians. Humanoid races are not rare in the universe, but an exact congruence between unrelated species is not to be expected. Perhaps Aureus would care to volunteer some relevant information."

"The Rralian physique is similar to that of the inhabitants of this planet. It is a matter of no consequence," said the robot.

Ben spoke up again. "Let me try to tell this story; otherwise we'll be here till dawn."

"How many are they?" asked Fomalhaut.

"Currently, there appear to be six."

"You mean six higher-order beings and a large number of secondaries, don't you?"

"No, I mean six. Those lesser beings you detected are in fact a rookery of penguins, brought into the fortress for Kern's amusement. Plus there are various parrots and other birds and pets."

Stingray broke into laughter. It might seem impossible for a being wearing an opaque helmet to look embarrassed, but Fomalhaut managed it adroitly.

"Six," said Stingray in disbelief. "Ben, that fortress of theirs is enormous. It has fifty times the volume of our Lighthouse, and you know how we rattle around in here. Why would six beings require all that space?"

"That's easy to explain. Their fortress, or 'polar redoubt' as they call it, was designed and built entirely by Kern. Most of it is empty. The rest is built on an unnecessarily grandiose scale. Kern's a romantic. He's the only member of the group with any real technical competence, but he fancies himself a poet. Their redoubt is the kind of structure you get from that combination." Ben's tone conveyed an obvious affection. Stingray's scowl only deepened.

Ben continued. "They plan to eventually fill the place with human advisors and students. After they're in charge, of course."

"You say only two are native to Rral," said Fomalhaut. "What of the others?"

"I said I saw only two. Aureus claims there are three. As for the others, Kroy dal Ren comes from somewhere in the Andromeda Galaxy. As I understand it, he was originally some sort of plasma-being who lived inside a star. Nobody quite got around to telling me how he got to be the way he is now, or why he looks so ridiculous, with all those bizarre features, like the bright yellow skin and teal hair.

"As for Cal-Cotavion—I didn't meet him, because you all showed up just as I was about to. I don't know where he comes from. I was told he is human, but not native to Earth."

"That seems very remarkable," said Fomalhaut mildly. "I'm not aware of any Human habitation on any other planet in this time period. Rouse?"

Rouse looked reflective to the point of being dazed. "Cal Cotavion. Yes, that was the name of the man I knew so long ago. He said—he told me he was from another planet, just as Ben says. But I remember so little from those days. You didn't see him, Ben?"

"Not clearly. He was cloaked, and turned away from me. I had the impression he was tall and thin. There is also a woman they call Dreamfarer." Ben lowered his eyes. "Her association with the Mariners is uncertain; her exact nature is unknown, even to them. She comes among them at unexpected times, sometimes as an apparently normal physical woman, sometimes as a vision or spirit. Her abilities are also unclear. She appears in dreams and visions to those who need guidance." He bit his lip and revealed nothing more of his experiences with Dreamfarer.

He gradually became distraught. Tears streamed down his face, his expression beseeching understanding from his comrades. Noticing the blaze in the eyes of Aureus, he winced, fearing that the robot was about to excoriate him for wasting their time with fanciful nonsense. But it kept its silence.

Raintree tried to continue, choked, and halted.

Rouse stood up. "Ben. You're exhausted. Let's finish this tomorrow."

"All—all right. But first please let me tell you about their newest member. And their oldest. He is from Earth itself. Or perhaps I should say he is *of* the Earth itself. He's used a thousand names over the millennia; none of them mean anything to him. The Mariners call him Endurance."

"Did you say 'millennia'?" said Standing Crane in a dry voice.

"I did. When I asked him how old he is, he could say only: 'if modern science is correct, I am about five billion years old'."

Fomalhaut kept silent for a moment. "And did you believe him?"

"Unreservedly. You'd believe him too if you met him. He is unforgettable."

"How do you account for such an immortal being?"

"I don't. Endurance himself remembers no origin. One day, so he says, he simply was."

"I suspect we could all say the same," said T'Ukudu.

The meeting broke up. Ben went to his apartment, where he was greeted by a lonesome lynx. The owl, of course, remained aloof, offering no more than a turn of her head to mark his return. He threw himself into bed. Uneasy dreams marred a restless night. Dreamfarer did not appear, neither to ease his mind nor to tantalize him further. He awoke as the first light of dawn turned his window into a rectangle of steel grey. His thoughts were still in turmoil. The braces on his legs produced just enough pain to remind him of their presence. He lay there miserably until he decided he'd faced too many early morning wolves in recent weeks; he must do something about it. He flung himself out of bed and went to his study, where he lit a plasma fire, sat down at his desk, and picked up the telephone. With a slightly foggy mind he calculated the time difference—an hour earlier. But this time it couldn't be helped. He dialed a number. It rang so long that he almost hung up just as the receiver clicked.

"Dad? It's Ben. Sorry to wake you...Oh, you were? I actually forgot how much daylight there is up there this time of year. How's Mom? That's good. Listen, Dad, you won't believe where I've been the past few days...okay, yes you would; you don't have to laugh that hard. I've been in Antarctica, visiting the Para-men, as their guest...Dad? Dad? Are you there? Yes, I'm all right. They're not monsters. No, I went there on my own...I wasn't a prisoner. Do you remember Thor? He was killed...killed in a plane crash; it was my fault. I know... Dad...what I learned down there...it's almost too much for me. Between them they have such wisdom...and beauty...Dad, did you know there's a man who's been walking this planet for the past five billion years? I met him.

"Dad...somehow, through pride or folly or whatever, I wound up as a member of the Vigil. I made a commitment to defeat the Para-men. And Dad, I don't know if my heart is in it. I love my friends in the Vigil, but I'm not sure we're able, or even worthy, to beat the Para-men, and I'm not even sure I want to. It's...quite a problem for me, Dad."

Cloud Raintree could offer his son little practical advice. But when he did not castigate Ben as a weakling or denounce him as a traitor to mankind, and when he expressed his faith in Ben's ability to come to a correct and honest decision, Ben felt better.

"Thanks, Dad. Give my love to Mom. I...love you both."

Quieter at heart, Ben was able to get a few more hours sleep. When he awoke he got dressed, called Fomalhaut on the intercom, and asked him to come to his apartment. His request was promptly met. They sat opposite each other across a low wooden table.

"Fomalhaut, I am resigning from the Vigil," said Ben solemnly.

"Ben, I do not accept your resignation."

Ben compressed his lips and said, "I don't think you understand, although I don't see how that's possible. My loyalties are frayed. I don't think you can consider me a reliable ally any more."

"I do understand that. As you've surmised, I was aware of your intentions when you went to Antarctica. In fact I knew of your previous contact with Valjhar and encouraged and facilitated it via whatever inconspicuous means I could devise."

"Why?"

"I saw in you my best chance of obtaining information on the Para-men. Your response to the knowledge you gained is not surprising; indeed it would clearly be difficult for anyone not to be favorably impressed with the Para-men as individuals. Nevertheless, my trust in you remains. I continue to believe it is important for you to remain among us, to serve as a bridge between the two factions."

"A bridge. I've heard that term applied to my role before. That will be a difficult role to play," said Ben.

"So it will."

"Fomalhaut, I have grave doubts about the wisdom or rightness of opposing the Para-men."

"So do I."

Ben did a double take at that. "Then why do you oppose them? And don't give me any rhetoric about the dignity of man and all that. What's your real reason?"

"To assure that my own species will be able to succeed the Human species at the appointed time. I don't believe I've ever made any secret of that."

"But Fomalhaut, you've admitted that this isn't actually your universe at all. It may be a near-identical parallel version, but it is not yours. In your universe your race rose to dominance, and that is fine and good. But perhaps in this one my species has a chance to survive and thrive. Where is the loss in that? You already exist, and your civilization had its full span of existence in its own cosmos."

"These thoughts have also occurred to me. But I do not know that in the unrecorded past of my own universe another version of myself did not organize another Vigil to oppose another group of Para-men, thus permitting the genesis of my species and ISAF. Nor do I know that this alternate Fomalhaut did not permit those Para-men to prevail, thus leading to ISAF via some other path. I do not even know whether my own cosmos contained that alternate version of myself, or whether he survived to return to the era to which he belonged. I admit that a large part of my motivation has been to assure that I will have an ISAF to which to return. But as yet I have no unambiguous knowledge of how to bring this about. In the face of such ignorance, it is impossible to know for certain what is the wisest course to pursue. We are left with only our good intentions and best judgments."

"And where do they lead you?"

"As before, to seek a negotiated solution with the Para-men. To avoid conflict and violence."

Ben nodded bleakly. "We must not fight the Para-men. It must not come to violence, even if we could win—and I don't think we can."

"Are they that formidable?"

"Any comparison between our groups indicates their advantage. How can we counter them? Their technology is unevenly developed, but generally superior. Among us, I'd say only Aureus is in their league in terms of sheer physical power. Nobody knows just what Tom is capable of doing, probably not even Tom himself. Then we have you, with your great intellect and Swiss Army Suit. Below that echelon we find T'Ukudu, who's unflappable and formidable in a brawl; and Stingray, with his mighty muscles and the power of a car battery locked up in his cells, and finally myself, brandishing the high-tech equivalent of a portable refrigeration plant." Ben looked glum at his own assessment.

"What about Rouse?"

Ben brightened momentarily. "How could I forget her? You know, I'll bet she could take on any one of them. But not more."

"If this disparity of power is as you say, why do you think the Para-men haven't acted to neutralize us?"

"I've thought that over at length, but I can only speculate. I suspect they just don't see the need. I believe they think that whenever they're ready to move, they can do so without worrying too much about our opposition."

"That is a troubling prospect."

"Indeed. I can tell you this: they claim a certain affection for us, and seem genuinely unwilling to risk our injury."

"That is generous of them," said Fomalhaut ruefully. "Yet perhaps we are not as helpless as they, and apparently you, suspect."

"That may be," said Ben pensively. He looked as if he were about to add something else, shrugged, and forged ahead. "This is highly subjective, but Valjhar left me with an impression I haven't been able to shake. He often looks up toward the stars with a look of expectation on his face. I get the feeling he's waiting for someone."

They sat in private silence for a moment. Then Fomalhaut said, "Ben, here is something I think you ought to know. As a condition of joining us, Rouse demanded that I show her my face and explain my exact nature. I did so.

When she had seen and heard, and I had described the Earth I left behind, she immediately consented to join."

Ben absorbed this surprise, fighting off the urge to request the same favor for himself, never doubting that Rouse Farewell might be entitled to confidences that he himself did not deserve.

"Thanks for telling me that. It eases my mind." Ben regarded the silent, motionless, glittering figure with something like cautious affection.

Chapter 36

Wakeup Call

Possum Perturbare shambled along in filthy, stinking clothes, his greasy hair hanging from beneath a dirty watch cap, his face unshaven. His odor and the mad gleam in his eye were enough to encourage passersby to give him a wide berth, while his incessant muttering practically demanded it. He cast a ruined glance at the Lighthouse, its beacon subdued in the bright Autumn sunshine. "I'll get you guys," he said belligerently. "You're in a heap of trouble, ooo-h-h-h boy, just see if you're not, just you wait." He followed his threat with a laugh that dissolved into a wet, phlegmy cough.

Veering into the park that fronted the east side of the Vigil property, he wandered its paths and fields, still muttering darkly to himself. A boy ran by on his way to retrieve a frisbee.

"Hey, nutcase," said the boy insolently, "who are you talking to?"

Perturbare fixed him with a wild stare and said, "I'm talking to my computer, you vile little twerp! Smartest one in the world!"

The boy turned toward his father, far across the field. "Hey Dad! This mental case says he's talking to his computer!"

Dad's voice came faint but insistent from the distance. "You get away from that man!"

The boy trotted off with a final smirk. Perturbare was left alone.

He made his way toward a grove of trees and collapsed at the base of one, lying on his back, staring up at the sky. He closed his eyes for a moment, then heard another voice.

"Hey, you there. Are you all right?"

He looked up and found a policeman standing over him.

"Oh sure, officer, I'm fine. Just catching a few winks on this fine day."

"Well, all right. But don't try to make this your permanent residence, okay?"

"No, no, I couldn't do that. I got places to go, people to see."

"Do you want a list of homeless shelters?"

"That's decent of you, but I'm sure I can find 'em if I need 'em."

"Okay." The policeman turned to go.

"Say, occifer," said Perturbare. "Tell me something. Is it just me, or does the sky look kind of funny to you?"

The cop turned back, then craned his neck at the sky. "Well—now that you mention it, it does. Darker—kind of shadowy."

"Yeah, that's what I thought." Perturbare propped himself on his elbows and looked around. Spots of sunlight filtering through the leaves had assumed a crescent shape. He grinned.

Even as they watched the sky grew murkier, taking on a purplish haziness.

"What do you suppose it means?" asked the policeman uneasily.

"I'd say the sun's going into eclipse."

"Eclipse? I haven't heard anything about an eclipse."

"Me neither," said Perturbare conversationally. "Unexpected, ain't it?"

By now everyone in the park was staring skyward in consternation. A confused murmur drifted their way.

A wall of shadow swept in from the east. Perturbare glanced at the sun; only a fragment of dazzling photosphere remained, the "diamond ring" effect. A moment later it too was absorbed. Prominences appeared as pinpoints of incandescent pink. The corona was a glorious flower of silver light.

"Ahhh," said Perturbare appreciatively.

"Holy God," murmured the policeman.

A hubbub of consternation arose: shouts, yelling, laughter, a few anguished cries. Headlights flicked on in the streets, but traffic soon snarled to a halt. A few cars rolled onto the grass, their drivers apparently too bemused to spare much concern for maneuvering their vehicles. Many trapped drivers lay on their horns for no imaginable reason —perhaps it was their attempt to drive out the dragon which had consumed the sun.

Perturbare enjoyed it all hugely. "Hey, officer. Maybe you'd better get out there and try to maintain some order." Without replying the cop trotted off into the strange twilight which had enveloped Boston. Perturbare laughed with blissful satisfaction.

A quiet voice sounded in his ear. "Doctor, I persist in my belief that it is dangerous for you to expose yourself during these proceedings. We cannot predict the degree of turmoil which will ensue."

"Objection noted, Brainchild," said Perturbare tolerantly. "How's it going?"

"We have encountered no difficulties. The fifty largest cities on the sunlit side of the Earth are undergoing simultaneous eclipse. On the night side, our mock suns have risen, turning night into day."

"I wish I could see that. It must be even scarier than what's happening here. Communications status?"

"Our altered news broadcasts make no mention of the eclipses or anomalous 'sunrises'. They show scenes of the cities in which nothing unusual is apparent."

"Good. Any official reaction?"

"It is fragmentary. I'm routing all phone calls intended for pizza delivery services to the White House and Pentagon, effectively disabling their phone systems. I am also interfering with other lines of communication from those sources."

"Status of the subsonic projection?"

"It appears to be inducing the desired degree of anxiety, if not more."

"True. How soon to maximum eclipse?"

"It is happening now. I am adjusting the orbits of all satelloons to put them into sun-tracking mode."

"Very good." Perturbare sprang upright and stretched, exulting in the sheer luxury of absolute control. He glanced again at the Lighthouse, its beacon now competing with the corona as a light source. But his gaze did not linger there; his anti-telepathy shield was facing that direction. Anything seen through its square plane of quantum disruption took on an unpleasant, sickening feeling of unreality.

"Doctor—there is activity at the Lighthouse. Fomalhaut has emerged and is flying on a course to the Boston satelloon."

"Fomalhaut—on his own?" He glanced up and saw a glittering dot rapidly dwindling in the murk. "Perfect. Wait till you can put him on a safe trajectory, then let him have it."

"No need to wait," said Brainchild. "Now activating." Perturbare envisioned Fomalhaut's dismay as Brainchild's diffuser field de-collimated his propulsion beams, destroying their ability to provide thrust. He arced up until his momentum was exhausted, then fell like a cannonball.

"I'm bringing him down not far from you."

"You're too kind," said Perturbare gleefully. "Just be sure to keep that anti-psi shield between us."

"Of course."

A second later a dull thud announced Fomalhaut's arrival. Grinning hard, Perturbare squinted and forced himself to watch as the shining figure pulled himself out of the sizable hole he'd dug in the turf. Recognizing Fomalhaut, the crowd which had accumulated in the field surged toward him.

"He's all right," said Perturbare. "Okay—begin phase two."

A tiny voice, ludicrously high-pitched, spoke in Perturbare's head. *"You're getting sle-e-e-e-epy! Obey the will of the Vigil, futile ant-like creature! Submit to those who are your superiors! You are in our pow-e-e-e-rrr! Render onto the Vigil your loyalty, your obedience, your goods! It is useless to resist!"* The voice went on in that vein, barely audible, but unceasing.

"It's working," said Perturbare, taking note of the mild tingling sensation in his jaw.

"I know. I can hear the voice emanating from your dental work."

"You will be to us as aphids are to ants! Ha ha ha!" squeaked the voice.

Perturbare brayed out an abrasive laugh and sprang upright. "Now. Let's see how much trouble we can make for our bubble-headed friend over there." He pulled off his stained, baggy jeans, filthy jacket and goose down vest; beneath them was a three-thousand-dollar suit. Next he plucked at his stubble; it peeled off as a film of transparent plastic. He pulled off his cap and wig and popped out the whole-eye contacts which had left his gaze rheumy and bloodshot.

Entirely changed, he marched decisively toward Fomalhaut and the crowd he'd attracted. Fomalhaut loomed in their midst, swaying uncertainly, the solar corona gleaming as a highlight on his helmet.

At the last moment Perturbare decided to adopt an English accent. "See here!" he bellowed. "Isn't this that fellow Foraminifera, or whatever he's called? He's the culprit behind all this foofaraw, that much is clear! And now he and his allies are attempting to dominate our minds!" Blustering and gesturing, Perturbare strode into the crowd, their attention temporarily his. He searched their faces, which were masks of confusion and fear, careful not to do more than glance at Fomalhaut. "What shall we do with this great glittering gawk? Shall we allow him and his cohorts to oppress us indefinitely? I say never!"

But if Perturbare had expected the peasants to take up stones, or to storm the Lighthouse with torches and pitchforks, he was disappointed. They merely stared at him in bafflement, or looked at Fomalhaut in consternation, or cowered beneath the baleful eye of the eclipsed sun.

One woman put out a timid hand and touched Fomalhaut's arm. "Sir? Can you tell us what's happening here? I'm really very confused."

"Madam," came Fomalhaut's calm answer, "the Vigil will provide full information as soon as it is available. In the meantime, you have nothing to fear, and I recommend you enjoy the spectacle of the eclipse. Do not view it once totality has ended, or eye damage may result."

A man spoke up. "What—what's this voice in my head? Am I going nuts, or what?"

"No, sir. The fillings in your teeth are being induced to produce this voice by means of a broadcast signal. Your teeth are being made to act like tiny radios. I believe it to be a prank, which I advise you all to ignore."

Everyone in sight relaxed visibly. It occurred to Perturbare that Fomalhaut's bland words might be reinforced by a power more subtle than speech. Balked, Perturbare tried to figure out how to regain control of the situation.

Then he noticed that Fomalhaut was standing a mere dozen feet away, facing him directly. Perturbare forced himself to squint at him through the shield.

"Hello, Dr. Perturbare," said Fomalhaut quietly.

Perturbare's spine froze; now he could not take his eyes off Fomalhaut. He was totally at a loss; it should be impossible for Fomalhaut to recognize him, know him, or call him by name.

As usual, Brainchild preserved his own presence of mind, even if Perturbare didn't. The computer's unruffled voice came through his ear pickup. "Doctor, I am prepared to encase Fomalhaut in full quantum isolation, should he make any threatening move."

Perturbare felt a sudden hot desire to do it anyway, to see how Fomalhaut liked the torture he himself had endured as a result of the Vigil's aggression. But Fomalhaut offered no threat. Perturbare's anger gave way to caution. He sub-vocalized his response. "It's a Mexican standoff. We can't hit each other with anything serious with all these people around."

Brainchild offered no reply. Fomalhaut continued to stand and wait.

"B-1. Turn off the diffuser field. Let him leave if he wants."

"Done."

Fomalhaut stirred as if in satisfaction. "Thank you. I'm sure we will have an opportunity to speak again, Doctor Perturbare." He assumed a flying posture and lifted off on beams of coppery light. The onlookers followed his skyward path, most of them smiling at the sight.

Perturbare turned and staggered aimlessly across the field.

Brainchild said, "Doctor, Aureus has appeared atop the Lighthouse."

Perturbare looked at his watch, which now displayed a tiny image instead of the time. The robot stood there, backlit by the beacon, looking up at the eclipsed sun.

Suddenly the screen went white. A glare cast shadows everywhere; a moment later a blast of thunder blew by, bringing startled screams and cries. The false dusk of the eclipse dissolved. Perturbare glanced up and saw a few black shreds melting before the solar disk. Scattered applause broke out among the onlookers.

"What happened?" he asked, although he thought he knew.

"The robot destroyed the satelloon with its tachyon weapon."

"From this range…" He shook his head, trying to clear it. "The fun and games are over. Destroy the rest of the balloons and the sun mirrors, and shut down all other Wakeup Call effects. I'm coming in."

He resumed his unsteady walk across the field, then veered suddenly to a clump of bushes, where he went to his knees and vomited miserably. He'd spent too much time staring through the damn psi shield. He sat and rested for a few minutes while waiting for the traffic to begin to move again.

Afterwards he tottered upright and walked down the street to his parked car, which resembled a white Maserati. Absently he tore up the parking ticket on the windshield, got in, and asked Brainchild to pilot him out of town. As traffic thinned out on the interstate, the synthesized engine noise began to irritate him; he flicked it off. When he was well away from Boston he left the highway for a minor country road, pulled onto the shoulder and waited. Seconds later a sleek white airplane descended, hovered over the car, and raised it through a belly hatch into a small cargo bay. Perturbare retracted the car's canopy and climbed out into the plane's cockpit. Brainchild set a southerly course as the shadows on the ground blended together and the clouds took on a dusky lavender shade. The plane did not betray its nature with a beam of orange light aimed out the tail. In this model, the low-power propulsion beam was fed into a high-efficiency photovoltaic crystal. The plane's only detectable signature was an unavoidable bit of heat.

Perturbare sat and brooded as stars crowded the sky at 100,000 feet. Finally he blurted, "That didn't go especially well."

"It seems to me that you achieved your major objectives," said Brainchild reasonably.

"Maybe." But Perturbare was not comforted. At the moment it was hard to remember what his objectives had been. "How the hell did he recognize me? Of course he would have known there was something odd about me from the presence of the shield. But how could he call me by name?" He shook his head, baffled. It was the last thing he'd expected to happen.

"He did not read you through the shield. It was functioning perfectly."

"He must have somehow tapped into our communications."

"But I never addressed you by your full name. I have thought of another possibility, though it raises as many questions as it answers."

"Let's have it. I'll try anything."

"Very well. When the robot destroyed me in the old laboratory, the isolation chamber you were in was automatically deactivated. Fomalhaut may then have detected you, read you, and so become reacquainted with your existence."

"Fine. Why then didn't he grab me? There I was, helpless, no more able to resist than a baby."

"I do not know. I can only suggest that you ask him. You might as well, since he is already aware of you in any event."

"Ask him." Perturbare chewed on that startling possibility for a moment. "I don't think so. I don't know enough about his capabilities. I'm afraid that if I give him a chance to explain himself, he'll pull some kind of Svengali trick on me and I'll wind up liking him or something."

"You could be shielded against telepathy."

Perturbare's stomach lurched at the thought. "Not again. Not for a while."

Disturbed, Perturbare pondered the day's events as the dark Atlantic slid by below. After a while he gave a big sigh. "I don't really feel like having any more adventures today, but the timing is right, and there's no sign of pursuit or attack from the Vigil. I suppose we might as well continue the plan."

"The Vigil is busy trying to deflect the blame for the Wakeup Call from themselves."

Finally Perturbare had an excuse for a quick smirk. "Who are they blaming?"

"Doctor Possum Perturbare."

That took him aback once more. "Hmmm. That's not what I expected out of this, but I suppose the publicity will do me good in the long run."

"They are having difficulty convincing anyone that a person of that name, of whom no one has ever heard, could be responsible for such chaos."

"I should think they would. It's an absurd claim, no doubt about it." He chuckled for a moment. "All right. I'm going to take a snooze. Wake me up when we reach latitude forty south."

The plane was inconspicuous rather than fast; it would be a long flight. Perturbare reclined his seat and dimmed the lights in the cockpit. Just as he was about to fall asleep the unwelcome thought returned and jarred him awake for a moment.

Why hadn't Fomalhaut taken me when he had the chance?

Chapter 37

A Power of One

Brainchild awoke Perturbare as requested. Perturbare sat up to find morning twilight in progress and a smooth cloud deck far below. After taking a few quiet minutes to banish the traces of unsettled dreams, he said, "Brainchild, bring up an unarmed White Wasp flyer. I don't want the Para-men thinking we're trying to sneak up on them in this stealth plane."

A few minutes later the flyer rendezvoused with them and mated with a hatch on the underside of the plane. Perturbare climbed down and entered the flyer; the plane banked away and headed home under Brainchild's guidance.

Perturbare spoke into a microphone. The coded signal was routed through his communications network to one of his satellites, whence it was beamed down to Antarctica. "This is Possum Perturbare calling Valjhar Cor. Please respond."

He waited. He'd already learned the true nature of the Para-men through Brainchild's access to the Vigil's data systems. The Vigil still had not knowingly disseminated that knowledge beyond themselves—one more reason to distrust them.

Valjhar promptly answered the hail. "Hello, Dr. Perturbare. What can we do for you?"

"I'd like to visit you. In person, now," he said, trying to put a decisive snap into his voice.

"That would be interesting. We are intrigued by someone who could come out of nowhere to wreak the mischief you have done. Come right along. Valjhar out."

Perturbare sat blinking. He'd expected to have to talk his way in, or at least provide some explanation. Instead he hadn't even had time to crack a joke. "Well, you heard the man—set the course."

"Course set; ETA forty-one minutes," said Brainchild.

Perturbare glanced down at the rumpled suit he was wearing and quirked his mouth in disapproval. He shucked it off, then turned to the flyer's tiny lavatory bay to clean himself up at the water hood. He then opened a storage locker which contained a spanking-new tunic, pants, and pair of boots, and soon had himself looking presentable.

As the flyer descended through broken clouds he was just finishing a breakfast of chocolate donuts, pretzels, and raw cauliflower. The meal did not sit well as he skimmed over the dimly-lit ice plateau. His throat felt tight. His palms were damp. He hadn't really prepared himself for the possibility of meeting the Para-men quite so soon. All at once the idea of presenting himself as their equal seemed absurd.

But then he straightened his back and cast his doubts aside. After all, if the meek and mild Ben Raintree could invade the forbidden sanctum and live to tell of it, he could do better still.

The Redoubt raised itself above the horizon and slid toward him rapidly. Perturbare took manual control of the flyer and circled the exotic structure at a low altitude. It occurred to him that he wasn't dressed to cross open ground in the subzero cold. Anyway he had no idea where to find an entrance. He flew around fretting, hating to appear to be at a loss. Just as he was preparing to break down and ask for instructions, the will of the Para-men was made known to him. A sizable gap opened in the tall, glowing dome which was one of the fortress's most prominent features. The periphery of this aperture was marked by movie-marquis chaser lights. He eased the flyer into the dome, its canopy immediately fogging from the heat and humidity within. Blinded, he relied on radar imaging to find a clear spot for landing, settling in for a gentle touchdown.

He retracted the canopy, revealing lush tropical growth, with *Mote* on its pedestal visible in the near distance. He looked with interest at the first faster-than-light vehicle he'd ever seen.

He looked around. Nearby were three Para-men, who regarded him with varying degrees of sobriety. Perturbare offered them a confident smile and clambered out of the flyer. A youngish man in an indigo tunic stepped forward to greet him.

"Hello, Doctor, I'm Valjhar Cor. These are my comrades Kern Harner and Endurance. Welcome to our Redoubt."

Perturbare shook hands with all three. Valjhar struck him as a cool, watchful character, while Harner's dark eyes looked into his with barely-restrained amusement. Endurance was an entirely different matter. Though his face was impassive, his eyes seemed to spear him with their scrutiny. He left Perturbare feeling as though he ought to apologize for something, though he couldn't imagine what it could be.

"Let's sit over here and discuss how we can be of help to you," said Valjhar. He led the way to a group of chairs. They had to brush away butterflies before they could sit.

"Doctor Perturbare. We monitored your recent spate of pranks with great interest. It showed a great deal of ingenuity in addition to an impressive technological prowess."

"Why, thank you very much," said Perturbare brightly. "But do I detect a certain ambivalence in your remarks?"

"Well. It did produce a lot of needless chaos and social disruption."

"That was the *point*," said Perturbare.

"I thought it was great," said Kern, more to himself than to anyone else.

Valjhar ignored the interruptions. "People were injured in the panics which occurred at some locations. A few were killed. The suicide rate has spiked sharply. Conditions haven't returned to normal in some cities even yet. No explanation will satisfy the inhabitants of Rio de Janeiro or Riyadh, for example, that your pranks were anything but acts of an angry God, and quite possibly signs of the end of the world."

Perturbare looked from one face to another. He conceived several possible replies to these charges, but none seemed advisable under the circumstances. In particular, Endurance's cold expression discouraged him from saying anything that might be perceived as callous.

Valjhar didn't keep him dangling too long. "But perhaps you didn't foresee these unfortunate effects."

Perturbare nodded slowly. "That's true, I didn't anticipate those precise consequences. I did mean to create a lot of trouble, make no mistake. But promoting death was not my intention." He risked a glance at Endurance, who did not appear mollified.

"Your effort to blame everything on the Vigil was a fiasco," continued Valjhar, speaking with cool equanimity. "In fact the result was to reveal your existence to the world, something else which I infer you did not intend."

Valjhar's matter-of-fact use of the word "fiasco" stung Perturbare, but he could not argue with his conclusion. "You're right, I did not intend that. Not that I consider it any great disaster."

"I'd like to compliment you on the thoroughness of your concealment before this event. Even now, we can find no trace or record of your previous existence."

Perturbare snorted. "You won't, either. I was subjected to quantum isolation a year or so ago. Thanks to the Vigil."

Kern's mouth dropped open. "Quantum isolation? I didn't know the Vigil had that capability."

"They don't. I did it to myself, to escape them when they tried to capture me."

Kern made no attempt to conceal his amazement. "Quantum isolation," he said again, turning to Valjhar. "I'm not sure I could manage that trick myself."

"Another reason for us to be impressed with our guest. But I'm sure he didn't come here for our evaluation of his conduct or capabilities." He leveled his grey eyes at Perturbare once more.

"You're right, I didn't. I came to tell you that I want to join your struggle against the Vigil."

Kern brightened at that, while Endurance's stare became still more discomfiting. Valjhar did not appear surprised by the announcement. "Why?" he asked simply.

"Two reasons. To get back at the Vigil, whom I consider to be a bunch of treacherous snakes, and to support your program of reforming human society. I don't see much hope for my species without it, unless I took it over myself. And I'd rather not. Mad scientist I may be, but world conquest is not my ambition."

"You consider the Vigil to be your personal enemies?"

"I started thinking of them that way the day they invaded my laboratory, tried to slice me to ribbons while I hung from an elevator car, killed my computer, and forced me into the Isolator," said Perturbare.

"Your computer. I assume you mean the notorious Brainchild?"

"That's right. He turned out to be not quite as dead as everyone thought he was, by the way."

Again Kern Harner reacted with surprise. "Brainchild the sentient computer? You made that? Oh! I want this person on our side. He's like Hephaestus and Daedalus combined!"

Perturbare studied the voluble Harner for a moment. "Yes, I made Brainchild. He was my first major invention. Everything since has been done in collaboration with him."

"Self-aware machines are neither common nor easily made," said Valjhar with a glance at Harner. "Aureus appears to be the only other example on this planet. Your achievement is remarkable, Doctor Perturbare." He was silent then, asking for no further clarification of Perturbare's motives.

"Tell us, Doctor, how you can contribute to our effort?" he asked after a while.

"Any number of ways," said Perturbare confidently. "I have a technological infrastructure that reaches to the moon. It includes massive facilities for research and manufacture. Through Brainchild, I have good access to the data systems of the Vigil, and complete penetration of all other worldwide networks—except yours. I've devised the means to defeat, or at least neutralize, every member of the Vigil, including Aureus. Possibly excepting Standing Crane. Finally, I point out that I'm from Earth—and human, and mortal; I mention these to distinguish myself from our friend Endurance. I know this culture, I know its sore points. I know how to get into the collective head of the human race and manipulate it in ways you haven't demonstrated yourselves. One last thing—I infer from Kern's remarks that I control certain technologies which you yourselves cannot match."

"All compelling arguments, I'd say," said Kern with a grin.

Valjhar's own reaction was more restrained. With a small shrug he said, "It's true, our own technology is somewhat uneven. Except for a few specific tools we acquired early in our careers, it is rather makeshift and cobbled up. *Mote*, for example, is far from the greatest starship we have encountered."

Perturbare found this last remark rather pointed, reminding him that he as yet had no interstellar technology.

Nor any great motivation to develop any, for that matter.

Valjhar lapsed again into an unnerving silence, studying him with a searching gaze. After a while he said, "What are your plans should we refuse your offer?"

Perturbare hoisted his eyebrows. "I don't know—I hadn't given the possibility any real thought. I suppose I'd just continue as I have—working up new equipment, making a little trouble here and there. Or maybe I'd go after the Vigil myself."

Valjhar looked a little pained by this answer. "And what would you expect for yourself in return for your help?"

"Why, nothing," said Perturbare, surprised. "I might make a suggestion on how to handle things now and then, but beyond that, I can't think of a thing I want that I don't already have."

Valjhar nodded. "Very well. We must take up your offer with the others before we can reach a decision. Thanks again for coming."

The three of them stood up. Perturbare did likewise, although he was feeling somewhat out of sorts. He'd never guessed there might be any delay in accepting his offer, let alone any question as to whether it would be accepted at all. Now as the three of them guided him toward his flyer he began to suspect he was getting the bum's rush. He became indignant. Valjhar was mildly supercilious, but it was Endurance whose narrow-eyed disfavor really irritated him.

Acting on impulse, he halted and rounded on the golden-eyed figure. "All right, Kid Eternity, you can stop trying so hard to conceal your distaste for me. If you find me so loathsome, why don't you just twist my head off?"

Endurance's gaze remained as unwavering as the pole star. "I do not kill," he said quietly. "But if you give me reason, I could follow you, keep an eye on you until you shrivel with age and cease to be a problem. It would be dull work for me, but tolerable."

Perturbare managed a sneer. "Dull for *you*...? I'd rather have a rookery of school-teaching nuns filing after me."

Endurance made no reply. Perturbare angrily turned away from the three and stalked toward the flyer.

Standing near it was a tall figure in a grey hooded cloak, white leggings, and a white doublet. Perturbare barely spared him a glance, muttering, "Sorry to interrupt your ballet lesson."

But then a glimpse of the pale hand which projected from beneath the cloak stopped him in his tracks. On it was a ring bearing a green stone of no great size, yet the very sight of that gem made him gasp for no reason he could rationally comprehend. He only knew that here was a singular object, a prodigy beyond any he had ever encountered. He searched for a face in the shadow of the hood, but it was well concealed. The cloak was clasped by a brooch containing a great smooth amethyst; the sight of that stone also struck him like a blow to the stomach.

To his astonishment and dread the figure took a step toward him and laid a hand on his shoulder. It was the hand with the green ring. Perturbare could only stare at that jewel resting on his collarbone as if it were an incandescent poker. His peripheral vision revealed glimpses of lights and objects he was still less willing to face.

"I am Cal-Cotavion of Colibdis," whispered a voice. "I see that you recognize the power of the Stones. If you can take into your hand the one I wear around my neck, we will know you better."

Perturbare forced his head around to look into the shadows of the cloak. Hanging from a fine chain was a great faceted teardrop of colorless crystal. It was the most terrible thing he had ever seen, and he recoiled from the thought of actually touching it. Cal-Cotavion cupped it in his hands, held it out and offered it to him.

Perturbare put out his hand, hesitated, then forced himself to clasp the Stone. It was icy, and its angles, though not acute, felt infinitely sharp. It filled him with a flowing coldness, as if he'd been rendered permeable to a stream of frigid, effervescent liquid. A whiteness welled from the Stone; it also filled him, obscuring his vision, even obscuring his thoughts. For a timeless moment he stood on the brink of inner worlds he had never suspected.

Then abruptly it was snatched away. He stared at his empty hand. His palm felt hot as fire in the Stone's absence. Bewildered, he looked to Cotavion.

"The reaction is neutral," murmured the pale man. "Take heart; I have known kings and queens less able to endure this Stone than you. Be glad I did not ask you to bear the Stone which burns my brow."

Perturbare did not look up. He didn't dare try to see what sort of Stone lay hidden in the shadows of the hood.

"There is no great evil in him," said Cotavion, his voice now ringing out clearly and forcefully.

"It has never taken an evil man to do evil deeds," answered Endurance.

Dazed, Perturbare stumbled into the flyer and into his seat.

"Shall I bring you back to base?" asked Brainchild. Perturbare could only nod. He lay back and ignored the liftoff and passage through the dome. He said nothing, only staring through the canopy as softly-lit clouds flowed by far below.

"Brainchild...could you see me handling that Stone that Cotavion gave me?"

"I could see it reasonably well."

"What did you make of it? Of the Stone?"

"It appears to be a cut crystal of some kind."

"And the light? That white light that came out of it?"

"I was aware of no such light."

That jarred Perturbare and gave him something further to think about.

As it turned out, he had not long to wait for the Para-men's answer to his offer. As his craft flung itself through the ionosphere over the Antarctic Peninsula, Brainchild interrupted his brooding.

"Doctor, the Para-men are sending a visual communication. Shall I display it?"

Perturbare frowned; suddenly the Para-men seemed like a distraction. But he rallied himself and asked to see the transmission.

Valjhar Cor's face appeared on a console screen, looking concerned and a little contrite. "Doctor Perturbare, I want to apologize for any discomfort you may have suffered at our hands. Cal-Cotavion acted on his own initiative to subject you to that test. I know it can be harrowing. I did not expect him to do it."

Perturbare made a flippant gesture toward the cockpit camera. "Forget it. I enjoyed it. Thanks for your concern."

"I'm also calling to tell you that we've decided to accept your offer of assistance."

That was it. Valjhar did not smile, offer thanks, or even congratulations. He merely looked out of the screen, his serious, earnest expression unchanged.

"That's nice," said Perturbare noncommittally. "Are you offering membership in the Para-men, or whatever you call yourselves?"

"No, we prefer a more informal partnership. Our group is small and cohesive; we feel it would be disruptive to add members at this time."

And yet somehow you recently found room to induct Endurance. Perturbare stared bleakly at the face on the monitor, toying with an impulse to invite Valjhar and his cronies to study Terrestrial mythology by means of an excursion to Hell.

But in the end he did not. "I see. I appreciate the offer, but I admit I'm having second thoughts. Before I commit myself to you I will require answers to a number of questions."

"That's reasonable. Do you want to discuss them now?"

"No. In a few days. And I mean to ask them in person."

"Fine. You're welcome to return at will. Just call ahead so we'll expect you."

"I'll contact you soon." Perturbare ended the transmission.

For the rest of the flight he sat rigidly, the muscles of his face uncomfortably tense, his fingers drumming an incessant tattoo on the arm of his chair. Brainchild kept silent, having learned to interpret these white-lipped moods and knowing better than to intrude into them.

Somewhere near the southern tip of South America the flyer dropped into the clouds.

Chapter 38

Joint Effort

Music awoke Raintree from an uneasy sleep. Confused, he looked around in the darkness for the source of the cheerful, tinkling melody that seemingly came from nowhere. "Lights!" he croaked. The illumination revealed nothing but the familiar furnishings of his bedroom.

The music ceased with an energetic flourish. At that moment Ben heard a loud click and felt a painful jolt in his legs. With a panicky yell he threw off the covers. The braces had snapped open and fallen off his legs. They lay beside him on the bed, looking unpleasantly alien. He ran his hands over his calves and shins. Reddish patches, only slightly tender, marked where white rods had penetrated flesh and bone just moments before.

He didn't even bother to get up to see whether he was truly healed; he had no doubt of it. He set the braces beside the bed, covered himself up again, killed the lights, and lay there. He couldn't help but smile at Kern Harner's caprice —making the braces play music to announce the completion of their task. But they'd picked an unfortunate time to decide their work was done. It was 3 a.m. Ben knew he'd never get back to sleep after being jarred awake like that.

He didn't remember what he'd been dreaming when the music sounded, but it hadn't been pleasant, he was certain of that.

The wolves of the hour, the only wolves he'd ever feared, took him in their jaws and shook out thoughts, images, and memories he'd rather have kept locked away.

He had met the Dreamfarer. The very thought seemed absurd, nonsensical. She was a fantasy, a waking dream whose details slipped away day by day, while his memories of the other Para-men grew more intense. Yet he *had* met the Dreamfarer—had sat next to her, spoken to her, even touched her body.

But even that memory lacked substance, was unconvincing. He might as well try to convince himself that he had met his own conscience.

And yet, despite all that, he looked for her in every shadow, in every beam of moonlight. But now she was silent, both in his waking hours and in his dreams.

They stood high in the Lighthouse, in a chamber where the beacon's light was muted by the pale glow of dawn, and the chill air of morning moved amongst the open columns.

"You know you can't stop me from going," said Rouse Farewell, breath smoking, green eyes on fire.

"I would not presume to try," said Fomalhaut.

"But I can't do it all alone. There are too many of them, and only one of me. Why not join me? Let this club of ours do some good in the world, rather than just sitting around waiting for the Para-men to pass wind."

"Rouse, this 'club' was constituted to prevent alien interference in Human affairs, not to foster it. And we certainly cannot afford to go to the rescue of those who seek the victory of the Para-men."

"Ahhh!" cried Rouse. "You bloodless cipher! How can you not expect these people to support the Para-men? They're treated worse than animals in their own country. Besides, has it occurred to you that saving their bloody lives would be a prime way of swaying their sympathies to our side?"

"I'm sorry, Rouse. If we did as you ask, there would be no end to it. We would gradually be forced to assume more and more responsibility for world affairs until we ourselves were in the position of despotism we seek to deny the Para-men. Or else we would become so involved in local politics that our vigilance over the Para-men would fail."

"All right then, all right! Sit on your hands if you must. But I thank God I can do something about this tragedy."

"That is appropriate."

"This is not over. I'll see you when I get back." She fired herself into the air, disappearing into the south.

If not before, thought Fomalhaut, his foresight prompting the thought as he looked after her dwindling form.

T'Ukudu's tendrils bent forward slightly in surprise. The alert was one which had never sounded before, and the icon which appeared on the communications monitor had also never previously been used. He sat down at the console and accepted the call. The monitor displayed a human face. Ben's descriptions of the Para-men allowed T'Ukudu to recognize it as the supposedly alien Valjhar Cor.

"Greetings, Valjhar. What is the purpose for your call?"

"T'Ukudu, isn't it? Good, you're said to be reasonable. I assume you're aware of the situation in Haiti," said Valjhar with some intensity.

"Actually, I am not."

"Then let me familiarize you with it. A mass movement has arisen in which thousands of the poor and powerless are demonstrating in favor of our proposed reformation of human society. This morning the government reacted, slaughtering anyone implicated in pro-Para-men activity. Hundreds have been killed already, and neither side shows any sign of backing down."

"That is unfortunate, but why does it provoke this unprecedented open communication between our groups?"

Valjhar's features took on a look of determination. "I'm calling to inform you that the Para-men will go to Haiti to intervene in the situation. We find it intolerable."

T'Ukudu hesitated. "It would be contrary to our doctrine to permit you to assert yourselves in a human conflict of that sort."

Valjhar's grimness intensified. "Nevertheless, we intend to do it. We will not permit innocent people to die in our name. If you insist on making this the trigger point in our relationship, then so be it. But we will go to Haiti."

"We do not wish to precipitate a conflict. Perhaps a compromise is possible."

"I was hoping you'd say that. Here is what we propose. Bring the Vigil to Haiti as well. We will confine ourselves to separate areas, but work with the same goal of stopping the killing. That way it will not appear that you have conceded to us the right to interfere in human affairs. You can even claim that it was you who invited us to take part in the operation—we will support you in that. Rouse Farewell is already in Haiti, doing what she can. I hope you will choose to join your comrade in her unselfish effort."

Valjhar's eyes were steady and challenging.

"The others must be consulted in this matter," rumbled T'Ukudu.

"Of course. But we leave for Haiti in ten minutes. Make your decision soon."

Stingray's sharp voiced blared from the intercom in Ben's apartment just as he finally fell asleep on the rug in front of the fireplace. It also woke Sasquatch and sent him dashing back and forth in alarm.

"Ben, grab your equipment and meet us in the flyer bay as soon as you can. We've got a fight on our hands. Understood?"

"Yes," mumbled Ben. "I'm on my way."

Five minutes later he arrived in the bay carrying a suit of cold armor and a cryogun equipped with his new turbo-blizzard modification. Stingray, Fomalhaut, and T'Ukudu bustled around a combat transport flyer, the model Ben called the Gyrfalcon, loading equipment and supplies.

"What's going on?" asked Ben through the disorientation of sleep deprivation.

Stingray grinned at him. "We're teaming up with the Para-men to overthrow the government of Haiti."

Ben's jaw dropped open.

"That's not quite accurate," said Fomalhaut stiffly. "We're not going in with the intention of overthrowing the government."

"No, but if we defeat the Haitian military it'll have the same effect, won't it?" asked Stingray acerbically. "It's practically a civil war down there."

"Teaming up with the Para-men?" said Ben in astonishment.

"Oh, not exactly," said Stingray. "We'll be operating in separate areas, but we will be pursuing the same goal. Don't look at me like that; I know it's crazy."

"Where are the others?"

"Rouse is there already. When I rousted Standing Crane out of that museum his apartment has become he said he could get there faster on his own. As for Aureus, I took the liberty of deactivating the damn thing. I doubt we could trust it to be on good behavior in such proximity to his quarry, and anyway I suspect its methods of dealing with the Haitian troops might be unnecessarily severe."

"Aureus isn't going to like this," said Ben.

Fomalhaut sighed, surprising everyone; it was a sound none of them had heard him make before. "At some point Aureus is going to realize that we may no longer be willing to permit him to arrest the Rralians. At that time, deactivation had better be our first option, not our last."

They scrambled into the flyer, opened the bay, and launched themselves into the early morning sunlight.

"T'Ukudu, since you committed us to this misadventure, perhaps you'd care to take tactical command of the operation," said Fomalhaut.

T'Ukudu seemed oblivious to Fomalhaut's resentful tone. "Very well. Our activities will be confined to the northern half of the nation, particularly the areas north of Port-au-Prince. Fomalhaut will operate independently, as will Rouse and Standing Crane. Ben, Stingray, and I will act in concert. The flyer will be left in a high-altitude hover, ready to provide covering fire."

Not long afterward the flyer descended to skim the barren, eroded hills of interior Haiti. Fomalhaut jettisoned himself and was soon out of sight. T'Ukudu then landed on a dirt road between a village and a column of soldiers in jeeps and trucks. The three disembarked and the flyer ascended to its station. It was a sweet morning, with wisps of fog just burning off in the valleys. A few cattle picked at the grasses growing among the tree stumps in the field, but their ears pricked up nervously as the rumble of the advancing soldiers grew louder.

Ben shared their misgivings. He pulled down the hood of his cold armor, viewing the world through its metallized goggles. Stingray and T'Ukudu wore armored suits of similar function—it wasn't wise to go unprotected when fighting near Dr. Borealis.

"What's that new gadget atop your cryogun, Ben?" asked Stingray casually.

"A new wrinkle. We'll see how it works."

The soldiers came into view over a rise in the road. They stopped short at the sight of the three bizarre figures blocking their way. The engines of their vehicles idled roughly.

"Perhaps we can turn them back without much violence," said T'Ukudu. He manipulated a control paddle. From high overhead, glowing cables of ERASER fire, in wavelengths selected for impressive visibility, cut into the road just ahead of the lead vehicle, spewing out clots of fused, incandescent slag.

The Haitians made a loud outcry, but answered with small arms fire that splatted harmlessly off the Vigil armor. Engines roared, and the jeeps surged forward. Soldiers leaped from the troop trucks and spread out rapidly.

T'Ukudu deactivated the flyer's weapons. The battlefield had become too chaotic to use them without the likelihood of fatalities.

"There's a couple hundred of them," worried Ben. "An awful lot."

Stingray made a disdainful sound. "If three members of the Vigil can't handle two hundred poorly-equipped Third World troops, we've no business pretending to oppose the Para-men."

My point exactly, thought Ben.

"Ben, attempt to immobilize the soldiers from a distance. Stingray and I will fan out and engage them at close range." T'Ukudu and Stingray were gone in an instant, running to flank their opponents with superhuman speed.

Ben raised the cryogun and sighted a tire on the lead jeep. He touched the targeting contact, then fired. The tire flashed white with frost and shattered. He subjected the other front tire to the same treatment, and suddenly the jeep was riding on its rims. He fired at the engine compartment and the engine seized and shattered. Ben stepped off the road for a better angle of view and began methodically destroying and disabling the enemy vehicles and weapons. It was an easy, impersonal process and his nervousness soon died away. He was so intent on his marksmanship that he was late in noticing twenty soldiers who ran up and started firing at him with light machine guns. At this range the impact was more than enough to knock him down. Gasping, he raised the cryogun, braced it against the ground as best he could, and triggered the turbo-blizzard. The recoil almost tore the gun from his hands, but he held on. The turbine shrieked as it sucked in air and blew it forward, while tachyon cooling whitened it with a sleet of frozen water and carbon dioxide. It blasted back his snow-covered attackers, sending them howling. Ben regained his feet and played the weapon like an icy fire hose. He was delighted—the spectacular yet relatively harmless turbo-blizzard gave him a greater feeling of power than the much more dangerous cryobeam ever had. Filled with confidence, he advanced into the thick of the fighting, alternating between the two weapons as appropriate.

He had a moment now and then to note the fighting styles of Stingray and T'Ukudu. Having never seen either of them put their physical abilities to full use, the sight was impressive and a little frightening. Stingray moved among the soldiers like a dog among rats, overwhelming them with speed and strength. He lifted them like children, throwing them about, hitting and breaking and battering. He zapped some with his bioelectricity; from their spasms Ben couldn't tell which method was the most merciful. Yet for all the savagery of his attack, Stingray left no corpses in his wake—though some might find themselves in that state if medical care weren't forthcoming.

T'Ukudu's style was smooth as oil compared to Stingray's brawling. Though scarcely less than Stingray in weight and strength, he seemed to flow among his opponents, hardly moving until the perfect moment for a decisive move. Then the merest touch on exposed skin would result in a downed enemy, put to sleep by the gentle agency of Touchtalk.

Enthralled by this spectacle, Ben noticed only peripherally when a man raised a rocket-propelled grenade against T'Ukudu, and by then it was almost too late. Ben swung the cryogun. In his fumbling haste he touched the wrong contact, and the soldier's head was instantly frozen hard as the moons of Neptune. By then the missile was on its way. It exploded against T'Ukudu, blowing off his right arm and shoulder, the shrapnel shredding a dozen men in his vicinity. T'Ukudu wavered and fell heavily.

"Stingray! T'Ukudu's down!" yelled Ben, his voice breaking. He had stood immobile too long; a squad of men rushed him from behind, yanking the cryogun from his grasp and pinning his arms. He glimpsed Stingray rushing in from the side, his face terrible with anger. But concentrated fire from three heavy machine guns caused him to stumble. A truck roared in out of nowhere, catching him from behind and smashing him down. Stunned, Stingray was only able to roll onto his back before the truck returned and ran up his crotch to plant its left front wheel on his chest. He grabbed the tire and bumper and strained, but the truck's weight was beyond his strength. The driver jumped out, grinning sadistically. Ben's captors hustled him toward the scene. The forty soldiers who were still standing gathered around the pinioned Stingray, laughing and firing their pistols into his armor. Stingray gave up trying to lift the truck and strained to reach them with his long arms. Another man with a grenade launcher strutted up and aimed it at Stingray's head. Stingray tried to throw himself from beneath the truck; it bucked and rocked but he could not escape.

The missile man said something in French. Ben did not understand it, but Stingray must have, for he made an answer that embarrassed the missile man and drew a laugh from the others. The missile man squeezed the trigger as Stingray made a last spasmodic effort to reach beyond his limits to strike the man down.

Suddenly a snapping electric arc leaped from Stingray's hands to the grenade launcher. Its handler yelped and dropped the weapon in alarm. Electric serpents danced from Stingray's fingers, banging, cracking, burning clothing and flesh, knocking men down and sending them flying. Ben's captors loosened their grip. He broke free and grabbed the cryogun from the hands of a scorched, unconscious man. He unleashed the turbo-blizzard, scattering the few soldiers who were still capable of putting up a fight. T'Ukudu, somehow back on his feet, walked to the truck. Between his single arm and Stingray's two they managed to overturn it. Then he sat down, content to watch as Raintree concluded the rout.

Peace suddenly ruled the field, except in Raintree's mind. Snow and frost covered everything for a hundred yards. Fuming frozen gases encased everything that had fallen to the cryobeam. Liquid nitrogen boiled in puddles.

Stingray remained supine, breathing cautiously. T'Ukudu continued to sit quietly, looking horribly asymmetrical with an arm and a good part of his upper torso missing. Raintree searched the field, spotted the detached arm, and brought it over to T'Ukudu, not knowing what else to do.

"There's no need to bother with that, Ben," said T'Ukudu quietly.

Ben silently agreed; there could be no hope for the gentle Servant of T'Utahn. He dreaded to look closely at the wound which had doomed him, but felt he must. He moved to T'Ukudu's side and knelt down, shaking.

His vague expectations of what he'd see went unmet. Instead of bleeding organs spilling from a ruptured chest cavity, there was a homogeneous mass like dense bread moistened with glycerin. The only evident structures were protruding bones. Ben gaped, scarcely knowing what to think.

"We Servants are not constructed with specialized, irreplaceable organs which might be vulnerable to attack," said T'Ukudu calmly, as if answering an unasked question. "For the most part, our metabolic functions are distributed evenly throughout our tissues."

"Are you telling me you might survive?" asked Ben in astonishment.

"I will certainly survive, assuming proper conditions. Further trauma of this magnitude might compromise my recovery, especially if inflicted during the next several hours. Also, my regeneration will require large amounts of raw material. I will be unusually hungry for the next few weeks.

"After all, why should the Makers send out emissaries of such fragility that the slightest mishap might jeopardize their mission?"

"No reason I can think of," said Ben, reeling with relief. "Stingray, how are you doing? It seems to me that truck picked a painful road to travel."

Stingray lifted his head and offered a rueful grin. "I'm not built exactly like you either, Ben. No external genitalia. Which is not to say that I'm feeling my best."

"No, I wouldn't think so." Raintree gingerly took the remote from T'Ukudu's belt. "I'm calling in the flyer. You two have done enough for one day."

"Agreed," said T'Ukudu. "The Para-men must be satisfied with our efforts on their behalf."

His comrades laughed, wondering whether T'Ukudu had intended the irony.

"So, T'Ukudu, what do you think of our planet so far?" asked Stingray.

"With a few individual exceptions, I have no great regard for the human species."

That blunt assessment killed any good humor that their survival might have fostered. Raintree found himself hoping he was one of T'Ukudu's exceptions, while Stingray lay silently, looking distracted and increasingly grim.

The flyer hissed down and hovered a foot off the ground. T'Ukudu and Stingray shambled aboard and were gone to the north.

Raintree suddenly found himself alone on the battlefield, faced with blood and pain and imminent death. He was neither a physician nor a miracle-worker; perhaps he should have flown out with the others. But no, there must still be something he could accomplish. He was still on his feet, while colleagues with ten times his strength were not. Perhaps Dr. Borealis was a more formidable persona than he'd realized.

A tour of the field soon quenched his self-appreciation. He stood over the body of the soldier whose missile had nearly destroyed T'Ukudu. The man's frozen head had snapped off when he fell, its features obscured by a thick coating of ice.

Raintree staggered away. Nearby were men who had also fallen to the grenade attack. Most were mutilated, horribly mangled, definitely dead. One was still alive, lying propped up against a jeep, holding his severed hand while the stump bled freely. He jabbered frantically in French as Ben approached. Ben's heart writhed in his chest. He stood over the man, wondering how he could help. All he could do was freeze things...he gestured for the man to hold out his handless arm and froze the stump, stopping the bleeding and ending the pain. Next he took the severed hand, wrapped it in a rag, laid it on the ground, and fired at the cryogun's lowest setting, chilling it to just above freezing. If advanced medical care could arrive in time, it was at least conceivable that the hand could be reattached. The man fainted.

It would take a squad of doctors to minister to all those here who needed care. Men lay with compound fractures, gasped with broken ribs, wept over electrical burns. He thought about going to the village for help, but realized it was a poor source of any real assistance, even if the villagers were willing to provide it. He walked about, doing what little he could to alleviate suffering with the cryogun, not daring to do very much for fear of wreaking worse harm. He pulled the hood from his face so the injured could see they were dealing with a human being, although his frost-haired pallid face did not reassure them greatly. He tore up rags for bandages, tied clumsy tourniquets, offered chunks of ice to suck or to hold against wounds. When the wailings of pain and fear reached too high a crescendo he wished he could freeze them all and send them on to peace and silence.

Somewhere to the west, Rouse Farewell veered north, drawn by the smoke that lifted from a burned-out village. Streaked with dried blood, her flight suit in tatters, she pushed herself through the stubborn air, hoping to save any villagers who might be trapped by the attack. She had already destroyed much of the Haitian military, and now her allies, though tardy in arriving, were adding to her efforts. She'd even heard from Fomalhaut that the Paramen themselves were operating in the southern peninsula.

That was a matter she'd have to take up later, for if the Vigil were here at the behest of the Para-men rather than at her own request, she would not be easily placated.

Her matchless eyesight revealed the worst—the town had already been razed. There was nothing she could do. A large military unit was approaching from the north, which seemed odd since the town was already destroyed.

Her wrath was subsumed by curiosity as she noticed a strange geometrical design on an open field near the town. She swooped in to find it was composed of human bodies carefully arrayed in concentric arcs. At the center of the figure was the one man still on his feet, Tom Standing Crane. Baffled, Rouse landed beside him at the focus of the rings of bodies—every one of them dead, by the look of them.

Standing Crane wore the brown-and-grey robes he'd affected in recent months. Again Rouse wondered at the changes that had overtaken the man. Once a stocky, vigorous man with a flushed complexion, he had in some sense waned, becoming wan and frail, his face almost as grey as his raiment. His hair had dried out and was coarse and grey, while his cheeks were sunken and his eyes mantled in shadow. Yet in another sense he had gained some perilous power. He was if anything taller than he had been, and those darkling eyes of his swiveled about with a chilling deliberation.

In the village itself were dozens of wounded: villagers and soldiers, men, women, and children. They lay prostrate or propped up against walls, or simply languished in ditches which carried raw sewage. Children cried and screamed; the adults were mostly silent, save a few who were delirious. The few who had the resources to open their eyes looked toward Standing Crane and his corpses without comprehension.

"Standing Crane, what the hell are you doing?" demanded Rouse.

He did not turn aside to answer. "I am preparing to send these people to their rightful destinations."

"What, you're conducting a funeral? This isn't the time; the living need your help!"

"What happens in death is more important than what happens in life."

"But you're a *doctor*. It's your solemn *duty* to minister to the *living*," she said with quiet intensity.

Standing Crane did not reply. Instead he walked around the rings of bodies, bending to brush their hands and hair with his fingers. He spoke in hollow tones, using a language Rouse had never heard.

"That doesn't look like any Native American funeral rite I've ever seen," she said uneasily.

"Why should it be? There are no natives left on this island. I think Columbus took care of that." For a moment he sounded like his old self again, then he fell back into his murmuring. Rouse could no longer resist a shudder.

The roar of motors distracted her. She turned and saw the Haitian mechanized column approaching. Wearily she made ready to lift off for battle, but Standing Crane stopped her.

"Don't bother, Rouse. I'll handle it from here." He extended his hand, fingers held out loosely. Immediately the trucks choked and died, while the foot soldiers slumped and fell in their tracks. The attack was over.

"How did you do that?" asked Rouse, her voice trembling as it hadn't since she was a young girl.

Standing Crane gave a dry chuckle. "Ah, Rouse. You of all people know how such things are done. I didn't arrive soon enough to stop men like those from massacring these villagers. But don't be afraid. Once the scales are balanced I'll help you with those who remain among the living." He went back to his work, moving calmly and methodically as one who weeds a garden or harvests an orchard. For a while Rouse could only stand and watch, trapped between anger, wonder, and—fear.

Standing Crane halted for a moment to turn her way. "Don't be afraid," he repeated.

Ben Raintree spoke urgently into his communicator, seeking medical assistance wherever he could find it. But in a place like Haiti there was little to be found, especially none mobile enough to arrive in time to do any good. He called the Lighthouse and asked that a flyer be sent down, but the Vigil did not possess any capacity for massive airlift. He called Tom Standing Crane, but received no response.

The Vigil was poorly equipped for an operation like this, Ben realized. Perhaps they could defeat the Haitian military, but they lacked the massive infrastructure needed to deal with the aftermath of such destruction. They'd saved many civilians, but doomed much of the army in the process.

A pervasive whine interrupted his thoughts. A dozen small flyers hummed into view and landed. Their hatches opened, discharging insect-like robots which scuttled about, located the worst casualties, and began treating them with spider-limbs bearing laser scalpels, spray jets, suction tubes, and micro-manipulators. They even spoke French, questioning the men, addressing them in soothing tones. Ben gaped at this sudden activity, wondering by what miracle his allies had provided it.

A larger flyer came into view, a graceful wasp-waisted form unlike any he'd ever seen, its fuselage emblazoned with a "P" emblem. Raintree stared and gulped, feeling suddenly very much alone. The flyer landed and its canopy slid back. A man in a spotless white tunic climbed out, looked around, noted Ben, and sauntered over. He put out his hand with a friendly grin.

"Ben Raintree? I'm Possum Perturbare. Glad to meet you."

Ben numbly shook hands. Perturbare appeared relaxed, casual, but alert.

"Say, you're quite the physicist." said Perturbare genially. He looked at the cryogun. "That trick of controlling the collapse of your tachyon wavefront—that's impressive. Wish I'd thought of it."

"Thanks," said Ben.

Perturbare stepped back and surveyed the battlefield with compressed lips. "I must say, you and your buddies did a number on these men. My partners and I usually get the job done with less havoc."

"Your partners?"

"He means us, Ben."

Raintree whirled. Approaching were Valjhar Cor and the tall, hooded figure of Cal-Cotavion. Valjhar smiled warmly. "It's great to see you here, Ben. We heard your call for medical help and decided to send in a few squads of Perturbare's Palliators."

Raintree let out a long breath. "I'm glad you did. How goes the campaign? I've been on my own here for hours and haven't heard much news."

Valjhar's smile showed satisfaction. "Haiti will never be the same. We've ended its military and rooted out the worst corruption in the government. Perturbare had no difficulty in discovering exactly who needed to be removed, and for what reasons. I think we've discouraged any other national leaders who might be tempted to oppress those who support us."

Ben gave a rueful smile at that. Valjhar noticed and laughed. "Yes, Ben, I guess that's a mixed blessing for you, isn't it? But don't worry. I think this is the start of a new era of cooperation between our groups."

"I hope so," said Raintree.

"And Ben...here is Cal-Cotavion. He can do things for these injured men that even the Palliators can't match."

Almost reluctantly, Raintree turned to face the cloaked figure. Without thinking he put out his hand. Cotavion's left hand slowly emerged from the folds of the cloak. Ben gripped it; it felt cool and strong. He peered into the shadows of the hood and found two silvery eyes shining out at him with a keen light. Abashed by that gaze, Ben lowered his eyes, resting them on Cotavion's hand. The fingers were long, the flesh white as wax; but it was the green ring that made him yank back his hand as if from an electric outlet. He gasped and stepped back, halting beside Perturbare, his eyes locked in fascination on the faceted bottle-green gem on Cotavion's finger.

Perturbare looked at Cotavion sidelong with narrow-eyed discomfort, then turned sympathetic eyes on Raintree.

They exchanged glances; Ben suddenly felt kinship with the man.

"The Stones are disconcerting, I know," said Valjhar quietly. "But when you see the result of their use you will view them with greater tolerance."

Cotavion turned toward the battlefield. He raised his ring-hand, and from the stone welled a greenness, an airborne essence of peridot that illuminated the fallen men like a leaf-green sun, infusing them like an elixir. Their cries and curses ceased. A rich, blissful silence took hold.

Cotavion put down his hand and closed his cloak. "Now they have new strength to sustain them until they can be moved to a place of care," he murmured. "I will not try them by the other Stones, though they are in sore need of it. They are still too weak."

"But if you would, please show them to Ben," said Valjhar.

Cotavion slowly turned, then flung back his cloak and hood, revealing the four gems he carried. Their power flowed out at Raintree like a cold wave, each, in its way, lovelier and more terrible than the rest.

"What—what are they?" he asked in a husky voice.

Cotavion again lifted his hand; his voice was low and soft. "This is the Stone of Life," he said, displaying the twinkling green stone. His hand moved to the great purple brooch at his throat, which somehow Ben had failed to notice before. It glowed dimly, a light not overwhelming, but commanding. "This is the Stone of Adamance." He lowered his hand, this time to indicate the great crystal teardrop which hung from a chain around his neck. Its glints and refractions seemed to come from within, as though it eschewed the ordinary illumination of day. "This is the Stone of Light."

"Of light?"

"Of Inner Light." Then Cotavion's fingertips wavered upward to lightly touch the small blue gem which burned from a silver fillet around his brow. "Here is the Stone of Truth," he whispered.

"But I don't understand," insisted Raintree, flinching from the glint of that sky-blue stone. "What do these titles mean? Do these jewels somehow control or represent the forces and ideas you name? Are they magic?" he blurted wildly, knowing he was lost in fantasy.

"Indeed, they are not magical, as I am well qualified to know," said Cotavion with a hint of amusement. "They are simply Stones, and as such they do not represent the powers which give them their names—they *are* those powers."

Raintree could only stare at Cotavion's lean, pale face, unable to accept such a statement as indicative of reality. He looked at Perturbare, but found no guidance there; the renegade looked aside, his face tense with his own disbelief, confusion, even distaste.

"Ben, there's little enough we can tell you about the Stones," said Valjhar. "They are, as Cotavion said, actual physical embodiments of various abstractions, expressed as physical objects which resemble gemstones."

Raintree turned back to Cotavion, who somehow stood erect beneath the weight of those four awful jewels. He forced himself to stare straight into Truth, the better to force into his mind the fact that the universe was capable of containing such prodigies—was capable, he supposed, of somehow bringing them into being. It was far more than he'd ever expected—merely to discover that such concepts as Truth and Inner Light were more than the wishful fancies of men, but were absolutes tied into the very structure of being—was an epiphany; to be in the presence of their physical embodiments was almost beyond endurance. His private universe had already expanded to encompass such wonders as Dreamfarer, and Endurance, and Rouse. Now it grew a hundred fold to make room for the Stones.

He looked at Cotavion, seeing him clearly for the first time. His face looked unhealthy and sallow, his mouth set in a line of abiding solemnity. Lank colorless hair hung over his ears and framed his high forehead. His eyes contained his main strength. Steady as moons, they contained glints of all four Stones. As he studied this weary but regal figure of silver, grey, and white, Ben wondered what sort of being it took to carry so terrible and wonderful a burden as the Stones.

Valjhar and Cotavion had departed, traveling in a tunnel of space collapsed by the device on Valjhar's belt. Raintree felt overloaded, utterly exhausted by events and revelations. He sat down on a still-frigid truck fender and stared numbly into space as Perturbare ambled about, checking the progress of his Palliator robots.

Soon a small fleet of boxy flyers appeared, landed, and let down ramps. These craft bore red crosses in addition to the Perturbare "P". Automated litters, suspended on small propulsion beams, emerged. Perturbare helped some of the most afflicted soldiers onto them, then sent them floating into the flying vans. When the field was cleared the vans lifted up and were gone. The Palliators re-boarded their own small flyers and also departed. Hands on hips,

Perturbare stood a hundred feet away, surveying the field, talking to some invisible presence, presumably his computer.

Presently he strolled up to Ben. "Well, those butchers certainly received more mercy from us than they would have offered their victims. That's the way Valjhar wanted it."

Ben did not respond. Perturbare studied him sympathetically. "It's those Stones, isn't it? I know. It doesn't seem right that things like them can actually exist. It's like a fairy tale." He gave an involuntary shudder. "I can't get used to them."

Ben looked up at him. "They are terrible, it's true. But they're also the most marvelous things I've ever seen or imagined."

"Oh, not you too." Perturbare chuckled. "But then, I'd heard you were a dreamy sort." He took one last look around the field. "Well, my work here is done. Do you need a ride?"

"No, I've got a flyer on the way."

"All right. I'm sure I'll see you around. Take it easy. Go home. Forget about Truth, Niceness, Sweetness and Light. Eat a blueberry pie, watch all five *Planet of the Apes* movies. The originals, of course."

Ben finally smiled. "All right. Thanks for your help. I've already got one death on my conscience. You probably prevented it from being a dozen."

Perturbare boarded his flyer and departed.

Raintree sat there musing while mists and vapors rose from the icy wreckage around him.

Chapter 39

The Faces of Rral

On the bridge of *Mote,* Possum Perturbare sat with Valjhar Cor.

"Dr. Perturbare, your assistance during the Haitian operation was invaluable and perfectly executed. Hundreds of lives were saved. The world now has an indisputably positive example of the good we can accomplish; even the Vigil may be disarmed. I admit I had some initial doubts about our association, but I now consider them resolved. We are in your debt."

Perturbare smiled with a lingering reserve. "Well, thank you very much. But please, call me Possum; everyone does."

Valjhar smiled back, though in fact the modes of Terrestrial humor usually eluded him. "Do you wish to take up those questions you mentioned earlier?"

"Actually, only one question is really weighing on me right now. Let me reconstruct my chain of thought so you may better understand my concern." Perturbare tilted back the bridge chair, which he found uncomfortably small, and gazed through the dome at the ice dome far above. "Here you sit, supposedly a native of the planet Rral, along with your friend Kern Harner. Rral, you say, is over two million light-years distant. And yet I look at you and have trouble convincing myself that you are in fact an alien. In fact, I have trouble convincing myself you're not a native of Kansas. You are not only humanoid, but as far as I can tell without analyzing your genes, perfectly human."

Valjhar offered a small embarrassed smile. "I must admit that we prefer to deal with beings who resemble ourselves. We might have settled down to rehabilitate a race of crustaceans, or jellyfish, or swirling lights, but in the end we selected creatures like ourselves."

Perturbare returned a look of skepticism. "But this isn't a matter of mere resemblance. Superficially at least, you are identical to the human race. Now, I believe in parallel evolution as much as the next man. I suppose the universe might be teeming with humanoid races. But you differ in no detail from my own species—not by an odd shape to the fingernails; not by a variation in the configuration of facial hair; not by the presence of an extra vertebra, not even by a difference in the cusps of your molars. To be frank, I'm not willing to accept that as coincidence. You can either explain how it is that the peoples of Earth and Rral are so closely related, or you can reveal the hoax by which you Earthmen present yourselves as aliens." He sat back and awaited Valjhar's response.

Now Valjhar grew red with embarrassment, but the smile did not leave his face. "Well, I see I won't dissuade you from your conclusions, although in fact you have overlooked one possibility which is in fact the truth."

"Which is?"

"That this is not the face I have always worn."

Perturbare's heart beat three times. "Oh."

"We thought it would improve our chances of gaining the trust of the human race if we recast ourselves in its image."

"Oh? In that case, why did you wait so long to reveal yourselves?"

Valjhar contrived a shrug. "Amateur theatrics on our part. We thought to maintain an aura of mystery and unapproachability, hoping to elicit a worldwide sigh of relief when we finally revealed we were 'human' after all."

"I see. So what are you really? Lizard men? Newts? Not bugs, I hope?"

Valjhar shook his head. "No no, nothing so alarming. I suppose I must show you." He sat in thoughtful silence for a moment. "There's someone I'd like you to meet. But first I must ask permission." He turned to the console behind his chair. "Kern? Perturbare has asked some pointed questions about our true nature, and I'd like to introduce him to Pimsehkia. Is that all right with you?"

...Pimsehkia? thought Perturbare, cocking an eyebrow. For some reason he could hear only Valjhar's half of the conversation.

"All right, I will, thanks.

"Pimsehkia, hello. Possum Perturbare is here and would like to meet you. Do you mind?

"Yes, him.

"I know you haven't. I'm sure it will be fine.

"Good, thank you. We'll be right there."

Valjhar broke off this communication and looked at Perturbare. "Shall we go?"

The bemused Perturbare followed Valjhar to a remote part of the Redoubt. They entered a corridor which was lit by a peculiar golden light. At its end was a carved wooden doorway, which they entered.

Valjhar and Perturbare stood in a low-ceilinged room unlike anything Perturbare had ever seen. It was all in wood, polished stone, and fabric, the wood carved with fanciful designs regardless of whether it made up a rafter, a chair, or even a floorboard. Colorful metallic foils were applied to these designs, defining them and lending the whole a subtly kaleidoscopic beauty. The shelves and tables bore all manner of intricate, whimsical objects made of hand-wrought metals, woods, and enamel, ornaments maybe, or perhaps toys. The room was not opulent, but it was certainly beautiful, exotic, and comfortable. Other doors gave glimpses into rooms of a similar character.

Valjhar indicated a tiny figure who perched expectantly in a chair.

"Pimsehkia Flam, may I present Dr. Possum Perturbare."

Up popped the oddest creature Perturbare had ever seen. She was humanoid, pale, graceful, slender, and under four feet in height. She had long tousled blonde hair that grew in a fine down on the nape of her neck and onto her back. Her ears were mobile and somewhat mouselike, set rather high on the head. Her nose was flat, little more than a small ledge over her upper lip, with the nostrils nearly hidden. Her mouth was small and delicate, her eyes large tilted ovals, with grey sclera, oval irises of gemlike aqua, and large central pupils. She wore a simple little peasant dress that matched her eyes and hinted at her small breasts.

"Hello!" she said in a voice which was little more than a squeak. She extended a tiny long-fingered hand; he took it most gently, marveling at its softness and warmth.

"Hello…Pimsehkia," said Perturbare, at a loss for words. He was suddenly aware of his nose, thinking of it as an absurd proboscis.

"So you're the great super genius! You're also the first human person I have met on this world."

"And you...are the first Rralian I've met who actually looks like one, or so I take it."

"Yes, yes. I take no part in the boy's antics as the 'Paramen'. I see no reason to reshape myself into your form when I'm quite happy as I am."

"And why shouldn't you be?" said Perturbare, staring. "You are the most exquisite—person—I've ever seen in my life."

Pimsehkia's laughter was a quick chiming titter. Her eyes shone up at him. "You are very handsome for a human."

"Pimsehkia is Kern's mate," said Valjhar in a bright, helpful voice.

"Oh?" said Perturbare. All at once he felt like a great, shambling oaf. "Then I'd say old Kern has done awfully well for himself. But Pimsehkia...doesn't it bother you to see Kern and Valjhar in these alien forms?"

"Well...not as much as it used to. They do seem awfully...big. But I still recognize them for who they are. The shape of their eyes has changed, but the spirit in them remains the same. That reminds me, how is Ben Raintree?"

The question took Perturbare by surprise. "Raintree? Uh...I only met him once, but he seemed...all right. Distraught, and rather dreamy, maybe, but then that is his reputation."

Pimsehkia laughed again. "Yes, that's true."

"You know him then?"

"No...not exactly. I feel as if I do though."

Perturbare looked around. "This apartment. Is it typical of a dwelling on Rral?"

"Typical? No, it's quite a bit nicer than what I was used to, but Kern spares no effort to keep me happy here. He

455

even made me this." She stepped over to an embroidered curtain and drew it back. A shaft of reddish light entered the room.

Perturbare approached this window, bent down and looked out. The viewpoint seemed to be from the side of a tall but gentle hill. Down below, a harbor city dreamed in a quiet afternoon. Great sailing ships sat placidly at anchor, or moved slowly out in the bay, their filmy sails lit by a large golden-orange sun.

"This is a simulated view of our home city on Rral," said Pimsehkia with a touch of wistfulness. "Kern makes sure that the view changes all the time. It reflects the weather, the seasons, and the cycle of day and night. Ships come and go. Sometimes a house even burns down, but it is quickly rebuilt, and I'm sure no one is hurt. It's really quite marvelous."

But to Perturbare it seemed that Pimsehkia Flam might not be far from tears.

"It's beautiful," he said. "It's a very beautiful city." Perturbare studied the little alien, noting her narrow shoulders, her long neck, her large eyes. Something about her form was familiar to him; suddenly he realized what it was.

"I just noticed—you look like Aureus!"

Pimsehkia flinched at this and drew back.

"That's not surprising," said Valjhar. "Aureus, as you call it, is a robot of Rralian construction."

"Neither of you look happy to hear its name."

"That thing has followed us relentlessly from one end of the Local Group to the other," said Valjhar in a tired voice.

"I hate it," said Pimsehkia. "If not for it, we might all be home right now, having a picnic, or singing."

Perturbare somehow knew that it was unusual for Pimsehkia Flam to declare hatred for anything. The words sounded distressing coming from her mouth.

"Why is the robot so intent on capturing you, anyway?"

"Because we dared to build a spaceship and leave our world," said Valjhar.

"Valjhar, I'm tired," said Pimsehkia. "I want to sleep."

"Yes, of course, Pimsehkia. We'll be on our way. Thanks for having us in."

Perturbare felt as though he were guilty of being harsh with a kitten. "Pimsehkia—I'm sorry if I've said anything to upset you. We hulking Earthmen are a little awkward when it comes to dealing with charming sylphs such as yourself."

Pimsehkia gave a tremulous smile. "You're very sweet. Goodbye, Doctor Perturbare."

They walked back through the empty corridors, with Perturbare quiet in thought.

"Pimsehkia. She seems a little—simple. Childlike."

"She is both those things, to a degree. But make no mistake. She is not stupid. There is no such thing as a stupid Rralian, as Pimsehkia is fond of saying."

"What does the poor girl do with her time?"

"Her waking hours are spent reading, and writing poetry and verse which is better than Kern's, which is one reason he loves her. She cooks, and draws, and watches many of your movies. Maybe someday she will wish to emerge into your world."

When they'd returned to the bridge of *Mote*, Perturbare said, "So. You're elves. Pixies."

Valjhar chuckled. "Come now. Have I been unkind enough to mention the troll-like aspects of the human form?" He touched a few contacts. An image formed in the air: a male Rralian, looking only slightly more robust than Pimsehkia, with brown hair and grey irises. "There you see a typical man of Rral. Myself, to be specific." He touched another contact. Another image appeared, this one red-skinned with black hair, but with a familiar look of wayward passion in his violet eyes. "Kern."

Perturbare studied the image in fascination. "And how did you work the transformation?"

"Kern introduced nano-scale devices into our bodies which visited every cell and rearranged our genes. After a period of adjustment we emerged in these altered bodies. Biochemically, we are still essentially men of Rral, with some modifications to suit this environment. Anatomically, we are human."

"I sounds like an unpleasant process."

"It would have been, if we had been conscious while it was taking place."

"And what about Kroy dal Ren? He looks like a twelve-year-old nerd's idea of a cool alien superhero."

"Ah." Valjhar lowered his eyes in embarrassment. "Kroy—was born on the planet Smerkesh, of Rralian stock. His body was taken over by the star-being who occupies it now, which was formerly a creature of organized magnetic fields inhabiting the interior of the local sun. We visited this system, and wound up taking Kroy, in his usurped biological body, with us when we left.

"When we decided to reshape our bodies for our mission to Earth, Kroy emerged looking as you see him now. Naturally, I had questions for Kern. Kern claimed that

Kroy was so oblivious to his physical body, so disoriented by his new state of existence, that he wouldn't notice any difference, as long as his body conformed roughly to humanoid norms. So far Kroy hasn't noticed the difference."

Now Valjhar looked more than embarrassed—he looked sad, if not downright haunted. Perturbare decided not to probe for whatever was being left unsaid.

They parted amicably. Perturbare sauntered to the bay where his flyer was parked, chuckling at the thought of Kroy dal Ren, unaware of the mischief Kern had worked on him. He entered his flyer and lifted off for the region of fog and stormy waters which concealed his home.

He fell asleep in his chair, where he had his first look at the opaque jade eyes of the Dreamfarer.

Chapter 40

Ultimata

The Vigil met in conclave; Ben Raintree held the floor. He stood at the angle of the new V-shaped meeting table and addressed his colleagues passionately.

"I want no part of a policy that insists on treating the Para-men with suspicion, of dealing with them as if they were criminals or lunatics. That path will lead us to open conflict, to war, death, and destruction. It would be a senseless war, without wisdom, and without much chance of success. I've described what I learned on the battlefield —about Cal-Cotavion and the absolute powers he controls, and how Possum Perturbare, with all his capabilities, has now allied himself with them. The time for trepidation and suspicion is past. Now is the time for decisive action to resolve our conflict." He held the gaze of each of the others in turn, his eyes alive with a turbulent light. His face was flushed, his jaw firm. None of the others had ever seen him assert himself so emphatically.

"But Ben," ventured Fomalhaut, "we cannot risk accommodating the Para-men too far. The risk to the future…"

Raintree shook his head vehemently. "To hell with your future! Face it, you don't know whether the future you anticipate will come about because of, or in spite of, anything we do. It may already be doomed. Despite your efforts to guide things in the direction you desire, you're only guessing. You don't really know what you're doing. I say let's do now what we know to be right, and let the future shape itself from that. Remember—this is not your universe. Your people, your culture, has run its course in its native universe. Let this one take its own form, whether it pleases you or not."

Fomalhaut made no reply.

Raintree continued. "I demand that the Vigil immediately take up negotiations with the Para-men to resolve our disputes. We must work out our differences in a peaceful manner. If we do not attempt this, I will resign. I'll join the Para-men myself!" A sudden uncertainty came over him; he looked away, haunted. "Or if that isn't practical, I'll go home to Canada, where sanity usually prevails," he said more quietly.

"It's been nice knowing you, Ben," said Stingray in a heavy voice.

"Ben, truly, you would be missed," said Fomalhaut mildly. "However, we cannot allow the demands of a single member to remake our policy so dramatically."

"Make that two members," said Rouse in a level tone. Everyone turned towards her.

Stingray's eyes bulged in disbelief. "Rouse! Have you fallen victim to the Para-men's glamour too? We can't just roll over and give them their victory without a struggle. It would be the end of freedom on this planet."

"How do you know that?" replied Rouse with a cool intensity. "Ben knows them; you don't. Ben doesn't seem to fear the loss of his freedom or dignity, and I'm sure he values his almost as much as you do yours."

Stingray made a noise of frustration and waved his arms. "But Ben...Ben's a hopeless romantic. He sees a dreamy woman and a set of glowing costume jewelry and he'll follow them anywhere." He cast an apologetic glance at Ben, who looked back stonily. "I'm trying to base my decisions on facts."

"What facts?" demanded Rouse. "The only facts we have are the ones Ben brought back and the results of the campaign in Haiti. Your stubborn prejudice against the Para-men has nothing to do with 'fact'. I doubt that you even understand your hostility toward them yourself. Facts? You don't even know your own origin, or history, or how you suddenly acquired the ability to shoot lightning. Oh, what a bountiful source of facts you are."

Fomalhaut interrupted quietly. "Stingray has a mental talent which enables him to induce a virtual positive electrical charge in selected objects. When the potential is great enough, the insulating capacity of the air is overcome and his natural negative charge arcs to the target."

"I do? Why didn't you tell me this before?" asked Stingray, amazed.

"It might have inhibited your natural discovery of the talent. Such things can rarely be taught, and are best left to emerge on their own."

"Will you please shut up?" said Rouse. "We are discussing something more important than Stingray's built-in wiring. Here is my point of view. I don't want to spend my life tied to this organization, waiting for it to do something constructive. I'm with Ben. Either start talking now, or I'm out."

Fomalhaut sat motionless for thirty seconds.

"Very well. I see that our best course at this moment is to put the matter to a vote. Will anyone disagree if I assume a vote of 'no', that is, that we shall seek no compromise, from Aureus? I feel we must still consider it a part of our organization, even if it is still immobilized."

No one made any objection. "Aureus and Stingray vote no. Ben and Rouse vote yes. T'Ukudu?"

T'Ukudu sat eating a wheel of cheese. His wound had skinned over, and the bud of a new arm had already appeared. "My purposes will not be served by coming to blows with the Para-men. I vote yes."

"Tom?"

Somehow they were all certain that, one way or another, Tom Standing Crane wouldn't be among them much longer. Whatever power had taken root in him was using him badly. Most of his hair had fallen out; his skin was going grey and dry as parchment. He sat wrapped in robes of grey and brown. Despite his deterioration he made no complaint, sought no salvation. Still, as he pondered his decision, a fleeting anguish moved in his sunken eyes. His mouth worked for a moment, trying to form words, but then an impassive serenity settled over his features.

"It is futile to delay a conflict which is foretold in the very movement of the air. I say no."

Ben groaned, started to rise, but Fomalhaut waved him back down.

"I see," said Fomalhaut. "Ben, Rouse, and T'Ukudu vote yes; Tom, Stingray, and Aureus vote no. The deciding vote is left to me. I vote yes. Ben's words and Rouse's vote have convinced me."

They all looked at him in amazement. Ben smiled tentatively. Rouse nodded in satisfaction, while Stingray assumed a scowl.

"Are there any here who cannot accept this result?" asked Fomalhaut.

Tom said nothing.

Stingray said, "I'll go along until you discover the folly of this decision. But tell me something, Fomalhaut. How much time do you spend dealing with panicky, outraged government officials after what we did in Haiti?"

"Approximately three hours per day."

Stingray nodded. "The U.S. Government tolerates us only because of our stated goal of countering the Para-men and preserving the status quo. If we make any sort of accommodation with the Para-men, that toleration will cease. The corporate and ideological interests which control the government will permit nothing else. At the very least, we will be obliged to move our headquarters."

"Yes. At the very least."

"As long we as we all understand where all this is likely to lead."

"Noted. Well then. Since delay has become so unfashionable in this group, I propose we immediately contact the Para-men to arrange for our colloquy."

"Wait," said Ben reluctantly. "Before we do that, hadn't we better decide what to do about Aureus?"

"I say we leave him just as he is—shut down and harmless," said Stingray. "I don't trust him. His goals and ours no longer coincide. Whatever we decide to do, he's a danger."

"And yet we did take Aureus into the Vigil. We did make certain promises; we did accept its help when it was convenient to do so," said Fomalhaut. "We don't even know that Aureus hasn't some valid reason to apprehend the Rralians."

"If he would deign to let the words spill from his gold-plated lips, we would know," scowled Stingray.

"Our chances of a successful negotiation with the Para-men may be diminished if they see we are capable of betraying one of our own allies," observed T'Ukudu.

Stingray said, "Even if that ally is their worst enemy?"

"Honor must not yield to expedience."

"Stingray, what are the limits of the control device to which Aureus is subject?" asked Fomalhaut. "Can you restore its mental function, senses, and speech apparatus while denying it movement or the use of its weapons?"

"Aureus's brain is a self-contained system, with no known way to shut it down. He's been free to think during every second of his immobilization. As for the rest, yes, I can do that."

"Then let us exercise our conciliatory skills on Aureus before we attempt their use on the Para-men."

Stingray nodded. "All right. Rouse—will you help me get him?"

Rouse accompanied him without argument. Evidently, Fomalhaut thought, Stingray meant to try some reconciliation of his own.

Ten minutes later Rouse returned carrying the contorted robot. Stingray followed, still limping from his rough treatment beneath the wheels of the truck. Rouse set Aureus on the angle of the table and resumed her seat. Stingray attached a console to the control interface beneath the robot's skirting and studied a readout. T'Ukudu joined him. Stingray touched a few keys, observed the readout, and said, "That should do it."

"Aureus," said Fomalhaut carefully, "do you hear me?"

Muffled words emerged from the golden mouth, which had not opened. "Yes, I hear you. In fact I have heard the entire proceedings of your meeting, as well as much else that has occurred since your latest treachery against me."

Everyone looked toward Stingray, who shrugged and grimaced in embarrassment. "All right. Apparently my understanding of its systems is incomplete."

"No matter. It saves us the trouble of explaining our intentions," said Fomalhaut. "You are aware of what we intend to do?" he asked Aureus.

"I am. My only concession to you will be this: release me, and I will resume my pursuit of the criminals without destroying you, unless you ever again threaten to hamper me, or in fact ever again come within range of my sensors."

Fomalhaut paused.

"We are not in a position of requiring concessions from you. It is you who require concessions from us. I observe Stingray fingering a control which I believe will open and activate your tachyon weapon, and I note that it is aimed at your midsection."

Aureus said nothing, but somehow seemed to glower despite being deprived of any capacity to move or even to show its face.

Fomalhaut continued. "I will lay out our intentions regarding the Rralians; you may then decide whether you wish to participate, under terms which we will define."

"And if I choose not to cooperate?"

"Regrettably, we must then leave you in your present state for an indefinite period, if only to preserve our lives."

"State your intentions."

"First you must clarify an important matter. What is your aim regarding the Rralians, and of what crime are they accused? You need not answer if it would compromise your integrity to do so. However, a failure to answer will result in your being returned to the closet."

"The criminals are in violation of the most fundamental law of Rral. They have uncovered, developed, and employed scientific technology beyond that which is permitted. My mission is to return them to Rral for judgment."

"You do not plan to kill them?"

"My mission is to return them unharmed. Killing them is a last resort, but one which I must pursue if the alternative is to let them go free."

"I take it then that you are a creature of Rral."

"I am a Prohibitor of Rral."

"Why is advanced technology illegal on Rral?"

"It has been found harmful to the well-being and development of the people of Rral."

T'Ukudu interjected a remark. "Note that the proscription is so absolute that the instrument of its enforcement is itself a mechanism. Living Rralians may not employ the technology necessary to apprehend offenders."

"True," said Fomalhaut. To Aureus: "Thank you for your candor, which greatly facilitates the resumption of a genial relationship between us. Now, as to our intentions. We will try to persuade the Para-men to abandon their plans and leave the planet. If we succeed at that, after three days we will release you to pursue them, according to your mission."

"And if they do not agree to give over their efforts, merely to please you?"

"That depends. If we reach some compromise whereby they remain on Earth, yet take no action which we consider damaging or objectionable, we will treat them as guests, or even allies, and therefore not subject to attack. You must then defer your mission until they choose to leave the planet at some future time."

Fomalhaut gave a sigh. "If, however, they persist in plans which we consider detrimental to the Human race, we will release you to take whatever action against them you consider necessary, as long as harm to others is avoided."

"I see. So, depending on their whim, or yours, I may either eventually regain the freedom to complete my mission, or languish indefinitely while you and your fellows consort with the criminals."

"That is essentially correct. Let me describe our immediate plans. Assuming we are able to arrange a parley with the Para-men, we will permit you to accompany us, as long as you pledge not to harm, molest, capture, subjugate, kill, injure, or threaten the persons of Valjhar Cor and Kern Harner. Perhaps through consorting with them you may at least obtain information which will assist you, should you ever resume your mission against them. These are our terms; they are not open to modification."

"I accept them without condition."

Fomalhaut prepared to urge Aureus to reconsider, realized what he'd just heard, and did a double take. The others also regarded Aureus with surprise, except for Stingray, who scowled in suspicion.

"I did not expect your acceptance to be so quick or complete," said Fomalhaut mildly.

"You said the terms were not open to debate. I choose to believe you. Would you prefer to argue the matter for a time?"

"No. Your answer is sufficient. But I hope you will not object if we leave the control interface in place until you have proven your compliance."

"How can I possibly prove my voluntary compliance if you are able to paralyze me at any time?"

Fomalhaut considered. "Very well. You are right. Stingray, please release Aureus and remove the interface."

Stingray stood up and folded his arms. "This is a mistake. I won't do it. Let T'Ukudu release him. I don't want to take the blame for it later."

T'Ukudu bent down and used his remaining hand to set Aureus free.

Aureus instantly straightened up and leaped from the table. With clanging footsteps its fluid gait took it into a corner, where it stood motionless, glaring at the others.

"You see, Stingray?" said Rouse in a voice of quiet irony. "Docile as a lamb."

"Aureus, I regret that it has been necessary to change the terms of our original agreement," said Fomalhaut in a conciliatory tone.

"I do not expect consistent behavior from organic beings."

Ben found that he was sweating profusely. "Well," he said with a slight quaver, "Now that that's settled, shall we contact the Para-men?"

Fomalhaut said, "Ben, I propose that you make the contact. You deserve the honor of initiating what I hope may become friendship between our groups."

Smiling, Ben left for the communications room. Ten minutes later he was back, still grinning. "Valjhar was— absolutely delighted by the idea, and he asked me to thank you all. We agreed to meet at a neutral site, and settled on central Australia. However, he wants to delay the meeting for ten days—to allow our injured members a chance to recover."

T'Ukudu reacted to this with equanimity; evidently he felt ten days ample time to grow a new arm. Stingray looked sour, as though he resented being coddled by his enemies.

As they left the meeting room Stingray leaned over to Raintree and grumbled, "Well, Ben, you got what you wanted. I never thought you'd be the one to take over the Vigil."

Ben frowned as he considered that, wondering if Stingray intended it as a left-handed compliment. He answered, "Well, Stingray, knowing me, it's probably all just a dream."

Fomalhaut stepped out into the beacon chamber high atop the Lighthouse. Standing between the pillars, he gazed down at the angular structures of Boston, their blocky forms softened by the hazy mauve light of dusk. After a moment he stepped to the brink and lifted off, heading for a favorite retreat in central Asia, there to contemplate the day's events and search for insights into their likely consequences. He launched himself into a suborbital ballistic arc, gazing wistfully at the stars as he hurtled high over the pale Arctic.

A pressure, a thought, intruded into his mind. Surprised, he opened himself to it and found himself in contact with the mind of Rouse Farewell, who asked to meet with him to discuss an important matter. Fomalhaut agreed at once, killed off his velocity, and dropped into the atmosphere to facilitate verbal communication. There he waited, adopting an upright posture in the air, balancing on his propulsion beams.

His wait wasn't long. His sensors detected Rouse's approach long before his eyes could sight her. Her flight was very powerful, ripping through the air with no concern for energy expenditure, as befitted someone whose power source was the universe itself.

A moment later she achieved an effortless hover a few feet in front of him. She floated gracefully, her hair streaming in a thin wind cold enough to freeze Fomalhaut in a moment if not for the protection of his suit.

"Rouse. I was not aware you were telepathically adept."

"I'm not. But I know you well enough that I thought if I concentrated on you, and 'saw through' in the right way, so to speak, I might establish contact. Just an experiment."

"It was well done. What do you wish to discuss?"

Rouse's expression was serious and intent. "What are we going to do to help Standing Crane?"

"Help him with what?"

"Don't be disingenuous. You know as well as I that he is being consumed by the thing that dwells within him."

"Yes—I cannot deny it, much as I would like to."

"But what can we do? He is a decent man being subsumed and destroyed by a force we don't understand."

"I am aware that you would like me to enter Standing Crane's mind and somehow grapple with this entity and cast it out. But I must tell you it is beyond my power to do so. I have looked into him and examined this presence, to the extent that I dared. It is very powerful. It is potentially the greatest power among us, on either side. When Standing Crane arrived and requested Vigil membership, I was immediately aware of his possession. I also foresaw that it might become a threat. Yet I felt compelled to accept him. To do otherwise was to leave him without direction, moderation, or control."

"I wish I could have a crack at the horrid thing, whatever it is," said Rouse grimly.

"It is not truly a personality, but more like a force of nature, and thus not to be overcome through effort of will or strength of character." Fomalhaut noticed Rouse's wry expression and reminded himself again of the source of her power. "Point taken. However, I still believe we have no recourse against this entity, certainly not without knowing its exact nature. I fear Tom must seek his own destiny, while we hope to direct his power to our advantage."

"That's a cold-blooded attitude."

"Standing Crane himself seems to be facing his impending demise with equanimity...assuming that demise is what he is indeed facing."

"I'm not sure how much of Standing Crane is left to face anything."

Fomalhaut hesitated. "Nor am I."

Rouse compressed her lips in dissatisfaction. "I just wish he'd stop looking at me the way he has recently. It's as if he knows something he isn't telling."

And then Fomalhaut, in an unwelcome moment of foresight, also glimpsed something in regard to Rouse Farewell, and the knowledge sent rare emotions burning through him. His only consolation was that she could neither see his face nor look into his mind to see the image that had afflicted him.

Chapter 41

Golden Rain

At the appointed time the seven members of the Vigil boarded a flyer for the trip to Australia. They departed in the dead of night, to rendezvous with the sunrise somewhere in the Gibson Desert. Even Rouse chose to ride. She was uncharacteristically pensive and seemed to want the company. The others were uniformly solemn and silent, though Raintree nurtured an optimism that the old conflict might be on the verge of ending at last.

A thousand miles later Rouse's small radio receiver chirped; she frowned and inserted the earpiece. She listened for a moment and muttered, "Damn."

They all looked at her, even T'ukudu from his place in the pilot's seat. Stingray said, "What's the matter, Rouse?"

"An explosion and fire on an offshore drilling platform in the North Sea. Oil is spilling and the crew is in danger. I've got to go."

Fomalhaut straightened up with unusual animation. "By all means, Rouse, attend to the emergency. No doubt we can handle the negotiations without you."

Rouse looked at him curiously.

"I'll come with you, Rouse," said Stingray earnestly. "You might need some help in the water."

Rouse brushed his cheek with her fingers and shook her head. "No, but thank you. The Vigil's business is as important as mine, and your place is here." She stood up in the flyer's cramped cabin. "Damn," she whispered again. "I hate these oil fires. They're like taking a trip to the underworld." She shook herself as if to fling off a veil of cobwebs. "I'll try to make it back to you before it's all over. Good luck to you."

"Take your time, Rouse," said Fomalhaut.

She cycled through the airlock into the vacuum a hundred and fifty miles above the Earth.

"Rouse is diving into the atmosphere," said T'Ukudu, studying a readout. "She is proceeding toward the North Sea at a speed of Mach 13."

Stingray shook his head in admiration, then caught Fomalhaut with a sharp glance. "You seemed awfully anxious for her to leave."

"Rouse now pursues her rightful mission in life," said Fomalhaut placidly.

Half an hour later the flyer landed on the tawny, scrubby plain of the Gibson. The six emerged and examined their surroundings. The sun was just up; every golden rock cast a long blue shadow. Two other vehicles were visible in the middle distance: a purple-black Para-men craft and a white wasp-waisted flyer bearing the emblem of Possum Perturbare. He and the Para-men stood in a loose group near their flyers, looking toward the Vigil.

Black specks atop the low hills on the horizon caught Fomalhaut's attention. His collar optics revealed their nature. "Look," he said quietly. "Those distant figures are native Australians."

T'Ukudu carefully scanned the horizon. "It would be interesting to know how they learned that an unusual event would take place here today."

Stingray squinted around with a frown. "Where are they?" he asked. "I don't see them."

"Indeed?" said Fomalhaut. He scanned again. "They have departed. I can sense their minds; they are retreating in apprehension."

"Primitive superstitious dread," said Stingray smugly.

"Perhaps. Shall we greet our counterparts?"

They began a slow walk toward the Para-men, who came forward to meet them. Raintree conceived a sudden and unwelcome mental image: the Clantons approaching the Earps at the OK Corral.

The two groups were still well separated when a gust of wind blew back Cal-Cotavion's cloak, permitting a glimpse of the Stones. The sight, brief as it was, stopped the Vigil in its tracks.

Raintree looked up at Stingray, who appeared shaken. Ben assumed a fierce grin. "Costume jewelry, eh, Stingray?" He chuckled happily; suddenly all cares seemed banished.

Aureus, walking a few steps ahead of the others, had also halted. Its head swiveled toward Cotavion and locked onto him. From somewhere within the robot's body came an eerie wailing note which his colleagues had never heard before. Its mouth slid open; words rolled out across the desert like the notes of great bronze bells, painfully loud for the members of the Vigil.

"CAL-COTAVION: YOU ARE IN POSSESSION OF ARTICLES WHICH ARE THE PROPERTY OF THE SCIENCE COUNCIL OF RRAL. I ORDER YOU TO IMMEDIATELY SURRENDER THE FOUR STONES. WILL YOU COMPLY?"

No one spoke while the echoes of Aureus's demand surged back and forth between the hills. Stingray swore under his breath and stared hard at Fomalhaut. Fomalhaut turned toward their flyer and stood motionless.

"Go polish your head!" came Kern Harner's faint reply. Cal-Cotavion said nothing.

Valjhar's voice, though low and mild, somehow covered the distance between them. "What do you intend to do with the Stones if we hand them over?"

"MY DUTY IS TO DESTROY THEM; FAILING THAT I MUST CONSIGN THEM TO A BLACK HOLE AND THUS REMOVE THEM FROM THE UNIVERSE."

Stingray angrily stalked over to Aureus, bent down, put his mouth to one of the domes which presumably represented its ears, and screamed, "Aureus! LOWER YOUR VOICE!" He slipped his fingers beneath the skirting on the robot's back, only to find the input terminals covered by sheaths of some insulating material. Aureus rotated its head and lifted its face. Stingray found himself face-to-face with the robot. A kind of scornful mirth was contained in its immobile features.

Across the way, Cal-Cotavion shook his head. "I will give up these Stones to one person and one person only, and she is not here."

Aureus wasted no more time in conversation. Configuring its flexible body for flight, it poised for lift off. At that moment the control interface which Stingray had devised floated out of the flyer. It wafted toward Stingray's open hand, but changed course to follow Aureus as the robot shot up and accelerated toward Cotavion. In a moment Aureus was moving too fast for Fomalhaut's mental impulse to guide the device with sufficient accuracy.

Stingray howled in frustration, turned to Fomalhaut and yelled, "Fire on that thing!" Fomalhaut hesitated for an instant, then unleashed twin ERASER beams which merely glinted dangerously from the robot's golden hide.

Aureus flew a ground-skimming course straight for Cotavion. Another figure stepped into its path, an incidental nuisance for the robot, which merely climbed a dozen feet to clear the obstacle. But Endurance had other ideas. He leaped up, his right hand lashing out and grabbing Aureus's ankle, sending the robot crashing face-first into the gravel. It immediately squirmed around and tried to regain its feet, but Endurance's grip was not so easily broken. They wrestled in the dirt, Aureus twisting and writhing like a golden starfish, but to no avail. Endurance took another grip on Aureus's wrist. He stood up, dangling Aureus before him in an undignified posture.

Fomalhaut suddenly stiffened. He sent his voice rolling over the desert with the aid of his suit's vocal amplifier. "EVERYONE TAKE COVER AT ONCE! VIGIL AND PARA-MEN SEEK SHELTER!"

"What?" Startled, Stingray looked aside at Fomalhaut, who was entering the flyer with all deliberate speed. He squinted back toward Aureus and barely made out the deadly glimmer of its opening Third Eye. That was enough to convince Stingray. He dashed toward the flyer, sweeping up a bemused Ben Raintree along the way and practically throwing him into the cabin. The hatch was barely closed when a blinding flood of light poured in through the cockpit canopy. The canopy darkened automatically, but Stingray was already dazzled. When his vision returned he found T'Ukudu at the controls, manipulating the flyer's external cameras. Screens showed a magnified view of Aureus, still trapped in the grip of Endurance, lashing his captor's body with a thin beam from the Third Eye.

"That's a low-grade tachyon beam—Aureus is trying to draw out Endurance's molecular energy—freeze him," muttered Raintree. The attack had no apparent effect on Endurance, who methodically inched his grip up Aureus's limbs without giving it the slightest chance of escape.

The tachyon beam intensified. Raintree winced at the thought of the power it represented. "That's the high-power tachyon emission. Aureus is trying to convert Endurance's substance directly into energy."

To Stingray's incredulity, this new attack did not phase the fragile-looking figure of Endurance either.

The screen flared white, then darkened to reveal a cataract of energy washing over Endurance. A powerful shock wave lifted the flyer and flung it through the air, sending the Vigil members crashing against the overhead as the vehicle settled on its side. Raintree thought himself lucky to land on T'Ukudu instead of vice-versa. The flyer continued to quiver and jerk but now seemed more stable.

Fomalhaut made his way forward and manipulated the controls. "The starboard cameras have been destroyed. Switching to the belly cameras." The screens again depicted Aureus, still buffeting Endurance with an incandescent wind. "Aureus has eschewed subtlety," observed Fomalhaut. "It is releasing some of its stored energy in its attempt to escape."

It was difficult to make out the figure of Endurance in that holocaust, but he was evidently still standing, still holding onto his captive.

"He's indestructible!" cried Stingray in amazement.

"Of course he is," answered Raintree tensely. "How do you think someone could survive for five billion years without being indestructible?"

"The flyer's outer skin is approaching the melting point," said T'Ukudu. "I suggest we attempt to lift off at once."

"Just another moment," said Fomalhaut calmly.

They crowded around the monitors while Endurance finally got a hand around Aureus's neck. His fingers dug into the gleaming substance, and suddenly the robot's energy beam ceased. Its mouth opened wide and it began to writhe and twist with renewed vigor. Endurance's inexorable fingers pierced the robot's transparent covering and ripped it open. A metallic golden liquid flowed from the rent to splash into the molten rock in which Endurance was standing. He continued to rip and shred, emptying the transparent envelope, scattering globules of the liquid gold.

In the flyer the radio snapped on. "This is Aureus requesting assistance. This is Aureus. Requesting assistance."

Raintree swallowed hard. Despite everything, it was not easy to stand idly by while one of his allies was being destroyed. Stingray noticed the stricken look on Ben's face and said, "If Aureus had been trustworthy, this wouldn't be happening." But Stingray's own troubled scowl did not abate.

In another moment Aureus's form had been reduced to a flaccid man-shaped envelope. But that was not enough for Endurance. He reached inside and ripped out the robot's internal components, crushing them, tearing them, throwing them aside. Finally he pried out the silver ovoid which functioned as Aureus's brain. With wrath burning on his face he began to squeeze. But here Aureus offered the only effective resistance it had managed so far. After a moment's frustrated effort, Endurance lifted the brain case and hurled it into the molten rock, creating a brief fountain of glowing slag. Then, staring into their camera, he began to approach the Vigil flyer with a deliberate tread.

"Events have gotten out of hand," observed Fomalhaut placidly. "We shall depart." He moved toward the flyer's cockpit.

Ben had brought along his equipment; he scrambled to a locker where he found his cryogun undamaged. He was pulling on his cold-armor when a spurt of melted metal and composites showed the path of an invisible beam which was slicing the flyer in two. Ben rolled aside. Fomalhaut, his suit fully mirrored, abandoned the console and stepped in front of the beam to deflect it outwards. "I suggest we prepare for battle," he said sadly. "Defend yourselves. Try to neutralize the Para-men without harming them. Appeal to their reason if possible. Remember, we started this."

"Hey, where's Standing Crane?" demanded Stingray, looking around as if he might find him under a seat cushion.

"Standing Crane felt no need to seek shelter," said Fomalhaut. He flashed out of the opening which had been burned into the Flyer's side.

Raintree was the last one out. His head was bare; the hood of his cold armor was lost in the ruins of the flyer. The air was corrosive with smoke and fumes from the molten pit where Endurance had casually destroyed one of the most powerful beings on Earth. Even at this distance Raintree could feel the pit's radiant heat on his face. Endurance was still approaching, still too far away for his expression to be read, but Ben remembered what he had seen on the monitor.

Possum Perturbare's flyer rushed by overhead, its invisible UV ERASER beam lashing out to finish off the Vigil flyer. Ben raised the cryogun and tracked the flyer, but did not touch the contact. As long as Perturbare confined himself to attacking the ruined flyer, Ben would not molest him. He looked around to gauge the general situation.

Only then did he notice "Standing Crane" standing nearby. Ben found it impossible to think of him as the same Tom Standing Crane he had known, but had as yet no other name by which to call him. Apparently most of "Standing Crane's" clothes had been blasted away in the conflagration; he stood wearing only a white loincloth which emphasized the damage his possession had done him. His body was lean and dry as a figure of weathered wood. The last wisps of his hair had burned away with his robes, leaving his scalp grey and parched. Even his ears seemed to have degenerated into shapeless flaps. He watched impassively as the Vigil and Para-men warily approached one another, his shaded eyes unfathomable.

"Why don't you stop this?" cried Raintree bitterly, for he suddenly had no doubt whatever that this creature easily could.

"It is not my task to stop that which must be," came the whispered answer.

"Really? Then why the hell do we need you in the Vigil?" He felt an urge to raise the cryogun and shatter the husk of Standing Crane's body; perhaps it would be a kindness. Yet an unreadable glance from those black eyes stayed his hand.

"Standing Crane" walked away, heading generally toward Cotavion.

And now it was time to deal with Endurance, who was close enough now for Ben to see the glitter in his eyes. To Ben it seemed a threatening, accusing gaze, difficult to bear. He lifted the cryogun, thinking to encase Endurance in a mass of frozen air. It wouldn't harm him, but might immobilize him until the situation could be sorted out. Endurance, seeing his intention, frowned and shook his head. Ben triggered the turbo-blizzard as a warning, a gesture of defiance or desperation, he wasn't sure which. But Endurance was at its extreme range; it had no affect on him at all.

And then Ben was aware of a presence beside him. He turned reluctantly, finding there the Dreamfarer, a figure somehow set apart from the world, lit by a cool gleam not shed by the Australian sun, her pale flesh free of the smoke and dust of the battlefield.

Ben's voice caught in his throat, but he managed to say, "You've got to stop this. Tell the others we mean no harm, that Aureus's attack was his doing alone. I'm afraid something terrible will happen here."

The Dreamfarer held her eyes shut for a long moment. Her eyelids were bruised like the skin around her eyes. "Ben...a creature of dream has little influence on those who are awake and angry."

Raintree felt his last hope dissolve away. Filled with grief, he tightened his grip on his weapon, ready to do whatever a freezing man could to ease the situation.

But Dreamfarer stopped him. "Ben—it's not fitting for you to take part in this battle. Please stay here, with me."

"What, loiter here while the others risk their lives?"

"You are a friend to everyone here. It would destroy you to take up arms against either group. Stay with me, walk in dream, and live—live to search for peace in the future."

He looked into those jade-green eyes, desperate to accept the peace she offered, fleeting though it promised to be. Beyond it lay confusion and uncertainty, and pain which he must face soon enough. He surrendered his resolve to fight, entering into the dreamscape he saw behind those eyes. After a few moments his grip loosened and the cryogun clattered down onto the rocks.

Puzzled, Endurance stepped up to Ben and looked into his eyes, finding them locked on infinity, oblivious to everything. Just as well. Either he'd gone catatonic or was the victim of the spirit called Dreamfarer. At least he was neutralized and out of harm's way.

Or so he supposed, until Perturbare's flyer hissed by again, its weapons continuing their pointless work of dissecting the hulk of the Vigil flyer. Endurance considered bringing down the flyer with a hurled rock. Perturbare had leaped too eagerly to the attack after the battle with Aureus, neither requesting nor receiving the agreement of the others. His intemperate action was almost as responsible for this debacle as was that of Aureus. Yet Endurance could not stop Perturbare now without risking his death. He settled for carrying Ben a few hundred yards away and laying him in the shadow of a large boulder.

That done, he turned his attention back to the battle, intending to neutralize whichever Vigil member was most dangerous. He suspected it was the thing they called Standing Crane, but that one was approaching Cotavion, who could be trusted to deal with the threat. That left Fomalhaut as the obvious choice. Endurance scanned the landscape and found him engaged in a simultaneous duel with Valjhar and Harner. Best to put a stop to that before someone got hurt.

He started forward, but after a few steps a powerful blow from behind knocked him face down into the dust and gravel. He rolled over to find an enraged Stingray looming over him.

"What did you do to Ben, nature boy?" Stingray demanded through clenched teeth.

"I put him out of danger." Endurance sat up and made to get to his feet, but Stingray snatched up a massive rock and smashed it down on him, knocking him flat again.

"Putting him into a coma in the process?"

"I did nothing of the kind. Ben is largely a victim of his own imagination. He's no warrior; it's best that he be put aside." Again Endurance tried to rise; again Stingray laid him low, this time with a powerful kick to the face. The next time he tried to get up, Stingray was ready with another boulder, which split into three pieces on impact. The blows did Endurance no harm, but he was kept off balance, unable to resist their force.

When Stingray attempted another kick, Endurance's hand flashed out and grabbed his ankle. He squeezed gently, grinding bones against one another and wringing a howl out of his antagonist. Still holding on, Endurance got to his feet, forcing Stingray to hop on one foot. Once fully upright, Endurance released his grip. Stingray instantly thrust in and delivered a blow that launched Endurance three feet into the air. Landing neatly, Endurance answered with a blow of his own, driving the wind out of Stingray with a fist to the gut. For a few moments they stood toe to toe, trading punches that sounded like sledgehammers striking wooden beams. But Stingray was soon panting and bloody, while Endurance remained unmarked and unruffled.

Finally Stingray stumbled back to glare at his opponent with a hot mixture of wrath, frustration, and bewilderment.

Endurance said calmly: "Stingray, you are valiant but misguided. I intend to end this madness, so that all may listen to reason. If I must break your bones or knock you unconscious to keep you from dogging my every step, I will do so, if reluctantly."

Stingray said nothing. His glare went unabated, but he made no move.

Endurance gave a nod of satisfaction, turned, and walked away.

A projectile flashed low over the battlefield. An instant later a great concussion smashed down and flattened everyone who was still on his feet. Possum Perturbare's flyer, caught in the vortex, rolled violently and made a hard landing on its side. Too fast for the eye to follow, the missile made a radical climbing turn and then another pass at a greater altitude. This time the sonic boom wasn't quite so shattering.

Stingray, his ears ringing, hauled himself up and gaped at the rocketing blur. Then he ran to the boulder that sheltered Raintree, stopping short at what he found there. Raintree lay with his head cradled in the lap of a pale woman with silvery hair and opaque green eyes. She looked up at him, her face radiating sweet innocence.

Stingray said, "Leave him alone, you mind-rotting witch, or I'll leave purple footprints on your immaculate white buttocks."

With a pout of annoyance the Dreamfarer vanished from sight. Stingray lifted Ben, shook him, slapped him lightly. "Raintree, wake up! Wake up, you useless mooncalf!"

Life returned to Ben's eyes; he stared blankly at Stingray for a moment. Then his face turned bright red and twisted with embarrassment.

"Save your wet dreams for later, Ben. Rouse is here! Now we've got a chance."

They staggered out from behind the boulder and saw Rouse Farewell streaking directly for Endurance.

"Oh no," moaned Ben. "She's picked the one Para-man she can't possibly defeat."

Rouse plowed into Endurance, the impact sending him fifty feet into the air.

Ben whistled between his teeth, wincing as the crack of the blow reached them.

"Damn it all, that won't hurt him," muttered Stingray.

But Rouse wasn't done yet. Before Endurance could begin to fall she did a tight, high-speed loop and delivered another blow, lofting him another fifty feet. The next time she returned he tried to grab her, but she was too fast, too nimble in the air, and Endurance only grabbed an armful of air. Again and again she looped back, returning from every direction, striking and striking again while Endurance made futile grabs. In seconds he was gaining altitude like a rocket, with Rouse providing another boost every second and a half. In moments they were merely two dancing specks in the heights, and then they were gone.

Their faces mirrors of incredulity, Stingray and Raintree gaped at the empty sky, and then at each other, eyes shining. From sheer relief they burst into laughter.

"I don't believe it," said Ben. "Endurance didn't have a chance against her. I wonder where she'll take him?"

"Into orbit, I hope. She's given us a chance. Let's get out there and win this fight."

"No!"

Stingray turned and looked down at Raintree with surprise.

"Stingray, don't let your blood run so hot. Our job here is to stop the fight, not win it. It's on our honor to do so."

Stingray scowled at Ben for a long, tense moment.

"You're right, Ben. I have gotten carried away. But there's just something about these Para-men that gets under my skin."

"We've all noticed," said Raintree dryly.

Stingray ran off to look for Fomalhaut and T'Ukudu. Ben followed, then turned aside to retrieve his cryogun, which was lying in the dust near the wreckage of the flyer.

"Ben."

He turned at the soft voice. There stood the Dreamfarer. He felt his legs going weak, his will slipping away.

"Ben. I'm not finished with you yet."

"Dreamfarer, don't do this to me," said Ben in a husky voice. "If you take me from my duty, you force me to become your enemy."

She did not relent, though a tear rolled down her cheek. The power she wielded was more than Ben Raintree could resist. He fell, unmanned, into the dust.

"Your true duty is not in the here and now," she whispered.

T'Ukudu climbed the rocky knoll atop which Kroy dal Ren sat watching the confusion on the plain. The creature turned to look, his head cocked at an odd angle, as T'Ukudu strode up to him.

T'Ukudu halted at a respectful distance. "Greetings. I am T'Ukudu, Servant of the T'Utahnti, and presently a member of the Vigil. I note that you take no part in the conflict below."

Kroy dal Ren stared at T'Ukudu silently, his head bobbing back and forth, up and down. T'Ukudu began to think he would not reply. Finally he answered in a warbling, poorly-controlled voice. "Valjhar asked me to wait here and respond to any emergency that might arise."

"I see. And how are you to deal with such an emergency?"

"I don't know. Valjhar did not tell me. I must act as I see fit, I suppose."

T'Ukudu regarded the agitated figure in thoughtful silence. Then he said, "How will you recognize an emergency, should one arise?"

Kroy dal Ren waggled his head. His dark, liquid eyes ended up staring at the pale blue sky. "I don't know that either. It's difficult for me to interpret events in your world. I see you approach; sounds emerge; you ask me questions. I answer as if you were real, yet I do not know that you are, or if you are anything more than some vagrant image formed by the balls of gel which have become my chief interface with the world. The thin, cold gas I inhabit vibrates and I interpret the vibrations as meaning." He pointed at the sun, still close to the horizon. "There is my reality. This place...I had no concept of it when I abandoned my native form in search of knowledge. I have found a word to describe what this realm is to me. It is a fantasy."

T'Ukudu said, "I wish to learn more of you and your kind. May I touch you, so as to facilitate communication between us?"

"It makes no difference to me."

T'Ukudu stepped up and laid two fingers on the yellow flesh of Kroy dal Ren's arm. He flinched back, then steadied himself, reestablished the contact, and stood in stolid communion with this enigmatic being.

Fomalhaut found it difficult to concentrate on his task. The memory of the destruction of Aureus was hard to dispel. He had quailed at that event; surrender had suddenly seemed an attractive option. Valjhar Cor stood a hundred yards away, so close he could see his grave, fretful expression without the need to sense his emotions. Yet communication between them was impossible. His duel with Kern Harner required all his resources. If he tried to fly, Kern would apply a magnetic or electrostatic force to bring him to ground. If he tried to walk toward Valjhar, Kern would launch proton bolts that would smash him off his feet. If he tried to approach Kern himself, Kern would create solid obstacles out of thin air to hamper him. Fomalhaut wished he'd equipped his exploration suit with weapons more subtle and powerful than simple SASERs and ERASERs. The suit was primarily defensive in function, and so far Kern's own suit had manifested no power able to harm him. But Fomalhaut suspected that was merely reluctance on Harner's part. Given the complete control over matter he had already displayed, Fomalhaut believed Harner could possibly unravel his suit's structure if he wanted to badly enough. Kern Harner was toying with him, and enjoying himself in the process, if the melodramatic poses he was always striking were any indication.

Fomalhaut sighed. Although he was loath to do it—for there was no malice in Kern Harner; not even any real anger—he felt he had no choice. He immobilized his suit, braced himself as well as possible against Harner's assaults, and shut down all sensory inputs. Suddenly isolated from the external world, he was able to concentrate, to reach out with senses more subtle than vision, there to find the refinement of the quantum flow that was Kern Harner. He reached out, thrusting at that semi-coherent zone of being, pushing into it like a hand into a balloon, stressing it, deforming it.

He reopened his sensory channels. Kern Harner lay prostrate. He and Valjhar Cor converged on the fallen figure from different directions. Fomalhaut arrived first, relieved to find that Harner was merely stunned. Valjhar then approached, his hand not far from the instrument of spacial manipulation which he wore on his belt, a terrible weapon. Although he was now within earshot, Fomalhaut decided to address him with the authority of naked thought.

Valjhar Cor. We must stop this. Aureus's attack was made on its own initiative, despite our efforts to preclude it. I would have destroyed the robot myself had I known its intention. Let us end this conflict before someone is killed.

Valjhar stared hard at the shining helmet. *I thought as much. More than once we have confronted the Prohibitor somewhere among the stars. Now at last it is destroyed. Let there be peace between us.*

The two came together, their hands extended in a gesture of amity which was common on the world they had adopted as home.

Valjhar offered a wry smile. "On Rral, major negotiations between rival parties are often preceded by an athletic competition. Perhaps we brought our traditions with us."

Before their hands could meet, they were distracted by a cry of hopeless anguish. They looked aside; a thousand feet away stood "Standing Crane" at the focus of a pencil of piercing blue light emanating from the cowl of Cal-Cotavion.

"What is the nature of that radiation striking my colleague?" asked Fomalhaut in a carefully controlled voice.

"It is the Light of Truth," said Valjhar soberly. "It's a bad sign for your friend that he reacts to it so badly."

Fomalhaut's sensors then alerted him to another interruption: the approach of a high-speed projectile from the edge of space.

"Rouse Farewell is returning," he said.

A sudden foresight paralyzed him with dread. Despite his certain knowledge of what was to come, he did his best to avert the outcome he foresaw. *Rouse. Turn back. Do not approach!*

Again he engaged his voice amplifier. EVERYONE TURN AWAY FROM KROY DAL REN. DO NOT LOOK IN HIS DIRECTION. SEEK SHELTER IF POSSIBLE."

T'Ukudu broke off his contact and stepped back, as troubled and uneasy as it was possible for his kind to be. He was not reassured when Rouse came stooping down from the ionosphere like her namesake raptor.

Kroy dal Ren followed her plummet with a smooth swivel of his head. "There is the person who defeated and removed the immutable one. Perhaps Valjhar would count her return as an emergency." He casually got up from his perch on a rock.

"What do you intend to do?" asked T'Ukudu, glancing over his shoulder at Rouse.

"I do the one thing I know how to do which reminds me of my old life." He touched a contact on a small device he wore on his belt. T'Ukudu instantly found himself looking into a large, mirror-like paraboloid which had materialized in the air.

T'Ukudu had no gift for precognition, but he knew this was a moment for desperate action. He sprang forward, intending to skirt the mirror-bowl and do whatever was necessary to incapacitate Kroy dal Ren.

But he didn't get the chance. Before he could reach it, a tiny sun formed at the focus of the floating silver bowl.

Somehow Kroy dal Ren had manifested a thermonuclear spark in the mirror field which hovered before him. A focused beam of outrageous power stabbed out and caught Rouse Farewell, blasting her back, sending her tumbling end-over-end. Fomalhaut frantically engaged his sensors to see where she would fall. To his astonishment, she did not fall, but recovered from her tumble, came around, and flew right up that terrible beam, her determination so powerful that Fomalhaut felt it resonating in his brain. He urgently wanted to tell her the battle was over, that she need not bear this trial, but he dared not risk breaking her concentration by intruding into her mind.

A great shock wave rolled over him, rocking the earth, followed by a blast of superheated air. Fomalhaut consulted his sensors: luckily, the flux of hard radiation was low; the air was absorbing the gamma rays which were the product of the fusion reaction and re-radiating them at longer wavelengths—X-rays and ultraviolet near the focusing field, mainly light and heat beyond. Fomalhaut's helmet was set to transmit only one hundred-thousandth of the available light—and it was more than enough to see by.

Rouse made a series of zigzags, dodging out of the blast, but it was nimble as a flashlight beam, and Kroy dal Ren soon caught her in it again. As long as she persisted in approaching him she could not long avoid that terrible light, and she showed no sign of breaking off her attack. Given no other choice, she pushed her way through incandescent plasma as if it were a hot wind out of the desert, the strength of her resolve beyond any which Fomalhaut had ever witnessed.

Suddenly he became aware that a weak tachyon beam was striking the fusion spark. Fomalhaut turned and saw Stingray, braced against a rock a thousand yards off, firing Raintree's cryogun. But he didn't seem to know how to operate it properly, and anyway, it was beyond the device's capacity to neutralize more than a fraction of the mini-sun's energy.

And still Rouse forced her way into that stream of power. Now she had closed to the point where she must be bearing the brunt of the X-rays near the source. And yet she did not falter—but how could she possibly resist such terrible punishment? It was beyond what any form of normal matter could endure. Fomalhaut focused his fine-scale sensors as she bore through the shaft of plasma. He read the state of the atoms of her body, ordinary atoms for all the magnificence of the soul they housed.

His findings deprived him of any acceptable options.

Fomalhaut knew how he felt about Rouse, and he knew he was the only person present who had a chance of saving her. The Para-men were apparently as unable to contain their errant comrade as he had been unable to contain Aureus.

He raised his weapons. A single shot should be enough to end this threat. And yet, he hesitated. Which would he rather do, kill for Rouse Farewell, or die for her?

Very well then. His exploration suit was not composed of any form of normal matter. He would subject its ability to protect him to its most severe test.

He fell forward and activated his propulsion beams, intending to intercept Rouse and force her away from that terrible beam and the death that awaited her. But as he hurtled toward her, another force gripped him, a force with the signature of Kern Harner, impeding him, deflecting him from his course.

And so Fomalhaut ran out of time.

With a feeling of regret he knew would never fully leave him, he pushed his thoughts into Rouse's mind.

Rouse. You are maintaining your physical integrity by mentally increasing the electromagnetic binding force of your atoms. If you increase it any further, your atoms will collapse, and you will explode into a cloud of neutrons, killing yourself and everyone present.

He could feel her surprise, her confusion—instead of veering off to safety, she relaxed her efforts—relaxed them too much. Still in contact with her thoughts, he felt the sudden impact of the beam, burning, tearing, cutting through.

And suddenly he found himself thrust deep within her mind, seeing it in its full splendor as never before: a vast, sunlit expanse, clean, brilliant, and uncluttered. Many other people had shared glimpses of the insight she had mastered, but for most of them it had been like putting a match to a pile of wet leaves...a brief spark, quickly extinguished by the sodden mass of disillusionment and time.

But not for Rouse Farewell. For her, that spark had flourished in a bed of tinder long and perfectly prepared through years of suffering and strife. The flame had taken hold, and spread, illuminating her in a light without shadow, revealing to her in perfect clarity the illusions underlying what passed for reality, and preparing her to use that knowledge to her great advantage, and to the advantage of all those other minds who still struggled to see the truth. And so she had. She had transcended the limitations of the world, yet she had not left the world behind.

Until now.

Again she was blasted back—and she was not afraid. She was never afraid.

Fomalhaut came back to himself and found that his hands were raised, his ERASER beams sweeping toward Kroy dal Ren. He turned them off just as the mini-sun went out and the mirror-field vanished. Fomalhaut spun to take in the situation. In the far distance he saw Valjhar Cor— standing at the end of a tunnel of space he had elongated with his dimension device, beyond the range of his partner's destructive power.

With no more room in his heart for the trivialities of the conflict with Valjhar and his allies, Fomalhaut lifted off for the site of Rouse Farewell's downfall.

Valjhar Cor allowed his tunnel to retract to its normal dimensions. He knew he owed his life to Fomalhaut's warning—without it he would never had survived the initial manifestation of Kroy's power, so disastrously unleashed. His eyes followed Fomalhaut's flight. He had little doubt of what Fomalhaut would find when he reached the spot where Farewell had fallen. Valjhar motioned for his three remaining comrades to meet him at their flyer. When he arrived he found Kern trembling and crying. Valjhar's own legs felt unstable. He turned to Cotavion, pointing to the place where Fomalhaut could be glimpsed as a small, glittering shape.

"Rouse is there. What does your green Stone tell you about that place? How many lives are there?"

Cotavion's cloak parted; the green ring was lifted and shed a faint light.

"Two are living, but one is preparing to depart, and no action of the Stones will stop her. No action of ours can save her, not this time. Her presence here—it was a curse upon this world."

Valjhar nodded slowly. "What we did for her—what you did for her—was not in vain. She gained years of the most glorious life it's possible for any Human, or perhaps any being, to live."

"I must go to her, to bid her farewell."

Valjhar shook his head. "I'm sorry, but no. I don't believe her allies are in any mood to accept our sympathy. Get in the flyer. We're leaving."

"What? No!" Having freed himself from his downed flyer, Possum Perturbare, wearing some sort of armored battle-regalia, clattered up to the Para-men. "I don't know what you guys are talking about. Why leave now? The

Vigil is finished! Let's end this while we've got the chance!"

"No. This has gone too far already. We came to make peace with the Vigil, not to murder them..." Valjhar found that he could not continue.

"Are you crazy? This wasn't your fault. If Aureus hadn't—"

"The only reason that robot was here is that we lured it here! I can't blame the Vigil for that." Valjhar stood reeling. "We have just killed the finest example of the race we came here to save. She was a friend. That is very much my fault. I never should have allowed Kroy anywhere near this place."

"She was my friend," said Cal. "We will not betray her further by harming her friends. That we were on opposite sides of this conflict will bring me regret for however much longer I have to live."

After a moment Valjhar steadied himself. "We are leaving. And so are you, Perturbare."

Perturbare looked from one face to the other and could make no objection. Chastened, he clumped away to his own flyer.

"Kroy..." said Valjhar. But as he faced the starling's baffled, birdlike stare he found there was nothing he could say. He turned instead back to Cotavion. "When we get back...try to isolate Kroy somewhere. Expose him to the blue Light. Somehow he must be made aware of what he has done."

Stingray flung down the cryogun the instant the mini-sun went out. It had turned out to be useless, although by looking into its sighting viewer instead of into the nuclear flare itself he had preserved some fraction of his eyesight. His clothes were smoldering from their bath of radiant heat; his hair and eyebrows were singed. He tore off his scorched rags as he staggered to the rock where Ben Raintree again lay lost in dreams. He spoke, but couldn't hear his own voice. He yelled as loudly as he could until his throat closed up with grief. "Raintree! Wake up, damn you!" He gave Ben a none-too-gentle kick. "Wake up I say!" He extended his hand; a spark leaped from his fingers and danced over Ben's chest. Ben gave a jolt and came awake, staring at Stingray.

"Get up! Rouse is down!"

Not yet certain is this were dream, reality, or nightmare, Ben pulled himself up and ran after Stingray. Stingray's dangerous intensity filled him with apprehension. His seared appearance was proof that while he himself had slept smothered in fantasy, his friends had suffered and fought. And Rouse... Ben shuddered, wanted desperately to rewind time, to recall events and set them right.

In the distance Fomalhaut huddled over some blackened mass—Ben gasped with horror, almost fainting. Fomalhaut's slumped, defeated posture was terrifying— Ben had never known him to be anything other than upright, calm, and in control.

Ben did not dare look Stingray in the face.

There lay Rouse, or at any rate her charred remains. Ben looked around wildly, his eyes bulging. *"Standing Crane!"* he screamed. *"Doctor Standing Crane! Get the hell over here!"* A thought scuttled spider-like through his mind: if he had been awake and aware of what was happening, he might have prevented this with the cryogun, not by firing at Kroy dal Ren, but at Rouse herself, cooling her and protecting her from the fire. He would never forgive Dreamfarer, and himself, for that...

"Ben...Standing Crane can't do anything for me...quite yet..."

Raintree looked for the source of that faint voice, and found that Rouse Farewell had indeed contrived to speak. Stingray fell to her side, put out his hand, and drew it back, afraid to touch her devastated flesh. Her eyelids creased open, but beneath them was nothing like functioning eyeballs. Yet somehow her hand reached out to touch his. "Don't—worry about me. I've gone this way before."

"Will I see you again?" asked Stingray with childlike desperation.

"You'll see me everywhere. Where is Cal? I know now he was the wizard I saw. The wizard of the mountains. I would like to tell him goodbye."

"He's not here, Rouse," said Ben quietly. "I wish he was."

Fomalhaut spoke in a quiet monotone. "No magic can help her now. Nor can any doctor. Her burns are fatal. The radiation has riddled every cell. Her words come from an effort of will that goes beyond life or death."

"Then where is T'Ukudu? He can ease her pain, at least," demanded Stingray.

"T'Ukudu is gone."

"Gone?" said Ben hollowly.

"Annihilated in the initial outburst of Kroy dal Ren's nuclear flare."

Stingray looked up. "They're leaving," he said in a tight voice.

"Who's leaving?" asked Ben through tears.

"The Para-men."

To Fomalhaut that statement was an igniting spark. He snapped upright and oriented himself on the Para-men's flyer like a cannon swiveling toward its target. He saw Valjhar Cor about to enter the vehicle; without hesitation he seized him with all the force of his mind. Valjhar was flung back from the doorway, roughly jerked about like a puppet in the hands of an irate puppeteer. Fomalhaut felt the flow of his victim's emotions: first shock, then confusion, then fear. His hand slipped toward the dimension belt; suddenly its lens was facing Fomalhaut and his allies. Fomalhaut instantly released his grip on Valjhar's body and mind, directing it to the weapon. He saw into its mechanism, a device of subtlety far beyond any quick scrutiny, left it and encountered a far simpler device: the catch which locked the belt around Valjhar's waist. He released the catch and snatched away the belt, bringing it soaring into his hand. Valjhar looked appalled, radiating first indecision, then intense regret as he turned and quickly entered the flyer, which hurtled away a moment later.

Fomalhaut stood staring after it, suffering from an unfamiliar and highly disconcerting welter of emotions. For a moment his self-control had been burned away. He did not even know why he had sought so violently to bar Valjhar's escape—whether to attempt to reestablish the aborted parley, or simply to seek retribution for the death of Rouse—he did not know.

He turned around and found Raintree and Stingray looking at him with plaintive grief.

"Isn't there anything you can do for Rouse?" asked Stingray hoarsely.

"I don't know. I will try." Fomalhaut drew a series of deep breaths, trying to purge himself of confusion and anger. If he were to attempt to enter Rouse's mind while she was so near death, he must not do so while wrapped in agitation.

When he felt himself sufficiently calm, he sought a bridge between Rouse and himself, and found it easily made. Rouse welcomed him. She was serene, full of anticipation, free of fear. Her thoughts brimmed with reassurance and understanding, with only the wryest sort of regret that her death had been unnecessary. In the end she even found the grace to thank him for stopping her from destroying the others in the course of her own stubborn rush to destruction.

She left more of herself in his keeping than he felt he deserved, or could ever fully understand.

Fomalhaut then withdrew, granting her the privacy she required. He felt utterly depleted, sinking down to squat beside Rouse's charred body. He found it difficult to speak, and when he did his words came in a choked monotone. "Rouse—is all right."

Stingray's expression intensified still further. "You mean she'll recover?"

"No. She will die. But for her, death is nothing to be feared."

And then suddenly "Standing Crane" was there, a grey, skeletal figure wearing only a dusty rag. In his right hand he carried a scale; with his left he reached up and plucked a strong wing-feather out of the air and laid it in one of the cups of the scale. Then he knelt and drew something out of Rouse: a filmy purity of being whose beauty was unbearable and irresistible all at once. He placed it in the other cup of the scale, yet its weight was as nothing, for the cup did not fall; the feather outweighed it absolutely. And then the spirit-presence lifted from the cup and departed from their ken. That part of reality which had contained the consciousness of Rouse Farewell was now a void

"She goes her own way," said "Standing Crane". "She is beyond my judgment, and has no need of my guidance or protection."

"Anubis," whispered Fomalhaut.

"What?" This was Ben's voice, thin, near to collapse. His anguish brought Fomalhaut out of the visionary trance into which he had fallen. "Standing Crane", or rather Anubis, was still present in the objective world, yet now he carried no scale, no feather. He merely sank down to the ground and regarded Rouse's lifeless body.

"Anubis," repeated Fomalhaut. "It is Anubis that has possessed Standing Crane's body."

"Anubis? The Egyptian god of the dead?" cried Ben in disbelief.

"Not exactly. Anubis served as judge and guide to the dead. It was Osiris who ruled the underworld."

Raintree stared at "Standing Crane", trying to understand how and in what sense he had been taken over by a god from an extinct mythology. "Standing Crane's" eyes were sunken and deeply shaded, but as Ben watched he detected a glimmer of humanity in their depths.

A bit of Tom Standing Crane emerged as Anubis slept. He looked down at his hands, and then at Rouse's body. He kept looking between them, and Ben saw anguish in those eyes, grief that he had not been able to preserve Rouse's life with the physician's skills he once had valued. Suddenly Ben felt compassion—he could identify with a man who had been invaded and defeated by a spirit presence stronger than his own.

Ben knelt beside him and laid a hand on his shoulder. "Tom," he said quietly. "I believe Cal-Cotavion could cast out whatever it is that has taken you over."

With an audible creak of bone "Standing Crane" turned his mummified head. Ben was cowed by the hopelessness and despair he found in those eyes.

"No, Ben," came the dry whisper. "It's too late for that. I could never endure those Lights. They would destroy me in casting out the jackal. It leaves me little room to exist."

As proof of that, the glimmer of life faded and Ben found himself staring into the black gaze of Anubis. He withdrew his hand, hastily stood up and backed away.

He looked around and discovered that Fomalhaut had departed. Stingray crouched over Rouse's corpse, his face a carving of bitterness and grief. Ben did not dare speak to him. It was all he could do to step up and rest his hand on Stingray's shoulder.

"I needed her, Ben," he hissed. "She knew something vital to me, something I must know if I am to survive."

"What's that?" asked Ben in amazement.

"How to endure the world. How to reconcile myself to its endless death and misery, to the horror of being either predator or prey. How to face it with the serenity she found."

Ben had no answer to this. A moment later Fomalhaut alighted nearby, burdened with the cryogun and a pair of unrecognizable objects. He stepped up to Ben. The two crisped, blistered objects turned out to be T'Ukudu's feet and lower legs.

"Kroy dal Ren's beam cut T'Ukudu off at thigh level, but the flesh above his shins was thoroughly carbonized by penumbral radiation. I excised that material," said Fomalhaut with preternatural calm.

Ben nodded, staring blankly at the gruesome bits of bluish meat which were all that remained of T'Ukudu.

"I have retrieved your cryogun. Please use it to chill these remains to a point just above freezing. Maintain that temperature until the flyer which I have summoned can arrive."

Ben humored this pointless request, trembling with the effort of restraining hysterical laughter at the ludicrousness of it all. Fomalhaut, apparently unable to remain engaged with them or their situation any longer, wandered away.

Stingray suddenly raised his head and surged to his feet. He caught Ben with a knifelike glance, covered the distance between them with three immense strides, and stood looking down at him with a careful scrutiny.

"Ben. I intend to defeat the Para-men, one way or another, at any cost. If necessary I'll do it alone. What I want to know is this: are you finally with me?"

For a long moment Raintree looked up into Stingray's face. With the stench of Rouse's burned flesh in his nostrils and a bitter wind in his heart he said, "Yes, I am."

Stingray nodded in grim satisfaction. He bent down and lifted Valjhar's dimension belt, which Fomalhaut had discarded. He gave it a cursory inspection, his lip curled in distaste. Then, with fingers like bronze rods, he bent the metal casing and crushed the focusing lens, tore open the housing and scattered its components. With a bleeding hand he flung the ruins aside.

"Now we must return to the world and inform it that its greatest hero is dead."

Chapter 42

Fomalhaut Speaks

Somewhere in the emptiness far from the plane of the Solar System, Fomalhaut, strapped into his Frame, activated and oriented its virtual antenna. In a formal voice he began to speak, using his birth language for the first time in years.

"I beam this message toward Deneb in the hope that, three thousand years hence, an ISAF Radio Telescope Multiplex will exist there to receive it. This must be an act of faith on my part, for I am by no means convinced that an analog of the galactic civilization which sent me on this mission will ever arise in this reality. Indeed, I am not convinced that my own species will ever come into being in this star system. If not, perhaps my own actions will prove responsible. My efforts to assure the normal, independent development of the Human species have gone awry. I have become a mover of events, rather than an observer. I have precipitated conflict which has resulted in the deaths of beings of surpassing quality. My self-control has been eroded; my objectivity is lost. I find myself motivated by goals and emotions which are not encompassed by the scope of my mission. At this time my chief desire is to accelerate to relativistic speed and attempt to return to the milieu which I know. However, I am constrained against taking this action. I have initiated serious events, and I must see them through to their conclusion. Moreover, I find that I must deprive myself of even the option of returning, at least for the present. We have attacked the Para-men, violated truce, stolen and destroyed their property. I cannot assume that they will show restraint in dealing with my equipment when I have deprived them of theirs. Therefore I must put the Frame beyond their reach."

Fomalhaut included in his transmission a compressed burst containing whatever information he had gathered which might be of interest to his contemporaries. It was plentiful, though much of it sounded unlikely enough: the existence of T'Utahn and its people; the presence of the immortal humanoid Endurance, the apparent existence of a second Human world somewhere beyond the galaxy; the tale of the Stones and their uncertain origin, and especially the secrets of the obscure planet Rral.

With that accomplished, Fomalhaut instructed the Frame to take itself into a galaxy void some three billion light-years distant, there to remain for ten years. He unstrapped himself and watched as the Frame vanished, lost to him for a long and uncertain period.

For hours Fomalhaut drifted in the darkness of stars, so soothing, yet tantalizing, for he could not immerse himself in that quiet blackness as deeply as he longed to do.

Indeed, he had only hours before he must face a dreaded responsibility. He oriented himself toward the warm sunlit core of the Solar System and set out at a steady one G acceleration for Earth. He approached the planet from the south, the Antarctic ice cap bright as a reflection on a steel ball. But that continent was not his destination— rather, he veered aside for the reddish-buff interior of Australia. Even at this distance he could see the puff of dust which marred the desert they had chosen for their meeting with the Para-men.

The funeral of Rouse Farewell, the Peregrine, had inevitably become a spectacle involving the world. As

Rouse had been without a permanent home, it was decided to erect her monument on the spot where she had fallen, despite the protests of New Zealand, her birthplace.

As Fomalhaut entered the atmosphere he looked at the runway that had been hastily scraped out of the desert. Even now more aircraft were arriving; already they had deposited thousands of mourners in the tent-and-pavilion city which had been erected to accommodate them. That Human presence would become permanent: there were plans to erect hostels for the use of those pilgrims who would come to visit the tomb. Also planned was a permanent monument, likely to be a tasteless, grandiose structure ill-befitting Rouse, her beliefs, or the way she'd lived her life.

The area, as it turned out, was ceremonially important to the aborigines, but their plea that it be left undeveloped went unheard, something Rouse surely would have hated.

Fomalhaut touched down at the central site of the funerary complex, where Rouse's remains would be temporarily interred during the construction of the monument. With him on the platform stood Stingray, barely in control of his rage; Raintree, pale, bleak-faced; and the being they had come to call Anubis, inscrutable, dressed in robes of grey and brown. Here was all that remained of the organization he had so carefully assembled from the greatest powers available on Earth. The death of T'Ukudu and the destruction of Aureus had been all but ignored in the face of the death of the Peregrine, and that, thought Fomalhaut, was just as well.

Fomalhaut looked over the throng of Humans who had come to pay their respects and to be seen on television: politicians, many of whom had been discommoded by

Rouse's independent and uncontrollable actions; leaders of organized religion, most of whom viewed Rouse and her apparently supernatural powers, which were based on principles and wisdom not encompassed by their beliefs, as anathema; businessmen, to whom Rouse and her non-materialistic way of life had been an enigma if not a threat. Yet there was also genuine grief here, impinging on Fomalhaut like a dismal cloud, difficult to shut out. The remnants of Rouse's family were also present, a few aged siblings and cousins who viewed her death with as little comprehension as they had viewed her life.

To Fomalhaut's surprise, the Vigil had suffered no loss of popular support as a result of Rouse's death. To the contrary, a mood of vengefulness seemed to have brought people more firmly to the side of the Vigil than ever before. Nor was there much sign that the general populace appreciated the fact of the Vigil's pitiful weakness. There had always been a tendency to perceive the Vigil's sizable Human staff as an integral part of the organization; the loss of a few of the "top" Vigil members was not seen as insurmountable.

In any event, Fomalhaut and his cronies were seen as chief among the bereaved, and were thus in charge of the ceremony.

The time came when they were expected to offer eulogies. Anubis of course had no inclination to do so—it was only through Standing Crane's residual influence that it was here at all. Stingray's expression remained fiercely set. Whatever thoughts and feelings he carried within him would remain there, and this was also for the best, for their expression would alarm many and bring peace to none. Raintree looked around, his mouth working, trying for words, but ultimately he too was silent, defeated by the event.

"I will speak for her," said Fomalhaut. He was briefly abashed by this impulsive gesture—an outsider presuming to intrude into the grief of the Human species. Yet it had to be done, and no one else had stepped forward.

"Rouse Farewell came as a great surprise to me when I first came to this planet. As you may know, my own people possess a wide array of what you would call 'psychic' or 'paranormal' mental powers. These are ultimately based on the interaction between the mind and the quantum underpinnings of all existence. These powers can be accessed or gained via several paths. Their attainment is something for which my people take little credit. The structures and mechanisms which permit them are built into our brains, and usually these powers manifest themselves.

"With Rouse it was different. I am sorry to tell you that the Human race possesses only a meager foreshadowing of the neurological equipment which provides for easy neuro-quantum interaction. Yet Rouse Farewell exhibited such powers, powers on a scale which I personally would find impossible to match. Nor had she ever heard the term 'neuro-quantum interaction'. Rouse came to her abilities through a process wholly unlike that which empowers members of my species, a process which the majority of humans can barely imagine, rarely pursue, and almost never attain. It was through Rouse Farewell's profound wisdom of the ways of the world that she was able to fly. Through years of strife and seeking she gradually cast aside the illusions of her physical being, and learned how to see beyond the limitations imposed on her body by the laws of time and space.

"But this was not Rouse's most admirable achievement. For, once she had attained this transcendence over the physical, what did she do with it? I assure you, Rouse could have bent this power to almost any end. Yet she chose only to fly, to enjoy the peace and beauty of the high regions of air and light which were her domain. She had escaped life's rigors; she had defeated her baser self; she could have had an indefinite existence of joyful solitude in the exploration of nature. Yet in the end she would not elevate herself above the travails of her fellow Humans. Time and again she plunged into the turmoil of Human affairs, bringing hope to the hopeless and inspiration to the cynical. In the end, her courage, generosity, and concern for Human welfare resulted in her death.

"I will always regret that the mission of the Vigil resulted in the death of Rouse Farewell. I regard her as the finest being I have ever known. I am humbled by her memory, and consider the omniverse enriched by the diffusion of her spirit into its substance."

Chapter 43

Perturbare Sees

Standing unnoticed in the crowd, Possum Perturbare glanced around to take in the reaction to Fomalhaut's speech. Even those who did not speak English had gotten the sense of it, perhaps by virtue of Fomalhaut's telepathic talents. Feeling subdued, impressed by Fomalhaut's oratory, Perturbare studied the distant, glittering figure throughout the remainder of the ceremony. He wasn't using a psi-shield, trusting the presence of so many thousands to keep him from Fomalhaut's notice. Still, he was careful to moderate his thoughts so as not to call attention to himself.

Presently Rouse Farewell was interred and the crowd began to break up. Perturbare made his way to his aircraft, a twin-engine Cessna turboprop which Brainchild had maneuvered to the front of the takeoff queue. He lifted off and steered south, waiting until he was well out of sight before jettisoning the wings and fuselage, revealing the compact prop-beam flyer beneath.

Perturbare remained pensive as he flew along. Eventually he remarked, "I'm glad I had no part in Farewell's death. I was peeved at her when she almost got me killed by knocking my flyer out of the air, but I think I'm ready to forgive her for that."

"I was most interested in Fomalhaut's explanation of her powers," said Brainchild. "The implications for the potential expansion of consciousness are unlimited."

"I never thought I'd hear old Formal Hat come so close to getting misty-eyed," said Perturbare, with a hint of mist in his own voice.

"I intend to further explore the interaction between the mind and quantum phenomena."

"Okay. You know, I've been vaguely aware of Rouse Farewell and her alleged powers all my life—but I was never quite sure whether to believe the stories, or how to account for them if I did. I guess I was never ready to believe that anyone could really be that good—that clear-minded. I wish I'd had a chance to know her."

"Doctor, are you returning to base?"

"No, we're going to pay a call on our partners at the Redoubt. I think it's time I finished up that project with Kern."

A short time later Perturbare and Kern Harner resumed work on upgrading the Para-men's computer and data-transfer systems. Pimsehkia Flam even emerged from her apartment for a short time to greet him and hover nearby as they worked. Perturbare strove to conceal his fascination for the little creature, a restraint made easier by the love that glowed in Kern's eyes whenever he looked at her. Her eyes, noted Perturbare, rested on himself, the exotic Earthman, a little more often than they did on her Rralian mate. Presently she gave a delicate yawn, a merry wave, and retreated to her own domain.

As usual, Kern Harner was a willing and capable assistant, but showed no great interest in the work. Perturbare had gradually realized that Kern's knowledge of the fabulous Rralian technology was spotty and rather narrow. Kern knew far more about *Mote's* star drive than Perturbare had as yet been able to take in, but Perturbare could see that *Mote* was a tinkered-together space jalopy compared to the full capability inherent in Rralian technology. Outside of that area, Perturbare matched and in many cases surpassed Kern's technical knowledge.

It was this advantage which enabled him to make certain precautionary modifications to the Redoubt's data systems without being detected.

Kern, who had lately gone on a Wagner kick, hummed "Siegfried's Funeral Music" as he worked, an unwelcome reminder of the Vigil deaths. With a pained expression Perturbare glanced over at his assistant, but Kern's earnest face killed his complaint on his lips. Kern's deep-set eyes were bright with a passionate love of drama and tragedy. Although he bore partial responsibility for the Peregrine's death, he seemed to have shrugged it off, as though it had been only the sad consequence of some game.

Perturbare had no reason to suppose himself the older of the two, but it was difficult to think of Kern as anything but a clever adolescent who saw everything through a haze of romance. Perturbare tried to imagine him in his true pixie-like guise, and found it easy enough.

Still, the lugubrious beat of that humming was getting on his nerves. To interrupt him, Perturbare asked, "Have you had any luck tracking down Endurance?"

Kern shook his head and could not restrain a small mischievous smile. "No—the Peregrine did a most thorough job of hiding him. We'd probably have to re-mate *Mote* to its drives and comb the whole inner solar system to find him. We've calculated that he's probably not in an escape trajectory, but most likely in a highly eccentric terracentric or heliocentric orbit. We'll keep looking and just hope his orbit brings him close enough to Earth for us to spot him."

"Gee, I sure hope you do," said Perturbare with patent insincerity. While he had no real desire to see Endurance marooned in space forever, neither did he care to subject himself to the immortal's minatory scrutiny. Perhaps someday he himself would search for and retrieve Endurance, thereby gaining his gratitude, or at least his tolerance.

"Well, Kern, I think you can finish up here by yourself, don't you?"

Kern looked up with obvious disappointment. "Yes, I suppose I can, if you have to leave."

"There's something I want to talk over with Valjhar. I'll stop back and see how you're making out before I head for home."

"All right," Kern said more brightly. "I'll see you later."

Perturbare paged Valjhar and got a quick reply. "I'll be in my quarters; we can speak there."

"Your quarters? Which wing are they in?"

"Oh—I mean my quarters aboard *Mote*."

"Ah. I'll be right there."

Perturbare climbed aboard the starship and found Valjhar seated at his accustomed place beneath the main dome. He offered the Rralian a grin. "Don't you ever leave this ship? The Redoubt must offer better accommodations than whatever cabin you have aboard her."

Valjhar nodded soberly. "That's true. But I'm still more comfortable here. Especially lately. I wish...I wish we could put this ship back among the stars, back where she belongs..." His gaze defocused, Valjhar stared into some inner world. After a moment he came back to himself and looked at Perturbare. "What can I do for you, my friend?"

Perturbare was distracted by an object Valjhar toyed with as he spoke. It was a transparent sphere the size of a billiard ball, lit from within by the milky glow of a twist of light which was embedded in the crystal. Perturbare frowned and squinted at the thing, trying to make out the exact shape of the twist, but it baffled him, threatening to leave him with a headache. "What's that?" he asked, although he suspected he'd rather not hear the answer.

"Well, that's a little difficult to explain. It's something I took away from Old Rral along with the dimension belt."

"But what is it?"

"I call it the Motionglobe. Briefly, it gives one the power to move through any dimension of space in any manner whatsoever."

"Oh," said Perturbare. "Well, that sounds useful."

Valjhar managed a rueful smile. Perturbare was surprised to notice a sheen of sweat on his forehead. "I haven't had much to do with the globe since I acquired it. The use of it is—disconcerting at best." He held the gently glowing sphere before his eyes, studied it gravely, then pressed it against his forehead with the palm of his hand. When he lowered his hand the globe was gone. Perturbare looked around as he might for an egg which had vanished through sleight-of-hand.

Valjhar tapped his forehead. "It's inside my head. Don't worry; it doesn't hurt; it has no problem co-occupying the same space as my brain. Now that it's in place..." Valjhar did something impossible which hurt Perturbare's mind to see, then shuddered. He jerked his head forward, and the Motionglobe flew out and landed in his lap. Perturbare goggled at it.

"I'm sorry," said Valjhar a little shakily. "My mind just isn't big enough to encompass this power."

Perturbare nodded mutely, his eyes still locked on the sphere.

"Would you like to try it?" asked Valjhar.

"No! No thanks. I have enough trouble with motion sickness already."

"I think I've distracted you," said Valjhar mildly. "What did you want to discuss?"

Perturbare shook himself and forced his mind back to the here-and-now.

"I think it's about time you explained why we haven't pressed our advantage. The Vigil was finished—the few left standing were on the ropes, totally demoralized. We could have ended it then and there. We could now be planning the future of Mankind instead of sitting here on our hands. Even now the Vigil is weak and vulnerable. Why aren't you doing anything?"

Valjhar shook his head. "I never should have agreed to that meeting. It was premature, and unnecessary. The likelihood of violent conflict was too great. And now…"

"Yes, and now Rouse Farewell and T'Ukudu are dead. It's a terrible thing, and I wish we could undo it, but we can't. But surely we must act to finish what they started?"

Valjhar shook his head again. "There's no need."

"No need? How can that be?" By now Perturbare was both baffled and exasperated.

Valjhar studied Perturbare for a long moment. Finally he said, "Very well. You've proven yourself trustworthy, if at times a bit impulsive. I'll tell you why we must wait."

"At last!"

"But first, will you walk with me? I don't think this is the ideal environment for what I'm about to tell you."

"All right," said Perturbare, chafing at the delay. Valjhar slipped the Motionglobe into a pouch in his tunic and led the way out of the ship. A few minutes later they stepped into a transparent blister high atop one of the towers. The night was clear, and for once the aurora was confined to a weak glow along the horizon, clearing the stage for the profusion of stars which shone through the purest air on Earth. The silver velvet of the Milky Way arched high; tiny puffs of nebulosity within it were apparent even to the naked eye. The smudges of the Magellanic Clouds stood as vanguards of the ranks of invisible galaxies which marched into infinity.

"Perturbare, what do you see when you look out at the stars?"

"What? I don't know—I've never actually thought about it much. I suppose I see the lights of a city."

"We know that the universe is actually a wilderness," said Valjhar quietly. "Hugely empty, with the majority of star systems barren of life, their planets either blasted rocks or balls of gas, either frozen or fiery. Of course there are islands of complex life, perhaps a million in this galaxy, few enough so that one must sift through a hundred thousand stars to find one that sheds its light on living beings who resemble us even remotely. But when you multiply that million by all the galaxies in the universe, and when you then multiply by infinity to take into account all the realms of the omniverse itself, of course there's no shortage of intelligent beings of every description. The point is—well. You ask why we are not more active in pursuing our ambitions for the Earth. The answer is—

we've not yet all arrived. There is still another Space Mariner."

For some in explicable reason Perturbare's breath caught at this news.

"You see, the omniverse is not populated solely by blundering, indecisive, morally ambiguous beings such as ourselves. True, we are in the majority in that respect. But if you look hard enough, beings of flawless idealism, of heroic character, are also to be found. I will tell you a story which will take you far beyond the dimmest star we can see. Once upon a time, a few beings found a way to turn the deaths of stars into instruments of unlimited potential. They learned how to extract the singularities from the centers of black holes, to strip away the event horizon itself, leaving exposed the naked singularity, an infinitesimal node of utter chaos, capable of anything. And they learned to master those singularities, to rein in their infinite potential, to subject and limit them to the will of whomever might be found with the strength to bear them. And they decided to dispense these instruments to worthy beings, and to disperse these beings throughout the omniverse, with their task to avert suffering and promote the well-being of intelligence wherever it is found."

Perturbare stared into Valjhar's eyes, looking for deception, for the least hint that he was being played for a fool. But the earnest, candid look in Valjhar's eyes did not waver; nor did their peculiar starshine gleam.

"It sounds like you're describing some sort of Cosmic Patrol," said Perturbare in a neutral voice.

Valjhar nodded. "Yes, but we generally call them the Singulars, or the Select, or sometimes, well, the Paladins of the Black Band."

"Hmm. Well, this is quite a story. But how does this organization of benevolent paragons relate to our present concerns, if I may ask?"

Valjhar smiled and dropped his gaze. "It's simple enough. From our first days as Space Mariners we had among us a woman, Shaula Alshain, who had been chosen as a potential member of the Singulars, or the Cosmic Patrol, if you prefer. As part of her training and testing, she had been assigned to a universe, our universe—"

"Wait a minute. These people are assigned to entire *universes*?"

"Yes...but you see, Shaula, wasn't yet responsible for the whole universe; she was still a trainee. Her mission was to accomplish as much as possible under strict limitations, in order to demonstrate her worthiness to carry a Universal Instrument. She traveled with us as a Space Mariner, growing and learning as she went, until eventually she became a magnificent example to us all. After finally proving her worth beyond any doubt, she was called back to be fitted with her Instrument, or Singularity Band. It's a long and difficult process, and we've been waiting for her to rejoin us ever since."

Again Perturbare studied Valjhar as he sat in the starlit silence of the blister, glowing with the love he obviously felt for this superwoman. Perturbare wondered how he himself would measure up against a woman who had the strength to rule over a singularity—a pinpoint of insanity beyond any prediction or analysis—without giving way to madness or megalomania. He had to admit he would probably be wilted by the comparison.

"And when is Miss Alshain expected to join us?" asked Perturbare gently.

"Soon. Very soon."

"But Valjhar—I still don't think you've answered my question. Powerful as she undoubtedly must be, do we really need to wait for her before we defeat the Vigil?"

"You don't understand. Once Shaula is among us, we won't need to defeat the Vigil."

The skin on the back of Perturbare's neck turned cold. "Why not?"

Valjhar looked up, shaking his head, grinning widely. He made a rather wild gesture. "The Vigil can't possibly fight against Shaula once she has her Instrument. She can simply neutralize them with a thought, or remove them, or better yet, bring them over to our side. For that matter, she can wipe away any dissent or resistance to our plans. Not through cruelty or compulsion, you understand; she can simply illuminate people's minds, make them see that our way is best. With her help, Earth can be a paradise in a very short time. We will have done our duty to ourselves and to this planet—and then we'll be able to resume our voyage across the stars, and perhaps even go home at last."

"I see," said Perturbare brightly. "Well, that really does answer my question. I'm looking forward to seeing it all happen. Thanks very much."

Perturbare whistled his way out of the Redoubt, forgetting all about stopping to say goodbye to Kern. He passed Cal-Cotavion in a corridor and offered him an absent nod, the import of the Stones scarcely entering his mind. Reaching the landing bay, he boarded his flyer and lifted off into the darkness. As he steered the craft his whistling became shrill and grating.

"Doctor, you have left the Redoubt," said Brainchild. "You may relax your frozen expression of good-humored acquiescence."

Perturbare's face abruptly collapsed into a haunted stare. "What do you think about this, Brainchild? Cal-Cotavion isn't good enough for them. Even the Stones can't illuminate, or brainwash, the whole planet at once. The Motionglobe just isn't powerful enough. No, the Para-men aren't ready to take on the Vigil and rule the Earth. Not until they're joined by some cosmic demigoddess so omnipotent she outclasses everybody short of God."

He looked out at the stars, which shone with an unblinking clarity he suddenly found chilling.

"It will be interesting to see if I can resist the mental manipulation which Valjhar implied that Shaula Alshain would employ. Of course, even if my mind is successfully modified by her, I may remain unaware of the fact," said Brainchild.

"I don't care for this one bit. I'm going to have to think about this situation very carefully," said Perturbare.

Chapter 44

The Vigil Hears

A Vigil flyer set down on the Australian battlefield, not far from the spot where Rouse's monument would soon rise. The door slid open and out came Fomalhaut, Stingray, and Raintree. They filed over to the site of the destruction of Aureus, an irregular circle of fused sand, still too hot to touch. Globules of liquid gold shimmered here and there. The only other traces of the robot were a few bits of hardware which projected from the glassy surface at odd angles.

They halted and looked at the scene in silence.

After a while Stingray said, "Do you still think there's any chance of repairing him?"

"I consider it a necessity," said Fomalhaut. "Without the power of Aureus, we stand no chance against the Paramen."

Stingray snorted. "With allies like Aureus, we don't need enemies. I'd rather leave him right where he is. But I admit we must make the attempt. Let's pick up the pieces. I don't want to remain in this wretched place any longer than necessary."

Fomalhaut raised his arms and fired infrared beams to re-melt the rock, a lengthy process. Stingray and Raintree were soon driven back by the radiant heat. Raintree looked uncertain as Fomalhaut waded into the molten pool. "Are you sure your suit will protect you from that?" he called.

"Quite sure." Fomalhaut fished around in the lava, coming up with bits of mangled debris which he simply tossed into a heap, already so damaged there seemed little point in treating them delicately. His biggest prize was the transparent envelope which had been Aureus's skin and container. He emptied it of lava before adding it to the pile.

Once the pool was cleared of solid debris, Stingray and Raintree went to the flyer and came back with a big mass spectrometer which floated on a propulsion-beam palette. Now protected by thermal armor, they prepared to process the lava through the massive machine. Soon the liquid rock was pumping through the device, which was kept from melting by Raintree's cryogenic technology. Drop by drop, or sometimes in gushes and spurts, golden liquid collected in quartz flasks. When each was filled, they carefully capped it and placed it in a rack.

They ran the lava through the mass spectrometer three times. By the third time no measurable quantity of the mercury-like substance was retrieved. Satisfied, Fomalhaut shut down the machine and studied the display on the weighing rack.

"We have recovered ninety-eight percent of the volume of 'mercurgold' which Aureus originally contained. We must hope that the loss of two percent will not be significant, for I doubt we can synthesize such an exotic substance ourselves."

"There's still one significant item we must recover," said Raintree.

"True," said Fomalhaut. "Endurance threw Aureus's brain case into the lava with substantial force. It penetrated into still-solid rock some distance below this pool. I must extract it." With that he plunged into the fuming liquid rock, vanishing beneath the tiny flames that danced across its surface. The ground trembled. Stingray and Raintree could only imagine by what means Fomalhaut pursued his prize.

Presently he splashed to the surface, the brain case cradled in his arm like a football. It appeared pristine, its mirror finish unmarred.

"Is it functioning?" asked Stingray.

"Yes."

They returned to the Lighthouse and moved the remains of Aureus into a laboratory. Stingray consulted the complex's locater system.

"Where the hell is Anubis?" he asked irritably.

"Who knows?" answered Ben. "Haunting some pyramid, maybe."

"You know, I refuse to accept that thing at face value. Why, of all the thousands of mythical gods that have infested human culture, should Anubis suddenly turn out to be real, and inhabit, of all people, an American Indian, a man unrelated to the culture that invented Anubis in the first place?"

"We cannot answer your question," said Fomalhaut. "But I can tell you this: whatever it is that has usurped Tom Standing Crane believes itself to be Anubis."

"But why Anubis? Judge of the dead—guide—whatever it's supposed to be—why not Apollo, or Quetzalcoatl? When will they pop up?"

"It's not every day that sees the death of someone like Rouse Farewell," said Raintree softly.

That stopped them all for a moment.

"In that case," said Stingray, "now that she is gone, would anyone care to guess why Anubis is still around?"

"And why didn't he conduct a weighing or judging ceremony for T'Ukudu?" wondered Ben.

"Perhaps because T'Ukudu was an alien. Or an artificial being," said Stingray.

"Or perhaps it is because T'Ukudu is not dead," said Fomalhaut.

They turned silent stares on the faceless figure.

"I withheld comment on this matter until I had some confidence in my actions. But I now think they are justified. Come with me."

They followed him into another laboratory, where lying submerged in a tank of translucent bluish liquid were T'Ukudu's feet, shins, and calves. Their severed ends were mossy with whitish tendrils that seemed to grow even as they watched.

"I don't believe it," said Stingray. "Fomalhaut, you are quite the optimist."

"That optimism was fostered in me by T'Ukudu himself. I suggest you reach into the tank and touch one of the legs."

With a quizzical expression Stingray reached into the thick warm liquid and brushed his fingers over the pale flesh. At first he gasped and flinched back, but then he reached in and gripped an ankle.

"What is it?" asked Raintree.

"It's Touchtalk—very strong. It's telling me how to prepare this emulsion, and to place his remains in it— amazing."

"It is an autonomic survival function of the Servants," said Fomalhaut.

"But what makes you think the result will be anything like our T'Ukudu?" asked Stingray.

"Much of the basic knowledge and skill of the Servant is encoded in its genome."

"So we might produce a generic Servant, but not T'Ukudu as we have known him."

"It seems better than nothing."

Stingray blew out a breath. "But wait—we have two feet! Why not grow two separate Servants in different tanks? That way we'll have a backup the next time we get one of them vaporized."

Fomalhaut studied Stingray's intense face and glittering eyes, unable to tell whether he was being serious by such superficial means.

"So," said Raintree gloomily, "despite everything, we might get Aureus back, and even T'Ukudu, sort of—"

"But not Rouse," finished Stingray.

"But not Rouse."

A few days later Fomalhaut sat hunched over the worktable that carried Aureus's various components. The brain case rested on a rubber pad. It alone was undamaged; everything else was smashed or mangled to varying degrees. A small tub of the metallic polymer they'd dubbed 'mercurgold' sat nearby, carefully filtered to remove all residual impurities.

So far Fomalhaut had only managed to repair Aureus's eyes, while Raintree had made some sense of its compact but incredibly powerful tachyon weapon system. At the moment Fomalhaut was laboring alone, his colleagues having temporarily surrendered to exhaustion and a sense of futility.

They could never restore Aureus to its original state of perfection. They could not replicate most of the materials used in its construction, and must use whatever substitutes were available. Thankfully, its energy storage cells, while bent and warped, had not been breached, or the resulting detonation would have blown a crater in the Australian crust. The cells appeared to be nothing more than simple black cubes, quite lightweight. Fomalhaut's sensors indicated they worked by storing energy in knots of distorted space within the cubes, another technology they could not match.

Now Fomalhaut struggled to understand the interface between the brain case, which lay there so serenely inert, and the systems of Aureus's body. The problem had preoccupied him since their repair project had begun, and he was beginning to fear it was intractable. Somewhere in the archives contained in his belt computer lay the clues he needed to decipher this technology, but he wasn't enough of a space-structure physicist even to recognize them, let alone understand them. If ISAF had wanted an observer capable of repairing a robot from a technology in some ways surpassing its own, he reflected ruefully, they should have chosen someone who had made a stronger effort to apply his intellect to practical matters.

And now, despite the efforts of his suit's de-enervator to sustain his energy and alertness, he began to fear that his mental acuity was waning. For how else could he explain his growing conviction that the spirit of T'Ukudu was haunting him? Surely he had been too long immersed in Human superstitions, if they could even be called superstitions when an extinct god turned up real. But could that alone explain his feeling that T'Ukudu was calling him, summoning him?

Frustrated, Fomalhaut switched off the stress analyzer he'd been using to determine which of the curves and kinks in Aureus's components were intentional and which had been caused by Endurance's abuse. He stood up and made his way to the dimly-lit laboratory where T'Ukudu's lower legs were putting forth the tendrils of their regeneration.

He looked into the tank and was jarred by surprise. The fibrous webwork of tissue had taken on the complete form of the Servant. It was an eerie simulacrum, like the ghost of his friend woven from fine, pale threads.

And now the call was stronger than ever. Fomalhaut belatedly realized that this disembodied nervous system was capable of a telepathic whisper. He submerged his hand in the emulsion and touched an ankle; immediately his mind was filled with familiar thoughts.

Fomalhaut. Thank you for responding to my call.

"T'Ukudu! You know me? What else do you remember?"

I remember everything up to my immolation by Kroy dal Ren. It is he whom I wish to discuss.

"But how is it that you retain such knowledge? There was nothing left of you but your feet."

Fomalhaut, you know something of the generalization of function of my tissue; for example, I am literally brainless. My mental processes are distributed throughout my body, with highly redundant memory storage in all areas, including my feet.

"I see. What do you wish to tell me about Kroy dal Ren?"

That being should be destroyed.

"You surely do not make this claim from a desire for vengeance?"

Of course not. In my contact with him I learned that he is insane. A humanoid brain is not a suitable vessel for a consciousness of his nature. His efforts to adapt himself to its limitations have become an increasing source of disruption and mental deterioration. Still worse from his point of view is the absolute variance between his native environment and ours. Beings such as he are in complete, instantaneous, and intimate communication with all others of his kind, through a means more perfect and pervasive even than telepathy. Note that this interconnection is not limited to the star-beings in a single sun, but to all similar creatures inhabiting stars throughout the universe. Not only that, but they are almost without sensory input of any other kind. For them the universe is a uniform medium of fusible hydrogen which is inhabited only by the massed consciousness of their fellows and themselves. They have no concept of motion, nor of space, nor of physical location. That Kroy dal Ren has been able to adapt himself to this environment to any extent is remarkable, but it is not enough. He is capable of manifesting hydrogen fusion on a much larger scale than he demonstrated in Australia, and he may well do so, on any pretext, or on none at all. For his sake, and for the welfare of this planet, he should be destroyed.

Fomalhaut considered this information. Despite his decades of deep space exploration, he had never discovered or been aware of star-beings such as Kroy dal Ren. Either they were not pervasive in his native universe, or they represented a vast fund of consciousness of which he and his culture were ignorant.

He sighed and resumed his communication with T'Ukudu. "Thank you for this information. I am most gratified that your identity was not obliterated after all."

I too am pleased at the prospect of resuming my mission. However, my full regeneration will yet require several weeks; I can be of little use to you until then.

"I understand."

Fomalhaut, thank you for acting on what must have seemed a series of ludicrous impulses, thereby preserving my existence.

"I'm sure you would do the same for me."

Five days later Fomalhaut, Stingray, and Raintree again gathered around the remains of Aureus, on which little further progress had been made.

"Do we agree, then," said Fomalhaut, "that we are incapable of completing the repairs on Aureus?"

"I don't see how we can," murmured Ben. "Despite all our efforts, we still have no understanding of the interface between the brain case and the command interpreter. We haven't even a theoretical idea of what influence passes between the two as a signaling medium. It certainly isn't electricity."

"That is true. The substance of the brain case acts as a perfect insulator. In fact, it has the properties of a permanent mirror field. The medium might be quantum-interactive or telepathic in nature, but if so I am unable to interpret it. To me Aureus's mental activity feels like a smooth continuum, the thought equivalent of white noise."

"Even if we could get his brain hooked up again, Aureus wouldn't have much to control," said Stingray. "The material of his transparent 'skin' appears to be beyond our analysis. I can't find any way to fuse or repair the damage."

The three sat there looking at each other glumly.

"Why not let me take a look at him?"

They swiveled as one to see who had spoken. Raintree's jaw dropped, Stingray grew wide-eyed, while Fomalhaut merely took in the situation.

Possum Perturbare stood in the doorway.

"Easy, boys," said Perturbare. "Formaldehyde, I'm going to drop my psi-shield so you'll know I'm harmless."

Stingray sputtered and said, "How did you get in here, traitor?"

Perturbare made a negligent gesture. "I've been into your computer system practically since day one, beach boy. You can't even be sure I haven't watched as you drifted in your water bed and went like this." Perturbare goggled his eyes and worked his mouth like a carp.

Stingray took a giant step in Perturbare's direction, but Fomalhaut stopped him with a word. "Dr. Perturbare, perhaps you'd better explain why you've come."

"I've come to offer my help."

"To us?" asked Stingray incredulously.

"Yes...I'm offering my services to the magnificent globe-spanning organization of the Vigil, though I can't imagine what I could possibly contribute to such a masterful crew," said Perturbare, conspicuously eyeing the three of them and the ruins of Aureus.

"You have a hard time deciding which side to be on, don't you?" said Stingray.

"Again, yes; when I don't have all the relevant information, sometimes I do."

Stingray rushed over to Perturbare and stood looming over him, a foot and a half taller and three times heavier. Perturbare flinched before his sudden fury.

"What the hell is going on here?" raged Stingray. "I'm supposed to just accept your change of heart, let you waltz in here and mouth off to us? Are you really just that special, that we should do anything but lock you up like the Quisling you are? Or maybe you're really trying to play both sides against the other, while you pick up whatever pieces are left when we're done? You're just lucky you had no direct role in Rouse's death, or I'd twist your head off right now."

Perturbare barely dared to raise his eyes. "Look. You're right. I was pissed at you guys for trying to nab me, or kill me in the case of your little hobby project here," he said, waving his hands at the remains of Aureus.

"What?" said Stingray. "When did we do any of that?"

"You did, trust me. You wouldn't remember."

"Now wait a minute…"

But Perturbare bore on. "And yes, I liked what the Para-men had to say, and yeah, I think human society as it exists now stinks to high heaven and ultimately can't be saved. So I was in a snit. But I'm not snitty enough to want to see some alien come along and rearrange everyone's thoughts to suit herself."

"What new information do you have, Perturbare?" asked Ben in a tone of quiet intensity.

With an uncharacteristic seriousness Perturbare related everything Valjhar had told him. "When I heard him speak, I realized that under his plan the human race would have about the same status as Kern's penguin colony—well cared-for, carefully optimized pets. I won't be a party to that. I'm not even convinced that I myself would remain unaffected by the modifications Valjhar intends his girlfriend to make."

"What course of action would you recommend?" asked Fomalhaut.

Perturbare assumed an expression of distaste. "My preference would be to present a worldwide, united front of resistance to Valjhar's plans. He's no monster—if it could be demonstrated that the great majority of the race is against him, I believe he'd give up. I also believe that, given time, I could engineer that kind of unanimity. But we don't have that time. Once this Shaula Alshain shows up, it's all over. And her arrival is supposed to be imminent. Therefore: I suggest an immediate surprise attack against the Para-men. Or at least immediately after I fix up the Gold Woodsman here."

"What makes you think it can be done?" demanded Stingray.

"What makes you think it can be done?" mocked Perturbare. "You'll be the first to know if I can't fix him, water boy."

"That's not what I meant. What makes you think an attack against the Para-men can succeed?"

"The Para-men are as weak right now as we're ever likely to see them again. Endurance is still missing, and Valjhar is trying to get used to a new weapon that he doesn't much care for and can barely handle. Plus, you'll have me on your side. That'll be a surprise."

"That doesn't answer my question."

"So what's *your* answer?" said Perturbare hotly. "To wait around until this cosmic goddess shows up to readjust your attitude?"

"No. I intend to fight them if I have to do it alone. I just wanted to know if you had any answers."

"What would be your objectives in such an attack?" asked Fomalhaut.

"Preferably to inspire them to leave the planet with their hides intact. If any of them gets hurt, God knows what this Alshain will do when she finds out."

"I concur. And unless anyone objects, I accept your offer of assistance."

"Not so fast, chromium domium," said Perturbare. "There's something I need to know from you before I commit myself."

"And that is?"

"When you invaded my old lab, you rediscovered my existence after the shutdown of the quantum isolator. You must have. Why did you leave me alone after that?"

Stingray and Raintree turned surprised looks on Fomalhaut. His answer was calm and reasonable. "When I discovered you, I naturally inspected you carefully, having no memory of you and being surprised at your sudden appearance. I found your desire for self-determination to be so strong that you were willing to suffer the blotting-out of your very identity in order to preserve your freedom. That being the case, I decided to forego the political advantage we had sought in trying to capture you, and to respect your privacy. I also recommitted myself to preserving the freedom and integrity of your species. I am happy to have this opportunity to apologize for our ill-considered attack, which was made at my instigation alone, and against Stingray's objections."

Perturbare stood abashed. Stingray had a hard smile for his discomfiture.

"In that case, I suggest we all get to work," said Perturbare.

Stingray and Fomalhaut turned away, apparently satisfied. Only Raintree continued to study Perturbare, his eyes filled with shifting greenish lights.

Perturbare returned the scrutiny. "What's on your mind, Raintree?"

Raintree shook his head. "Until now, I've seen myself as playing the role of Judas in this farce. Now I don't know what to think."

Perturbare gave a slow nod and maintained his level gaze. "Okay. As soon as your ethical crisis helps you to reach a useful decision of some kind, let me know what it is."

Three days later, Aureus, looking complete and intact except for the vacancy in its brain cavity, lay on a table in the main Vigil laboratory. Perturbare reached into the robot's cranium and attached a device to the command interpreter. An optical cable ran from it to a small Brainchild terminal nearby.

"You know, Doc, if our tools and equipment are really as inferior as you claim, I don't see why you insist on doing the work here instead of at your fabulous secret headquarters," said Stingray.

Perturbare shrugged. "My place isn't ready to receive visitors. For one thing, you'd dent all the doorjambs by bashing your forehead into them. Anyway, the place has been all but shut down for the past few days. It's taken most of Brainchild's processing power to decode Aureus's command language. And that's saying a lot."

"My guess is that 'secret' was the operative word in my description."

Perturbare looked up in injured innocence. "What—would I keep secrets from you, my faithful allies and companions? Stingray, your cynicism alarms me."

Fomalhaut and Raintree walked into the room. "Nice to see you boys," said Perturbare. "We're just about to put our puppet through his paces. Brainchild, are you ready?"

The computer's voice emerged from the terminal. "I am ready."

"Good. Proceed with the test routine."

Aureus's eyes flickered and illuminated. The Third Eye slid open. The Vigil trio flinched, but the eye remained dark. Perturbare chuckled as the lid slid shut again. "Can you see anything?" he asked.

"I can see very well," answered Brainchild. "The audio inputs and other sensors are also functioning. I would say that Aureus has enjoyed an unusually rich and complete set of sensory stimuli."

"That must be why he was always such a joy to work with," said Stingray.

"Proceed with the articulation sequence."

Brainchild fed tiny electrical charges into the liquid-filled compartments of the robot's envelope. The mercurgold within them expanded along lines of least resistance, producing the equivalent of muscular motion. The robot's hands, arms, and legs flexed and writhed; its torso bent; its head pivoted and tilted. Its mouth fell open, and Brainchild's voice issued from it, having gained a bell-like tone. "I appear to have full motor control." The golden body reclined again and grew stiff and still. "The mercurgold compartments are now fully charged. Stingray?"

"This will be my pleasure." He picked up a fifty-pound sledgehammer and brought it down on Aureus's chest with all his strength. The blow produced a loud *clang* but made neither bend, dent, nor ripple. Indeed, one angle of the sledgehammer's head was flattened. "He's solid."

The robot relaxed and went fluid again. "I have full control over Aureus's systems," said Brainchild.

"Excellent. Thank you, Brainchild," said Perturbare, reaching in to disconnect the interface cable.

"Now wait a minute," said Stingray. "We need Aureus's weapons, not his personality. Why don't we leave Perturbare's computer in control? I daresay it'll be more reliable that way."

"Brainchild would have to control the robot remotely, as it did just now," said Fomalhaut. "That would leave it open to interference, or even takeover, by the Para-men."

Besides, said the thought that intruded into Stingray's mind, *I am not yet prepared to grant Perturbare full control over a weapon strong enough to destroy us all. The future is not so clear to me.*

Stingray made no further comment.

"Well, gentlebeings," said Perturbare, "are we ready to lay the silver egg?"

"I suppose so," said Fomalhaut, "as long as we're prepared for a quick shutdown in the event that Aureus finds some reason to blame us for its defeat."

"Then we're ready. Even Stingray's old control gadget was good enough to provide that." Without ceremony Perturbare picked up the brain case and plopped it into place. The final touch was to replace the crystal cage which enclosed it. When the robot's internal force fields took hold of the cage and locked it into alignment, Perturbare knew the monster was about to reawaken.

Sure enough, its eyes took fire. Aureus stood up with a motion so quick and fluid it could scarcely be followed.

"My teleportation system is dysfunctional," it announced.

"That is true," said Fomalhaut. "Of all your systems we understood it least. We were unable to repair it."

"I see. In general you have done a creditable job of reconstruction."

"You're welcome," said Perturbare.

"What is our projected course of action?"

"We plan an immediate attack on the Para-men," said Fomalhaut. "In addition, we release you from your vow not to attack the Rralians, Valjhar and Kern."

"That is irrelevant. I was unaware of the presence of the Stones on this world. Their destruction takes precedence over all, and must be my first priority."

"Are you saying that the Stones originated on Rral?" asked Raintree.

"They did, and they were the bane and curse of that world."

"This is just as well," said Fomalhaut heavily. "I doubt that any of the rest of us could stand against Cal-Cotavion in any event."

"All right then," said Perturbare. "We're as ready as we're ever going to be. Only one thing left to be done — sucker the Para-men into putting themselves into an exposed position."

"And of course that would best be done by someone whom they trust," said Stingray.

"Ben...?" said Fomalhaut.

"No."

"Well, Ben says 'no', and it sounds like he means it," said Stingray. "As for myself, I'm obviously out. Perturbare is also inappropriate. It would be pretty suspicious for him to suddenly be trying to arrange a meeting between us. I'm afraid that leaves you as our most credible remaining spokesman, Fomalhaut."

"So it does." Fomalhaut turned, hesitated, then walked quickly out of the lab.

"What's his problem?" asked Perturbare, looking after him.

"His problem? Perhaps members of his species feel a measure of remorse when reduced to treachery," said Raintree bitterly.

"Ah. I see," said Perturbare, nodding at him with bland acceptance.

"Don't look at me that way. Yes, I've been guilty of consorting with the enemy, but I've never actively taken their side."

"Well, Ben—I've been too busy lately to shop for sackcloth and ashes, but I do hope to eventually purge myself of evil, given time."

"Shut up, both of you," said Stingray. "The next time you feel like indulging in guilt or blame-casting, think about Rouse."

Ben subsided, but still smoldered at Perturbare. The grin that lurked just beneath Perturbare's placid expression was infuriating.

Presently Fomalhaut returned. "The Para-men agree to meet us on the ice near their fortress. Valjhar offers his profound apologies for the deaths of Rouse and T'Ukudu."

He sighed.

"We attack as planned."

Chapter 45

Nike Descends

Scant hours later Raintree found himself boarding a
flyer bound for the Antarctic. He'd spent the preceding
hours brooding, not daring to sleep for fear that the
Dreamfarer would come to him and discover his plans.
Now his throat felt tight and dry. Nausea threatened to
overwhelm him. Cold sweat felt like panic trying to seep in.
But somehow he managed to do what was required of him,
and if he were even paler than usual, no one pointed it out
to him.

Stingray, however, did take note of what he attached to
the storage racks on the flyer's bulkheads. "Two cryoguns,
Ben?"

"In case one breaks," Ben muttered.

"Like carrying coals to Newcastle, isn't it?"

"You know better than that. Antarctica is a furnace
compared to what these guns can do. What about you?
How long do you expect to last in that outfit?" Stingray
wore a suit of body armor that left his arms and legs bare.

"Indefinitely. I was made to survive in a much more
heat-hungry medium than a little chilly air."

"Ben, please pilot the flyer, if you would," said
Fomalhaut.

Ben welcomed the assignment, as it would distract his
mind. Stingray took the copilot's seat, while Fomalhaut sat
in the cabin. Ben guided the vehicle away from the landing
stage atop their headquarters. Aureus would follow under
its own power. They dared not approach the Para-men in

the robot's company for fear of revealing their hostile intent.

"I still wonder if we shouldn't have dragged Anubis along," said Stingray.

"Have no fear," said Fomalhaut. "If Anubis feels his presence is required on the battlefield, he will make an appearance. I hope not to see him."

As they flew down the east coast of North America, Ben studied the urban incrustations which crept up its bays and waterways like some skin disease. He found himself wondering what he was about to do in the name of those who dwelt there. But finally honesty prevailed, and he admitted to himself that it was not for his fellow men that he was prepared to fight, but for Rouse, and against the Dreamfarer, who had tried to make him a traitor, who had played on his weaknesses and left him unable to defend his comrades.

The coast fell away into the mists in the west. "Stand by," said Ben. "I'm about to accelerate into orbit." He pitched the flyer's nose up forty five degrees, then fed power to the main propulsion lantern, more than was really necessary. He felt the weight of acceleration bearing down on him, pushing him into his seat back, making it difficult even to maintain a grip on the control yoke. He was by far the weakest of those in the flyer, yet he was determined to bear as much as they.

"Ease up, Ben," said Stingray thickly. "There'll be more than enough punishment where we're going."

Soon the mass of the Antarctic ice cap gleamed along the horizon before them. They descended, and the sun dropped with them, until it and they skimmed just above the ice, the sun's horizontal beams casting elongated blue shadows from every ridge and crack.

Only the Redoubt's uppermost spires were still in sunlight; below was a clear shadowless twilight. Fomalhaut came forward and stared through the canopy. After a moment he pointed and said, "There they are." Ben steered in the direction indicated. Soon he detected a group of tiny figures, mere fragments of ash almost lost on the expanse of purple ice.

"They're all together," said Ben. "Stingray, take over the piloting." He removed himself from the pilot's seat, leaving Stingray no choice but to obey or suffer a crash. "Slow to fifty knots and pass them on the left at a hundred feet of altitude." He yanked one of the cryoguns clear of the rack, opened a panel in its side, and flipped several switches, causing the weapon to whine ominously. Stingray looked back. Fomalhaut made no objection to Ben's plan. Shrugging, Stingray began to execute the maneuver.

Ben pulled the hood of his cold armor over his face. He keyed open a loading door in the side of the fuselage, grabbed a railing, and leaned out to look ahead. There stood four figures looking in their direction. He also caught the unmistakable glint of the Stones. With gall rising in his throat he swung the barrel of the cryogun out the hatch. By now its whine had climbed to an eerie wailing. He braced himself and triggered the weapon, which emitted a terrible hollow shout as it froze a huge mass of air with the Paramen at its center. The flyer shuddered and swerved as a great volume of air was pulled in and compressed into that crackling, fuming hemisphere. The cryobeam cut out. Ben leaned out even further, looking back to access the results of his deed.

So, he had done it. He had committed the most aggressive act against the Para-men that Doctor Borealis possibly could.

"Ben, you're on fire!" cried Stingray.

In fact it was the cryogun that was smoking and spitting flame, overloaded and burned out by that one massive burst. Raintree shrugged off its shoulder strap and tossed the ruined weapon out the hatch. "Turn us around," he ordered. Perhaps his purpose was achieved—perhaps with one shot he had preempted the conflict. The question now was whether his frozen victims could ever be revived.

The flyer yawed about and headed back toward the great hemisphere of solid air. Ben stared at it with narrowed eyes, while behind him loomed Fomalhaut.

"It was a worthwhile effort, Ben," said Fomalhaut, "but it did not work. The dome is hollow, and there is activity within."

"All right then," said Stingray, "let's get down there before they can escape."

But even as the flyer began to brake, the mass of ice lit up with the incandescence of a sun. A solid column of blazing, ionized gases erupted from the side. "That would be Kroy dal Ren, I expect," shouted Stingray, wrestling the controls as the flyer was buffeted by shockwaves.

"Look!" yelled Ben, pointing toward the Redoubt. Like angry gnats, a dozen flyers swarmed around it, testing and probing its defenses with brilliant threads of energy.

"Perturbare's timing is good," said Fomalhaut.

The flare of radiance from the Para-men's frozen prison subsided, leaving the area fogged with steam and vapor. Raintree squinted. He thought he saw a fleeting shadow heading toward the Redoubt, but wasn't sure.

"Valjhar has dispatched Cal-Cotavion to defend the fortress," stated Fomalhaut.

"Then that's where Aureus will go," said Stingray.

"Valjhar is down there with Kern Harner and Kroy dal Ren. I do not believe Valjhar is using the Motionglobe which Perturbare described. My friends, the hour has come. We will now either succeed in our goal, or fail. Both possibilities carry with them bitter consequences. Our honor has been expended. Let us try to behave ourselves as though this were not the case. I will now depart. Gentlemen, good luck to you." Orange light beamed from his shoulders as Fomalhaut dived from the flyer.

Fomalhaut continued to probe the minds in the mauve-lit mists below: Kern Harner, excited, alert to opportunities for melodrama; Valjhar, confused, hurt, distressed; Kroy dal Ren—indecipherable, disconcertingly so. Fomalhaut bypassed him and focused on Valjhar, planning to impose a surrender directly on his mind, to force upon him a realization of the futility of his plans. He established the contact. Valjhar, reacting with unexpected force and facility, managed to expel him through sheer fury and moral outrage.

Then Fomalhaut's sensors overloaded as he was smashed back by the full impact of Kroy dal Ren's nuclear beam. His mirrored exploration suit was so far able to fend off this level of radiation, but the flux was increasing rapidly. Kroy dal Ren, he realized, was the major threat here, and Fomalhaut had been craven to aim his first assault at the relatively helpless Valjhar Cor.

Very well then. He had already suffered too much at the hands of Kroy dal Ren. He would suffer no more.

With T'Ukudu's warnings in mind he turned his attention to the incarnate star-being. It was pointless to fire his weapons directly at him; the mirror field Kroy used to collimate his energy output was also an effective shield. Instead Fomalhaut directed his SASERs at the ice around the creature's feet. At full power they turned it into a quaking slurry of ice, water, and steam. The solar beam faltered and went out. Grimly, Fomalhaut forced his way into Kroy dal Ren's mind.

To his great surprise, Kroy welcomed the contact with something like joy. Fomalhaut encountered no resistance as he probed the limits of Kroy's consciousness. His intention was to pinch it off at the root and cast it out to dissipate in the quantum randomness outside the brain. All the while Kroy attempted to engage him in intellectual and emotional discourse, oblivious to the deadly nature of Fomalhaut's maneuverings. At this intimate level, Kroy's mentality was not nearly as difficult to grasp as when interacting with the physical body he wore so maladroitly and the spoken language he found so foreign. It was clear to Fomalhaut that Kroy dal Ren had suffered greatly from lack of the communion he had known as part of the cosmos-spanning network of star-beings, a communion to which no other class of being was privy.

Kroy's brain contained mere scraps of the personality which had originally inhabited it, too few for that person to ever be resurrected. If only the two could have shared that brain and body, there was no telling what sort of being the hybrid Kroy dal Ren could have become.

Fomalhaut broke off the contact, his plans suddenly changed. He probed the small mirror field generator which produced Kroy's collimator, activated it, and reshaped the paraboloid into a sphere with Kroy dal Ren at its center. That done, he fused the controls to prevent any further change to the field. He took a firm telekinetic hold on the mirror bubble, lifted it twenty feet into the air, wrapped himself around it and propelled it skyward with the full power of his propulsion beams. He drove on until they were surrounded by blackness and the Earth was a distant luminous disk. Only then could he relax; the interplanetary medium should be too thin for Kroy to find anything to fuse. Still, he must not delay; the Para-men were not without resources. What he proposed to do was outside his previous experience, but there was no time for hesitation or meditation. He turned his attention to the sun, forming a pathway, a column of space-time whose quantum frothiness was temporarily smoothed out and made coherent. Holding that in mind with the utmost difficulty, Fomalhaut turned all his remaining resources to Kroy, reestablishing contact. It should now be a simple matter of forcing out Kroy's consciousness, whose mind should then be transmitted into the space-time "wire" he had formed, to reconstitute in its proper form in the solar plasma, if it could.

Yet something deterred him. This was still the killer of Rouse Farewell. He did not wish this creature to inhabit, and perhaps colonize, the sun of Earth. Therefore he let the space-bridge collapse. While holding Kroy's consciousness with one part of his mind, he used what remained to build another bridge to the nearest star whose planets he knew to be lifeless: the star Fomalhaut. The bridge was tremulous, and not to be long maintained.

Fomalhaut cut the silver thread that bound Kroy to his humanoid body. The creature's consciousness flashed away at transcendent speed.

Only then could Fomalhaut fully relax, floating exhausted beside the bubble containing Kroy's now mindless body. He had found unknown strength to achieve a feat few of his fellows could match. His own mind felt like it was in danger of evaporating into the void as well.

Yet despite his weariness, he still had responsibilities on the distant blue-white planet Earth, and was about to return when he was distracted by what seemed to be traces of Kroy's consciousness echoing in his mind. For a moment he feared that Kroy might have managed to invade and infiltrate his own mind. When he opened himself he was astonished to eavesdrop on the pervasive chatter between all the star-beings in the universe, though he could make almost no sense of it. His contact with Kroy's mind must have sensitized him to this form of communication, which was something like the Transsend employed by ISAF, although infinitely more polyphonic. Had the voice of Kroy dal Ren rejoined this chorus? He attempted to sift through the multitude in search of a tone he could recognize, finding it by virtue of the fact that it was crying loudly, calling for help in a voice which Fomalhaut thought might well escape the confines of the universe itself.

A response was not long in coming: a true Transsend, or Transcendental Signal, though it had a beacon pattern which Fomalhaut had never known to be used by ISAF or by anyone else in his native universe. With a thrill of apprehension he realized the truth: Kroy dal Ren, returned to its native environment by Fomalhaut, had demonstrated its gratitude by summoning a member of the organization Perturbare had dubbed the Cosmic Patrol.

Their flyer battered and buffeted by the pillar of fire erupting nearby, Stingray yelled, "Ben, let's set this thing down before they burn us out of the sky."

Ben shouldered his second cryogun as Stingray landed the flyer. They leaped from the hatch. The flyer was soon lost in the mists which still seethed throughout the area. Ben was glad of the cover.

The ground trembled. A sudden silence came almost as a shock to the two stalkers.

"Kroy's stopped firing," whispered Ben. "I wonder what happened."

"I don't know. Let's just hope we find him before he fires again," muttered Stingray.

Ben nodded in agreement. They crept forward, listening intently, wary of every shadow and fold of fog. They looked at each other as a thin hissing sound grew louder behind them. Their eyes communicated what they both already knew—it was Aureus in flight. Sure enough, an instant later a blur of gold shot by overhead. An instant after that, a bar of power slammed out of the mist, caught Aureus like a battering ram, and sent it tumbling out of sight.

"Hah!" The cocky cry of triumph came from a place not fifty yards away.

"Damn!" whispered Stingray. "Kern's proton beam."

"Do you think Aureus survived it?"

"The old Aureus would have shrugged it off. Now, who knows? Come on, let's go nail Kern."

They continued on, though Ben was uncomfortable with the idea of "nailing" Kern. They found him soon enough, and also Valjhar, who knelt in the fog cradling Kroy dal Ren's inert body in his arms. Raintree knew then that Kroy had been destroyed, for while his twitching body still held life, his eyes betrayed the presence of no sort of consciousness, not even the incomprehensible intelligence of the star-being. Then Kern, who had been staring blankly at the tableau of Valjhar's grief, noticed them. Ben raised the cryogun; Kern frowned in disapproval and made a gesture even as Ben touched the contact. The cryogun throbbed, the anti-energy poured out, but it had no detectable effect on Kern or anything else. Ben's arms went slack, appalled at the ease with which his only weapon had been neutralized.

Then Kern turned to find Stingray loping toward him like a great hunting cat. To Ben's astonishment, Kern reacted with a smile. "Stingray!" he cried, but it was almost a welcoming sound, not a cry of fear or enmity. He made other gestures, and Stingray found himself charging up and off a ramp which had materialized before him. Stingray rolled on crashing to the ground and was back on his feet, charging again. This time Kern created a maze, through which Stingray blundered with many loud curses. Kern laughed merrily, but as Stingray finally found his way out, Kern manifested a huge spear which he brandished dramatically. "Brünnhilde Flam!" he cried. "In thy name I battle the fearsome Fafnir!" Stingray gave a roar which would have done credit to that very dragon and darted up with inhuman speed. Lightning crackled from his outthrust fists. Kern flew back with a *"whuuf!"*; his spear went flying. Stingray was on him in an instant, straddling him. Ben winced to see the huge form dwarfing and dominating the much smaller Kern. But inexplicably, Kern reacted with another laugh.

Disbelief sent Stingray's eyes bulging, his skin pale and waxy with a rage Ben had never seen him show before. "Surrender, you little buffoon. Deactivate your engineering suit!"

"Never!" Kern kept laughing in Stingray's face, a reckless, carefree laughter that to Ben seemed insanely inappropriate. Grimacing with anger, Stingray struck him a blow with a single finger, little more than a tap, even for one so slight as Kern.

"Oh! Even the strongest blows of the mighty Stingray fail to deter the scarlet-clad hero!" chortled Kern.

"Why do you laugh at me?" demanded Stingray.

"You big oaf, I know you can never really hurt me."

"Is that right?" Stingray raised his fist for another blow. The sight of the muscles knotting along his arm sent Ben running towards him yelling "No!" but he could never reach him in time, His legs moved with dreamlike slowness. His mouth could not form words fast enough to accommodate those that tumbled from his mind. Valjhar, he saw, had somehow materialized on Stingray's back, and was pummeling him with all the force he had, but he might as well have been trying to hamper a water buffalo. Stingray's fist came down, the only fast-moving thing in existence, and Kern's head snapped to the side, blood spurting.

Then Stingray raised both arms, flinging Valjhar aside. In the thinning mists Ben saw something terrible, the shadow of Anubis. He screamed hard enough to tear his throat, but there was no stopping the dreadful thing now taking place; indeed, it only got worse as he watched. Slits opened on the undersides of Stingray's wrists, and narrow black blades swiveled into view. His eyes afire with madness, Stingray thrust these spines into Kern's throat.

That act somehow broke the spell that had magnified time. Ben ran up and stood there, looking down at Kern, who tried to speak, but choked and spit blood; tried again but managed only a rasping murmur.

His face relaxed. Suddenly he looked no more than a child.

Stingray stared down at the corpse, his face a void of incomprehension. One of his spines had detached and lodged in Kern's throat. Stingray lifted his other arm and regarded the spine that still dangled loosely from the slit in his flesh. It dripped a mixture of blood and a black slime that coated the serrated blade.

Stingray turned a stricken look on Ben, as if mutely asking what he had done.

"Ben," he said hoarsely, hopelessly. "Kern's last words...they were in Rralian. And I understood them. He asked me—why I killed him. I remember now. *I was one of them.* They took me from the sea, an ignorant savage, and brought me up to walk among the stars. And Kern...he was not a brooder, not like Valjhar, nor solemn and burdened like Cal. He was happy just to travel among the stars with his friends, with his lover, helping when he could, and he was...my friend. He never held anything against me...not my ungainly size, not my bad attitude, nothing. Unless I'm dreaming it, he and I explored the ruins of civilizations that perished before the Sun was born. We admired the colors in nebulae and I listed to his poetry and tried not to laugh. And now..." He grabbed the remaining spine, ripped it free and cast it away; he also pulled out the one in Kern's throat, handling it with the utmost revulsion. Then he gathered up Kern's body, and clutched it to him, lost in agonized sobs.

Ben looked at Valjhar, seeking a reprieve, pleading for redemption of some kind, but found there only wrath of such intensity that he felt withered. But before Valjhar could offer any accusation, Stingray looked up, catching Valjhar with a gaze of equal ferocity.

"If you had listened to me—and abandoned your plan to take over my planet—you need not have robbed me of my memory, need not have cast me from the heavens, need not have sown this misery. Rouse and Kern would still be alive, and I would not be a murderer."

Valjhar's anger appeared short-circuited by Stingray's words. Looking stricken and lost, he wandered away. Raintree could not bring himself to follow.

Stingray spoke no more, but hovered over Kern's body as if seeking to shelter it from the cold. Ben pondered him for a moment, then wandered over to the living shell which had been Kroy dal Ren, examining it listlessly.

"Now do you see why I sought to keep you from this struggle?"

Ben turned aside. There stood the Dreamfarer, regarding him with sad eyes of jade.

"You loathsome succubus," he whispered. "You've invaded my mind for the last time. You've weakened me, subverted me, made me doubly a traitor. But I swear I will tolerate you no more."

Dreamfarer lowered her head, and with no further word dissolved away. Ben stood looking bitterly at the place where she had stood, then turned away. She was gone, absent from his heart, and with her went the last of his innocence, he feared.

He glanced at Stingray, who was still lost in misery, as thoroughly unmanned as Ben himself had been the last time the two groups had met. Anubis lurked nearby, he knew; presently he would come forth to deal with Kern, and perhaps Kroy dal Ren, as he had done with Rouse.

With a coldness of heart exceeding the coldness without, Raintree walked clear of the blanket of vapors. He peeled back his hood, glad of the icy air which flooded his lungs, and searched his surroundings. Undulations of the snow field and the uncertain lighting hid anyone who might be nearby. The only sign of activity was the flitting of Perturbare's flyers as they worried the Redoubt's defenses. Their numbers were reduced, and as Raintree watched they were reduced still further, withered and crumpled by forces seen and unseen. In a few moments all were gone. So much for the efforts of the brilliant rogue technologist, thought Ben.

But that thought had barely dissipated when a hundred more flyers, each larger than the last, breasted the horizon in ominous formations. They opened fire, their beams spread into partial hemispheres by the Redoubt's diffuser fields. But those vehicles too fell prey to the fortress's apparently inexhaustible defenses. In a few minutes the skies were empty and peaceful yet again.

There was a hushed silence, and then, in waves and curtains, a thousand flyers moved in like white locusts, their propulsion beams forming a complex and shifting webwork of fiery threads across the sky. The hugest of them landed and disgorged great roaring mechanisms which rolled toward the fortress and deployed hosts of automated diggers, sappers, melters, and batterers. Still the Redoubt's defenses flared out, crippling many of

Perturbare's vehicles, but unable to deal with more than a fraction of the attackers at any given moment.

Raintree stood in grudging awe of Perturbare's capabilities. He could only imagine the results if those forces had been turned against his allies and himself.

Despite that distant thunder and tumult, a nearby pit in the snow caught Raintree's attention. He walked over and stared at the small, narrow footprints which led from it toward the fortress. His face bleak, Ben began to follow Aureus.

In his hidden command post far from the scene of battle, Possum Perturbare observed the monitors which displayed his assault on the Redoubt. His ERASERs were effectively neutralized by diffusion, but the ram-beams were more effective. Though somewhat defocused, they were still able to exert damaging force, especially against those parts of the structure that Kern had frivolously constructed of ice. Brainchild, in control of every weapon, was careful not to damage the tall silo that sheltered the main hull of *Mote*. It would not do to deprive his erstwhile allies of their only means of escape.

Yet all of this was of mostly academic interest to Perturbare. In fact, he had not yet bothered to deploy his newer and subtler weapons.

"How's it going, Brainchild?"

"I am reasonably certain that all aspects of the Redoubt's defensive systems have now been exercised. I detect no surprising or unexpected capabilities or command systems."

"Good. Withdraw the battlefleet while there's still something left of it."

Brainchild complied. In minutes the only sign of the robotic battle was the wreckage of the hundreds of downed flyers which smoked and sparked all over the ice.

"There'll be a heck of a cleanup job for somebody when this is all over," said Perturbare. "Okay, shut down all their defenses."

Brainchild complied. All sensors confirmed that the fortress was suddenly inert.

"Excellent. They never discovered the command interfaces that I installed."

"Or perhaps they never considered the possibility that you might do such a thing," said Brainchild with its usual equanimity.

Perturbare winced. "Maybe not." He stood up, walked down a short tunnel, entered a cockpit, and seated himself before another console. He touched the controls; the flyer rose up, a mantle of snow sliding from it in sheets. He set a course for the Redoubt, skimming just over the ice. Keying the communicator, he spoke into the air. "Possum Perturbare to Vigil. How goes the struggle?"

There was a pause. "Raintree here."

Something about Raintree's tone wiped out Perturbare's self-satisfied smirk.

"What's happening, Ben?"

"Kern Harner is dead," said Ben lifelessly.

A brutal hand squeezed Perturbare's heart. The flyer dipped dangerously. Brainchild took over the piloting.

"Oh. Damn. Damn."

"Stingray killed him, and now he's out of it too, completely un—uncommunicative," continued Ben. "Kroy dal Ren is also a vegetable, but not dead—I s-suspect Fomalhaut is responsible for that, but I can't find him or contact him. I don't know what Valjhar is doing. Right now I'm trying to find Aureus and Cotavion."

"Ah—" Perturbare hesitated to ask the next question. "What is your present status, Ben?"

"It too closely resembles yours. Raintree out."

Feeling numb, Perturbare landed beside the fortress, disembarked, and walked unprotected through the cold to the nearest entrance, where he took possession of his conquest.

Fascinated by the onset of a power beyond any he had ever encountered, Fomalhaut remained adrift in cislunar space, searching for signs and portents. The body of Kroy dal Ren had already vanished through some means he could not analyze. Now the entire Solar System quivered beneath some inescapable scrutiny. Space itself seemed to ring like a bell as it was quartered and searched. Somewhere in the direction of Hercules the search met with success. A few minutes later, an object moving at a substantial fraction of the speed of light hurtled through space on a direct path to the Antarctic. Fomalhaut took note of its passage but did not seek to follow; his attention remained directed outward. Aware of the approach of Shaula Alshain, he prepared a mind probe with much trepidation. But before he could launch it, he himself came under mental scrutiny, a probe so deep and thorough that he knew Alshain for a telepath equal or superior to himself. Seeing little chance of blocking her probe, and having no compelling reason to attempt it, he laid himself bare, at the same time taking advantage of that intimacy to learn what he could of her.

Alshain found within him no sin which could not be forgiven. She took special note of his recent act of mercy toward Kroy dal Ren. Fomalhaut suddenly lost his feeling of ambivalence for that deed. It had been well done.

A thought entered his mind: *You belong to an admirable race. It will be my privilege to guard it, should my tenure in this universe be so long.*

Fomalhaut reacted to this sentiment with a flood of incompatible emotions: gratitude, exhilaration, but also foreboding, a dread which was not due to the Para-men victory that now seemed inevitable. Marshaling all his resources, he deepened his probe, seeking out the most recent modifications to this intellect, changes which went to the heart of Alshain's ability to gain victory by reordering reality itself. He sought out her link with the Universal Instrument, shying away from the utter chaos of the implement itself, but studying her mastery over it. And he discovered that her link was tenuous, her mastery incomplete. He trembled in the grip of absolute dismay — he could imagine nothing more dangerous than a being in imperfect control of a Universal Instrument.

Aware of his knowledge, Alshain acted; the link between them was ended. Even Fomalhaut's knowledge of her imperfection was expunged from his mind.

Somewhat dazed, Fomalhaut watched as she proceeded Earthward, in despair of following, for he could not hope to match her speed. Alshain, perhaps realizing this, reached out and carried him in her wake.

An arc-light glare from high overhead suddenly burned into and blurred the white landscape. Raintree glanced up in time to glimpse a hurtling spear of light which fell to earth and penetrated the ice a few miles away. He knew enough to fling himself down in the twilight that followed.

The shockwave rolled over him seconds later, carrying clouds of ice crystals which hissed against his armor like sand. When he thought it safe to rise he stared at the pillar of plasma and vapor that issued from the pit.

Hands shaking, he raised the cryogun and peered through its sight, raising the magnification to its highest setting. The bright plasma thinned and faded, but the steam still made it difficult to see anything. Raintree fumbled with the controls, defining a narrow cryobeam which cooled and condensed the steam into snow. The scene briefly cleared, enabling Raintree to make out the figure who emerged from the pit, looked around, and set out toward the Redoubt at a walk. It was Endurance. The sight of him filled Ben with fear of the unknown, not due to Endurance's return *per se*, but from wondering what agency could have returned him thus to this time and place. He suddenly regretted his solitude on the ice plain, doubting his capacity to survive whatever was about to unfold. Even the presence of the Dreamfarer would be a comfort at this moment. But she did not come.

Raintree's solitude was ended even as he conceived the wish. Hearing a rush of air and a muffled impact, he looked to the side. There stood Fomalhaut, newly returned from God-knew-where. From behind came soft footsteps. Ben turned to behold a less welcome presence: Anubis, his grey, withered face grim and shadowed. And finally another unexpected arrival: Valjhar Cor, his face alight with expectation.

Before a word could be exchanged between them, the heavens opened up in glory. A figure descended, wrapped in lights and blazes, clad in curtains and coronas of light, a female form as grave and beautiful as Athena, as fell as Nike descending onto the battlefield.

Ben dropped his cryogun, unconsciously reacting to its futility. All their fates would surely be decided by the exalted being now coming into their midst. Eyes flashing green fire, she lifted her hand, which was bound by a dark metal band containing an orb of perfect darkness.

The god Anubis witnessed her coming and was disturbed. Here was an interloper, a factor from outside the universe which might interfere with events as it had foreseen them.

Tom Standing Crane, inhabiting the small corner of his own mind and body that had been allotted him by Anubis, was startled out of oblivion by the strength of this reaction. Rousing himself to peer out through his own eyes, he found he still possessed enough of himself to be awed and moved by the splendor of this strange woman.

Anubis was not so moved. Standing Crane followed its cool, austere mind as it probed into Alshain's reality in an effort to determine how to deal with her threat. The source of her power was a singularity, capable of anything, including the dissolution of Anubis itself. Yet the singularity was itself vulnerable—it was simply a knot in space, a knot which might easily be untied, especially since this woman had not yet learned how to guard its integrity from such interference. Anubis prepared to untie the knot. Never before had it contemplated taking so active a role in determining the course of life and death, not even when the sorcerers and demigods of its native world had offered temptations to do so. But Shaula Alshain came from beyond the pale. She was foreign. She was not his responsibility; she could not be allowed to challenge the fate which this universe had contrived for itself and its children.

Standing Crane saw all this as well, and more. He saw that Shaula would not survive the destruction of her Instrument. There was no difference between undoing the Instrument and murdering Shaula.

Without hope of success, Standing Crane rallied himself against this force that had invaded him, this intellect which was deep but narrow, implacable and remorseless in its goals. The memory of the lifeless face of Rouse Farewell inspired him. He had done nothing to save her; he could not permit his own body to destroy another person of such worth.

Although captivated by the spectacle of Shaula's descent, Fomalhaut could not ignore the psychic eruption within the shriveled figure beside him. Anubis emitted a thin wail of distress—or was that Standing Crane? Fomalhaut was startled by the rictus that contorted the withered face. Here, he sensed, was a unique opportunity. After a moment's preparation he sent his consciousness into that hairless skull. The passage was easy.

Fomalhaut—? For love of all gods, help me expel this thing.

And that Fomalhaut did. The mind of Anubis was reminiscent of a dimly-lighted hypostyle hall—huge, monumental, but ultimately not complex. Anubis was, he was surprised to find, so narrowly driven and single-minded as to resemble a primitive computer program. And yet its hold on Standing Crane's body was strong and pervasive. Within the framework of the pillared hall metaphor, Standing Crane's consciousness wandered like a ghost, wan and depleted, yet driven to desperate exertion by the fear that Anubis meant to destroy Shaula Alshain. Now Standing Crane held Anubis at bay, creating such turmoil and stress throughout his body that Anubis was effectively paralyzed, unable to apply its powers to the task it had set itself. But Standing Crane was meeting no success in actually expelling Anubis from his body.

Fomalhaut took advantage of this stalemate to further explore the mind of Anubis. Its thoughts, he discovered, were so lucid and fundamental that it had access to all the essential forces of the universe — Anubis indeed commanded the power of a god. Yet something in the very structure of space was inimical to it, which seemed to explain why it was forced to occupy a Human body and brain, rather than manifesting itself in a form not subject to the interference of a prior tenant.

Fascinated, Fomalhaut delved deeper into this labyrinth of being. He discovered a series of "annexes" to the main hall, or perhaps a series of subroutines appended to the main program. Entering one which seemed unusually well developed, he found there the dormant characteristics of another god from ancient mythology — Hermes, the Achaean deity of theft, medicine, and dreams — Hermes, herald and messenger of the gods — Hermes, who guided the dead into the underworld...

Even as he considered these qualities, the personality of Hermes seemed to stir, as if taking life from Fomalhaut's mere contemplation of it. This, as Fomalhaut soon realized, was a personality far more complex — far more "mercurial", indeed, than the dusty implacability of Anubis. As Hermes stirred and gained strength, he became aware of Fomalhaut, and saw the situation that prevailed outside in the world of space and time. His reaction to the intentions of the part of himself which was Anubis was decidedly ambivalent.

Fomalhaut hastily disengaged from Hermes and returned to the "main hall", where the foundations of the consciousness of Anubis were trembling. He made contact with Standing Crane, who was now merely a dismayed bystander within his own body.

Fomalhaut! I held the thing as long as I could. What is happening now?

"Anubis is not the only god you carry within you; you contain multitudes. Now another of them seeks to assert his dominance over Anubis."

There was a sudden psychic convulsion; Fomalhaut was nearly expelled by the turmoil.

"Standing Crane—?"

Fomalhaut...Anubis...is leaving...!

Fomalhaut instantly disengaged. In the external world half a second had passed. Where Anubis/Standing Crane had stood as one, now they were two. One figure resembled the Tom Standing Crane who had applied for Vigil membership so many months ago: a weathered man, exhausted surely, but not wasted. Beside him was the dry-skinned thing into which he'd degenerated. The contrast between them was horrid, now that both could be seen at once.

Yet it was Standing Crane who slumped onto the ice, while the mummy stood straight and tall, its eyes boring steadily into the descending radiance of Shaula Alshain, eyes that remained shadowed despite the celestial glory that shone into them. The division had been so swift that no one else had had time to notice it. Fomalhaut watched helplessly as Anubis, now rid of all interference, reached out and loosened the knot of spacetime at the heart of Shaula's Universal Instrument.

Shaula gave a shriek of anguish as her light was extinguished. "Valjhar!" she cried, falling the last few feet onto the ice as a flame that had been quenched. Valjhar ran to her and took her in his arms. She stared into his face with an agonized emptiness that chilled Fomalhaut's blood. He dared not enter her mind for fear of the chaos and devastation he knew were within it. It was hard enough merely to look at her as she lay perishing. She was tiny and fragile compared to her exalted condition of a moment before, an elfin creature of the native Rralian type. He couldn't help but be moved by her beauty, even in its dissolution.

As Shaula gazed into her lover's eyes she managed to speak. "Valjhar! What trouble have you gotten yourself into now? I see your plan for this planet...Valjhar, my dear love, I never would have used the Instrument to reorder things as you intended. That is not the way of the...of the organization I have so—wretchedly failed...Valjhar..."

Suddenly Raintree was at Fomalhaut's side, looking at him with a crazy gaze. "Can't we help her either?" he rasped.

"No," said Fomalhaut with forced calm. "She came here unprepared, prematurely, in response to an outcry from Kroy dal Ren. Shaula's fusion with the Instrument was incomplete. A complete union would have allowed her to defend it, or even to transcend its loss. As it is, the Instrument defined her reality. Without it she is lost, cut adrift, living in a fading, unsustainable dream. She will die."

"Then at least this damned monster Anubis is here to conduct her to wherever she must go next."

"He will not," said Fomalhaut with infinite regret. "As a native of a foreign universe, her fate is of no concern to Anubis."

Raintree scanned the horizon, his eyes afire with a fanatic gleam. "I know someone who can help her," he muttered. "I will not return unless I bring him with me." So saying, Raintree ran off toward the Redoubt, grabbing up his cryogun in mid stride.

Fomalhaut paid little heed to his departure. He only stood and observed Valjhar's grief as Shaula's mind gradually dissolved into chaos.

Whistling uneasily through his teeth, Possum Perturbare slunk through the eccentric maze of passages Kern Harner had devised for his fortress. The section ahead was dimly lighted. On one wall were seven spots of light, one in each color of the rainbow, pure and beautiful. They seemed to be projected from seven pinholes on the opposite wall. A guard device, or an internal sensor of some kind? Perturbare shook his head. He stepped into the beams, slouched down (the beams were at Kern's eye level), and let the colored rays enter his eyes. He shook his head again in appreciation. Kern had installed this trifle merely for the pleasure of drinking in these colors should he happen to pass this way. It was one of many sensory confections Perturbare had discovered already. He'd miss Kern; the boy had shown real possibilities. It was hard not to think of Kern as a boy, although in reality he had probably been somewhat older than Perturbare himself.

The Redoubt's internal locator system was no longer working. Perturbare was unsure whether the voice intercom was still reliable, but he still tried it whenever he passed a console.

"Pimsehkia? Pimsehkia Flam! I'm looking for you. I need to get you out of here."

So far there was no response. Perturbare wished he could remember exactly where Pimsehkia's apartment was, but without the locator system he was reduced to wandering in the right area and hoping to get lucky.

Perturbare turned a corner and confronted the most desolate-looking creature he had ever seen. The look in Pimsehkia's eyes made him feel that justice, not luck, had arranged this encounter.

"Pim—Pimsehkia...you have to leave. This place has been shot to hell. It could all come down at any time."

"Why don't you mention that you're the one who did the shooting?" she hissed, tears streaming down her elfin face.

Perturbare flinched back, speechless.

"I know that Kern is dead."

"Stingray—Stingray did that..."

"Stingray was led here to battle by you! *You* betrayed us, you, with your blue eyes and your ingratiating grin. And for what? I knew Shaula would never go along with Valjhar's plan. I tried to tell Valjhar that, but he was too lost in his fantasy to listen to me, silly little Pimsie Flam! As if he could possibly understand Shaula Alshain as well as I do. I knew that as soon as Shaula arrived she would straighten out this whole mess you boys have made, and without anyone getting hurt. All you had to do was *nothing*, and all would have been well. Instead Kern is dead. The most harmless, the most innocent person among us is dead. Ben, Stingray, and Valjhar are devastated. And I—when I sleep... Get out of my sight, Dr. Possum Perturbare. Go back to your lab, tinker with your gadgets, talk to your computer, because your ability to interact with living creatures is very poor."

"It's not safe here," said Perturbare in a chastened whisper.

Pimsehkia made a wild gesture. "Kern Harner was not so poor a builder as you seem to believe. Don't worry about me. I am no concern of yours."

She turned and ran down the corridor, weeping.

Perturbare stood looking after her for a few minutes.

With no particular sense of motivation he wandered away, approaching a more-or-less T-shaped junction of corridors. He turned right, glancing behind him to discover an empty corridor. Looking ahead, he found himself face-to-face with Endurance.

Perturbare's mood of mellow sadness for Kern, Pimsehkia, and especially himself evaporated. For an instant he considered how he might dissemble his way out of this, but the look of reproach in Endurance's eyes dissuaded him from trying. For the first time in his life Perturbare knew the cold tingle of the nearness of death. He had no illusions—his life was totally accessible to hands that had eviscerated Aureus. No amount of guile would preserve him from whatever vengeance Endurance might care to exact.

Thus Perturbare concluded that only honesty might serve him, or at least, at this moment, cost him nothing.

"All right, Endurance. Maybe I deserve death for betraying you and the others. But if you do kill me, you'll have accomplished nothing but murder. The Para-men are defeated. Your cause is lost; it can't be recovered by my death. Let me live. I tell you that I plan to devote myself to helping humanity as best I can. That's the only good you can salvage from this debacle."

Endurance glowered at him. Perturbare labored to maintain eye contact with those fell golden-brown eyes. Every muscle in his body was rigid with tension as he forced himself not to turn and flee.

After a harrowing pause, Endurance brushed passed him and walked away. Perturbare turned to watch him go. Endurance shot back a final sidelong look of freezing wrath.

Perturbare slumped against the wall, his head spinning. It seemed to take minutes for his heart to start beating again, and then it tried to hammer its way out of his ribcage. He breathed heavily, savoring the continuation of his existence. Even cold sweat seemed like something to appreciate.

He would never forget the look in Endurance's eyes.

"Brainchild. In the future, please remind me to make a real effort to stay off Endurance's bad side."

"Doctor, could you explain how you determined that you were threatened by him?"

"It was his eyes. The look he gave me."

"I hope someday to be able to analyze the nuances of facial expression with such facility."

Raintree panted as he ran. It was ironic that he, who had access to the planet's most advanced technology, was reduced to running while lives were literally in the balance. At least he'd been able to pick up Aureus's trail once again, though the glare and roar of the robot's tachyon weapon as it thundered into action would have been enough of a guide.

"No!" he cried. He had hoped to reach them before any such pointless battle could be joined. It was too much; he sobbed like a child as he stumbled along. The ground heaved. He squinted in the brilliance and cast the cryogun aside, a mere trinket compared to the powers he was approaching. He pulled up the hood of his cold armor. It muffled the din, and provided protection against the waves of furnace heat which rolled in from the still-distant battlezone. Crevasses opened in the ice; he leaped over them without thinking. Other Lights mixed with the searing energy of the tachyon beam: colored glows which in their way were still harder to endure. Shockwaves blew the tops off ice-ridges and knocked him off his feet. Over the thunder of the beam came a series of sharper concussions like the blows of a titan's hammer. Raintree scrambled up, terrified, desperate to run in the opposite direction, but compelled to continue toward the violence ahead. He crawled over a ridge and for the first time saw the tiny figures of silver and gold as they battled in the distance. He put up his hands, squinting between his fingers, lest he be blinded.

Aureus relentlessly probed and blasted with its terrible beam, alternating between its vampiric negative-energy mode and then spewing out what it had drained as coherent energy that threatened to ignite the very air. Somehow Cal-Cotavion was standing up to that fury, every Stone blazing. The purple Stone of Adamance was ascendant, and the Light of Life also glared a hot green. All the Stones were afire, terrible to look upon. Clearly they were Cotavion's shield against Aureus, but Aureus itself showed no susceptibility to their unworldly power. And why should it? For Cal-Cotavion, Aureus was a true nemesis—a machine intelligence, neither alive nor anti-life; not evil, nor anti-truth. Aureus was merely implacable and extremely powerful, too much a creature of pure physics to be affected by such abstract forces, no matter how absolute.

Yet by the way Aureus kept its distance from Cotavion's pale staff, Raintree guessed that Cotavion did not lack a means of offense. And indeed Cotavion suddenly lifted the staff and rammed it into the ice, a blow far beyond all that was humanly possible. Sheets and chunks of ice tore themselves loose and jumped into the air for a hundred feet around him. Aureus went tumbling even as the tremor reached Raintree.

When his eyeballs stopped vibrating, Raintree saw Cotavion standing over the flailing robot. Holding the staff two-handed like a bat, Cotavion struck Aureus such a blow that Raintree didn't know whether to cheer or scream. The sound alone was like being struck by a bag of cement. There came another such blow, and another, and then, just as Raintree was convinced that Aureus must be destroyed, the tachyon beam flared out again, this time so powerful and deadly that Raintree moaned, turned his head and slid back down the ice ridge, for he could not stand even the nearness of that avid, eerie power. He curled up and sheltered his head in his arms, trembling and cursing fate.

The clamor finally died away. Ben could hear nothing but the turmoil in his own mind. For long minutes he dared not move or even open his eyes. His vision was crisscrossed with pulsing lines and vague forms that had been burned into his retinas by the brilliance of the battle.

Finally he forced himself to claw his way to the top of the ridge, where he opened his tearing, blurry eyes through an act of will. He saw Aureus standing before the prostrate form of Cal-Cotavion. From the robot's hands dangled the four Stones.

The sight was intolerable. Raintree heaved himself up and over the ridge, lurching across the shattered ice and snow. Aureus turned its head to regard him as he approached. It stood as if otherwise paralyzed, unable to decide how to deal with the Stones.

"He refused to surrender the Stones," it said. "He said he must return them to his Queen, and if he could not do that, so he must die."

Raintree could recall no previous occasion when Aureus volunteered any information about anything at all. He glared at it. The robot's transparent openwork helmet was cracked; the jewel or lens in its throat was missing; and its skin had several ruptures. Some of its "muscles" were flaccid, with mercurgold lying scattered in globules and small pools.

Yet in contrast, Cal-Cotavion appeared unharmed, even pristine, lying on the ice as though arranged in state. His hood was thrown back, and the violet light of the polar twilight lay softly on his face. In the few previous glimpses Raintree had had of him, Cotavion had always appeared alien, unhealthy, and grim. Now he lay serene and beautiful, noble as a fairy-tale prince, wise as a wizard. On his forehead was a circle of blackened skin. There must the Stone of Truth have burned him, yet he had carried that Stone and all the others, using them well, defending them valiantly. Raintree stood staring at him, wishing he had known him better, praying to someday possess some fragment of his strength.

He whirled on Aureus. "Give me the Stones."

"I am obliged to retain them."

"Damn you, hand them over! They are needed. Take them back later if you must." Raintree took three emphatic steps forward and held out his hand. "I demand that you give them to me, or be prepared to use them yourself." He glared at the robot without blinking, his mouth set, prepared to face the same death that had taken Cal-Cotavion, and expecting it.

"I am not suited to the use of the Stones. I am unable to destroy them. Very well, I put them into your care."

Raintree's jaw dropped open. He sputtered and stammered, completely at a loss. "You—you will give them to me?"

"As long as your use of them is not contrary to the parameters of my mission." Aureus extended its hands and opened its fingers. There gleamed the ring, the brooch, the pendant, and the fillet.

Beyond all expectation, Raintree faced the reality of actually taking possession of the Stones. Now that the moment had arrived, he wasn't sure he was up to it. The mingled Light of the Stones was the distillation of all that was good and strong and proper in the universe, and it was uncompromising—among them was no Stone of Mercy.

And yet he did step forward and clutch them in his hands, grateful for his cold armor, which at least spared him from having to touch them with his bare skin. He stared into their depths from inches away. Suddenly, he realized, he had access to absolute powers.

"Now you must withdraw at once," said Aureus. "The energy I absorbed from Cal-Cotavion exceeds the safe limits of my storage capacity, and I must discharge it immediately."

Raintree looked into the robot's crimson eyes, so unreadable, and nodded. He hobbled away, still shaky, not daring to tap the Stones for the strength he knew they could provide, afraid of unleashing forces beyond his ability to control, half convinced that the Stones would discover his unworthiness and annihilate him.

Yet somehow, when Aureus, not yet a hundred yards behind, released its pent-up energy in a cataclysmic pillar of incandescence that bore straight up into the sky, Raintree was not immolated. He managed to stay on his feet, and his gait grew steadier.

The tableau of Shaula's dying was unchanged. Suddenly it was lit in glaring chiaroscuro as a rod of power leaped starward from somewhere near the Redoubt. Valjhar glanced angrily over his shoulder, and was still looking that way when a wall of hot, compressed air rushed by at the speed of sound, whipping before it a mist of warm water, buffeting and pummeling them for a moment before it swept past. Valjhar winced and turned away. Somehow he knew that Cal-Cotavion, errant wizard and reluctant nobleman of Colibdis, had met his end at last. He returned his attention to Shaula, whose words and mind had lost all coherence. Her eyes rolled back in their sockets. Her mouth was locked wide open, and drool spilled over her lips. Her body was rigid and trembling, and remained so until at last, mercifully, she died a moment later.

Valjhar Cor looked up at the two passive figures who stood nearby. Cal-Cotavion was dead. So was Shaula, and even Kern. Kroy dal Ren was a vegetable; Endurance was missing; Dreamfarer was not in evidence; Pimsehkia's fate was unknown. Nearby stood Fomalhaut, smug and aloof in his reflective armor, and beside him was the shriveled monster who had so callously destroyed the woman whom Valjhar thought of as queen of the stars. Not far off was Stingray, whom he and his friends had taken in and nurtured, and who now had repaid them with murder. Out of sight, yet doubtlessly nearby, was Perturbare, a worse traitor yet, if possible. Finally there was Aureus, the Prohibitor—that soulless thing that had dogged them across the galaxies, finally catching up to enforce the repressive edicts of Rralians long since dead and forgotten.

Of all the Space Mariners, only one remained who might still exact vengeance, and that was himself. Yet he could not do it in his present state of helplessness. He must take upon himself a power he had wished to avoid. He reached into his pouch and extracted the Motionglobe. Before anyone could react he held it up and permitted it to pass into his skull.

Valjhar's world changed. Everything was suffused with a dreamlike confusion and haziness. The world flickered as if a shutter were being whirled in front of the sun. He seemed able to see in directions he never knew existed.

Yet there were his enemies, frozen in various awkward attitudes. There was Stingray, the savage murderer of an unresisting Kern Harner. Struggling against a flow of time suddenly more viscous than amber, Valjhar forced his body upright and through the thick syrup that enveloped him. A hazy pink-orange glow brightened before him and made vision difficult. Refractive waves of air expanded from his path like languid ripples. Snow and ice churned beneath his feet in a welter of vapor and plasma. Before he could even approach Stingray, some influence lifted the giant, tearing him from Kern's crumpled body, throwing them both across the ice like loose-jointed puppets.

Shaken by this violence, Valjhar halted and discovered a capacity to project himself directly through space without destructive interaction with his environment. As in a dream he flitted over the ice, transient and insubstantial as a ghost. He came upon Raintree's discarded cryogun. With a sickening upheaval of his perceptions he found he could see inside the device. Reaching through the fourth spacial dimension, he grabbed handfuls of components, eviscerating the weapon from the inside.

He contemplated doing the same for Anubis—"god" or no, the creature responsible for Shaula's death. As he approached the wizened figure, it somehow turned its head and regarded him with hollow black eyes. Apparently Anubis was not constrained by the limitations of time. Chilled by this, Valjhar decided to switch targets, selecting Fomalhaut, the architect of the entire disaster.

But as he neared Fomalhaut's gleaming form, another figure somehow interposed itself—Endurance. As Valjhar passed by, moving with an agonizing subjective slowness, Endurance reacted to his presence. Moving with the slow inexorability of a starfish, he wrapped himself around Valjhar, clasping him in an unbreakable grip. Valjhar struggled, seeking escape through higher dimensions, thrusting palmfuls of ionized air into Endurance's face, even trying, and failing, to reach inside him as he had the cryogun. But Endurance was immune to all such tricks and tactics. Valjhar found himself blind with rage and tears.

"Stop. You must stop now. It's over," said Endurance softly as Valjhar wept.

"Endurance! What have I done—I've led us into disaster. We led the grandest life it is possible to live, out among the stars—and now all lies in ruins. It shouldn't have happened this way. We came here to do something great, to save a world and a race. Now my family is dead. They were everything to me, and I led them to their deaths. Why am I still alive?"

"Valjhar—for you, the passage of time will erase all pains and errors."

Valjhar looked into Endurance's coppery eyes, and what he saw there put his own pain into some perspective, for the solace of forgetfulness or death could never come to Endurance.

Unable to tolerate its disorientation any longer, Valjhar extracted the Motionglobe from his skull and returned it to its pouch.

"Look over there," said Endurance.

Valjhar turned and gasped with a hope so poignant it was almost worse than despair. Ben Raintree loped into view carrying the four Stones. He ran up to Shaula's body. With a shaking hand he pushed the ring of Life onto his finger.

"Ben, she is dead," said Fomalhaut.

With a fanatical gleam in his eye, Raintree sought out the source of those words. "Fomalhaut! Get over here and monitor her mental activity."

Fomalhaut complied without objection. Another figure approached: Tom Standing Crane.

"Tom—? I'm sorry; I forgot all about you. Are you all right? You must be frozen, dressed as you are."

"No, I'm fine." But Standing Crane was not unchanged. He bore a keenness of expression none of them had seen before, and the shadow of a smile touched his lips. "I'm back to being a doctor again, too."

"Excellent! Can you monitor her vital signs while I use this on her?"

In answer Standing Crane knelt down beside Shaula and placed his fingers below the angles of her jaw.

Raintree raised the ring, crying out as its spring-green Light flooded out, bathing Shaula's motionless body. Still her head lolled and her eyes stared blindly. It was almost more than Valjhar could bear to watch. He'd never known Cal-Cotavion to restore life with the Stones, or even to attempt it. Yet the glory of the Light was compelling; the mere reflection of it seemed to bring new strength flowing from the bones of his body. In that Light, hope could never be forbidden.

Quivering with effort, Ben pushed the Stone into Shaula's forehead and into her breast. "Live!" he cried, his voice hoarse but powerful. Suddenly he turned his head and looked full into Valjhar's face, his eyes narrowed with a fierce determination. He flipped his wrist, and an ovoid purple object tumbled through the air, landing in Valjhar's hand.

"Valjhar! Use that on both of us!"

Valjhar strode forward. Without even being aware of it he raised the Stone of Adamance, though he had never before wielded such a thing. Raintree seemed to drink in its violet diffusion, then bent with redoubled effort to the task of pouring the green fire into Shaula.

"She has a heartbeat," said Standing Crane calmly.

"Ben—! I detect minimal brain activity," said Fomalhaut, sounding as rattled as anyone had ever heard him.

"Ahhh!" The green Light guttered and died. Valjhar wasn't sure if Ben's outcry indicated joy at victory or relief at cessation of pain. Whichever it was, he sank to his knees. Valjhar walked forward slowly, desperate to see the return of Shaula's spirit to those mad, glazed eyes.

But he was disappointed. Shaula merely resumed the spasms she had suffered just before her death. Seeing this, Raintree again invoked the ring, this time as a gentle, sustaining shower of green.

A flyer touched down nearby. Possum Perturbare emerged and sauntered up. No one greeted him or paid him any heed.

"She lives," said Fomalhaut, "but her mind remains deranged."

"I had some contact with her while Anubis was still within me," said Standing Crane. "It may be that the damage done to her is beyond even the reach of the Stones. I suspect that only those who fitted her with the Instrument have any hope of repairing her sanity."

"No!" said Ben. "These other Stones—Truth and Inner Light—"

"Truth is the last thing she needs now," said Fomalhaut. "Do not confront her with the finality of the separation between herself and her Instrument."

"Fomalhaut is right. Shaula's mind must be reconstructed, and we lack the means to do so," said Standing Crane.

"We also lack the means to return her to wherever this 'Cosmic Patrol' keeps its headquarters," said Ben bitterly.

"You know," remarked Perturbare, "I'll bet Valjhar's Motionglobe could get her there. Or anywhere else, for that matter."

Everyone turned and gaped at him for a moment.

"Perturbare is correct, of course," said Fomalhaut. "And we have a logical candidate to take her where she needs to go."

"Exactly right," said Raintree.

Valjhar said in despair, "I can barely control the Motionglobe. I cannot imagine how to command it to take me to a foreign universe. I will try..." He shuddered at the prospect, but of course he had no other choice.

"No, Valjhar," said Raintree. He stood up then, straight and tall and wreathed in light, a figure, thought Valjhar, comparable in splendor to Cal-Cotavion, but without the grey cloak to shield it from sensitive mortal eyes. "Fomalhaut, that logical candidate you mentioned is yourself."

"What?"

"Who else?" challenged Raintree. "You alone among us all have crossed from one universe to another. Your space-faring experience makes that of the Space Mariners look like a walk around the block. You have that outfit which allows you to survive in the most extreme conditions. You have the giant intellect necessary to understand and control the Globe. Are those sufficient reasons?"

"I have no idea how to find one particular universe out of an infinite multitude."

"Leave that to me." Ben turned back to Shaula, and with great deliberation lowered the fillet of Truth onto his brow. With haunted eyes he unleashed its power as an azure pencil of radiance, difficult to look upon. But rather than probing directly into Shaula's mind, Raintree directed the beam at her hand, into the inert metal band which had housed the singularity. After a moment the beam winked out. Raintree jerked the fillet off his head. On his forehead was a spot of blackened flesh. "Fomalhaut. Take the information from my mind," he said hoarsely. "Is it enough?"

"It is enough. I see the band's origin place, and I have some sense of it. Valjhar? Will you give up the Motionglobe?"

Valjhar stepped forward. He found himself placing into Fomalhaut's hand the ineffably strange relic of Rral. Fomalhaut held the Globe before his mirrored helmet and released it. It hovered before him, he stepped forward, and it passed through the helmet without resistance.

"Shaula Alshain will need protection," said Fomalhaut tonelessly. "Her present costume might suit one equipped with a Universal Instrument, but it will not sustain her on a journey such as this."

Possum Perturbare dumped an armload of metal and fabric into the snow beside Shaula. With a crooked grin he said, "Just happened to have this spare suit of space armor in my flyer. It may be a tad big for her, but it should do."

A few minutes later Fomalhaut stood in the center of the small group with the armored Shaula Alshain cradled in his arms.

"I shall return as, and if, possible."

With that Fomalhaut and Shaula somehow folded into themselves and were gone.

Which left Raintree, Valjhar, Perturbare, Standing Crane, Anubis, and Endurance standing around staring at each other.

"Kern!" cried Raintree. He ran off toward Kern's twisted body, with Valjhar and the others following. Taking Kern by the shoulders he turned him over and lay him on his back. The sight of his staring, blood-caked face sickened them all. Nevertheless, Ben again wielded the green ring, with a vehemence at least equal to what he had brought to bear on behalf of Shaula.

But Standing Crane approached, kneeling in the cone of verdant light, searching for a pulse, examining Kern's eyes for pupil response.

"I'm sorry, Ben. It's too late—there's too much damage here for even you to overcome."

"That one has already walked the path," said Anubis.

Raintree quieted the ring and whirled on Anubis. "Thanks for sharing that information!" The green ring smoldered. Ben looked as though he were considering its possible effect on death's doorman.

"Ben," said Standing Crane. "You might try using that jewelry on Stingray. He's the one who really needs it."

Ben leveled a last dire glance at Anubis and trotted off toward Stingray, where he sat huddled on the ice.

Raintree halted beside Stingray, whose bruised, battered face betrayed no awareness of his presence. Ben raised the Stone of Inner Light, anxious to banish the anguish and dejection so evident in every line of Stingray's body.

There was a rush of motion and Stingray vanished. An instant later Ben found himself looking up into blazing blue eyes, his wrist caught in a painful grip.

"What are you doing?" demanded Stingray in a rough voice.

"I—I wanted to use the Stones on you—bring you past this—show you the truth…"

"The truth? The truth is that I'm a murderer. That I became a savage animal to destroy one of my dearest friends. You want the truth? The truth is that we, supposedly the most advanced beings on Earth, were reduced to clawing at each other like animals to gain our ends. Like apes. Like humans."

"But that's not the whole truth," Ben insisted. "Let me use the…"

"Let me find my own truth!" thundered Stingray. "I can do that for myself, without the help of any pretty colored lights."

Ben drew himself up. "These Stones do far more than produce pretty colored lights."

"I don't care what they do! They have nothing to do with me." He released Ben and turned away. "I'm leaving. Going back to the sea. Back to where I belong—as a sea ape." Ben said nothing. Stingray took a few steps and looked back over his shoulder. "Goodbye…" His voice disintegrated into raggedness. He shook his head and strode away.

Ben looked after him, his throat constricting with sorrow. Then he stared down at the phenomenal objects he carried, considered his own desire to bathe in their healing glows, and rejected it.

The others had gathered around Kern's body. Valjhar bent down beside it and tried to close those staring eyes, but the lids were frozen.

Raintree returned, his expression bleak. He said, "I think it'll be a while before anyone hears from Stingray again. Whatever his crimes, he is paying for them now."

The air quivered, and a form unfolded into being. It was Fomalhaut, alone.

"You are all still here," he said softly. "Still waiting."

"It's only been a few minutes, Fomalhaut," said Ben.

"Ah. Of course. My subjective experience of the time elapsed is otherwise."

Fomalhaut turned, stepping away a few paces, unsteady on his feet. They all looked at him in silence as he stood wavering, his hands reaching out tentatively, as if to brush away cobwebs.

After a while he turned back to them. "Valjhar...Shaula Alshain is alive. I returned her to the place of her empowerment, but the damage was severe, and the course of her healing will be long and uncertain. The beings in control there swear they will do their best for her. I can tell you little more."

That was enough for Valjhar. Tears froze on his cheeks. "Thank you...Fomalhaut...Ben...Standing Crane...thank you all."

Fomalhaut reached up and produced the Motionglobe. "You may have this back. It is a remarkable artifact of unlimited potential, but I will not regret its loss."

"You—return it to me?" asked Valjhar in amazement.

"Of course."

"Don't anybody mention that suit of space armor," said Perturbare. "Glad to provide it." No one seemed to hear.

Raintree noticed a modification to Fomalhaut's exploration suit: on one shoulder was a four-pointed golden star against the background of a silver ring.

Fomalhaut was aware of Raintree's curiosity. "The —'Cosmic Patrol'—granted me an honorary commission in recognition of my help to Shaula." He sounded oddly embarrassed about it.

"It's time to deal with that creature Anubis," said Endurance. He stepped directly to the mummy-like figure, who did not react. Endurance looked over his shoulder at Fomalhaut.

"What kind of thing did you ally yourself with? Did you even know?" he asked accusingly. He reached up and grasped Anubis's face, his fingers entering its eye sockets and mouth. He pulled; there was a dry ripping sound, and puffs of dust spurted out. The grey parchment skin crumbled and tore away, revealing nothing but an empty void. Endurance pulled the skin away like a mask, and the void assumed the jackal-headed shape of the classical Anubis.

"You don't belong in this world. Cross back through the door; go back where you came from. Haunt the temples and towers of Ammon, and trouble us no more."

Words emerged from the terrible form. "First there is a service I must perform."

Eyes far older than the god Anubis bore into its darkness. "Do what you must. Then go."

Anubis, the lightless silhouette of a man topped by the long-snouted head of a jackal, turned and walked off toward the Redoubt. With varying degrees of enthusiasm the others followed. At his heels were Endurance and Standing Crane, who regarded the incarnate spirit which had so recently possessed him with something like mirth.

Trailing them all was Possum Perturbare. His stride was listless, and after a while he faltered and stopped. He stood watching as the others marched toward the horizon. No one looked back at him.

He turned back. A few minutes later he lifted off in his flyer and was gone.

Presently they advanced on the glittering figure of Aureus as it stood near the body of Cal-Cotavion. The robot's legs wobbled like weak springs. It looked at them unsteadily as they approached.

Grimly Valjhar reached into his pouch to retrieve the Motionglobe. Fomalhaut simultaneously mirrored his exploration suit.

"No!" To his surprise, Ben found himself defending Aureus. "He gave me the Stones to save Shaula."

They both turned to study Raintree. Valjhar dropped the Globe back into the pouch. Fomalhaut's suit resumed its normal appearance.

Anubis stepped up to Cal-Cotavion, passing and ignoring Aureus. Raintree glimpsed the body and was startled, for it seemed to have been replaced by a superb marble statue, a work of majesty in its depiction of a hero in death. Then he realized it was in fact Cotavion's body, its contours smoothed and whitened by a sheath of frost.

Anubis manifested the scale, and plucked from the air a white swan feather, which it placed in one of the cups. Bending down, it extracted from Cal-Cotavion an essence resembling the combined Lights of all the Stones. To Raintree's eye, it lacked the absolute purity which had been so apparent in Rouse's spirit. Anubis placed it into the other cup of the scale, which tilted in neither direction.

"This spirit is not unstained," said Anubis, "and is as yet a small thing, kindled from the cosmic fires late in his life. I go now, to guide him on the roads of cleansing and growth. Then will my duty to him and his people be fulfilled."

The figure of Anubis stood motionless. Some quality of animation faded from its substance, and it slipped from being like a shadow displaced by light.

"So much for Anubis," whispered Raintree. He began stripping himself of the Stones, placing them in a pocket of his cold-armor.

"Aren't you planning to wear the Stones, Ben?" asked Valjhar.

"Absolutely not. 'Stained' as perhaps he was, I'm no Cal-Cotavion. I'm not fit to wear them for any length of time. I haven't the strength. But I'll keep them safe. Maybe someone else will come along someday, someone worthy of carrying them. It's not any of us."

Valjhar shivered. "True. Here's the fourth." Valjhar handed over the Stone of Adamance.

"What will you do now, Valjhar?"

Valjhar managed a wan smile. "Somehow *Mote* survived this conflagration. I'll find Pimsehkia and take her home to Rral at last, where I hope we both can heal. And perhaps someday I'll be reunited with Shaula. I will wait for her."

"I hope so." Ben and Valjhar gripped each other's hands tightly.

Valjhar then turned toward Aureus. "That, at least, is my plan, unless the Prohibitor of Rral proposes to stop us...?"

Aureus said, "My teleportation system is dysfunctional. I have suffered substantial damage. Nearby stand persons able and, I think, willing to destroy me if I attempt to apprehend you. Using the Motionglobe, you could easily elude me. I must consider my mission a failure. You are free to depart. However, I invite you to remain on this planet, or someday return to it, so that I may monitor your activities in partial compliance with the parameters of my mission."

Valjhar blinked in confusion. "Thank you," he said uncertainly.

"Or take me with you."

Valjhar was startled. "No, Prohibitor. Even if I were willing to consider it, Pimsehkia would never abide it."

"I did not wish to kill the Colibdian."

"And yet you did."

"Recovering the Stones is the highest priority of any Prohibitor. I will remain near them now. They must never again return to Rral."

Valjhar then turned to face Endurance. "My friend... what will you do now?"

"I need to think things over. My attempt to assist the human race as a whole was not a success. All this fury unleashed, all this death and misery, and the only thing accomplished was to preserve the status quo. Never before have I seen so much effort and ambition expended only to result in so much futility. I haven't walked the mid-Atlantic ridge since before the rise of civilization. I think I'll go take a look at it."

"Then goodbye."

Endurance turned to go, then looked back.

"One last thing—"

Valjhar halted.

"That thing you carry...the Motionglobe...may I see it?"

Valjhar fished out the glowing sphere and placed it into Endurance's hand.

"I've seen this before," said Endurance.

Valjhar's jaw dropped. "You—what did you say?"

"When I first opened my eyes...I saw this light, this object, floating before me in space. I stared at it for a while, and finally reached out to touch it, to hold it. But my coordination was poor; I bumped it too hard...it floated away, and I had no way to follow. I never saw it again until now. I always wondered what became of it. Well, goodbye." He handed back the Motionglobe.

"Wait!"

Endurance turned again.

"You were obviously meant to have this."

Endurance considered this, and nodded.

"Don't you want it?" said Valjhar.

"Do you have any use for it?" asked Endurance.

"Well—yes, I suppose I may."

"Then you hold onto it."

Valjhar was flabbergasted. "You mean to say—after billions of years of separation, when you finally find this thing, against incredible odds, you're just going to walk away from it?"

Endurance gave a small smile. "You aren't seeing this from my perspective. As you say, I've waited billions of years. A few more years, or a few more million, won't mean much to me. Don't worry; when the time is right for me to possess the Motionglobe, it'll come my way again."

THE END

Joe Bergeron

Appendix

The Rise of the Vigil

The great clash between the Vigil and the Para-men has been one of the central events of my fictional universe ever since I was a boy.

The first superhero I ever created was the Pteranodon — yes, the same guy who was so quickly dismissed for membership in the Vigil. The next two had more staying power, maintaining active roles in my personal mythos to this day. They were Stingray and the Red Proton. At the time (mid 1960s) my odd concept for this pair was that they were actually one boy who, when the need arose, could split into two separate and very different superheroes: Stingray, an ocean guy, and Red Proton, an energy guy. This duality concept was dropped fairly early, leaving the two characters to develop along their own paths. Red Proton eventually dropped his hero name and became known as Kern Harner, who still wears red and still fires the occasional proton beam. My current notion is that they were best friends while both were among the Space Mariners.

Many other characters followed these three. A large gang of young heroes included such non-entities as the Spook, the Devel (deliberately misspelled so no one would think him a Satanist), the Black Cat, and even Chordate Kid, who could turn into any chordate animal, which includes all vertebrates as well as certain obscure critters such as the sea squirt. Also on hand were Kroy dal Ren, who was originally a Spock-themed alien who could process solar energy with his chlorophyll-laden green hair, and the Dimension Kid, a brown-haired lad who wore an indigo tunic and carried the Dimension Belt. Together, they were known as—the Kid Crusaders!

For a while, anyway.

After some time this bunch turned into space travelers as well as superheroes. Some of the lamer members fell into oblivion, while other more grandiose characters popped up in their place, including Mega Lad and Super Nova. Eventually these characters all became so powerful they evolved into a pack of gods with names like the Psychalien and Power Paragon, quickly losing all value as fictional characters.

By this time, the late 1960s, I was also fooling around with other super groups of a more earthbound nature. One was called the Para-men. These uniformly-dressed characters each exemplified one human ability or quality, hugely magnified. Their names, as I recall, were Motion, Strength, Endurance, Beauty, Vision, and Skill.

At some point I extracted a few of my favorite old characters from the ranks of cosmic gods and conflated them with the Para-men. My idea was that these were former space wanderers who had settled on Earth. The Dimension Kid assumed the identity of Motion. The Red Proton and Kroy dal Ren tagged along. Endurance began to develop his long separate history of wandering the Earth. Beauty gradually morphed into the Dreamfarer. Strength, Vision, and Skill went away forever.

My other major group at this time consisted of Tukudu (not yet T'Ukudu), Stingray, Anubis, Aureus, Dr. Cold (Ben Raintree) and Captain Fomalhaut. There were also a few peripheral members who eventually dropped away, such a

Ahura Rama Singh, a Sikh mystic, and Jim Levi, the Psychedelian, who, like the Pteranodon, was rejected for Vigil membership in the current novel.

This group was called the Allies.

Some of these characters were quite a bit different than their current incarnations. Anubis was simply Anubis, with no Tom Standing Crane or any particular back story. He looked like a papery grey bald man who wore a picture of a jackal on his grey tunic. Captain Fomalhaut was still a superman from the future. He has since dropped his military rank, though I slyly retained this detail in *The Vigil* by means of Fomalhaut's honorary commission in the "Cosmic Patrol". The original headquarters of the Allies was three floors high in the Prudential Tower in Boston. When visiting Boston I would often go to the Pru and ride the elevator to those floors, imagining that in some parallel universe my heroes were just on the other side of the door. Perhaps the Vigil rented offices in the tower while waiting for the Lighthouse to be constructed.

With two super groups inhabiting the Earth, it was natural to think they might be rivals, fighting over the destiny of mankind. Both groups continued to evolve and gain new members. The Allies acquired a flying hero who played the same role that Rouse Farewell plays in the current novel, being killed in battle against the Para-men. He was later reincarnated after a fashion as Stormdevil, a weather-controlling spirit. The Allies also gained the services of Peregrine, who was originally supposed to be an actual peregrine falcon turned into a powerful flying woman.

I eventually removed the flying guy from this "Endurian Universe", plunking him into his own world and his own novel, *The Way of an Eagle*. His function in the Allies was taken over by Peregrine, who was rethought into the Endurian version of the (name in flux) flying hero, with a similar origin, which is only hinted at in *The Vigil*.

The Para-men gained Cal-Cotavion, who was originally called Titan-Man. By this time the basic story of the Allies versus the Para-men was pretty well established. While in high school in the early 1970s I drew a comic strip about the battle between Aureus and Cotavion on the ice near the Antarctic fortress of the Para-men. It's similar to the battle described in the novel, and shows the Stones in all their glory.

Another major character in *The Vigil* had his genesis a few years earlier while I was in the ninth grade. There I started drawing a grinning, crew-cut scientist-trickster called Possum Perturbare. The drawings and the name both got around, and for a year or so I was more-or-less affectionately known as "Doc Possum" to many of my classmates.

While in high school I invented Captain Universe, an absolute paragon who was a member of the Cosmic Patrol. Not an entirely serious character, he was the subject of satirical voice recordings I made to amuse some friends. The character of Shaula Alshain descends directly from him.

Sometime in the late 1970s I wrote a story called "Cold Christmas" featuring Perturbare and Raintree. It serves as a bridge between *The Vigil* and its sequel *Acts of the Vigil*, and will have to be re-written someday. The late John Gardner, who was one of my creative writing teachers in college (among other things), described it as "a more grown-up version of the Hardy Boys".

Many details of plot and character percolated through my mind over the following decade. I had always realized that "The Allies" was a bland sort of name for a super group (not to mention a source of confusion for scholars of the World Wars). I eventually came up with the Vigil, a name which has grown on me over the years. Considering the proliferation of comic book super groups since then, I'm lucky that no one else has appropriated the name.

I started writing *The Vigil* in 1991, finishing it the following year. I then began sending it around to publishers. One prominent editor liked it, but suggested that the mob of characters was too confusing. He advised me to keep Fomalhaut as the viewpoint character throughout the book. He also didn't think that such a comic-booky novel was quite right for his publishing house. I'm sure he was right...after all, comic book material never did become very popular, did it?

After that I fiddled with rearranging the book so that the introductory stories of the various characters would be kept together, instead of having the chapters alternate between them. Ultimately I decided I preferred the present structure. I take as my model *The Many-Colored Land* by Julian May, which also has a crowd of main characters and begins by introducing them in their own little stories.

Note that Ben Raintree is one of a number of extraordinary cousins stemming from the Raintree family. Leonard Ronar, hero of my novels *The Astronomer Who Didn't Like Magic, The Astronomer Who Hated a God,* and *The Astronomer Who Would Not Be King*, is one of them. Another cousin is mentioned in *The Vigil* but not identified as such. Even Sapphire is a cousin! *The Vigil* also contains other connections to the world of Colibdis. Anubis, Dreamfarer, and Cal-Cotavion all come from there.

The saga of the Vigil continues in *Acts of the Vigil*, and concludes in *Behold the Vigil*. Alas, my original ending for the series was somewhat anticipated and pre-empted by Alan Moore's *The Watchmen,* requiring me to re-think my plans to a degree. But I still got the job done.

Joe Bergeron

May 19, 2011

www.ingramcontent.com/pod-product-compliance
Lightning Source LLC
Chambersburg PA
CBHW052344020726
47503CB00001B/97